FLIGHT OF THE SPARK

FLIGHT OF THE SPARK

EVELYN PUERTO

Cover by George Long
Map by Jeremy Bullard

ISBN 978-0-9909715-4-2

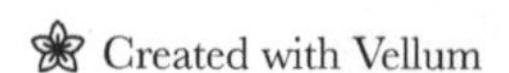

CONTENTS

River Mirna
River Selenga
Tlefas

1

Iskra wasn't sure about many things, except one: This would be a day she'd remember her whole life. She stared at her mug of tea, lost in anticipation. Today, for the first time in her fifteen years, she was going to leave the village of Gishin.

People didn't often travel from village to village; it was considered an unnecessary risk, which made no sense to Iskra. The idea of seeing a new place and new people seized her imagination and sent tingles down her spine. She was confident that the thrill of something new would be worth the discomfort of a few hours on a wagon.

At first, her mother had been adamant: Iskra was not going anywhere. Undaunted, Iskra put her mind to convincing her mother. Every time her mother complained about the quality of candles, Iskra reminded her that better ones were to be had in Shinroo, along with soft woolen stockings and shawls. And she'd heard a rumor that the shoemaker in Shinroo was already selling summer shoes, and Luza needed a new pair.

By some miracle, and perhaps by Iskra's zealous attention to her chores and tireless arguing, her mother relented. In fact, she had no idea why her mother had granted her permission . . . maybe she'd decided to indulge her daughter just as she'd indulged in a little too much wine that night at the inn.

Whatever the reason, Iskra didn't care. Her heart raced at the thought of just seeing something, *any*thing, beyond drab Gishin and its surrounding fields. For once, she'd taste the illusion of being free from the rules that constrained her every move. She lost herself in a daydream of what was out there, what wonders she might see in Shinroo, a town two or three times the size of Gishin.

Then she heard whispers, the words arriving as if on a cold breeze, breaking into her happy reverie:

"Old Cassie was taken last night."

Iskra jerked her head around, seeking to find the speaker. She scanned the faces of the women sitting to her left on the worn wooden benches, all huddled over the meager breakfast of runny porridge and pine needle tea the village provided. The women all looked the same, garbed in shapeless, faded, and mouse-colored dresses and aprons over woolen leggings, all with hair cropped under their ears and across their foreheads. The only variations were the colored bands that circled their left sleeves at the shoulder to announce their professions.

"That's right," said a thin woman hunched over her tea. "She's gone."

Iskra noticed the woman's shaking hands and pale, fearful eyes. She wondered if Cassie was someone the woman had been close to.

The words repeated themselves in Iskra's mind, cramping her stomach. She stared at her half-eaten porridge, no longer hungry. *Old Cassie was taken last night.*

A hand grabbed her shoulder and brought her back to reality. "Are you coming? We'll be late."

"Yes, Tavda," Iskra replied. She shook herself as if to free her mind from the fear that had gripped it and followed her friend through the crowded hall in the inn where most villagers ate their meals, since cooking was considered to be unsafe. The hall didn't seem as noisy and energetic as it had just a few moments ago. She shivered as she stepped onto the dirt street, a chilly breeze puffing in her face, making her blink. She drew her threadbare, slate-colored shawl closer.

Iskra hurried to catch up with Tavda, passing rickety wooden stalls displaying withered apples and potatoes with sprouting eyes, pottery and candles, shoes, and shawls, past people wearing their drab gray clothing. She caught up to her friend just as Tavda burst out from between the rows of stalls into what the village of Gishin called a main square. The town's monument to safety stood in its center, a statue of a man holding a sword in one hand, his other arm held out to protect an old woman and a little boy. Iskra thought the woman and the boy looked as though they didn't think the man could protect them from a cockroach. She frowned at the monument, noting it was shabby and worn down, much like the village.

Six or seven wagons were lined up to one side of the monument, some empty, others piled with the coarse earthenware made in the village, along with stacks of newly cut wood. Brown-clad traders piled goods on wagons or checked harnesses. Tavda and Iskra sprinted to the third wagon, where Tavda's mother, Revda, was negotiating with a trader.

"These girls are only fifteen," Revda said, pointing to the white bands on the girls' shoulders that marked them as students. "You'll look after them?" Revda looked hard into the man's eyes.

He smiled, his grizzled eyebrows almost completely hiding his eyes. "Like they were my own granddaughters."

Revda didn't smile back. "Make sure my other daughter meets them." She handed the man a few coins. "She'll pay you the rest when you get there." She hugged Tavda. "I'm still not so sure about this."

Iskra felt her knees grow weak. If Revda didn't allow

Tavda to go, her own mother was sure to forbid the trip. She'd looked forward to this excursion for weeks and winced at the thought of it being denied at this last moment.

Tavda pulled on her mother's sleeve. "Mam, you promised I could visit. We'll be fine. See all the guardsmen?" She pointed to the opposite end of the square, where ten guardsmen wearing their dark brown leather uniforms sat on their horses. "Ten men to protect us. We'll have no problems on the road."

Tavda's mother pursed her lips and shook her head.

Iskra hadn't thought about the bandits known to prowl the road between Gishin and Shinroo. It just now occurred to her to wonder if going to Shinroo *was* such a good idea. Her mouth felt like she'd eaten dust for breakfast. Her enthusiasm for travel started to evaporate like dew on a hot summer morning.

"Humph." Tavda's mother scowled at the guardsmen as if she doubted their ability to protect anyone.

"Besides," Tavda said, "you know the candles in Shinroo are safer than the ones here. Just like the darning needles. And you did want me to try to find a new teapot."

Guardsmens' cheers interrupted her answer. Kaberco, the Ephor of Gishin, strode through the market, his long black cloak swirling around him, his leathers creaking, the gold chain of his office draped over his shoulders glinting in the sun. Kaberco walked down the line of the caravan, placing his men at the front and rear of the line of wagons. He stopped when he saw Iskra.

"Peace and safety, Iskra."

"Peace and safety to you." She smiled at the huge man who'd been like an uncle to her after her father died.

Kaberco looked from her to Tavda. "Tavda is staying in Shinroo for a week. But you? You are coming back today?"

"That's right," Iskra said. "Tavda's staying with her sister.

She asked me to ride with her, since I've never seen Shinroo before. I'll be back on the afternoon caravan."

"Are you sure this is safe?" Revda pushed forward to get closer to Kaberco.

"Of course. My guardsmen will make sure they arrive safely. You have nothing to worry about."

Iskra felt the knot in her stomach relax. She was silly to be concerned. Kaberco was right. He always was. She smiled at him, grateful for his reassurance, her excitement about leaving the village stirring back to life.

Kaberco smiled at Revda and the girls. "Peace and safety." He turned and continued his progress along the line of wagons.

A loud horn cut through the crisp air.

"Here, it's time we got ready," their trader said. He boosted the girls onto the wagon's wooden seat. He settled into place beside Tavda. "Don't worry," he said, looking down at Revda, "they'll be safe."

A few more minutes of jostling horses and shouted goodbyes, another blast of the horn, and the caravan set off.

An hour later, Iskra was nodding off, the slow rocking motion of the wagon and the warmth of the sun having lulled her into drowsiness. She let her thoughts wander, barely paying attention to Tavda's chat with the trader.

Old Cassie was taken last night.

She hadn't realized she'd spoken out loud until Tavda poked her with her elbow. "What did you say?"

Iskra shrugged. "That Old Cassie's gone. Taken. At least, that's what I heard." She grabbed the wood rail of the wagon as it lurched over a pothole. She hoped they wouldn't break an axle passing over the holes and ruts that pitted and scored the road. Dried leaves from last fall spilled onto the dusty surface, twigs and branches scattered about bore testimony to winter storms.

"How do you know?" Tavda asked.

"About Cassie? People in the inn were whispering about it this morning."

Tavda nudged the trader with her elbow. "Is it true? Is Old Cassie gone?"

"'Tis true." He shook the reins to spur the horses to move a little faster.

"It's about time," Tavda said.

Iskra gaped at her friend. "How can you say that?" Tavda couldn't mean what she was saying. She often didn't.

"She was old," Tavda said. "And crazy and slow. I hated to get behind her in the market. She'd study each raisin, inspecting it for anything wrong before she'd put it on the scale. Took her half an hour to buy half a pound." She shook her head, shaking her wavy auburn hair. For what seemed like the hundredth time, Iskra noticed how the prescribed haircut of cropped hair and bangs flattered Tavda's round face. The fact she also had thick curly hair and large dark eyes didn't hurt, either. The short hair didn't look well at all with Iskra's straight dirty blond hair and long oval face. She thought the cut made her resemble a horse.

"It's not so crazy to not buy moldy raisins, is it?" the trader asked. His voice was low and he spoke slowly, mimicking the cadence of the horses' hooves.

"Maybe not," Tavda said. She picked up her basket and started adjusting the perky red bow she'd tied around the handle. "Maybe she's sick, and they'll send her back."

Iskra pressed her lips together. She didn't think so. When the healers came for sick people, they usually told someone, a family member or neighbor, and announced when the person might be coming back. But Cassie hadn't been ill, so no healers would have come for her. That only left the Prime Konamei's Guard, which removed the worst troublemakers.

Those people were gone, taken in the middle of the night. Never to be seen again, not even to be spoken of. Simply taken. People who committed lesser crimes at least got a trial. Iskra wondered what kind of horrible crime an old woman could commit, barely aware of Tavda and the trader swapping gossip.

"Maybe," Iskra said. "Maybe she really is crazy."

"Who?" Tavda asked.

"Cassie." Iskra wrinkled her forehead, frowning. "Yesterday she grabbed my arm and demanded to know when I'd give her the 'de-zeer-uh-dun,' whatever that is." She shivered at the memory of Cassie's wide, wild eyes and menacing tone.

The trader dropped the reins and stared at Iskra, mouth open, brows drawn together. "The what?"

"The dezeerudun. She said I had it, or would have it, and she wanted me to give it to her." She leaned back and blinked a few times when she saw how pale the trader's face had become.

"Better forget you ever heard that, girl. Don't tell anyone. Ever." He practically spit the words out.

"But—"

"Hush. A guardsman's coming." He picked up the reins and clucked to the horses.

Iskra noticed the trader's beefy hands were shaking.

She watched the guardsman ride past their wagon, a burly man on a large horse, armed with a short sword and a bow. Iskra had always been told the Prime Konamei's guards were there to protect the people, but somehow today she felt a sense of unease when they drew near. A cloud slid in front of the sun, casting a chilly shadow over her, making her shiver. The guardsman glanced at Iskra, Tavda, and the trader, then he moved along the caravan.

When the guardsman was a few wagons away, Iskra asked, "Why should I forget? What's a dezeerudun, anyway?"

The trader's face reddened. "It's dangerous. Don't talk

anymore about it or I'll put you out and you can walk the rest of the way." He slapped the reins against the horses' rumps. "Forget the words of a crazy old woman." He leaned over to glare at Iskra. "Do you want to be taken, too?"

She bowed her head, shivering under his anger, cringing at his disapproval. She most certainly did not want to be taken. Then Cassie really is gone, Iskra thought. No one had been taken for several years. But in the past six months, four people had vanished and the village gossips whispered they'd been taken.

Iskra hunched over her basket as another guardsman approached. He passed their wagon, then guided his horse alongside the wagon in front of them. "Hey! Trader!" the guard shouted.

The trader spun to look. "Yes, if you please?"

He sounded nervous to Iskra. She would be, too, if a guardsman yelled at her that way.

"What's that you have there? A sword?"

"No, if you please. Just a knife. For cutting ropes and such." The man's hand shook as he pulled the knife out and held it up.

"Huh. Make sure that's all you use it for. It would be a shame if you weren't here to trade this route any more." The guard touched his heels to his horse's sides and urged it to proceed up the line.

Suddenly the spring air didn't feel so warm anymore, the spring sunshine barely able to penetrate the shadows of the trees lining the road. Iskra huddled in her cloak, clutching it tightly around her, thinking. Iskra wondered that the guard would threaten a trader like that. Did Kaberco know his guards did that? He must. No doubt he only took people who threatened others' safety.

The wagon jolted over a rut in the road. Iskra clutched the edge of the wagon. Tavda fell against Iskra, laughing. Iskra sighed. Tavda didn't seem at all bothered by the trader's warning. Her own thoughts were as unsettling as the uneven road.

She glanced at the trader, who was still scowling. She didn't dare ask any more questions; no sense getting him even angrier. She had no desire to walk to Shinroo. Or to have to explain why the throbbing vein in his forehead burst.

But something didn't seem right. Everyone knew that the taken were unsafe to be around or wanted to overthrow the Prime Konamei. That didn't seem to fit Cassie.

She swayed back and forth with the bouncing of the wagon, letting her questions jostle each other in her mind like chickens in a box. She jerked upright, startled by the thought that maybe some of the people who were taken didn't know what they had done was a crime, like asking about the dezeerudun. One way or another, she determined to find out. But who could she ask?

Iskra was still lost in thought when the sound of a different horn blared over the rumble of the caravan. They passed through the Shinroo town gate and stopped in the market. The trader helped the girls down from the wagon.

"Don't forget what I said," he said to Iskra. "And best you ride back with someone else."

2

A few hours later, Iskra tugged on Tavda's hand. "Hurry up! I don't want to miss the caravan." She pointed to the sun, now past its high point and starting to descend.

"What's the rush? Say, there's a woman selling pasties. Maybe she has the ones with cabbage. Do you think she might have cookies, too?"

"Tavda, we ate with your sister. You can't be hungry."

"When did you last eat a pasty? It won't take long."

With a sigh, Iskra gave in to Tavda's insistence. The aroma of fresh pasty was too good to ignore. They stepped around some puddles, pushing through the crowd of people strolling along the lane. The girls each put two small bronze coins called sheaves in the pasty seller's rough hand, and chose crescent-shaped pasties stuffed with cabbage, still warm from the oven.

"Aren't you glad we stopped?" Tavda asked.

"Sure am." Shinroo's market had lots that Gishin's didn't, pasties and cookies and iron candleholders, instead of the earthenware ones sold in Gishin. Iskra assumed it was because Shinroo had twice as many people as Gishin and was a little less remote. What was the same were the clothes the villagers wore, everyone except traders and guardsmen all in drab gray, plain and shapeless, everyone alike.

Tavda finished chewing her last bite of pasty. "I don't see why you don't spend the night and go back tomorrow."

"You know I didn't get permission from Kaberco. Besides, I don't think your sister would like it."

"Oh, she loves company."

Iskra smiled to herself. Maybe Tavda's sister did, but probably not her husband. "You sure about that, Tavda?"

"Oh, yes." She laughed, then shrugged. "Well, maybe. I don't know. I don't care."

The raucous horn signaling the caravan's imminent departure sounded, preventing Iskra from retorting.

"Let's see who has to wait for who!" Tavda jerked away from Iskra and ran toward the town square. Iskra shoved the rest of her pasty in her mouth and followed close behind. They sped past a woman selling pottery and plates, men carrying trays of bread and sacks of coarse flour, and dodged children playing games and dogs in search of food.

"Watch where you're going!" one man yelled at Tavda after she jostled him off balance. She kept running and crashed into a pyramid of potatoes piled high on the front shelf of a stall, knocking most of them into the mud.

"Now see what you've done, careless girl! No sense of safety." The woman selling the potatoes grabbed Tavda by the neck of her dress and gave her a shake. "You've ruined my display."

"We're sorry," Iskra said. "We'll pick them up." She set her basket down and waved for Tavda to do the same. Then she began collecting potatoes, piling them into her apron.

"Those are her potatoes, Iskra. Let her take care of them."

"But it was our fault. Don't you think it's only fair we help?"

"You're the one so worried about being late."

"We'll be done faster if you help." She stood and stacked potatoes on the rough table.

"You're doing it wrong." The old woman waved a bony finger at the pile. "Big ones on the bottom." The woman tugged at the orange band on her shoulder, as if to emphasize her status as a market vendor who knew her job.

Iskra bit her lip. "Here, why don't you stack while I pick up the rest?"

She ignored the old woman's grumbling and scurried to gather the rest of the potatoes. Tavda wandered a few stalls down. Iskra wished she would help, but knew it wasn't worth arguing about. She dumped the rest of the potatoes into an open sack next to the woman's table. "I'm so sorry, I have to go." She grabbed her basket and ran after Tavda.

"Come on," Iskra tugged at her friend's arm. "Now I'm really late." She peered nervously at the sun, now well past the high point in the sky and half shrouded in dark clouds.

"Look! Plums!"

"Great. You can get them later."

"What are you talking about? This time of year, you're lucky to see anything but wrinkled apples. If I don't get them now, they'll be gone before I get back." She shook her head at Iskra. "What are you worried about? The second horn hasn't sounded yet."

She haggled for three tiny plums. Iskra paced outside the stall, glancing nervously at the sun, struggling to keep her breathing steady. As soon as Tavda handed over her sheaves and put the fruit in her basket, Iskra seized her hand. "Come on."

The girls sprinted past the last row of market stalls into the square. No line of wagons. They sped over the stone pavement and past the monument to Fairness that stood in the center of the square, the tall statue of a man holding a pair of scales. They dashed up to the main traders' post and found the clerk locking the weatherbeaten door.

"Where's the caravan for Gishin?" Iskra asked.

"Left quarter of an hour ago. Didn't you hear the horns?"

"We only heard one."

"Don't know what to tell ya. We sounded all three. It's gone."

"Do you think she could catch it?" Tavda sounded like she thought running after it was a good idea.

"If she ran after it? Maybe. But it would be worth my job if I let her. A girl running down the road? No." He shook his head. "Against the rules, you know."

Iskra stared at him. "But I need to get home tonight." She swallowed hard, gulping back the panic that rose in her throat. "I'll be in so much trouble." Kaberco had always been kind to her, but to stay overnight in Shinroo without permission, what would he say? And her mother. Iskra closed her eyes, cringing at the thought of her mother's wrath.

"Don't think you'll make it."

Iskra stared at the man. "What do I do? I can't break the rules!"

The man shrugged. "You can hang around here, see if any other traders come by. You might be able to hire a ride."

Iskra didn't like the sound of that.

"I'm goin' for my dinner. I'll ask at the inn, all right? You stay here and wait."

Iskra nodded and sat down on the stoop outside the trader's post.

Tavda sat down with her. "What are you worried about? If you can't get home tonight, you can't. Kaberco will understand."

"He might. Maybe. He'll be so disappointed in me. But my mother?" Iskra squeezed her eyes shut, trying to blot out the thought of Luza's anger. She sat on the steps leading to the trading post and put her head down on her knees so Tavda couldn't see her tears.

Iskra listened to the dripping of the water clock mark off half an hour, then another quarter. Her restlessness increased with every drip and she struggled to keep herself calm. She idly untied the yellow-green ribbon on the handle of her basket and retied it, working out some of her nervous energy in the mindless task. *Time drags faster than a rock erodes.*

At least Tavda had stopped pestering her and was flirting with the baker's apprentice, wiping a dusting of flour off his face with one graceful flick of her hand. That left Iskra free to sit and speculate about the punishment for people who left the village overnight without permission. She bounced her foot against the stoop, wishing the clerk would come back with some good news that would save her from the consequences of missing the caravan.

A shout startled her from her gloomy reverie. "Hey, where's the caravan?" Iskra looked up and saw a short, fat, dark-skinned man wearing the brown clothes of a trader sitting in a wagon loaded with two elk carcasses.

"Gone." Tavda pointed toward the village gates.

"Think I can catch them?"

"They left a while ago," Iskra said.

"Can you take my friend with you?" Tavda asked.

Iskra shook her head, attempting to get Tavda to stop.

"Not a good idea," the trader answered. "If we're attacked, I can't protect you. It wouldn't be safe."

"But you'll catch up with the caravan," Tavda said. "It's still early. The bandits won't attack before dark."

"I don't know." He frowned and shook his head.

"She really does need to get home tonight."

"If you're sure." The trader gestured to the seat next to him.

Iskra bit the inside of her cheek. "I don't know. What if we don't catch up? Then we'll have to go the whole way alone.

That wouldn't be safe." Her heart pounded and her breath coming faster.

"If you hurry, I'm sure you'll be fine," Tavda said.

"But is it safe?"

Tavda took Iskra's basket from her and handed it up to the trader. "Yes, of course. What could possibly happen? They're barely half an hour ahead of you. Well, maybe a little more."

Iskra shook her head at Tavda's overly optimistic estimate. Easy for her to talk. She gave Tavda a quick hug and climbed to the seat next to the trader.

The trader slapped the reins against the horses' sides. "Git up!"

Iskra blew out a deep breath at the sight of the clouds moving in, dimming the sunlight. Everyone knew bandits loved to attack lone wagons. Before she'd had a chance to protest, here she was, riding on one.

After they rode out of the village gates, Iskra relaxed her grip on her basket and sat up a little straighter. She glanced from side to side at the bare fields lining the road. At least here there weren't too many places for bandits to lurk. She knew if the bandits attacked she'd be frozen with fear.

"You don't have to be so nervous," the trader said. "There's not been a raid on a caravan lately."

"That's good, isn't it?"

"Hmm." The trader let out a deep breath. "I'm not sure why they've been so quiet. Maybe it's because the last time they tried it the guardsmen killed six of them. The bandits they took alive, they tied to trees and left for the warboars' lunch."

Iskra shuddered. She'd never heard of guardsmen doing such horrible things. She shrank into her seat and crossed her arms over her chest. She cringed at the thought of warboars, tusked beasts with the bulk of oxen and the speed of wolves. They roamed the mountains that towered over the villages nestled in the foothills. "Will the warboars attack us?"

"Not likely, this time o' year. They move up the mountains in the spring. Come fall, they prowl the lower slopes. That's when you haf to be careful." The trader glanced at Iskra. "Why'd you miss the caravan?"

"My friend was bargaining for plums."

"While I was bargaining for elk. Greed's got us both in a fix." He gave her a half-smile. "What took you to Shinroo?"

"I went with my friend, who's visiting her sister. All I wanted was to see something other than Gishin."

"And did you?"

She wasn't sure if the trader was laughing at her. "Different people wearing the same clothes, different kids playing in the same mud, different monument making the same promises."

"Disappointed, are you, in your first travels?"

She sighed. "A little. I was hoping for . . . I don't know what I was hoping for. Something exotic. Or exciting." She snorted. "Missing the caravan wasn't what I had in mind. Will we catch up with it soon?"

"My horses are tired, that's fer sure. I drove 'em hard, hoping to get to town in time. It may take us a while."

Iskra bit her lip. "Do you really think we'll be able to, before we meet any bandits?"

The trader shrugged, the shifting of his bulk making the wagon seat jiggle. "Hard to say. Depends if they feel like stayin' home or not."

"Where's that?"

"No one knows. Some say they keep moving, others think they have camps on the cliffs or in the wilds between towns." He pointed at the top of the mountain. "One thing's certain. They don't live up high in the mountains, near the Riskers."

"I wouldn't want to live near them, either."

"Nor I. Filthy barbarians, those Riskers."

They rode silently, following the road nearly due north through open fields. The trader looked from side to side constantly, alert for any sign of approaching beasts, human or otherwise.

Never again, Iskra promised herself, *will I do something this dangerous. Even if I have to break the rules.* She clasped her hands together and watched shadows made by the clouds scamper across the horses' backs and along the road.

After what seemed to Iskra to be half a day of fearful waiting, but in reality could only have been about an hour, they approached the bridge that crossed the river Mirna.

"Now, listen to me," the trader said. "Sometimes bandits hide under the bridge. Stay real still. If you hear anything, jump out and run. Don't look back." He wiped his face and neck with a dirty brown rag, the sweat dripping from the rolls of fat under his chin.

Iskra wondered why she'd wanted to even try to get home. She held her breath as they ascended the slope of the bridge, hearing each clop of the horses' hooves, the protesting creak of the wood planks, the faint echoes of their steps. The scent of damp decay rode the cool breeze. Iskra wrinkled her nose, stifling a sneeze. She let her breath out in a long sigh once they had reached the other shore.

"So far, so good," the trader said. "Maybe they've got business elsewhere. Let's hope it's far away."

"We're safe now, aren't we?"

The trader slapped the reins on the horses' backs. "Safe? Nope. Not 'til we get to Gishin."

That's not reassuring, Iskra thought. She listened for dangers from the woods that surrounded the road that twisted through the trees. Every caw of a crow sounded like a warning of a warboar's approach; every creak of a tree branch swaying in the wind sounded like a bandit on the move.

About half an hour later, the horse on the left stumbled and slowed. "Steady now." The trader pulled the reins to stop the horses and jumped from the wagon. He felt the horse's legs and studied its feet. While he worked, Iskra shifted her glance from the road ahead to the forest on their right, drumming her fingers on the seat beside her.

The trader frowned as he gently touched the underside of the horse's hoof. He let out a slow breath. "He picked up a stone. Hand me my bag, will you?"

Iskra found the trader's leather bag under the seat and passed it to him. He rooted around in it and withdrew a metal spike with a hooked end. Taking the horse's front leg between his knees, he dug into the underside of the hoof. Iskra winced at the sound of the iron scraping against the metal horseshoe.

"Whoa." The trader put a calming hand on the horse as it tried to shift its weight. He dug a little more and pried out a large rock. "That's all I can do now. We'll have to do the best we can."

"Can he walk?"

"He can." The trader swung back into his seat and picked up the reins. "We'll be a bit slow. Not much chance of catching the caravan now. You're not afraid, are you?"

Iskra clenched her hands together so he wouldn't see them shaking. "No." *Just terrified.*

The trader laughed. "Well, I am. But we'll have to hope for the best."

"Do you think we should turn back?"

"I been thinking about that. But the afternoon's half gone, and we're more than halfway. We'd have to cross the bridge again, which is the most likely place to run into trouble." He paused, surveying the road behind them. "We're best off taking our chances going on."

As they traveled north, the pine trees huddled closer to the side of the road. Iskra peeked between them, searching for signs of movement. She licked her lips and pressed them together, concentrating on keeping her breathing even.

The wind picked up, raising goose bumps on Iskra's arms. It rocked the branches of the trees that stood behind the pines back and forth, rustling the leaves, sounding to Iskra like a thousand whispered threats. She clenched her teeth to keep a moan from escaping her throat.

A few miles on, Iskra noticed the trader shifting in his seat, leaning forward, peering through the trees ahead. "What's wrong?" She gripped her basket harder so the wood handle bit into her hand.

"There's something ahead. Maybe it's the caravan, stopped for some reason. Get ready to move if there's trouble. Run up the hill, then cut left and keep going north. Walk about an hour, you'll be close enough to Gishin to turn back down to the road."

"But the warboars, and the Riskers. . .." Iskra didn't know which would be worse. Her knees were shaking so badly she wasn't sure she'd be able to run.

"You can climb a tree to get away from the warboars. The Riskers won't hurt you if you stay away from 'em. Better either of them than the bandits."

"But we haven't seen any bandits at all."

"That's starting to bother me," the trader said. "I reckoned they'd want revenge after what the guardsmen did to the last lot they caught. Last month, with all the mud, it made sense the bandits weren't about. I wouldn't have wanted to be on the road in that if I could have helped it. But now the road's drying out." He shook his head. "And no sign of them today. See? There're the wagon tracks." He pointed to the lines in the dirt road, then off to the side. "And the marks of the guardsmen along the edges. I been watching the whole time, but no one has tried to come onto the road." He shook his head. "I don't like it. Something's not right. I got a bad feeling about this."

Iskra squeezed her eyes shut. The one time she got her way with her mother, this disaster had to happen. Why, oh why, had she insisted on going home? She hadn't gotten permission to leave the village for the night. Big violation of the safely rules. The ephor had to know where everyone was, to keep them safe; he would understand why she stayed, though; he would. This was all Tavda's fault, making her miss the caravan.

"Quick, girl, run for it!"

She snapped open her eyes. They had rounded a bend and caught up with the caravan. The caravan that was now being plundered. Bandits were looting the wagons and all the traders and guardsmen Iskra could see were dead. She stared, unbelieving.

The trader shoved her out of the wagon and jumped down beside her. When she didn't move, he slapped her shoulder as if she were a horse. "Run!"

3

Iskra ran straight up the hillside, toward the lower slopes of the mountain. Over the noise of her gasping breath she heard the bandits' shouts. The trader ran behind her, panting hard.

"Don't try to get away, fat boy!" a bandit called.

"Wait," the trader called to Iskra. She turned back to see him leaning against a tree, face purple and sweaty, chest heaving. He broke a cord around his neck and handed the bag that had hung there to Iskra. "See that my wife gets this, will you? Now run!"

Iskra stood motionless, clasping the bag. "Run, I say!" The trader slapped her face and pushed her toward a faint trail leading up the hill.

She ran like a scared alloe rat scurrying for its burrow. Behind her she could hear the trader making his way up the mountain, churning his way along the trail, stomping through the underbrush when the trail faded out. The sounds of pursuit grew closer, and the shouts and taunts of the bandits grew louder when they caught up to the trader. She heard a brief argument, a scream of pain. Then silence. She froze, too afraid to move farther. Wrapping her arms tightly around herself, she ducked her head, clutching the trader's bag.

"Was he alone?" she heard one bandit ask.

"I thought there was someone else, mebbe a girl. See that mark on his neck? I'll wager he pulled his money bag off and gave it to 'er."

"I'll go. If she's pretty, you kin have the money."

Iskra choked back a scream. She crept into a thick stand of pine trees and inched her way up the slope. Behind the pines the hillside turned into a rocky cliff about twenty feet high that looked like a pile of untidily stacked massive blocks. She thought if she could get over the cliff without being seen, the bandits would give up looking for her. She shoved the trader's bag into her pocket and pushed the branches of the nearest pine to make a way through the trees. A flock of birds took flight from its upper branches, squawking.

"Better not run, little girl. I know where you are!"

The bandit's shout spurred Iskra into action. She gave up trying to be quiet and ran with all she had, shoving the prickly branches out of her way, trying to ignore the sting of the needles as they scratched her face and arms.

She clambered up the cliff, using its jagged face as a ladder. At the top she seized the root of a tree that twisted around the rock like the talon of a huge bird's claw. She hoisted herself over the edge. She glanced back.

The bandit had gained on her. He was nearing the base of the cliff, his wide grin mocking her. "Don't make me work too hard for you, pretty girl."

She started to run forward, and stopped. She smelled smoke. Who would have a fire up here in the hills? Bandits, perhaps. Or Riskers. No use to hope for anything good from either one. She started to run again, the smell of smoke growing stronger. She glanced around, searching for the fire. *Maybe the bandit won't venture near it.*

His heavy footsteps cracking downed branches told her

she was wrong. Gasping for breath, she ran on, scrambling over fallen trees, breaking the underbrush as she staggered on the uneven ground. She felt as though she couldn't breathe, her panic squeezing all the air from her lungs.

"You're makin' me mad, girl." He was close behind her, his breath loud and rasping. "Ugh."

Iskra heard a heavy thud and the crackling of underbrush. She spun around and saw an arrow in the bandit's knee, blood staining his pants. She looked around wildly to see where the arrow had come from. The bandit sat up and wrenched the arrow from his leg. He seized his hunting knife and pulled his arm back, as if to hurl it at Iskra.

Another arrow lodged in his eye and he fell backward. A muscular, dark-haired man ran up and slit the bandit's throat.

A taller man carrying a bow joined him. He pulled the arrow from the bandit's eye and picked up the other one. "What made him come this far from the road?"

The first man pointed at Iskra. "She's his prey, I'll warrant." He took a step toward her, concern etched on his copper-brown face. "Are you hurt?"

She stepped back, holding her shaking hands out in front of her. "No. Don't touch me."

He laughed. "As long as you're not a bandit or a warboar, you're safe enough with us. I'm Tarkio, and I think I've seen you in Gishin."

"Yes, I'm Iskra." Now she noticed he wore the brown clothing and short boots of the traders. "You're a trader, right?" She lowered her hands slowly. Maybe she wasn't going to come to some horrible end in the forest today.

"That I am." He pointed at the other man. "This is Xico."

"Hee-co?" She repeated the strange name. He was a little younger than Tarkio and had vivid green eyes and dark hair that fell in loose curls around his golden tan face, much longer hair than a village man's. He wore a leather vest over a red shirt, not the clothes of a villager. Who was he?

Xico studied her for a moment. "Come with us. We can take care of the wounds on your face."

Iskra touched her burning cheek. Feeling the wetness, she pulled her hand away and gasped to see blood on her fingers. "You're not a bandit, are you?"

"You would call me a Risker. But we aren't what you think."

She stared at him wide-eyed as he turned and walked to the campfire, Tarkio following. Iskra stayed where she was, watching the two men walk a short distance between the trees. They doused the fire and picked up their bundles.

Xico called to her. "Coming? I live not too far from here."

"Here? In the woods?"

"In Zafrad. A Risker camp."

She looked from him to Tarkio. Go with a Risker? Impossible. "Tarkio, I can't. It's not allowed." Villagers were strictly forbidden to associate with the savage Riskers. "It's not safe."

"Then you can stay here with the warboars or wait for more bandits," Tarkio said. "If you think that would be safer." He smiled at Xico, and the two men started walking along a trail through the trees.

Iskra stood motionless. She'd spent her whole life striving to stay out of trouble, and now she was about to commit one of the worst crimes a villager could commit. *How will I get over the shame?* She knew her mother would rather she died in a bandit attack than associate with Riskers.

She looked around at the deepening shadows, listened to the rustling trees. With no other choice, hand pressed to her mouth to keep her fear in check, Iskra stumbled after Tarkio and Xico, accompanied by the raucous cawing of a crow.

4

Trotting to keep up, Iskra could hardly believe what she was seeing. Tarkio strode up the steep trail in front of her, laughing and joking with Xico. With a Risker, a barbarian. How could he be friendly with such a person? Didn't he know it was forbidden? She hoped she'd be safe enough with Tarkio, who, as a trader, was at least a known quantity. Maybe.

Over half an hour passed as they tramped through the woods before she realized they were approaching the Risker camp. Exhaustion battled with her fear. She didn't think she could walk any farther. She didn't expect to find any rest with the uncouth Riskers.

By now the sun was starting to sink toward the tops of the trees. Long shadows crossed the streets of the camp, shading the houses. She frowned. From what she'd been told, she expected the Riskers to live in caves, or maybe tents. Not houses made of . . . what? She ran her hand along a wall. Stone, with some wood. Glazed windows, too. And there were so many houses, fifty or more. The camp was about the size of Gishin, but with wider streets and bigger yards around each house.

Xico opened the door to one of the houses, letting the smell of a savory stew float into the lane. He smiled and motioned for Iskra to enter. She approached warily. All she'd ever been told was stay away from the Riskers, *it's not safe*. She grit her teeth and walked in.

"Xico, who's this?" a woman's voice asked.

Iskra stared wide-eyed at a middle-aged woman with dark blond hair pulled back in a bun, stirring a pot sitting on what looked like an oven. She was cooking! That was dangerous enough, but in her own house, that was far worse.

Iskra shifted her gaze from the oven to the woman. Her dress was green like pine needles and was pulled in at the waist by the ties of her yellow apron. Risker women were supposed to be unkempt and dirty, not neatly dressed and clean like this one.

"This is Iskra, Mam. She was running from a bandit when we found her."

"Oh." The woman looked steadily at Iskra. Her eyes were as green and as kind as her son's. "You're hurt."

"No." Iskra shook her head. "Not really."

The woman raised her eyebrows. "Xico, why don't you and Tarkio go find your father and sisters? Supper's about ready." She waited until Xico and Tarkio left, then turned to Iskra. "You're not hurt, you say? Then what's that blood on your face and sleeve?" Iskra looked at her arm and saw what the woman was talking about: Her sleeve in bloodstained ribbons, little trickles of blood drying in rusty lines that extended to her wrist.

"Sit down there." The woman gestured to a wooden bench facing the table. Iskra slowly stepped away from the door and sat down. The woman took Iskra's arm, pulled back her sleeve, and held the arm up to the sunlight coming through the window.

Iskra looked at the long scratches in her arm. "How did that happen?"

"You ran through some igla pines, didn't you? They don't call them needles just because that's what they look like." She dropped Iskra's arm and fetched a woven basket from a shelf over the bench. "Where are you from, Iskra?"

"Gishin. I was in Shinroo and missed the caravan." She hunched her shoulders. "We were attacked by bandits and I had to run. I don't have permission to be out all night. What am I going to do?" She surprised herself, talking so openly with this Risker woman. Something about her kind and gentle manner made Iskra relax a little.

"Let's get you fixed up first, then we'll worry about that."

"If you please, you don't have to go to any trouble."

The woman laughed. "No *wahalu* at all, dear." By that Iskra guessed she meant helping her was no trouble at all.

As she talked, the woman crushed dried herbs between her fingers, then poured oil on them and mashed them with a mortar and pestle. She wiped the blood from Iskra's face and arms with a damp cloth and dabbed the oil mixture on the cuts. Then she removed a cord from around her neck and held up something shaped like a dragonfly that flashed green and lavender as it reflected the light. "May the power of the sky-god heal her, may the power of the sky-god protect her, may the power of the sky-god see her home," the woman chanted. As she sang, she passed the jeweled dragonfly over Iskra's wounds.

In spite of her pain and fear, Iskra tried not to laugh. Silly superstitions these Riskers have. They may not be savages, but they are ignorant.

"Do you want something to eat?" the woman asked as she replaced the dragonfly around her neck.

"Yes, if you please."

The woman turned back to the fire and Iskra took the opportunity to look around. The floor was pine, polished and shining, as were the tables and chairs. She ran her fingers over the smooth surface of the table, tracing the rounded edge. She noted how solid and sturdy the bench was, not making a move or creak as she shifted her weight. Braided rag rugs made bright splashes of color on the floor, the reds and yellows of autumn leaves mixed with green, brown, and white. A huge brick oven filled most of one side of the room. Rows of tiny plants in pots sat on the windowsills. A ladder rested against a wall, leading up to a loft. Iskra felt the room embrace her in a warm and comforting hug.

Maybe the Riskers weren't so bad. Iskra bit her lip. No, they're barbarians. I can't let them fool me.

Iskra watched the woman as she opened a small door on the side of the oven. Heat from a roaring fire wafted through the room. The woman tossed some wood in and shut the door. Tilting her head to the side, Iskra shook her head. These barbarians made cooking over a fire safer, enclosing the fire so no one would accidentally get burned. Why are none of our fires built like that?

The door flew open, and Iskra jumped. She jerked her head around to see a silver-haired, thicker version of Xico stride into the room. He was followed by three young women, Tarkio, and then Xico himself.

"Cillia," said the man, "I hear from our son we have company."

"You hear right." She smiled at him, then pointed at Iskra. "This is Iskra. Iskra, this is my husband, Osip. Sit down, all of you. It's time to eat. Xico, open the *ikkuna*, please."

What's *ikkuna*? Iskra wondered. Maybe it's some horrible wine they'll force me to drink. She wasn't left to speculate long. Xico reached up and opened a small pane set within the larger glass pane of the window.

How clever, she thought. They can have fresh air without creating a draft. And they have glass windows. No one has glass in the village, except the ephor.

The next thing she knew, Iskra was seated next to Osip and across from Tarkio and Xico, eating food she'd never imagined. The pale-brown bread was soft with a crunchy crust. One of the girls poured a steaming sauce from a pot into a clay dish. Iskra watched as the others tore off pieces of bread and dipped it in the sauce. Not wanting to be rude, she imitated them, then gasped as she tasted the warm sweetness, like honey mixed with a darker kind of sweet. She had barely swallowed when Cillia set a clay pot the size of a large apple on the mat in front of her and handed her a spoon.

The stew in the pot was like nothing she had ever tasted, a stew with a sharp taste that created a pleasing heat in her mouth, mixed with a subtle sweet. Iskra imagined it probably was made with some kind of wild game. She hoped it wasn't warboar.

"This is so tasty," she told Cillia. "What meat is it?"

"It's just our old cow." Cillia laughed as Iskra blinked. "And a few herbs."

"Herbs? You eat medicine?"

Cillia smiled. "They're good for you, but I wouldn't call them all medicine." She pointed to the pots on the windowsills. "I forgot, you don't use them in the villages. Pepper and basil and anise, that's what I used tonight."

Osip reached over and stroked his wife's cheek, brushing back a few strands of hair that had escaped from the bun on the back of her neck. "It's a blessing to me, whatever you use, woman. Keep feeding me like this and I'll always come home."

Cillia swatted his hand away with a smile as she stood up. "Oh, get on with you."

Iskra stared at them. They seemed to have affection for one another. Shouldn't barbarians be brutal and curt? She watched Cillia pull another tray of little pots out of the oven and offer the steaming stew to her family.

Riskers eat with such abundance? I was told they lived on roots and nuts. And what makes that sauce so sweet?

"Tuli, fetch some candles, will you?" Osip asked.

One of the girls stood and walked to a shelf, then returned with a metal candlestick that split into three branches. The three branches supported a ring. Sitting on the ring were three pale yellow-green candles, held in place by delicately wrought metal leaves that surrounded the candle. Iskra had never seen such a graceful candlestick. Tuli lit the candles. To Iskra's surprise, they gave off no smoke or odor.

It was all so strange, she thought. What gives the candles that earthy color? And why don't they smoke or smell like rancid fat?

She took another bite of stew, savoring the flavors. Far better than anything she'd ever eaten in the village, and the food seemed to have no limit. Most villagers ate their meals at the inn, since cooking was so dangerous. Portions were strictly rationed out so everyone got their fair share, no more, no less. But here everyone just took what they wanted.

Confused by what she was seeing, she listened to the chatter of the three girls, who she soon learned were Xico's older sisters, Veressa, Fialka, and Tuli. She could see the family resemblance in every attractive face, all with skin in varying shades of golden tan, the girls with blue eyes like their father's, and the same confidence that stamped Xico's features. Xico seemed to be a year or two older than Iskra; his sisters were a little older.

She puzzled a little over how old Tarkio was. He'd seemed about twenty-five when in the forest. Now, teasing Xico's sisters, he appeared to be about their age.

As the girls talked, Iskra glanced from one to another, endeavoring to match these lively, pretty girls with the uncouth savages she had always imagined Riskers to be. They all wore their long dark hair in different ways, not cut short like village girls. One even had braids. Their dresses were as different as their hair, one blue, one crimson, the third a rich brown with some kind of complicated pleating on the bodice. No one Iskra knew had clothes that fine.

She pursed her lips, wondering. Perhaps what we've been taught isn't right? She shook herself. No, those are unsafe ideas. The Prime Konamei and our ephor wouldn't lie to us. These Riskers must be dangerous.

She looked around the table. Both Xico and his father were clean-shaven. She'd expected barbarians to have scruffy beards. Their tanned skin told of an outdoor life. Tarkio was a few shades darker, his skin more the color of burnished copper.

A few giggles from the girls pulled Iskra's attention to the other end of the table. The girls were telling their mother something about a house.

"Yes, it has rooms and a floor," said the youngest.

Her sister chimed in. "And can you imagine, there's even a roof."

The girl called Veressa shook her head at them and turned to her mother. "And, Mam, it even has an herb closet off the kitchen, just like yours."

The two other girls smirked. "You're planning on spending a lot of time drying herbs?" Even the men joined in their laughter, some kind of joke Iskra didn't understand. Veressa blushed and laughed along with them. What could be funny about herbs and medicines? She wrinkled her brow, gazing at Veressa, who didn't seem at all put out by her sisters' teasing.

Then Iskra saw Xico staring at her, his eyes the color of the fields in late summer just as they start to turn from green to yellow, ripening for the harvest.

She felt the heat rise in her face. To hide her confusion she looked down at her stew, noticing for the first time her pot was decorated with a pale blue flower painted on one side. Even what they eat out of is pretty, she thought.

"So, Da, I've thought it through," Xico said.

"I'm not so sure, Xico," Osip said.

Iskra looked from Xico to Osip. What were they debating? Whether they would let her go or not?

Xico waved his spoon in the air. "I went scouting the other day, east of the lake. It's teeming with game."

Osip nodded. "I'm sure it is." He held up a hand. "An' yes, I'm sure you'll catch a lot an' end up with more furs than you've ever had. But think, think about the bandits."

Xico shrugged. "I saw no sign of them."

"This time. If there's as much game as you say, they'll be after it. When they see one of your traps, they'll be sure to set one for you."

Iskra's eyes grew wider during this conversation. Cillia leaned over to her. "Xico, like his da, is a trapper. They've been arguing for weeks about trapping off to the east, deeper into the mountains."

"Isn't that dangerous?" Iskra asked.

As the light outside faded, the shadows deepened in the room, making everyone look other-worldly and strange under the flickering candlelight.

"Only if you think warboars and bandits are dangerous," Tarkio said. "Like most people do."

"If you want something, you'll have to take a risk or two," Xico said. "Isn't that what you taught me, Da?"

Osip picked up a piece of bread. "I did." He broke the bread in two pieces. "I also taught you to consider carefully what risks you'll take."

"Xico never met a risk he didn't like," said one of the sisters.

"I learned that from you, Tuli." Xico reached across the table to ruffle her hair.

Fialka stood to help her mother clear the table. She returned with four candlesticks topped with tall candles.

Extravagant, these Riskers, Iskra thought. Four more candles! She watched, fascinated, as Fialka lit them with a brand from the fire. Who are these people?

"Son," Osip said, "you're a grown man. I won't tell you

what to do. But if you go much past the lake, please don't go alone."

Xico opened his mouth, glanced at his mother, then closed it, nodding. "Yes, Da."

Iskra stared at him, jaw hanging open. "You don't mind if bandits attack you?"

Xico grinned. "It's not so bad when bandits shoot at you. They usually miss." He tossed a grape into the air and caught it in his mouth.

Iskra could think of no reply to that. She looked around the table, amazed that no one seemed at all surprised by Xico's attitude. She turned her attention back to her stew, letting the conversation flow over her. She felt she had landed in some upside-down world where risks were good and safety was unimportant. No wonder visiting Riskers was forbidden. It was too confusing.

When the meal was over, Cillia stood up from the table and rubbed Osip's neck, resting one hand on his shoulder. "Are you too tired to see our guest home?"

Before he could answer, Tarkio spoke up. "I was thinking about that. I need to go into Gishin this week, and I may as well go tonight. I'll take her down the Guarded Trail."

"Are you sure about that?" Cillia asked. "It might be too much for her."

"It's the shortest way," he answered.

Cillia frowned. "Are you afraid of heights?"

Iskra knew this question was directed at her. "Of course I am, everyone is. Heights are dangerous."

"You see?" Cillia said to Tarkio.

Osip shook his head at her, then turned to Iskra. "You told Cillia you had to get home tonight; you didn't have permission to stay out. If we take you down a gentler slope, the long way around, it would take much longer. You might not get back in time. And we could run into bandits. The Guarded Trail is well-protected."

"By who? The Prime Konamei's Guard?"

Osip smiled. "No. By Riskers. We take care of ourselves." His face grew serious. "The trail is steep and rocky, but it's the quickest way for you to get home."

Iskra hung her head. After fleeing from bandits and eating with Riskers, she didn't think she could take a hike down a treacherous path. What if she slipped and fell? She closed her eyes and tried to suppress the tremors that shook her body.

"I'm sure she'll be fine. I can help her over the steepest parts. We'll have no problems," Xico said.

Iskra looked at him, wide-eyed, amazed at his confidence, feeling a release of the tension she'd been holding for hours. Looking at him, she almost believed she'd get down the mountain safely.

Osip and Cillia exchanged a long glance. Then Osip said, "All right. But Xico, you go just to the foot of the mountain. No farther. Take no chances. *Samatale*?"

Xico nodded. "*Samatale*."

5

Iskra followed Xico as he strode along the path that ran north along the steep side of the mountain. He carried his bow and three arrows in one hand and wore a full quiver slung at his hip. He hummed as he walked, cheerful tunes that made Iskra feel like she could face down a bandit. Maybe an old and feeble bandit, but a bandit nonetheless. She was relieved to see that even though the sun had nearly set, it wasn't as dark as she had feared. There was enough light to see where she was putting her feet.

Suddenly Xico disappeared. Iskra stopped, heart pounding. What was he up to? He wouldn't attack her now, would he? But, that's what barbarian Riskers did. They jump you when you least expect it. But he didn't seem like the kind of person who would do such a thing.

Tarkio, a step behind her, nearly ran into her. "Just keep going. You'll see."

Sure enough, a few steps on Iskra saw that the path turned abruptly around an outcropping of rock. Xico was walking slowly, kicking rocks to the sides of the trail. A bird whistled, and Xico whistled in return. "The guards know we are here. Come. Be careful on the steps." He held out his hand to Iskra.

She hesitated a moment before putting her hand in his. It was bad enough to eat Risker food, but to touch one of them was worse. Or so she'd been told.

She let her fingers wrap around his, feeling a sense of security from clinging to his strong hand. Her heartbeat slowed and her breathing steadied.

The path abruptly changed from a gentle slope to a steep incline, with a few uneven steps chiseled into the stone. *He calls them steps. They seem more like notches to me.* She could barely fit her heels on some of them.

She caught a glimpse of the path winding down the slope of the mountain, and fought back a wild urge to throw herself down to end the dizzy sensation in her head, to stop the pounding of her heart. She paused, gasping as if she'd been running and put her hand against the side of the cliff.

Xico looked up at her. "You can do this. Just put one foot in front of the other. One in front of the other." He squeezed her hand and smiled.

She gasped as she felt a tingling sensation race from her hand all the way to her toes.

Xico tugged gently on her hand. "Come on."

Iskra wasn't certain she'd make it down the mountain. What she did know was she wanted to see Xico smile at her again. She gripped his hand tighter and cautiously took a step.

"Good, just keep going. One foot in front of the other." She cautiously took a few more steps. With each step, her confidence grew. She looked up to see Xico smiling at her, with not just his mouth but with his large green eyes. Suddenly feeling confused, she looked down and skidded a few feet on some pebbles.

"Not so fast." Xico laughed as he steadied her, wrapping an arm around her waist to keep her from falling. "One step at a time."

She froze in place, head tilted back so she could look into his eyes. A Risker has his arm around me. Worse than that, I like it. She felt a flush spread across her face. "Um, sorry," she said. She stepped back from him and took another step, her attention torn between the feeling of his hand holding hers and trying not to trip and fall.

As they made their way through the lower part of the path, Iskra felt her fear ebb. She shook her head, trying to understand why she felt calmer; surely, it had nothing to do with the Risker holding her hand.

Xico pulled his hand from hers at the foot of the mountain. "You've got quite a grip, girl." He shook his hand and flexed his long fingers. "Iskra, I'm glad we met you. Hope to see you again. Goodnight, Tarkio." He turned to begin the climb back.

"Xico, wait," Iskra said. "I haven't thanked you for saving me, for helping me."

He waved a hand in the air, smiling. "Think nothing of it. You'd better get going before they lock the gates." He nodded his farewell and started trotting up the slope.

"He's right, we don't have much time. Can you walk fast?" Without waiting for an answer, Tarkio strode toward the road.

Iskra scurried to keep up with him, not wanting to lose him in the twilight. Rustling leaves in the forest set her imagination running, conjuring up images of fierce bandits and ferocious warboars. An image of her mother popped into her mind, an angry, scolding woman Iskra feared all the more because she was real. So far, she'd survived her adventure without too much trouble. She could only hope she could get home safely and forget all about it.

TARKIO WAS silent as he strode along the road. It was one thing to rescue Iskra from bandits, another to explain to her mother what had happened. This girl was probably in for a bad time. He chewed on the inside of his mouth. It would be his fault for taking Iskra to the Riskers, breaking all the rules. Not that he'd had much of a choice. He'd have to do what he could to see she didn't get in trouble.

"Iskra, listen to me. You know villagers and Riskers are forbidden to mingle."

"You seem to know them. Why is it all right for you?"

He frowned. Interesting that this girl who seemed as timid as an alloe rat wasn't afraid to ask questions. "I'm a trader. I have a special license to trade with them, so it's all business. I go there nearly every week. It's different for you. Maybe it would be better if you don't say much about the Risker camp."

"Lie to my mother?"

"No, we'll tell her the truth. Let me do the talking. But I saw your face, how you enjoyed your time there."

She shrugged, tipping her head to one side. "I liked Cillia, and them."

"They're likable people. But you're not supposed to have anything to do with them. Do you want to upset your mother?"

"No, but—"

"You do know you broke the rules by even going to the Risker camp. Some people have been taken for that."

"But why? What's so bad about it? Besides, it wasn't my fault."

"I know. Not everyone will believe you." He stopped to look Iskra in the face, her features well-lit in the moonlight. "Think about it. It wouldn't be safe if people knew you'd been there. Not safe for you, or for your mother." Not to mention, could put his trading license in jeopardy.

When she changed the subject, he knew he'd won the argument. "Tarkio, what was that word they used? *Samatale*?"

Tarkio laughed. "It means 'We agree.'"

They continued along the trail in silence, the only sound the muted rustle of the birch leaves overhead. A few minutes later they reached the road just a few hundred yards from the gates of Gishin. Tarkio heard the creak of the gates being pulled shut, the heavy doors scraping the stone surface of the road. "Quick, they're locking up." He grabbed her hand and began to run.

The gatekeeper frowned as they dashed up. "Tarkio, what are you doing? Where's your wagon?" His eyes widened when he saw Tarkio's companion. "Iskra? Weren't you supposed to be with the caravan that got ambushed?"

"I'll come back and tell you later, Uyar," Tarkio answered. "I've got to get her home." He hustled Iskra past the gates. "Where to?"

She led the way down a narrow side street to the two-room house she shared with her mother, a tiny cottage that looked like every other in the village: one story, wood frame, thatched roof, weatherbeaten and badly in need of a fresh coat of paint. Through the slats in the wood shutters that covered the small window, he saw Iskra's mother sitting at the battered kitchen table, head bowed, gripping her short iron-gray hair with both hands. A single candle stood in a chipped brown clay dish, flickering and smoking, casting jerky shadows.

Iskra opened the door. "Mam! I'm home!"

Luza sprung up from the table and turned. "Where have you been? Don't you see how worried I've been? Why didn't you get here sooner? And who is this?" She pointed a long, skinny finger at Tarkio.

He stepped closer to her. "My name is Tarkio, and I'm a trader. You must have heard the caravan was attacked by bandits."

"Yes, I know. Two of the guardsmen escaped and brought the news. They didn't know anything about Iskra."

"That's because she missed the caravan."

Luza turned on Iskra. "What kept you from catching it?"

"Tavda was buying plums, and—"

"Tavda was buying plums. You know how dangerous it is to even go to another village. But you had to loiter around the market with Tavda. You promised I could trust you to catch that caravan. But no." Luza raised her hand as if to hit Iskra, then dropped it when Tarkio caught her eye. "Are you sure that's the truth? Plums? What were you really doing that made you late?"

Tarkio sucked in a breath. This woman's daughter barely escaped with her life, and all she could do was berate her about fruit. He interrupted Luza's tirade, trying to divert her thoughts. "It's a good thing she did miss it, don't you think?"

"How did she get back?"

"There was a trader who also missed the caravan," Tarkio said. "He offered her a ride back with him."

"Where is he?"

"They caught up with the caravan just in time to interrupt the bandits' looting. Iskra and the trader fled into the woods. From the sound of it, this trader sent Iskra ahead and let the bandits catch him, to give her time to get away."

Luza pressed her fist to her mouth and glanced from Tarkio to Iskra. "Is that true?"

Tarkio didn't allow Iskra to answer. "One of the bandits went after her. I was on the hill for business when I heard someone running up the slope, and some shouting. When they got closer, I saw what was going on and fought the bandit off. She was pretty shaken up. I took her to the Risker camp to let her catch her breath. It took us a while to make our way here." He noted with some relief that Luza seemed to be calming down. "I'm sorry you were worried, but I did the best I could to keep her safe."

Luza looked at him through narrowed eyes. "I know what kind of business goes on up the hill. Trading with Riskers." She spat out the word "Risker" as if it burned her lips. "Well, I thank you for helping my daughter. I am in your debt."

"Think nothing of it. Peace and safety to you."

As he closed the door behind him, he saw anger in Luza's eyes, anger mixed with fear simmering under her cold courtesy. He hoped she wouldn't take it out on Iskra. If she did, it would be his fault. Maybe he could have said something different to calm the woman down. He shook his head. Poor little timid Iskra.

6

Iskra watched as her mother leaned against the closed door, her hands pressing into the rough wood as if to shut out Tarkio, Riskers, bandits, and whatever else lurked in the dark night.

She took a deep breath as Luza slowly turned to look at her. "Explain."

Iskra crossed her arms, hugging herself. "Mam, you heard what Tarkio said."

"I did. He said precious little about what went on in that Risker camp." Luza took a few steps away, then turned back abruptly, wrinkling her nose like she smelled rotten eggs. "What happened there?"

"A woman cleaned up my scratched arm and face, and gave me dinner. And they helped me down the Guarded Path—"

"What scratches?" Luza took a step forward and waved a finger in Iskra's face. "Show me."

"I cut myself on some igla needles when I was running through the forest."

"I see the ripped sleeves. But there's not a mark on your face."

"Sure there is, Mam. See the blood on my dress?"

"Bloodstains, yes. But your face is as smooth as it was when you left. See for yourself." Luza grabbed Iskra by the elbow and dragged her over to a tiny, polished brass plate hanging on a nail.

Iskra stared at her reflection. Her mother was right. Even in the dim light, she could see there wasn't a mark on her face. No scratches, not even a streak of dried blood or trace of the oil Cillia had used.

"And what's this story about igla needles?"

Iskra pushed the torn pieces of her sleeve aside. "And here, too, I was all scratched, some of them deep."

Luza grabbed her wrist and twisted her arm to shine more of the candlelight on it. "I see nothing. Not a scrape, not a cut, not a single drop of blood on your skin." She dropped Iskra's arm and seized the other one. "No marks here, either. Whose blood do you have all over you? You'd better tell me the truth."

"I am." Iskra took a deep breath. Then she looked straight at her mother and tried to speak slowly. She wished her mother would believe her. "I was all cut up. Cillia washed the blood off, then she mixed some herbs, and chanted something. The herbs made it feel better right away."

Luza's knees buckled and she nearly collapsed on the floor. Iskra grabbed her to keep her upright, surprised at how heavy her scrawny mother was. Luza pushed her away and staggered to the table. She leaned against it, breathing in shallow gasps.

"Mam, are you all right?"

"All right? My daughter breaks all the rules and goes to a Risker camp." Luza moaned and lowered herself onto a wooden stool. "She then allows them to practice their superstitions and use their dangerous drugs on her. Those potions can take over your mind, you know. She follows this up by violating all our laws and eats with a Risker family. Then she asks if I'm all right?" She leaned forward and put her head in her heads.

"What else could I have done?"

Luza jerked upright and glared at Iskra. "Stupid girl, you could have asked Tarkio to bring you straight home. If he insisted on going to that camp, you could have refused food or treatment until he was ready to bring you back. He should have known better. You should have known better."

"That would have been rude. And my arms hurt. Aren't you glad they're better?"

"Don't try to distract me. That's what you always do." Luza narrowed her pale blue eyes. "You're impossible. I'm trying to keep us safe." She grabbed Iskra's arm and twisted it. "Don't ever tell anyone you even saw a Risker. If anyone asks, Tarkio found you in the woods and brought you home." She released Iskra, pushing her away.

Rubbing her arm, Iskra asked, "Why can't I talk about the Riskers?"

"Your father was another one like you. Always asking questions. Selfish. Careless. Just stop it, Iskra. Don't say a word to anyone." Luza put her head down on the table.

Iskra stared, noting how her mother was shaking so badly she was rocking the table, the stool creaking under her shifting weight. Why was she so frightened? And what could her mother mean about her father? She was still formulating a question that wouldn't provoke more anger from Luza, when a loud rap sounded at the door.

Her mother bolted upright. Hands shaking, Luza stood up, leaning on the table.

Another knock. "Luza, are you there?"

Luza gasped, and rushed to the door, flinging it open. "Kaberco!" She leaned against the door jamb, shaking.

"Hold on," Kaberco said. He pulled Luza into the cottage and closed the door, his bulk filling the tiny space, his black cloak making him seem even larger. "I heard about Iskra. Is she safe?"

"I'm here," Iskra said. Kaberco had been a good friend to Iskra after her father died, almost like an uncle. Usually just his presence, his wise, observant eyes and solid, tall frame made her feel safe. At least with him in the house, her mother would stop yelling at her.

Kaberco glanced at her, then led Luza to the table and helped her onto a stool. "Well, you don't look hurt," he said to Iskra. "What happened?"

Iskra took a deep breath, heart thumping to find herself the center of attention, and told him about missing the caravan. "I was so upset that I hadn't asked you for permission to stay overnight. All I knew was I just had to get home." She twisted her hands together, looking into his hazel eyes for a response.

"I'm glad you were concerned about safety." Kaberco nodded for her to go on.

Encouraged by his approval, she told about riding with the trader, her flight up the hill, and rescue by Tarkio, leaving out any mention of Riskers. She didn't think he'd be so approving of that part of her story. "Then Tarkio brought me home. Mam was so worried about me, and I'm so sorry."

The wrinkles on Kaberco's forehead smoothed as his whole face relaxed. "Don't worry, there's no harm done." He patted Luza's shoulder, straightening the tan band on her shoulder that marked her as a builder's clerk. "Is there?" He didn't wait for an answer. "Iskra, I'm happy you made it back safely." He put his arms around her and gave her a gentle hug.

She pressed her face into his chest, stifling a sob. *At least he cares about me.*

Kaberco took a step back and ran a hand over the lower part of his face. "You can see why it's important that I know if someone is traveling, right? If I thought you were staying in Shinroo, I wouldn't have been worried. I was getting ready to send someone to look for you when Uyar reported you were back. That's why we have the rules, you know, to keep people safe." He looked straight at Iskra. "Which is why we need everyone's cooperation, you see?"

She nodded. "I understand." To her relief, she saw a kind smile on his face. *Good, he's not angry with me.* She hated being criticized, especially when her mother was involved.

"Good. Luza, I'll leave you two. I'm sure you're both tired."

Luza nodded weakly. "Thank you, Kaberco. You're a good friend."

He took her hand and squeezed it. He nodded to Luza. "Peace and safety." He turned and let himself out of the house.

Luza stared at Iskra, eyes narrowed, mouth compressed. She rocked slightly on the stool, as if to add the creaking of the stool to the chorus of accusations against Iskra. "You may have fooled him, but not me. Never again, do you hear me? Never again will I let you go off with Tavda or anyone else. You will stay safe. You will not put me in danger. I will see to it. Now go to bed." She put her head down on the table.

Iskra hesitated, then walked to her mother. She laid a hand on Luza's bony shoulder. "Mam—"

Luza jerked upright and batted Iskra's hand away. "You pestered me for weeks. 'I just want to see what another village is like.' What's wrong with you? The life we have here, Gishin isn't good enough for you? See what happened, all because you were curious." She curled her lip. "Go to bed. I don't want to see you."

Iskra stared unbelieving into her mother's angry eyes, then turned away. *What did I do that was so horrible?*

She sighed and shuffled into the room they slept in. Two piles of straw covered with rough fabric served as beds. Iskra pulled off her dress, hung it on a nail and settled onto her straw, pulling her worn brown blanket over her.

She thought about the events of the day. First the trader, infuriated about something crazy Old Cassie had said. Then Tavda, making her late. She shuddered, thinking what could have happened if the bandits had caught her, if not for Tarkio and Xico. She shook her head. That Risker family reminded her of Tavda's, always joking and teasing each other, not afraid to show affection. Not at all like her mother.

She shook herself. How could she be admiring something about Riskers? She should be revolted and disgusted with herself for not being repulsed by them. But she'd seen nothing to despise.

Or to fear. Yes, she had to admit, she was afraid walking down the mountain path. But it wasn't impossible, and not dangerous if you were careful. Or had someone's hand to hold. It seemed to her the mountains weren't forbidden because of the trails. Warboars and bandits, they were a different story.

Which left the Riskers. Try as she could, she couldn't understand why they were forbidden.

There was much that confused her. From the mysterious healing of her wounds to the puzzle of the not-so-savage Riskers, people who ate tasty food and had houses that smelled like savory stew and fresh flowers, not musty straw and sour ashes. Risker girls with long hair and pretty dresses. A Risker boy with green eyes who gave her confidence and stirred her senses in a way she couldn't understand. She was a little unsettled that she liked the way he looked at her.

She shoved those thoughts away to consider what her mother had said, that her father was always asking questions. She knew little about the father who died when she was five. Kaberco and his sister had stepped in, caring for Iskra while her mother was too distraught to do anything. Iskra and her mother would have been lost without them.

With a start she realized that behind the anger in her mother's eyes was something like fear. Her mother had been angry at first, then terrified. Her fear had grown like a wind that quickened before a storm, a subtle breeze that intensified to an overpowering force. The fear only got worse when Kaberco arrived.

Kaberco. Her mother's loyal friend. He'd always been like a protector to Iskra, but it seemed that he was warning her about something. Iskra sighed. There's something not right here, she thought. How do I find out what it is without getting more people mad at me? Or getting taken myself?

KABERCO strode through the chilly night air, the gold chain he wore draped over his shoulders as a badge of his office jingling slightly. Now he could breathe easier, knowing Iskra was unharmed. He winced, thinking of little Iskra in the hands of bandits. She didn't seem to be harmed by her experience, just nervous, shifting her weight back and forth, not looking him in the eye. He frowned, trying to remember every detail of her behavior. Did she tell him the truth about what happened?

Her worry about not having permission to stay overnight in Shinroo was genuine, that much was clear. He waved at a guardsman on patrol and made his way down the quiet street. As he walked, he thought through the conversation again. Iskra had always been docile and obedient, quick to cooperate with all the safety rules. Nodding, he thought it was good most people were like her, wanting to comply.

Maybe that's it, he thought. Luza probably came down hard on her over missing the caravan. That's why Iskra seemed so uneasy.

He chuckled to himself. If he knew Luza, she'd make sure that there'd be no more close calls. No one in the village was more concerned with safety and following the rules than Luza.

Except himself. He let out a sigh and turned his face to look up at Dabrey and Zlu, the two moons that brightened the night sky. Dabrey was waning, now just a sliver, while the smaller Zlu was still full. Together they gave almost enough light to cast shadows. He liked these clear nights when both moons showed themselves. It was easier for his guardsmen to patrol the streets of the village and the outside of its walls.

These bandit attacks, they were a worry. He'd have to send an account in the morning to the Prime Konamei, and the local konameis, the Gishin council members. At least he wouldn't have to report a young girl's capture. He shuddered and grit his teeth. After what happened to his sister, he'd do anything to prevent that from happening to anyone ever again.

He bit his lip as he approached his house. How to word his report? The Prime Konamei never liked to hear about loss of life or property. He just wanted the population kept safe and everyone obeying the laws. In the two months Kaberco had been ephor, he'd done the best he could. But it never seemed to be enough.

A puff of a breeze cooled his face and stirred the hem of his cloak, and brought with it a spark of an idea. Best to emphasize this was the first attack in weeks. But how to explain that only two guardsmen and a young girl survived? Not to mention the gruesome end some of the traders had faced. That's going to take some finesse. He knew he was in for a long night of writing. *I can't afford any mistakes right now. Not now.*

Iskra sat primly on the bench in the corridor of the town hall just outside Kaberco's office the next day, swinging her feet. She thought back to the many times she'd come to visit him over the years, a small, timid girl grateful for the attention of the man who promised to keep her safe. Since he'd become the ephor her visits were less frequent, as she sensed his busyness and felt a little awed by his new importance.

But this afternoon she'd overcome her shyness and gone to see him. The clerk told her to wait, pointing to the rough wooden bench. She ran her fingers over it. Not smooth, like the table in Osip's house. The Riskers aren't savages. Why are they forbidden to mix with us? She'd tried to ask her mother earlier in the morning. Big mistake. That just loosened a downpour of harsh ranting from Luza, and the command never to say the word "Risker" again.

All of which made Iskra's thoughts churn like water in a washerwoman's tub. Lots of action that went nowhere, just stirred up dirt in the water.

Which was why she decided to seek out Kaberco. He'd always had answers to her troubles in the past. When she broke a toy, or lost her basket, or couldn't do her homework, Kaberco was the one she turned to. As she grew older, he listened to her talk about how she wanted to serve the village. One week it was as a baker, the next a vendor in the market. He always listened, advised, and encouraged.

She toyed with the yellow-green ribbon tied around the handle of her basket. If only he'll tell me what I want to know. She felt a fluttery sense in her stomach. There's no need to be nervous, she told herself. It's just Kaberco.

The door to Kaberco's office opened and the clerk came out. "You can go in now," he said.

Iskra stood, "Thank you." She walked into Kaberco's office, smiling.

He was seated behind his rough wooden work table, his big frame dominating the room. Simple, drab matting covered the stone floor, the uneven plastered walls bare of any decoration. Very much like Kaberco, Iskra thought. Plain and direct, all business, gets the job done.

Mounted on a side wall was a mechanical clock, one of only two in the whole town. She was fascinated by that clock and how it counted off the minutes. She knew Kaberco treasured his minutes and doled them out sparingly to people who came to see him. Which told her that while he valued her visits, she needed to use the time as efficiently as he did.

He returned her smile. "I haven't seen you in weeks, and now twice in two days. I hope today's visit is for a happier reason than last night's?"

"What? My safe return wasn't happy?"

He leaned back and laughed. "You know what I mean. What's on your mind?"

She sat on the stool facing him across the table and reached into her basket. "I brought you something. Well, really, us something." She pulled out two warm pasties. "I got the ones you like, the ones with honey."

He reached out for the pasty. "Well done, Iskra. I haven't had one of these in months. No one else thinks to bring me sweets." They both took a bite and chewed in silence.

She looked down at the pasty in her hand, trying to decide how to start the conversation. "Kaberco, do you like your job?"

He raised his eyebrows and nodded. "Of course I do. Why do you ask?"

"Because it could be dangerous. You know, fighting bandits. Or warboars. Or Riskers."

He nodded. "Yes, there is some danger. But those of us who choose to serve the village by protecting it know that the risks we take are to keep everyone else safe. This way only a few people have to be in danger."

"I've heard of you fighting warboars, and bandits, but never Riskers." The flutters in her stomach grew stronger.

Kaberco didn't seem to notice her nervousness. "That's because we have a treaty with them. Believe me, I wouldn't ever want to fight with them."

Now he had her interest. "Why not?"

"Because unlike warboars, they are smart. And unlike bandits, they are disciplined."

"Smart? Disciplined? I thought they are barbarians."

"Just because they are uncouth doesn't make them stupid. No, Riskers would make ferocious enemies. Better to avoid them altogether."

She thought about what he said. It seemed he wanted to change the subject, but she wasn't satisfied with his answers. Her pulse pounding, she asked, "Have you ever been to a Risker camp?"

He looked at her, pulling his brows together, searching her face as if to read her mind. "Why?" He pointed a finger at her. "What's this sudden interest in the Riskers?"

She swallowed, hoping he wouldn't figure out she hadn't told him the whole truth the night before. "Well, when the trader and I realized the bandits were coming after us, he told me to run up the mountain. I asked him about warboars and Riskers. He said the Riskers wouldn't hurt me if I stayed away from them."

"He's right."

"But being up on the mountain got me curious and I thought I'd ask you, since if anyone had been there, it would be you."

His face softened a little. "No, Iskra, I've never been up there. I've never had any need, or desire to go there. You shouldn't either."

She lowered her head and looked at her hands. He wasn't going to answer her.

When she didn't answer right away, he went on. "Don't let your curiosity lead you into danger, Iskra. Concentrate on staying safe, helping to build our safe, fair, and prosperous society by serving the village." He leaned forward. "You know I only want what's best and safest for you."

She looked up and smiled at him. "I know you do, Kaberco."

"Now, tell me about your apprenticeship," he asked. "Who are you working for this week?"

The fluttering in her stomach ceased. He wasn't going to press her harder about her new interest in the Riskers. *Except he didn't tell me the whole truth, that some traders go to the Riskers. Was that to keep me from asking more questions, to keep me safe? Or is there another reason?* She smiled at him and launched into an account of the market vendor she'd been working for and his great love of buttons, shoelaces, and little scraps of string.

7

Three days after he rescued Iskra, Tarkio joined a caravan headed for Trofmose, a large town at the confluence of the rivers Mirna and Shin, a day and a half journey from Gishin. He noted and approved the extra guardsmen on duty. *Maybe these will be more intrepid than the ones guarding the caravan Iskra was meant to be on.* He had heard that two of them had fled at the first sign of trouble. Shaking his head, Tarkio thought they must not have considered their pay was worth fighting for.

As usual, he took a spot toward the back of the caravan. He had spent the day before conveying barrels of honey down from the Risker camp, enough to fill a borrowed wagon. His own wagon was still in Shinroo where he'd left it before he went on foot to the Riskers to see about their honey harvest.

He'd hidden bags of Risker baked goods in between the barrels. They took the rough rye flour the villages produced, ground it to a finer texture, and mixed it with ground nuts, milled as fine as powder, and created light and moist bread and cakes. Most villagers didn't even know that anything other than coarse black bread existed. The Riskers' baked goods were reserved for the ephors and other members of the village councils. Tarkio's special license to trade with the Riskers let him in on secrets he knew the Prime Konamei wouldn't want many to know. He wasn't sure he wanted to know them, either.

When the road widened, Tarkio moved his wagon to travel alongside Waukomis, a tall, red-haired trader from the south. "Let me pass you, Waukomis," he said. "I'm tired of smelling your fish."

"I'll live and die in the stink of smoked fish," Waukomis replied with a grin, smiling all the way to his dark brown eyes. "It's worse today, with all this sun." He wiped his forehead on his sleeve and scratched his head, tugging at his short red hair. "You might not like the stench, but to me, it's the odor of successful trades and good times ahead. How goes it with you?"

"Can't complain. Should be good trading in Trofmose if it doesn't rain." He looked up at a cloud twisting overhead.

"If it rains, it will be good for the crops. They say the rye will be plentiful this year."

"They say that every year. Every year it's worse."

They rode in silence for some minutes, the only sound made by the creaking of harnesses and the horses' hoofs on the dry road. A cloud passed over the sun, putting them in shadow, giving them a little relief from the glare. The guardsman riding behind them spurred his horse to pass them, to change places with one of the other guards.

After the guard passed a few other wagons, Tarkio asked, "Have you heard from Poales?"

"Yes. He's just back from Litavye. He's been talking to anyone who will listen, from here to there."

"And?"

"A few traders down there agree with us, that the guardsmen need to do better protecting us given all the sheaves we pay them. They'll back us up with the guild."

"Good. What about the capital?"

Waukomis swatted at a fly. "So far, no. The guilds there are all too comfortable, living off the rest of the country. They have a good life, why should they speak up, risk it for anyone else?"

"Can't blame them, somehow."

"I hope if I were them, I'd still want what's fair for everyone," Waukomis said.

"Me, too." Tarkio glanced over his shoulder. "No sign of anyone coming from behind. I'll breathe easier once we get past these hills and come to the river."

"Did you hear about that caravan that got attacked three days ago? This time they didn't kill all the traders, they tied them to trees for the warboars to eat. The guardsmen from Gishin got there too late."

Tarkio snorted. "I more than heard. I was up in the hills when a girl came running, chased by one of the bandits. Xico and I killed him, then took her home."

"Home, meaning?"

"Xico's."

Waukomis looked at him in disbelief. "You didn't."

Shrugging, Tarkio said, "Yeah, what could we do? We couldn't just leave her there on the mountain, not with the sun going down. Cillia cleaned her up, gave her dinner, then I took her back to the village."

Waukomis shook his head. "Maybe we will have a good harvest this year. Or a third moon will grow in the sky. Tarkio the Perfect did something crazy."

Tarkio laughed. "It wasn't that crazy. We had to help her somehow." He caught the smirk on Waukomis' face. "She's just a kid. Fourteen, maybe fifteen. We couldn't leave her alone in the woods. It wouldn't have been right." Sensing Waukomis didn't believe him, he added, "Besides, she's a scared little rabbit. She'll never break the rules again."

Waukomis smiled. "Would be fun to see if she could be convinced, though."

Tarkio jumped when Waukomis voiced what he'd been privately thinking. Quickly, he started to respond. "Probably not a good idea—"

A shout interrupted him. A pack of bandits was hurtling down from the hills, fifteen riders armed with longbows and battle axes. The guardsmen rode to meet them, spearing two with their lances.

Tarkio and Waukomis grabbed their bows. Tarkio pressed his lips together, forcing himself to take even breaths, waiting for a bandit to ride within range. His first shot missed the man, but lodged in the horse's flank. The roan stumbled and fell to the ground. It rolled, crushing his rider.

Two other bandits rode toward them, eluding the guardsmen who were clustered near the center of the caravan. Tarkio and Waukomis shot arrow after arrow, some bouncing from the leather protecting the bandits' chests and legs. The trader in the wagon in front of them fell, screaming, an arrow lodged in his shoulder.

"Kill the horses!" Tarkio shouted.

Two more arrows were enough to down the horses. Their riders leapt free of their wounded animals, and ran toward the wagons, swinging their battle axes.

"I'll take the big one with the yellow beard," Waukomis said. "Wait 'til you can smell them."

Tarkio had to smile at that. Waukomis would go to his grave cracking jokes. The two of them nocked an arrow each and held two others ready as they pulled the bowstrings taut.

The bandits ran toward them. When they were fifteen yards away the morning breeze brought the scent of stale sweat to Tarkio's nose. "I smell 'em now," he said.

Tarkio's first shot dove into the bandit's arm. The second went through his neck, spilling a river of red on his dusty ash-colored shirt. Waukomis hit his man in the knee. With a shriek, the bandit dropped his axe and fell to the ground. Tarkio pulled out his knife, leaped down from the wagon, and ran to slit the man's throat. He turned to make sure the other was dead, slitting his throat to be certain. He wiped his blade on the bandit's worn leather shirt.

They looked at each other, panting, then along the line of wagons. Two guardsmen were fighting with two bandits, the others firing arrows at three bandits fleeing for the hills. One bandit lost his head, sliced off by the guard's sword. A well-placed thrust of a lance ended the life of the other. A few traders were slumped in their seats, killed by bandit arrows. Eight bandits lay dead on the ground.

Tarkio let out a long breath and dropped his hands to his sides, holding his bow loosely. He leaned against the nearest wagon, feeling the tension wane and his knees go weak.

After a few minutes, he joined Waukomis. They picked up a few arrows, then hitched the dead traders' horses to follow wagons of traders who'd survived. Then they shifted the cargo to other wagons. The guardsmen collected the bandits' weapons, and the two horses that had survived. Other traders searched the corpses for money, or anything they could sell.

"That's enough, move along," the guard captain said. "We don't want to wait for them to come back with friends."

Tarkio and Waukomis walked back to their wagons.

"These guardsmen fought," Tarkio said. "The other day, they didn't. Strange."

"Strange, indeed." Waukomis wrinkled his forehead, brows drawn together. He held up one of the bandits' arrows he'd picked up from the ground. "And since when do bandits use red arrows?"

THE CARAVAN PULLED into the Trofmose market, the province's main town. In spite of everyone's fears, they had suffered no further bandit attacks and spent a peaceful night camped along the road. When the lead wagons finally passed through

Trofmose's iron gates in between twin guard towers, traders and guardsmen alike cheered.

Tarkio drove his wagon into the market and signed his bills of lading for the honey, turning it over to his usual customers: assistants of the konameis, as the town council members were called. He parked his wagon behind the livery stable and left his horses in the care of the stableboy. Then he took his bundles of baked goods and delivered them to the ephor and other konameis. After his last stop, he stood thoughtfully, shaking the coins in his hand. Five bundles of bread brought in nearly a third of what a wagon full of honey did. How much money did the konameis have, that they could pay so much?

He shoved the coins into his bag and walked back to the market. *Better get my wife something,* he thought. *Then she'll be happy to see me.* The market was crowded, even for Sheshanbe, the seventh day of the week. Most people should be working. He wandered through the stalls, ignoring the chilly wind, looking for something that might please his wife. She didn't need any pottery. Maybe some cotton cloth? Her taste was so particular he was afraid to choose something she would wrinkle her nose at. He looked idly at candles and lamps. The last time he'd bought something for the house, his wife scolded him for buying something she'd purchased the week before. "If you were home more, you'd know what we need."

Almost every time he came home it was the same. The complaints. The anger. The sobs. Like being trapped in a dark alley at night with no way out. Then suddenly, like turning a corner, the lights would come on, her mood would change. She'd show a zest for life and fun few others could imitate. It didn't seem fair he never knew what made her mood change, or that she always blamed him when she was down. He rubbed his jaw, wondering why he always seemed to fail at reading his wife's moods.

He wandered along another aisle of stalls, not really seeing the goods on display. It wasn't fair to her, either, this life they led. She wasn't cut out to be a trader's wife, not with her moodiness and fears. He should have picked someone with a bit more backbone, a bit more even keel. But at seventeen and grieving the loss of his father, loneliness urged him to marry the first pretty girl who wanted him. Two years later, he had to admit her companionship wasn't always enough.

He pressed on, hoping to find the perfect gift. He stepped around mud puddles and panting dogs. He smiled at the baker's daughter flirting with the butcher's son, ignored people shouting out prices in an effort to entice passersby to stop, to look, to buy. An hour later he was chilled through, but still searching, seeking that perfect something that would put his wife in a good mood. He realized if he didn't get home soon, no gift would be enough to ensure peace in his house. Why was this so difficult? With a sigh, he bought a small bouquet of early spring flowers, the vivid orange ones Groa usually liked.

He turned to walk to his house, a house like every other villager's, rough wooden walls, two rooms, and a thatched roof. What was different about his was the drama that raged within. He pressed his lips together and his steps slowed like an exhausted mule's, unwilling to move quickly. Who would he find when he opened the door? Smiling happy Groa, or the scowling, angry one? Or would she even be home? As a market vendor, her days off weren't regular. He took a deep breath and went in.

His wife was sitting at the wood table by a window, mending one of his shirts, her dark red hair hanging limp around her bronzed face as she bent over her sewing. A few spools of dull brown thread stood on the table next to a pair of scissors. A good sign, he thought. She at least felt enough for him to mend his shirts.

"Groa, I'm home."

She looked up at him without smiling. "I see."

"How are you?"

"The same. You?"

He took a step toward her. "The trading was good. The Riskers harvested some honey, so I had a full load."

She went back to her sewing. "I heard another caravan was attacked. Were you on it?"

He laid the flowers on the table. She glanced at them, then made another stitch. Tarkio realized he was dealing with Melancholy Groa. At least she wasn't Raging Groa, who threw insults and the iron teakettle at his head, who might try to stab him with her sewing scissors.

"No," he said. "I was already with the Riskers." He pulled out a stool and sat down, wondering how much to tell her. Maybe if he trusted her with a secret, she'd trust him more in turn, and maybe even warm up a little. "Now that you mention it, a funny thing happened."

She drew her thin eyebrows together over her obsidian eyes. "What's funny about a bandit attack?"

"Well, not humorous. Odd." He waited to see if she was at all interested. "Do you want to hear about it?"

"If you want to tell me."

He pulled his stool closer to her. "I do. But, Groa, you have to promise not to tell anyone."

She set her sewing on her lap and looked at him. "No one?"

"No one, not even your sister. Promise?"

A little smile formed at the corners of her mouth. "Promise. Now what's this all about?"

"I was in the woods with Xico. We'd gone to see if we could find beehives they hadn't harvested before. Then we heard shouting and the noise of people running through the underbrush."

"Bandits?"

"One. He was chasing a trader and a girl."

"What girl?"

"A girl from Gishin. The trader was caught and killed. Xico and I finished off the bandit."

"So you got to play hero for a girl, while I sit here by myself. Is she pretty?"

Tarkio suppressed a sigh. Groa's jealousy flashed as unpredictably as lightning. "Not really." He shrugged. "She looks nothing like you." He saw a flicker of a smile in response. "Here's the part you can't tell. Ready?" He waited for her nod, then continued. "She was scratched up some, and from what she said, the caravan had been plundered. No sense taking her back to it. We were fairly close to the Risker camp, so we took her there, to Xico's house."

"Tarkio! That's against the law! How could you do such a reckless thing?"

"What could we do?"

"You could have thought a little first. What would I do if you lost your license? Or were taken? Then what would happen to me? Did you ever consider that?"

"Groa," he said gently, "you wouldn't have wanted me to leave that child alone in the woods?" He paused, waiting for her scowl to soften into a frown. "Besides, no one knows. Just Xico's family, the girl, and now you."

"Did you leave her there?"

"No. Cillia gave us some dinner, then Xico and I walked her down the mountain. I brought her home and left her with her mother."

"You wanted to meet her mother, did you?"

"No. And after meeting her, I have no desire to see her again." He leaned forward, smiling. "Truth be told, I think the girl only had eyes for Xico." He leaned over the table and ran his hand through her short auburn hair, stroked her full lips, and dropped his gaze to her lush curves, visible under the plain gray dress she wore. "Like I only have for you."

She brushed his hand away. "Flatterer." She looked at him out of the corner of her eyes, dimples forming in her brown cheeks. "Are you hungry?"

He nodded and leaned back, finally feeling a little warmth sink into his bones. He'd seen the pleasure in her smile. Perhaps his time at home wouldn't be so bad. And someday he'd find the right way to keep Groa happy.

8

The following week Iskra went to meet the caravan from Shinroo. She hopped from one foot to the other as she stood under the monument to Safety. Iskra scowled at the statue, wondering just what the man thought he was doing to keep the others safe.

Would the caravan never come? She paced back and forth, oblivious to the people jostling her as they made their way through the market past the wooden stalls, greeting neighbors and scolding their children. The wind shifted and brought with it the smell of fried grains mixed with the odor of drying blood. Iskra wrinkled her nose and moved farther from the butcher's stall.

At last she heard the horn announcing the caravan's approach. She'd paced all the way around the square four times before the guardsman leading the caravan came into view, followed by the line of wagons and guardsmen on horses. Iskra ran down the line, searching for Tavda. The caravans came from Shinroo three times a week. She hoped Tavda was on this one.

"Iskra!"

She whirled at the sound of her name. Tavda was waving from a wagon. She ran toward her friend as Tavda jumped down. Before Tavda could say a word, Iskra grabbed her hand. "Come on, I have to talk to you."

She dragged Tavda past the livery stable to a place behind the blacksmith's forge, ignoring Tavda's protests.

"Iskra, what's with you?" Tavda said. "What are you doing?"

"Listen, just listen." She took a deep breath. "I need to tell you something, but you can't tell anyone. All right?"

"Yes, I promise. But why here?"

"Because it's noisy. No one will hear us." Sounds of clanging metal from the forge affirmed her words. She proceeded to tell Tavda of her adventures of the week before, relating everything about the bandits and meeting the Riskers. She left out the part about Xico, his green eyes and encouraging smile. She was never going to admit the tingles she felt when he held her hand.

Tavda scratched her head. "That's the strangest thing I've ever heard."

"Isn't it? Why would they tell us the Riskers are barbarians when they're not?"

"I don't know." Tavda worked her mouth back and forth. "Are you sure?"

"Yes. The house was bigger than ours, it had at least four rooms, maybe more."

"Maybe they're an important family, like the ephor."

Iskra frowned. "I didn't get that idea." She waited while the blacksmith hammered on something that made a loud clang with every blow of the hammer. When he finished, she went on. "The table was wood, but it was so smooth. They ate off some kind of smooth plates that shone, not wood or tin like ours." She shook her head. "They had better food, too. Bread that wasn't dense and black. It was soft and tan, almost white, and the crust crunched. And the stew! I've never tasted anything like it."

"There must be some explanation," Tavda said. "The Prime Konamei wouldn't lie to us."

"That's not all." Iskra looked around to make sure no one was near. She stepped closer to Tavda, then told her about Cillia and how she healed her with the amulet.

"And there you have it. That's why," Tavda said.

"That's why what?"

"That's why they tell us the Riskers are barbarians. They have silly superstitions that are a waste of time."

"I thought so, too, at first. The scratches on my face and arms didn't hurt anymore, but I figured that would have happened anyway. Then I got home." She twisted her hands together. "Even though there was blood all over my sleeves and on my neck, there was no mark on my face or arm. See?" She turned her face to show Tavda her cheek, then pulled up her sleeve.

Tavda ran her finger along Iskra's arm. "Not a mark." She looked down at the ground, then rubbed her chin. "Well, we need to ask."

"Ask who?"

"Edalia, next time we have Oppidan lectures."

Iskra gasped. Her yearning to know the truth was like a splinter under a fingernail that wouldn't allow her to think of anything else. Edalia *would* know, but Edalia was in charge of making sure they all understood their responsibilities to promote safety, order, and fairness. If there was some conspiracy to hide the truth from the people, wouldn't she be in on it?

She rubbed her mouth. "I don't know, Tavda. Do you think she'd tell us?"

"She won't if we don't ask."

"I could get in trouble for being with the Riskers."

"True." Tavda twirled one of her curls around her finger. "But how can it be against the law if you were in trouble?"

Iskra frowned. "You would think so. But people get in trouble for breaking laws they didn't know about. I'm afraid to chance it."

Tavda let out a long sigh. "You can ask the questions without saying you were there."

Iskra shook her head. "Maybe." She remembered Kaberco's words: *I hope you want to stay safe*. With a start, she realized while she wanted to stay safe, she wanted to know the truth more. Tavda was brave to even think about risking Edalia's displeasure. "I just don't know."

"If you don't want to ask, I will. I can truthfully say I've never met a Risker. I'll say I just heard market gossip, or some such thing."

"Will you?" Iskra tugged at the hair at the back of her head. "But what if asking questions like this is against the law? And we get taken?"

Tavda frowned. "You might be right." She shook her head. "No. Even if it is against the law, we won't get taken. We're too young. They'll just come up with some kind of punishment, extra work or something."

"That would be horrible! No, forget I said anything." She looked up into Tavda's face, searching her brown eyes. "Please."

"Why? I think we should ask. If they make fun of me, you'll have to back me up. Say you've heard the same rumors, too."

Iskra's heart started to beat faster, like a drum warning her of danger. A series of clangs ended with a splash and a loud hissing sound. The blacksmith had finished whatever he was making. "Are you sure about this?" She tilted her head back to look up into Tavda's eyes.

Tavda nodded, making her short dark curls bounce. "Of course. Edalia's always asking if anyone has questions. So, we'll ask questions. She'll give us an explanation, and that will be the end of it."

"I hope so." Iskra bit her lip. Yes. Yes, Edalia would explain everything. Then she could forget all these confusing thoughts about Riskers and their strange ways.

ON NORMAL DAYS, Iskra enjoyed the Oppidan lectures she and the other fourteen-and-fifteen-year-olds attended. They'd all left school years earlier, once their group had mastered the basics of reading, writing, and a little addition. Since then, they'd worked in the fields and shops, assisting farmers and market vendors, or craftsmen like the blacksmith and baker, learning different trades.

Their workdays were shortened twice a week for Oppidan lectures. They gathered in a room in the town hall covered with posters listing safety rules hanging on its rough wood walls. Benches lined three walls of the room, allowing the class to sit in a squared semi-circle around the instructor. There they learned the history of Tlefas and how to find their role in building it into a safe, fair, and prosperous country.

As Iskra took her seat, she glanced at the tattered map of their country of Tlefas that hung in the front of the room, showing the River Mirna that flowed from Gishin to Trofmose on its way west to the sea. Just east of Gishin stood the mountain range that formed the eastern border of Tlefas—the mountains where the bandits lurked and Riskers lived.

Edalia, the teacher, picked up the lecture where she'd left off a few days earlier. "You remember how after the Endless War destroyed everything, the wisest leaders chose to cross the mountains and create Tlefas." Short, dumpy and constantly in motion, she paced back and forth on the scuffed wood floor in front of her eight students. "Determined never to be in danger again, they set about establishing laws to keep all the residents safe."

But they haven't succeeded, Iskra thought. What about the bandits?

"Oyamel, are you listening?" Edalia rapped her ruler against the wall over the head of a chubby boy whose eyes were closed and mouth hanging open. "Sit up straight. Perhaps you continue."

Oyamel pulled his head up, blinking. He looked around the room with a sheepish grin, then stared at the ceiling. "Uhh, for the past three hundred years we've been building a safe society. When we have achieved that, um, we can build a prosperous one."

"Perfectly correct. We are all patiently waiting for the day of peace and safety; our leaders will know when that happens. Then we will all enjoy the wealth of Tlefas. Continue."

Oyamel stretched his neck from side to side. "Well, one problem was that the people who settled Tlefas were from all of the warring countries. Many were the lighter-skinned Easterners. Some were the tall, red-haired Southerners. Others were the darker-skinned Westerners and Northerners. Our leaders were concerned they would bring the old racial, religious, and civil disagreements with them, preventing true peace and fairness."

"Very good, Oyamel," Edalia said. "Can anyone tell us how our leaders solved that problem?"

A girl with deeply tanned skin and black eyes raised her hand. "Our Prime Konamei, Pallu the First, decreed that people could not cling to their own groups. Marriages were arranged so the different races from the old country interbred. That way, the Prime Konamei removed all chance of discrimination and oppression, so that everyone would be treated fairly and be the same."

They still arrange marriages, Iskra thought. *That doesn't seem fair to me. Why do they still need to do that?*

"Good, Carmi. You've remembered well." Edalia looked around the room. "But there were other obstacles to setting up a safe and fair country. Who can tell us about another one?"

Oyamel raised his hand. "Another problem with safety was the other people who followed our leaders across the mountains. Their descendants are the bandits and the Riskers."

"Correct. Why did these people come to Tlefas?"

Another girl, one with ash-blond hair and pale-brown eyes raised her hand. "They were also fleeing the war."

Edalia nodded. "Can you tell us how that war started?"

"Yes. People of one country believed one superstition. In a different country, they believed something else. A different superstition. The rulers of a third country realized that these superstitions were making some people poor and others very rich. They tried to stamp out these dangerous beliefs. In their ignorance, many people fought to be able to continue to believe in fairytales and to live in an unjust society."

With a smile, Edalia nodded. "Perfectly correct, Maizie." She looked around the room. "Then what happened?"

Oyamel raised his hand. "All four countries went to war. After about sixty years, some of their leaders realized continuing to fight was hopeless, and they came here."

"Right. I see you were paying attention and not sleeping." Edalia looked around the room. "Unfortunately, as Oyamel pointed out earlier, they were followed by Riskers and bandits. Cruel and violent people who have stupid superstitions."

"What kind of superstitions?" Tavda asked.

Iskra's heart began to beat faster.

"You don't need to know about them," Edalia said. "It is a waste of time."

"But are we sure they are wrong? Don't their amulets have power?" Tavda asked.

"What do you know about amulets?" Edalia asked, narrowing her eyes.

Tavda shrugged. "Oh, not much. I just hear people talk,

you know, in the market. The old women say all kinds of things about Riskers and their amulets and what they do with them."

Iskra's heart pounded in her ears and she struggled to keep from gasping for breath as her classmates sat up to stare at Tavda. She had seized their attention like a cat grabs a mouse.

"Tavda," Edalia said, "what do the women in the market say the Riskers do with their amulets?" The warmth had left her tone, as if a cloud had obscured the sun.

Tavda scratched her head. "I don't know exactly. Heal people, maybe?" She looked at Edalia with wide, innocent eyes. "Do you think they can? Heal people, I mean?"

Edalia's eyes narrowed and she frowned. "What do the rest of you think?" She pointed her ruler at Oyamel.

"Riskers are barbarians. They believe in all kinds of nonsense that is untrue and unsafe."

"Good answer. Tavda, what do you believe?"

"Well, I know that's what we all say. But if it's true, why do some people tell these other stories like they are true?"

Edalia tapped her ruler on the palm of her hand. Iskra wished Tavda would stop. Edalia wasn't about to say anything different than what she'd always told them. She clutched her hands together as she watched Edalia pace back and forth, her face reddening, eyes blazing.

"Why do people tell these tall tales? Because they are not fully committed to our country's goals! They are looking for some easy way out. But there's no way to create a safe and fair society without sacrifice and hard work." She looked around the room, gazing into the eyes of each of her students in turn. "Do you understand? Does anyone have any questions?"

"I do, if you please," Tavda said.

Iskra shrank lower in her seat.

Edalia looked at her coldly, her gray eyes like dirty ice. "Yes?"

"If the Riskers are ignorant and wrong, then why is it dangerous to visit them?"

Several people gasped, and all turned to stare at Tavda.

Edalia shook her head. "What do the rest of you think about that?"

"You're joking, right?" Oyamel sneered.

"No, I want to know," Tavda said. She caught the threatening look in Edalia's eye. "If you please."

Iskra stared at Tavda, wide-eyed, amazed by her composure, how she didn't flinch under all the attention and criticism.

Oyamel laughed. "You must be stupid. If we know they are barbarians and dangerous, why would we want to visit them?"

"But how do we know they are dangerous?" Tavda persisted.

"Because we do." Oyamel folded his flabby arms across his chest and nodded. "We do."

Others chimed in. "What other fairytales do you believe in?"

"Do you have a secret amulet? Maybe one to make you less ugly?"

"Pretty dumb, to even think Riskers and bandits would know something we don't."

"Everyone knows Riskers share their huts with rats and stinging beetles, and feed their grandparents to the warboars."

Iskra sat huddled in her seat, head hanging. She had promised to back Tavda up. But she couldn't. If she did, she'd be a target, too. She listened as the others repeated all they had learned about the danger of Riskers and the wisdom of staying away from them, mocking Tavda for her stupidity for even questioning what everyone knew to be true.

She should speak up, say she heard the same rumors, maybe try to get Tavda to admit she shouldn't listen to gossip.

The problem was Iskra knew much of what they were

saying was untrue. How could she lie and say it wasn't? Her stomach knotted and she wrapped her arms around herself tightly. If she backed up Tavda, Edalia would despise her and she'd lose her good standing in the class. She took a breath and held it, trying to keep her body from shaking.

Edalia allowed the taunting for a few minutes before she interrupted. "Only barefoot, uneducated people believe in those superstitions. They have no power, no meaning." She looked around the room. "I need to know what you all believe. Who believes the Riskers have magic amulets that work like artifacts from fairytales?"

Tavda put her hand in the air. The rest of the group stared at her.

"And who believes the Riskers are dangerous barbarians?"

All except Tavda raised their hands. Iskra's chest tightened. She slowly raised her hand and peeked out of the corner of her eye at Tavda, who was glaring at her.

"We're done for the day," Edalia said. "You can go." As the group stood to leave, Edalia pointed at Tavda with her ruler. "Not you."

Iskra filed out with the rest, head hanging. *Tavda will be so angry. I need to do something to make her understand. She'll be furious I let her down, let her take the abuse alone. What have I done? I have to make this up to her somehow.* She lingered by the door to wait for her friend. She was able to hear every word.

"What do you know about amulets?" Edalia demanded.

"Nothing, I just heard people talking."

"Don't listen to gossip. You probably heard that from the traders. They're great ones for tall tales and fairy stories. There is no magic, no amulets."

Tavda sighed. "How can I be sure?"

Iskra's heart sank at those words. She felt even worse as she listened to Edalia's response.

"You'd better be very certain about this." Edalia paused. "You're fifteen now. They'll be making your work assignment soon. And a marriage assignment. This is not the time to be asking foolish questions."

ISKRA SAGGED against the wall of the dimly-lit corridor. That could have been her, the target of Edalia's scolding and her classmates' mocking. She didn't have long to consider what might have been. Tavda stormed out of the room and hurried away, her footsteps echoing on the stone floor, hitting Iskra's ears like blows to the head.

"Tavda, wait," Iskra called.

Her friend didn't even look around, but kept walking, head down. Iskra scurried after her. "Tavda, wait." They were out on the street before she caught up and grabbed Tavda's arm.

Tavda jerked away. "Thanks a lot."

"I'm sorry. I didn't know what to do."

"You could have said you thought there was something to the stories, like you promised." Tavda shook her head. "No, you just had to leave me there alone."

Iskra twisted her hands together. "Tavda, I was going to. Really."

"Why *didn't* you, then?"

"Because it was clear Edalia wasn't going to tell you anything. She just went on with the same stuff she's always said."

Tavda ran her hand through her hair. "How could you tell?"

"Once she got on the bit about tall tales, I knew."

After stepping back to allow two guardsmen to pace by, Tavda curled her lip. "Aren't you the smart one."

"I was hoping you'd see it, too, and stop. But you didn't."

"Now it's my fault?" She shook her finger in Iskra's face. "You just let me take all the abuse by myself."

Iskra flinched, putting a hand up as if to ward off a blow. "Tavda—"

"Letting them make fun of me, like I was the only one who had questions."

"Couldn't you see how scared some of them were?"

"Of what?" Tavda stepped back from Iskra, frowning.

"I don't know. Edalia, maybe, or the ephor."

"Was that any reason to chicken out on me?"

"Not just them. My mother would be so angry."

"So?"

Iskra squeezed her eyes shut and shook her head. "You wouldn't understand."

"You're such a mushroom. You'd do anything to save your own skin."

Iskra's chin quivered under Tavda's anger. Of course Tavda didn't understand. Her mother was actually kind. She tried another argument. "They made you the center of attention, put you in a dangerous place. Why didn't you stop?"

Tavda stared at her. "Because we agreed. I thought we were friends."

Iskra blushed. "We are. But you should have been more careful. You know how touchy they all are about the Riskers."

"You put me up to this."

"It was your idea." Her words started to tumble out of her mouth. "Besides, it's all your fault, anyway. If you hadn't wanted to buy plums, I would have been on the caravan, and none of this would have happened."

Tavda stepped forward with narrowed eyes. Iskra took a step back, suddenly afraid.

"If I hadn't stopped for those plums," Tavda said, "you'd probably be dead now." She stepped back and held up a hand as if to push Iskra away. "Stay away from me." She turned and ran down the street.

Iskra watched as her friend vanished around a corner. She walked home in a daze, head hanging, confused by all that had gone on. She didn't want to admit it, but Tavda was right. Buying the plums probably had saved her life.

And I betrayed her.

She rubbed her hands together, as if trying to make them clean. She felt dirty, disgusted with herself. How could she make it up to Tavda? Her throat clenched and her eyes grew hot. *What have I done? Tavda's in trouble, and it's my fault. She's right. I am a miserable, cowardly mushroom.*

Thinking about that was too painful, so she forced her thoughts to Edalia. Iskra had always admired her, a woman who gave up the man she loved because the ludi—the official in charge of marriages—said it would be better for the village if she married another. Sacrifice for the creation of a safe state, then a prosperous one, that's what Iskra had been brought up to value. Edalia was a living example of that kind of sacrifice.

But if the leaders really kept them safe, then they would have done something about all the bandits. People should be able to travel freely from one village to the next. If it's so important to build a safe and prosperous country, why do they take people? Wouldn't they be of use somewhere, somehow?

And the Riskers. They weren't foul or uncouth, sharing their homes with vermin. There were more rats in the village market than she'd seen at the whole Risker camp. Osip was the kindest man she'd ever met. There was no denying it, Cillia and her herbs or amulet or something had healed her wounds far better than the village doctor could have done.

She hesitated when she came to her house. She didn't want to talk to her mother quite yet, while she was feeling so desolate and ashamed. She ambled down the dusty street, looking at the houses as if for the first time. They were all the same, two-roomed, shabby, huddled together like scared barn cats. Close together for their own safety. Every one alike for fairness.

"Follow the rules and be safe."

Every child in Tlefas learned that. But the rules about the Riskers didn't make sense; everyone could benefit from whatever they used for healing. Maybe there was something dangerous, something Iskra hadn't seen yet.

Follow the rules and be safe. Iskra had always believed that. Now she wasn't so sure.

9

Two days later, Iskra picked her way through the market, stepping carefully to avoid mud puddles, pushing through the throngs of women carrying baskets, men laden with sacks and barrels, and children racing from stall to stall. A juggler stood at a corner, taking wagers on how many balls he could keep in the air. Even with the drizzling rain, the market was more crowded than usual as it was Hafsanbe, the eighth day of the week. It seemed to Iskra that everyone in Gishin had decided to spend their free time visiting the market. Everyone except Tavda.

Iskra hadn't seen Tavda since the day she betrayed her. Tavda had been assigned to the tailor, while Iskra had been busy helping the baker. Hopefully she'd find Tavda somewhere in the market and make up. In truth, she wouldn't be surprised if Tavda was still angry. What she'd done was despicable. There was no other word for it. Her mouth grew dry as she rehearsed what she would say to Tavda. As she dodged a man carrying a sack of beans on his shoulder, she heard a startled gasp.

"She's only fifteen! Since when do they take children?"

Iskra jerked her head around to spot the speaker. It was

the woman who sold dried fruit, talking with Tavda's mother, Revda.

She approached the women, but before she could say anything, Revda saw her, and shrieked, "You!" She seized Iskra's arm and slapped her across the face.

Iskra was too startled to do anything but stare in amazement. Revda's usually kind brown eyes were narrowed and angry.

The fruitseller caught Tavda's mother by the arm before she could hit Iskra again. "Revda, that's enough." She leaned forward to whisper to Iskra, "You'll have to forgive her. Tavda was taken two days ago."

Iskra felt that news like a blow to the stomach. She struggled to take a breath and stepped back. Shaking her head vigorously, she said, "No, no, it can't be." Even as she spoke, she knew the truth. The dark shadows under Revda's red, swollen eyes bore witness to the woman's grief and pain.

"It is," Revda said. "And it's your fault."

"Mine?" She clapped a hand to her mouth with her hand and felt her face grow hot. A sense of shame flooded through her, making her knees weak and her hands tremble. "How can that be?"

"Tavda came home all upset the other day. *You* had questions about the Riskers, and *she* asked Edalia about them. Everyone made fun of her." Revda paused, her breath coming in ragged gasps. "And now she's gone."

"But—" Iskra opened her mouth to speak, but no words came out. She swallowed hard and tried again. "What did she do wrong?"

Revda stepped close enough to Iskra to put her face directly in front of Iskra's nose. "She asked questions that shouldn't be asked." She put her hands on Iskra's shoulders and pushed her back. "Are you really that foolish?" With narrowed eyes, she stabbed Iskra in the chest with one pointed finger. "Go away. You're too dangerous to be around."

ISKRA BACKED AWAY FROM REVDA. She put her head down and splashed through the puddles, ignoring the glares and insults of the people she collided with. She wanted to run far away to escape Revda's anger and her own guilt.

Ducking around a corner into a narrow, roofed alley, she leaned against a wall, gasping for breath. She had escaped the piercing stares of the other villagers, but the oppressive feeling of shame still burned her. She dropped her chin to her chest, covering her eyes with her hand. Tavda was gone. Taken. It was all her fault. She felt her knees weakening and slid down to sit on the damp ground. She laid her head on her knees.

Why had she agreed to let Tavda ask Edalia about the Riskers? She knew better. The trader, Kaberco, her mother, everyone told her to not ask questions. She squeezed her eyes tight. *Now Tavda's gone and I'm to blame.*

She let out a long breath. What had happened to Tavda? Where did people go when they got taken? She dug her fingernails into her arms, gouging the pain made her moan. *If I'd backed her up like I promised, I'd probably know the answer to that question.* She shivered at the thought. *I'm still here because I'm a wretched, loathsome coward. No wonder Revda hates me. Everyone probably hates me. I can't blame them.*

Her chest tightened and she felt a wetness around her eyes. She rubbed her fists into her eyes, struggling to keep from bursting into sobs.

She sat still, watching the rain drip through a hole in the roof into a puddle in front of her, disturbing the muddy water. After a few moments, her thoughts turned in another direction. She puzzled over the fact that all Tavda did was ask a few questions. And for that she was taken. There must be secret laws that if you break them, you get taken. No matter how old you are. That just didn't seem fair. She wondered why there was all this mystery, why they couldn't be clear.

Iskra rubbed the back of her head and pulled at her hair. What was so wrong with asking questions? If the Prime Konamei really was doing everything that was best for the people, to make them all safe, then there should be a good answer if someone had a question.

I need to find out. It's the least I can do for Tavda. But how?

A horn sounded, cutting through the damp spring air like a sudden ray of sunlight shines through a cloud. The caravan was getting ready to leave. The caravan. Traders—Tarkio. *That's* where I'll start, she thought.

She jumped to her feet, brushed off her backside, seized her basket and hurried through the market, searching for Tarkio. She ran as if pursued by hungry warboars, driven to find him before the caravan left. She snaked her way through women carrying baskets and babies, old men chatting, and young men watching the young women selling pasties and jams. She dodged a baker carrying a large tray covered with loaves of black bread, slipped around a cat toying with a mouse, and bumped into a man carrying three bottles and a burlap bag.

"Oh, I'm so sorry!" Iskra said.

"Watch where you're going. You could hurt someone," the man said.

She scrambled to help him pick up the bag she'd knocked from his hand. Her apology was drowned out by the blare of the horn, signaling that the caravan was about to depart. She raced around the corner to the square and tore along the length of the caravan, looking up into each wagon as she scurried past it. Finally, she found Tarkio near the end, talking with some of the other traders.

"Iskra! This is a surprise."

"I'm so glad I found you. I need your help." She leaned against a wagon, panting to catch her breath.

"What is it?" His smile encouraged her to explain.

She pulled a money bag from her basket. "This belongs to the trader I was riding with last week. He gave it to me and asked me to give it to his wife. I forgot all about it until after I got home."

"And?"

She shook the bag a little. "You see, I don't know where his wife lives. I didn't even ask him his name."

"Why not?"

She was sure from his grin he was laughing at her, despising her for being so timid. "We started talking, and then later, when I realized I didn't know it, I thought it might be rude to ask. You know, after we'd been talking so long." She flushed and shuffled her feet.

Tarkio stroked his chin. "Well, I can help you. He's the one who had elk, right? His wife lives in Shinroo, and I'll be going there next week. She'll be glad to get this, you can count on that."

"Aren't you going today?"

He looked at her, studying her for a moment. She had the feeling that he was debating with himself, like he wasn't sure about what he wanted to say next.

Suddenly he smiled and took her arm. He led her a little distance away from the caravan, then leaned close to whisper to her. "I'll let you in on a secret. I'm leaving when the caravan leaves, but I'm not going to Shinroo. I'm going to Cillia and Osip's daughter's wedding. Would you like to join me?"

She sucked in a quick breath. A chance to go to the Riskers, to find out more about them was just what she needed. "I can't go back there."

"Why not?"

"You know the rules." She lowered her eyes to avoid his gaze and stared at his worn brown shirt and coat. Traders always wear brown, she thought idly. Why not gray like the rest of us?

"You'll be back before they lock the gates, I promise." He shrugged. "I thought you enjoyed your time there."

"I did." She shifted her weight from one foot to the other. "But to go to the Riskers, I don't know."

"Why? Afraid of a few barbarians?" He raised his eyebrows, making his large dark eyes appear even larger.

"No. And they're not barbarians, at least, I don't think so." Her voice trailed off and she bit her lip, staring at the ground. This was all so confusing. If she went, it would be a chance to find out what got Tavda into trouble. And she wouldn't have to go to the Riskers alone. She looked up when Tarkio started to speak.

"Risker weddings are a lot of fun. Not at all barbaric. Aren't you curious to see one?"

She was, she really was. "Yes. No. I can't." She shook her head. "It's dangerous."

"If you really believed that, you wouldn't still be thinking about it." Tarkio's brown eyes held hers captive. "Are you sure you don't want to go?"

"I'll be back in time? You'll keep me safe? You promise?" Maybe she could get some answers and not get into any trouble.

"I promise. Whatever problems come our way, I'll handle them." His calm, mellow voice reassured her like no words ever could.

She looked at him, thinking, noting his steady, calm gaze and well-muscled body. He would know what to do about warboars or bandits. She hesitated, "But what if I get caught? I could be taken!"

"We'll make sure you don't get caught."

She bit her lip. It's the least I can do for Tavda. She nodded.

He smiled. "Then let's go. We've got some climbing to do."

10

Never had Iskra seen such a feast. Wooden tables had been dragged to the green space on one side of the Risker camp, arranged under a large white tent. They were piled high with carved meats. Some, like chicken and pork, were familiar to Iskra. There were some enormous joints Xico told her were warboar. He laughed when he saw her startled reaction, so she was not sure she could believe him —even the Riskers must know warboar meat is poison.

She shrugged off the thought to marvel at the rest of the spread. There were roasted potatoes, not just the usual white, but red and yellow and purple ones. All kinds of chopped vegetables, cabbages, carrots, onions and even tomatoes. Loaves of soft white bread, twisted into fantastic shapes. Mounds of pears and grapes, and fruits Iskra had never seen. *What kind of people are these, who eat so well, and can make such things?* No one was checking to see how much anyone ate, to see if everyone got their fair share. Wouldn't this cause trouble? She'd seen fights break out in the village inn when someone felt they didn't get their full ration. These Riskers didn't seem to worry about that.

There was more than food to marvel at. The bride,

Veressa, wore a bright yellow dress, not pearly-gray like village girls wore to their weddings. This dress had tucks and lace and fit Veressa well, making her look graceful and beguiling. All the Risker women had dresses like that, Iskra noticed, each one a different color, all cut to flatter their wearers. She looked down at her own plain gray dress and frowned over its straight lines. Why do we all have to dress the same?

She let her attention stray from listening to the chatter of Xico and his sisters to the houses that edged the common area. They all looked fresh and clean after the morning's rain, now gleaming under the midday sun. While the houses were all built of stone with thatched roofs, they didn't all look alike. Some had two stories. Many had carved wood trim around the windows, carving that looked almost like lace. Most had window boxes with blooming flowers of red, yellow, and pink.

The doors to the houses were painted in bright colors, and some had elaborate paintings. A vivid red door had crossed swords painted on it. A pale-blue door had a graceful flowering tree with exotic-looking birds perched on its branches. One house even had a round room on one side. The eaves of the roof extended out, creating a shaded area. A bench hugged the curve of the room, providing a place for someone to sit. Iskra imagined the woman of the house sitting there, visiting with friends as they knit or sewed. She sighed and looked around. People laughing, joking, no one concerned with being the same, no one constantly looking around, afraid of some threat to their safety.

After dinner, while the women cleared away the dishes and leftover food, Osip pulled out a six-stringed fiddle and began to play. A few other men joined in, one playing a flute, another drums, and Tarkio plucking metal prongs attached to a small piece of wood.

"My da plays well, doesn't he?"

Iskra jumped at the touch on her shoulder. "Oh, Xico, I didn't see you there. Yes, he does. Where did he study?"

"Study?" Xico shook his head. "Nowhere. His father taught him, as his father taught him."

"Do you play?"

"No, I'm no good at it. The drums are more for me. My older brother, now he's almost as good as Da. What about you?" He sat down beside her, sitting close enough that their legs were touching, making Iskra's breath come a little faster.

"Oh, I can't. I didn't go to the music school, you know, in the capital."

"Why not?"

"I wasn't chosen. They only take children with talent. No one from our village has been chosen for a long time. There's no talent in our village."

"Does no one play anything?"

"Just the professionals. The best ones come once a year for Arrival Day and give a concert." Seeing Xico's frown, she added, "We have some professionals who play in the inn every evening." She could tell from the way Xico was shaking his head he didn't think much of what she was telling him. Was he disturbed by the lack of musical talent in Gishin? Or did he think something was wrong with her, that she couldn't play an instrument?

She tried to come up with a way to ask him, but while she was thinking, Cillia and her daughters approached bearing large trays of something cut into squares. It was some kind of baked product like bread, only it was pale yellow, light and moist. Two sections of it were stacked, one on top of the other, joined together with red hopberry jelly, and the whole creation was covered with a thick white cream, almost like soft butter. Xico called it cake. Tarkio nodded his acceptance of a piece and Cillia set it on the table next to him. The musicians finished a tune and set down their instruments.

"Wine for me, woman, if you want to give me some," Osip said.

"Whatever you like, old man. Your daughter Fialka will be happy to bring you some."

"Better send Tuli. She'll get the wine back here tonight. Fialka'll be likely to go chasing flowers or some such nonsense."

Fialka ruffled her father's hair. "You like the flowers around the house, admit it, Da."

"You've lost that round, Osip," Tarkio said. "You're still outnumbered, even with Veressa getting married." A shadow crossed his face as he spoke, fleeting like a ripple on a pond. He turned to pick up the plate with his cake, only to find it had disappeared. They all laughed at his surprise, all the more because Apango the flute player was calmly eating it.

"Hated to see good cake go to waste. Seemed to me like you were going to talk all night," Apango said.

Iskra braced herself for an angry fight. She sat wide-eyed, watching as Tarkio clapped Apango on the shoulder and laughed. "Tuli, sweetheart, can you fetch me more cake? And put it on this side, far away from my friend the *cumberground* here." He picked up his instrument and idly plucked the prongs. "What shall we play next?"

Iskra turned to Xico. "*Cumberground?*" That sounded like an insult to her.

Xico swallowed the bite of cake in his mouth, then answered. "A person who just takes up space."

Ah, it was an insult. Such strange words these Riskers use. And no one seems to take offense.

Tuli returned with a large piece of cake and set it next to Tarkio. "Well, now, Tuli," he said. "I suppose you'll be the next one married? Have your eye on anyone?"

"Oh, that would be telling, Tarkio," she said, tossing her long dark hair gathered in tiny braids. "There's one or two that would have me, but I've not decided."

"Who assigns marriage partners?" Iskra whispered to Xico.

"Assigns? What are you talking about?"

"Doesn't someone assign marriage partners? That's what we do. To make sure the match is in the best interest of creating a safe society."

Xico stared at her, then laughed out loud. "That's *baldotery*! Here no one assigns anything. People choose for themselves."

Iskra wasn't sure what he meant by *baldotery*, but knew it wasn't a compliment. "But how do *you* know you chose the right person?"

"Well, they spend a lot of time in each other's homes. Veressa lived in Lilio's camp for three months, staying with his aunt. Then he came here for three months. He was a big help to us last winter, after my da hurt his arm. You get to know a lot about a person when you work with them, live with them."

"Do the families decide?"

"No, they just advise. Some people get married even if their parents don't approve. Works out sometimes, sometimes doesn't."

Iskra stared at the men lighting a bonfire in the middle of the green. No expert telling you who to marry. People having to decide for themselves. How could they make such decisions? Without experts to help, people would get themselves into all kinds of trouble. "Do you pick your own trade, too?"

"Of course. My da's a trapper as well as a farmer, so I'll be trapping. My older brother will inherit the farm."

"Can you live off trapping?"

"Oh, sure. I'm getting good at tracking the rabbits and foxes. Lots of people want the furs."

Iskra stared at him. "But traps are dangerous! Aren't you scared?"

"Nah. No need for fear if you know what you're doing."

Fialka, walking by carrying two wine bottles, overheard his last comment. She reached over and patted him on the head. "That's my little brother, the tracker. He's got other talents he's not telling you about. He's pretty inventive. He came up with a new trap that kills instantly and doesn't hurt the fur. He'll do well for himself, even without a farm," she said. "Tell her about the bees."

"Bees?"

Xico nodded. "Their hives are in the faces of the cliffs, and we harvest their honey."

Iskra stared at him. "You climb up a cliff and take honey from bees?" She looked at Xico with a mixture of horror and awe. "You aren't scared?"

Xico smiled. "It's fun. Do you want to see the cliffs sometime?"

"No, I can't." Seeing his face fall, she added, "Well, maybe if you wanted to show me. . .?" Why am I so worried about pleasing him? He's just a Risker.

By now the sun was moving lower in the sky. A group of men who stood in the center of the green space with fiddles and drums began playing lively music. Others gathered around it and started to dance, a wild free dance in lines that circled the musicians. Some of the women held small wooden hoops with metal pieces attached to the sides. They shook the hoops, making a wildly exultant sound that stirred Iskra's desire for something, she didn't know what.

"Want to dance?" Xico held his hand out to Iskra.

"I don't know how."

He took her hand. "Come."

The warmth that flowed from his hand to hers made it impossible for her to refuse him. She allowed him to lead her to join the dancers. The dance itself wasn't too difficult, circle around, back and forth, raise hands, circle again.

When the tune was over, the dancers stepped back to allow Veressa and her intended, Lilio, to stand in the center of the circle. Cillia and two other women, all holding dragonfly amulets, joined them.

They circled the newlyweds, chanting, "Sky-god, bless them. Give them power. Give them love. Give them joy.

Give them peace. Bless them with children. Bless them when they go out and when they come in. Let them never forget you."

Iskra didn't know what to think. She squirmed, embarrassed for these kind and joyful people. They believed a ridiculous superstition, the old myths from long ago that every child knew were just stories.

As the chanting continued, more people joined in, forming rings around Lilio and Veressa. A beam of green light came down from the sky, bathing them in its glow.

Iskra blinked, rubbed her eyes, and blinked again. The light was still there.

Veressa's yellow dress was yellow no more, but glowed blue-green. The light from the sky was changing colors to the pale green of new spring growth, to the dark green of the pine trees. Then it faded to the cheers and laughter of the circling people.

Iskra watched, fascinated, as Lilio took Veressa into his arms and kissed her. She tugged at Xico's arm. "What does that light mean?"

"That the sky-god blesses the marriage."

They really did believe in this sky-god myth. But it was hard to ignore a green light from the sky.

"Are you ready to go?"

Iskra turned to see who had spoken. "Yes, Tarkio, I suppose so."

They made their farewells with Osip and Cillia. Xico walked with them toward the Guarded Path.

"Sure you can't stay longer?" he asked.

"Oh, no, I'd be in so much trouble if I was out past dark."

"Who would notice?"

"My mother. If I keep breaking the rules, she'll have to report me."

"Your own mother?"

"Xico, it's a different world down there," Tarkio said.

"They've turned their backs on the sky-god and have their own rules now. Time will show if they are better off or not."

"I think it's clear now," Xico said. "But I won't argue." He turned to Iskra. "That Tarkio, he's always right." He laughed.

Iskra's eyes widened.

Tarkio didn't seem to be offended. "I generally am." He shrugged and winked at Iskra.

Xico leaned close to Iskra to whisper. "Iskra, can you come back next Hafsanbe? I could show you how we get the honey."

She opened her mouth to say yes, then stopped herself. She hadn't seen anything in the camp that would explain why Tavda was taken, so there would be no point to her coming back. Except maybe a wedding was something no one would talk about. Maybe another time she could bring the subject up.

She opened her mouth to agree, then realized she couldn't. "Oh, no, I can't. It's Volunteer Day." The regret she felt surprised her.

"What's that?"

"The last Hafsanbe of the month is Volunteer Day. We all volunteer to help around the village. Sweep streets, clean the village hall, scrape snow and ice off the streets, whatever needs to be done."

"So, if it's voluntary, you don't have to do it."

"But I have to. It's the rule." She frowned, wondering why he couldn't understand.

"Funny kind of volunteering. I'm sure it would be fine if you skipped, just once."

"Xico, I can't."

"Can't, or don't want to?"

She couldn't tell if she saw anger or hurt in his eyes.

Tarkio broke in. "Xico, that's not fair. You can see she does. Rules are rules, right? The Treaty of Separation is clear; the penalties are harsh."

"But you brought her up here."

Tarkio stopped walking and turned to face Xico and Iskra. "I did. And I shouldn't have. It was a mistake."

Xico laughed. "That doesn't happen often. How will you fix this one?" He turned to Iskra. "Tarkio is on a mission to fix the world, to right all wrongs—" He broke off when Tarkio grabbed his head in the crook of his elbow. The two of them wrestled for a moment, then broke apart, laughing.

Tarkio shook his head at Xico. "Iskra, I really shouldn't have brought you here. It's not safe for you to come."

"You're right. Rules are rules. And I intend to follow them. It's safer that way."

"Really?" Xico asked.

Iskra gasped and shook her head.

Xico went on. "*Agliff*, are you?" he asked.

When Iskra didn't answer, Tarkio said, "He's asking if you're afraid."

I am, she thought. I could be taken. She looked at the ground, then into Xico's green eyes. Out of the corner of her eye she could see Tarkio's frown, the late afternoon sun accenting the shadows on his face. Either way, I'll displease one of them. She thought of her mother's anger, the mocking of her classmates, the warm companionship of Xico's family. What do I want?

That Xico never learns what a coward I am.

"Yes," she said slowly. "If I can, I'll come."

11

Three days later, Iskra strolled along Gishin's main street, debating with herself. She'd eaten her lunch at the inn and had some time before she was due to return to her duties helping the cleaners in the town hall. Should she go home? Or take a walk outside the village gates? The sun was shining, the fields greening, a fresh breeze blew that reminded her of the freedom she felt on the mountain with the Riskers.

She wanted to get away from the rules, the confusion of what she'd been told compared to what she'd seen with her own eyes. She wanted to flee from the question of why her heart beat a little faster when she thought about a Risker who had beautiful green eyes and contagious confidence.

Most of all she wanted to know what had happened to Tavda.

"A sheaf for your thoughts." Kaberco's deep voice broke into her thoughts.

She jumped and put a hand on her heart. "Oh, Kaberco, I didn't notice you there."

"You were thinking hard about something. Maybe I should offer you three sheaves for such weighty musings?"

His warm smile made Iskra feel guilty about her visits to the Riskers. "I was trying to decide if I should go for a walk or go home."

"I can help you with that. Come walk with me a little. I've been inside all day and would welcome a little sun."

They made their way through the gates. Kaberco waved at the guards and led her down the road that led to Shinroo. "Now, Iskra, when I met up with you, your forehead looked like a newly plowed field. Surely the question of whether to walk or not was not that engrossing."

"You're right." Iskra gave him a small smile. *Now what do I say? Asking questions of Kaberco was like stepping on ice. If I'm not careful, I'll end up going a lot faster or further than I intend. I can't just ask about Tavda, because people who were taken are never to be spoken of again.* "I was wondering about that caravan I was with, the one that was attacked." She swallowed. "Is it really true? No one survived?"

"I'm sorry to say that's right. Only you and the guards who came to raise the alarm." He shook his head. "When I got there with more men, the bandits were gone. Everyone dead. We found a lone wagon, just at the bend in the road."

Iskra cringed a little, hearing the anger in his voice. He didn't seem to notice. "Until you got back, we didn't know what to make of that. And we did find the body of the trader you were riding with." He paused, then added in a gentler tone, "I'm sorry."

Iskra hung her head. "It really was frightening."

"Believe me, I'm doing what I can to make sure it never happens again."

"What do you do with the bandits? I mean, the ones you catch?"

"They are questioned. Then taken."

"Which means?" She held her breath, waiting for his reply. Maybe Kaberco would tell her something, anything that would shed some light on what happened to Tavda.

"Taken. Gone." He frowned. "What's the interest in bandits?"

Iskra's heart beat harder. His next question will be about Riskers, I'm sure of it. "They're, they're scary." She shivered.

He put his hand on her shoulder. "Don't worry about them. The ones we catch, you'll never see again. You can count on that."

Iskra drew her breath in sharply. "That means—" She stopped herself from finishing the sentence.

"That means what?" There was a note of suspicion in Kaberco's voice.

"It means . . .."

"Iskra. Answer me." Kaberco's voice was harder than she'd ever heard it before.

"Kaberco, I know I'm not supposed to talk about her."

"Her?" His eyebrows were so tightly drawn together they nearly met over his nose.

"Tavda," she whispered.

"You're right, you shouldn't talk about her. Not unless you want to end up where she is."

"I don't. But, Kaberco, why? Why is she gone?"

He didn't answer her right away. Instead, he stared at her, a stare that made her feel like he was trying to force her into a confession. One more minute and she'd end up confessing the whole story. Her knees wobbled and her lip quivered. What would he do to her if he found out where she'd been?

"What did Tavda tell you?" Kaberco spoke slowly, his deep voice menacing.

Iskra's eyes widened and she gulped. "Nothing, she told me nothing."

He continued to stare at her, then relaxed. "I'm glad of it. I wouldn't want you mixed up in anything that could make life unsafe for you." He looked into her eyes. "If people do things that risk the safety of the village, they have to pay the consequences. Consequences that can be severe, as your friend found out."

Iskra's knees shook. What horrible thing happened to Tavda?

"You understand, you can never speak of her again."

She felt his words like a vise around her heart. Her head drooped and her shoulders sagged.

Kaberco put a hand on her shoulder. "Please believe me, I'm doing everything I can to keep the village safe and happy. Those who follow the rules have nothing to worry about." When she raised her face to look at him, he chucked her under the chin. "Can you smile for me? I like to think I'm keeping you safe and happy."

She returned his smile, hiding the sadness and guilt inside. *Which means I'll never see Tavda again. And if I try to find out why or what happened to her, I could be taken, too.* For a moment, she thought about doing as Kaberco advised.

No. I have to know. I can't stop now.

ISKRA NEVER KNEW JUST when she decided to skip Volunteer Day. She wavered all week, torn between her fear of getting caught and her desire to know more about the Riskers. *Maybe,* she thought, *the taken are sent to the Riskers. That's why we can't have any contact with them. Maybe they know where Tavda is.*

Her stomach churned and she cringed just thinking about Tavda, flushing with shame. *The least I can do for her is find out. No matter what the danger to me.*

She left her house early in the morning and set out for the section of the village square she'd been assigned to sweep. Passing through the market, she saw the caravan leaving for Shinroo. There were fewer wagons, she noticed, but she couldn't see if Tarkio was among them. It seemed there were more guardsmen, all riding brown horses and wearing black cloaks.

Her hands shook as she thought about what she was about to do. Biting her lip, she told herself the smart thing to do was to stick to sweeping.

The blast of a horn jolted her. She watched the creaking wagons move toward the town gates.

Until that moment she hadn't realized she wanted to leave, too.

She sidled up behind a group of people walking behind the caravan, as if she had a task to perform outside the village. *Pretend not to be afraid.* Clenching her jaw tightly, she forced herself to move slowly. If anyone saw her, they'd think she was just doing her volunteer service.

But no one will notice, she thought. *No one ever notices me.*

Once outside the gates, she strolled along the road, picking a flower or two as she walked, adding a sprig of leaves to her bouquet, the bright green leaves of spring. Past the village, she ambled along the road, trying not to attract any attention by running, and reached the turn for the Guarded Path.

With a quick glance over her shoulder to make sure no one was near, she stepped in between the trees onto the path. She paused at the bottom and looked up the rocky trail. It's really not that big a risk. I've done the hard part. I'll just have to make sure I get back before anyone notices I'm gone.

She hid her basket behind some trees and started her ascent. After a few minutes of climbing, another idea came to her. *I hope they let me in,* she thought. *What do they do to strangers who climb up uninvited? Do they shoot them? Or just turn them away?*

She slowly made her way up the path, forcing herself to not look down, to think about nothing but climbing. She repeated Xico's words to herself. *Put one foot in front of the other.* She took a few steps, then looked down, surprised to see how far she'd come. Her mind filled with terrors of falling, of smashing on a rock, and lying battered and broken at the foot of the hill, slowly dying in great pain. She slipped on a stone and fell, sliding back a few feet before she came to a stop in a bend on the trail, her flowers scattering along the path. Her heart thumped in her chest and she clutched the rocky side of the trail.

Sitting on the path, watching blood seep from a scrape on her knee, she reconsidered. She still had time to get back and sweep. No one would say anything if she was just a little late. She struggled to her feet, and looked down the trail. It looked a lot steeper going down. She took a step down, then turned and went up a few steps. The cut on her knee stung.

This isn't a good idea.

She turned to take a step down, stopped. She realized if she didn't go on, she'd never know why the Riskers were forbidden, let alone why Tavda was taken and what happened to her. If she stopped now, she'd never have the courage to return. And Xico would be disappointed. That was the thought that convinced her to go on. She stuck her chin in the air and started up the trail.

At the top, she saw Apango, who'd played the flute at Veressa's wedding. He smiled in recognition, waving lazily for her to go on to the camp. When she arrived at Xico's house, Cillia was packing bread, cheese, and fruit into a large basket.

"Iskra! I'm so glad you came today!" Cillia gave Iskra a quick hug. "We're all going to help with the honey harvest." Giving Iskra no time to protest, she wrapped her in an apron and thrust a large tan basket covered with a pine-green cloth into her hands. A long sling was attached to it instead of handles.

Slinging another basket on her shoulder, she said, "Come on. The others are already there."

12

Before she knew what had happened, Iskra was tramping along a trail through the woods, feeling the warmth of the breeze and the sun on her face. She wondered if there were bandits or warboars nearby. Cillia didn't seem to be worried. She was humming a cheerful tune, one that made Iskra feel happy just to hear it. Iskra noted that Cillia's apron matched her own borrowed garment, an apron made of a thick, coarse fabric that completely covered her dress and had short sleeves. She also saw Cillia had a bow in her hand and a quiver on her hip.

"It's good you're here," Cillia said. "The girls will be glad of your help, now that Veressa's gone."

Iskra wondered if she'd be of any use to them, if she'd make a mistake or ruin some of the honey. Or get stung by a bee. She had a mental picture of herself running down the Guarded Path, chased by a swarm of buzzing angry insects. At least the bees would keep the bandits away.

Presently they arrived at the foot of a steep cliff. Iskra bent her head back and could barely see the top. Tuli and Fialka had built small fires at intervals along the cliff, fires that gave off smoke that smelled like pine. Iskra joined the girls in searching for wood to keep the fires burning.

"The bees don't like the smoke," Fialka explained. "When they leave their hives to escape it, we can get the honey."

"Where is it?" Iskra asked.

"In the face of the cliff. The bees like to build high, away from animals that also like honey, and facing to the west, for the sun."

"Are you going to climb up to get it?"

Fialka laughed. "Not me! Tuli might, given a chance." She shook her head. "That's a job for Xico and Tikul." Seeing Iskra's puzzled look, she explained. "Our older brother. He missed the wedding because his wife's father was ill." She picked up a few more twigs. "I think that's enough for now. Let's go back."

Iskra spotted two flimsy rope ladders hanging down against the cliff. "Fialka, did they climb up those ladders?"

"No, they climb down. The boys and my father left early this morning and took the trail to the top. Da stays up there to lower the baskets, while my brothers come down the ladders. They poke the honeycombs with long poles to break pieces off and catch them in the baskets. When they're full, they lower them to us." She pointed up. "See, here comes one now." Slowly a woven basket full of honeycombs lowered down to them, suspended by a rope. Tuli ran up to it and steadied it, tugging gently on the rope.

"That's to let them know we have it," Fialka said. She carried a bucket to her sister, and the two girls shifted the honey from the basket to the bucket. After another tug on the rope, someone at the top pulled it up out of sight.

Iskra was astonished. She had no idea gathering honey was so dangerous. No wonder it was so expensive! When the next basket came down, she held her breath, hoping no bees were hovering around. She helped Fialka move the honey to a bucket. Then she rubbed her hands together to get rid of the sticky sensation.

Tuli picked up a honeycomb and broke a piece off. "Here, have a taste."

"Are you sure it's allowed?"

"Of course. Have as much as you like."

Iskra accepted the honeycomb and licked it. A smile broke across her face and she licked her lips. These Riskers were generous, that was one thing they had over the villagers. Never had Iskra worked so hard, with so much pleasure.

After an hour or so, Cillia placed some of the food she'd packed in the basket and sent it back to the top. "I think I'm ready for some lunch, what about you?" she asked. She handed around pasties stuffed with meat.

Iskra and the other girls ate in between emptying baskets, Tuli and Fialka keeping up a stream of banter and teasing. Iskra listened silently, taking it all in. These girls could choose their own husbands, their own lives. They could choose how they wore their hair and what color dress they put on. *Why does the Prime Konamei have to dictate all these things to us?*

After a few hours, she looked up to see Xico on the ladder fifty feet above her. He was wearing a large hat with a veil and held a long, thin pole in heavily gloved hands. Leaning from his ladder, he poked at a beehive and toppled a large honeycomb right into the basket. Iskra was amazed at how fearlessly he hung from the ladder, letting it sway with each shift of his weight, how he seemed to pay no mind to the stray bee that swarmed around his bare feet or the smoke that drifted upward. Most of all she admired his dexterity. He never missed the basket. Every honeycomb he knocked down fell right where he wanted it to go.

Finally, he worked his way to the ground. He jumped from his ladder and a grin spread across his handsome face when he saw Iskra. "You came!" he said.

"Yes, I just had to see the bees you were talking about," she said. "You're really quite . . .. You're very brave, to climb so high."

"Really?" He motioned to another young man who had jumped off the other ladder, pulling off his hat and veil. "Here's my brother, Tikul."

As Tikul approached, Iskra could see he had the same determined chin as Xico, but not the brilliant green eyes. He nodded to Iskra, then turned to Xico. "Hurry and collect all the buckets, will you? I'll get the horses."

Xico shrugged, smiling at Iskra. "My big brother. Loves to be in charge." He grinned. "He's just mad that he dropped a few honeycombs and I didn't." He tugged one of the ladders, and tipped his head back to watch as his father pulled it up. Then he placed all the buckets in a neat row near the trail.

Soon Tikul returned with two horses. He and Xico loaded them with the buckets of honey, stacking them on a small platform attached to the horses' backs. A sudden shout from Xico seized her attention. Xico was pulling a honeycomb out of his tousled curly hair, while Tikul and their sisters laughed. He winced as he pulled the sticky mess out of his hair.

Iskra tensed. There'd be a nasty fight now.

Shaking his head, Xico smiled at his brother. "You got me that time." He tossed the honeycomb at Tikul, who batted it down, laughing. Tikul took the lead of one horse and led it away, followed by Xico with the other.

Iskra walked down the trail with Xico. She listened as he told her stories of harvesting honey, of the times he nearly fell, or when the fires below went out and the bees swarmed back, ready to defend their hive.

She listened, fascinated, full of admiration. She was so taken with his stories she didn't notice how he slowed his pace until his mother and sisters passed them by.

He stopped just before they came to the outer edges of the

camp. "You've been quiet. Care to share what you're thinking?"

Harvesting honey is dangerous. It's exciting to watch someone drop the honeycombs into the basket. Thrilling to see Xico's green eyes light up when he talks to me. "It's been an interesting day."

"Are you glad you came?"

Yes. No. I didn't learn what I wanted to know. I should be disgusted with myself for enjoying the company of a Risker. But I'm not. She looked down at the ground, to give herself some time to collect her thoughts. "Yes?"

Xico laughed. "Sounds like you're not sure. But I am."

"You're what?"

"Sure that I'm glad you came here today."

She felt a warmth radiate through her chest and smiled at him. He returned her smile and took her hand. He turned it over and kissed her wrist, on the spot where the blue veins were visible through her skin. She felt breathless and weightless, like she could float all the way to the top of the cliff.

Xico squeezed her hand. "We'd best be getting back before Tuli comes to drag us home." He didn't let go of Iskra's hand as they walked.

By the time they returned to the house, Iskra told Xico she had to return to the village before she was missed. He went to help Tikul put the honey in the barn, while she went inside to say goodbye to Cillia.

"I don't need to ask you if you enjoyed yourself," Cillia said.

"Thank you for taking me. This was so fun! But I really need to go."

"Will they have missed you?"

"I don't think so. But, it's just, you never know what's going to happen."

"What do you mean?"

"People get taken, and we don't know why. Old Cassie did.

She started raving about a dezeerudun or something, and then she was gone. That doesn't make any sense to me. And a friend of mine just disappeared for asking questions about, uh, you all. The Riskers."

Cillia seemed to hold her breath a moment before answering. "I wouldn't put much stock in the rants of an old woman." She turned away from Iskra and stared out the window.

Iskra had the sense that Cillia was hiding something, or that she knew more than she let on. She tried to think of a question she could ask, one that would get Cillia to tell her. Maybe Cillia knew what happened to Tavda.

"Cillia, do you know what happens to people who get taken?"

Cillia looked at Iskra with pain in her eyes. "No. I don't."

Iskra felt a sinking sensation. *The Riskers don't know what I want to know. There's no point coming back here.*

"Before you leave, I want to give you something." Cillia pulled a basket down from a shelf and poked around in it. "Here, I would like you to have this."

Iskra reached out her hand to take the object from Cillia. It was surprisingly warm to the touch. She turned it over and saw that it was a small dragonfly amulet.

"I think this will help you, protect you," Cillia told her. "Just let the power of the sky-god flow through it to you."

"Thank you," Iskra said, tucking the amulet into her pocket. *I can't be rude; she's been so kind to me. I won't tell her she believes myths and fairytales that have no power to help or harm anyone.* "I-I guess I won't see you again."

Cillia pulled Iskra to her in a warm hug. "That's a wise decision, sweet girl," she said.

Iskra rested her head on Cillia's shoulder. This approval, this embrace, how she'd longed for them from her mother. Here with the Riskers was the only place she felt such peace. Should she really turn her back on them?

After a minute, Cillia stepped back and held Iskra by the shoulders, looking into her eyes for a moment, then said, "Thank you for your help today."

Somehow Iskra didn't think that was what she meant to say.

13

Iskra hurried through the drab village, hurrying to get home before the sun set. She hoped her mother hadn't finished her own Volunteer Day duties and would never know Iskra had skipped out on hers. She ran up to her house and peered in the window, pausing to catch her breath. No luck.

She watched her mother walk to the fire and set a small pot of water on the trivet over the flames and turn to pick up a mug.

Taking a deep breath, Iskra opened the door and walked in.

Luza turned to her, scowling. "Where have you been, girl?"

Iskra's lip trembled and she took a step back. "Oh, Mam, I was—"

"Don't tell me you were sweeping. Oyamel came by looking for you."

"I can explain."

"Tell me." Luza spoke quietly, her quiet tone not revealing the rage Iskra knew was building up within her as Luza's pale skin flushed. "Tell me now."

"Mam, I was busy."

"With what?"

Iskra stood up straight and looked directly at her mother. "If you must know, I helped with the Riskers' honey harvest."

Luza stood, frozen in place, grinding her teeth. "Why did you do that?"

"I don't know."

Luza hurled the cup in her hands to the floor. Iskra jumped at the sound of the smashing crockery, and hunched into herself. Her moment of courage wilted, leaving her feeling limp as paper left out in the rain. "You don't know? Look at me. Look at me, girl. Straight into my eyes." Slowly Iskra raised her eyes to do as her mother demanded. Luza raised her voice to a screech. "You went back to those Riskers against all the rules. Then you deliberately did something dangerous, like harvesting honey. Around bees! You might have been stung. And look at you! Honey all up and down your sleeves. What if someone had seen you?" She kicked a fragment of the broken cup.

Iskra stared at the golden splotches on her sleeve. "I didn't notice—"

"You didn't notice. Of course not." She shook her head. "Why, tell me *why* you went back to those barbarians?"

"She, Cillia, they've all been very kind to me."

"And I'm not? What about you being kind to me?"

"What do you mean?"

"You've become friends with these, these Riskers. Cippia. Who's that?"

"Cillia, Mam. She's the mother. She's been so thoughtful."

"And me? What am I? I've sacrificed for you, done so much for you. This is how you thank me." Luza dropped onto a stool and stared blindly at the table.

"Mam, I don't understand. I know the rules, but the Riskers aren't like what we've been told. What's so wrong about being with them?"

Luza sat silently, as if thinking about Iskra's question. Iskra studied her as if she'd never seen her before. Luza's wrinkled face was purple now. *The supposed barbarians are kinder than you, the model villager,* Iskra thought.

"Clean up that mess, the mess you made me make." Luza's voice grew higher and shriller with each word she spit out.

Iskra got a broom and began sweeping. She knew her best course of action was to do as her mother ordered until she'd calmed down a bit. She felt her mother's steady glare like a burn on the back of her neck as she scooped up the broken pieces of pottery and threw them out the window to the trash heap behind their house.

"Iskra, you must promise me never to go to those Riskers again."

"Why?"

"Don't ask questions. You're just like your father. Do you want to end up like him?"

Iskra drew her eyebrows together. "He died of grippe, Mam. You don't get grippe from questions."

"That's what I told you, and tried to convince all the neighbors. Some know it's not true." Luza clenched her fists, then pressed them into her eyes.

"Then what happened?"

"How do I know I can trust you not to tell anyone?"

"Mam, you need to tell me what happened to Da!" Iskra dropped to her knees in front of her mother and grabbed her hands. "Tell me!"

"You can never tell anyone, you hear me?"

"Yes, yes. I won't tell anyone."

"Your da asked lots of questions, just like you. Why does everyone have to be the same? Why is it taking so long to build a safe society? Why, after three hundred years are we still living hand-to-mouth? Are we sure the old myths are just that? And what's wrong with the Riskers?"

"Da knew the Riskers?"

"I don't know if he ever met any or not. He wanted to."

"What happened?"

"He was taken one night. They came for him, like they always do, on cloudy nights when there is no moon. A knock on the door, men in masks. 'Brisen Mukujuk. Come.' That's all they say."

"Was he sick?" Iskra's stomach churned.

"No, not at all. I knew it was his questions that brought them there. It wasn't like we had no warning. The ephor had been watching." She slammed her hands down on her thighs. "But your father wouldn't stop."

"What happened to him?"

"I never found out. I told all the neighbors he had grippe. The ephor told me I would be wise to stick to that story. Kaberco had just apprenticed to the ephor then, and interceded for me. If he hadn't, I would have been taken, too."

"Why didn't you tell me before?"

Luza slammed her fists on her knees. "So you wouldn't ask any questions! That's how I've kept you safe. Don't you see? He made his choice. He got what he deserved." Luza grabbed Iskra's chin and pulled her face close. "Don't you understand? If people knew he'd been taken, you'd be suspect. And so would I. I did all I could to keep the neighbors from guessing."

Iskra froze in place, kneeling. You cared more about the neighbors than your husband? She longed to voice her disgust but didn't dare further provoke her mother.

Luza pushed Iskra away from her. "Accept it. This is all we have and all there is. Now go to bed and forget your questions and Riskers and anything else." Luza's breath was coming in gasps, as if she was about to sob. "Your friend Tavda was taken for asking questions in class, and you think it's just fine to ask whatever you like. On top of that, you go to the Riskers.

You care nothing about what the neighbors will say, what this could do to me."

She continued her complaints for a few more minutes, and finished with, "I'm expecting your obedience. If you don't give it to me, then don't count on my protection. Now that Kaberco's the ephor, he can help a lot. But I won't ask him to save a wanton risktaker. You need to stay on his good side." She scowled at Iskra. "Go to bed."

Iskra stared at her for a moment, then complied. Unable to sleep, she tossed and turned on her bag of straw. The close, stale air of the house pressed on her, making her long for the fresh air up on the mountains.

And the sense of peace and freedom she never found in the village.

14

A little over a week after Veressa's wedding, Tarkio pushed his way through Trofmose's crowded market, eyeing the goods for sale. Several caravans arrived at about the same time, coming from all parts of Tlefas. Caravans from the central plains carried rye and corn, leather and livestock. From the far south came cotton and dried fruit. Tarkio smiled at a display of dried pelba, a fruit that only grew near the sea, available in Trofmose because of the traders bold enough to trade with the pirates who sailed up river, today to trade, tomorrow to raid.

Dangerous business, trading with pirates, Tarkio thought. The ones who did it successfully knew how to make the pirates think they got the best of the bargain. The ones that didn't never traded again.

The market smelled of sweaty horse hair and baking bread. His stomach rumbled. Food first, then company.

"Tarkio!"

He turned to see Waukomis, his red-headed friend with laughing eyes, carrying three loaves of black bread. He handed one to Tarkio, and resumed gnawing on another. "Stuff's as hard as a warboar's tusks. Any sign of Poales?"

"No, not yet. They said he came yesterday with the caravan from Litavye, but they haven't seen him since."

"What's that inn he likes?"

"I checked already. The innkeeper saw him go to his room last night. This morning he was gone, long before anyone got up."

"Odd. He knew we were comin' today."

"Unless he felt the urge for some company in the middle of the night."

Waukomis laughed, then shook his head. "Not something our friend Poales would do."

"Yeah. Something's not right." Tarkio scratched the stubble on his chin. "Let's pay a visit to Nunkini."

Waukomis nodded. Nunkini was a street sweeper who cleaned around the market and stables. While he was at it he collected gossip. If anyone in Trofmose wanted to know what their neighbors were up to, Nunkini was the first person they asked. "This could be fun," he said.

They strolled along the streets of Trofmose, a town of tens of thousands, a hundred times the size of little Gishin and a hundred times dirtier. They passed through the main square, with its towering monument to prosperity, a statue of a beaming man holding bread and fruit in the crook of one arm, holding a lamp over his head with the other. Around its base, rats battled for scraps of bread, dogs fought over dead rats.

Tarkio felt the prickling of the hairs on the back of his neck rising, making him feel someone was watching them. He nudged Waukomis and raised his eyebrows.

Waukomis casually turned his head about, as if stretching his neck. He rubbed the back of his neck and muttered, "I don't see anyone following us, but it sure feels like it."

"I caught a glimpse of two men with red shoulder bands just now."

"Red? Why would judges' clerks be loitering in the market this time of day?"

They walked a little in silence before Tarkio spoke again. "Is it my imagination or are people looking at us funny?"

"People always look at you funny." Waukomis smiled at his own joke, then grew serious. "I do get the sense people don't seem to want to notice us."

"Or maybe they're spooked, just staying away from all traders." *Am I right to be nervous, or imagining things?*

"Do you think it's dangerous even talking to Nunkini?"

Tarkio sucked in his breath. "Maybe. We'll just have to be careful." They turned down a narrow alley that reeked of sour milk and rotting fish.

The early summer heat made everything smell worse, Tarkio thought.

Emerging from the alley behind the town hall, they saw a scrawny youth with dirty-blond hair sweeping the pavement in front of an inn that stood across the street.

Tarkio nodded to Waukomis and approached the young man, who didn't bother to look up at their approach. Tarkio dropped a coin in front of the youth.

"If you please, you dropped this," the youth said. He stooped to pick it up, then gasped when he looked up at Tarkio's face.

"Thank you, Nunkini," Tarkio said, holding out his hand for the coin.

"I don't want to talk to you," Nunkini said, glancing from side-to-side. "It's not safe."

"Not much is, these days," Tarkio said. "Especially for traders. Is there any news of our friend Poales?"

"No news. None that I know, anyway."

"Is there any news you don't know?" Waukomis asked.

"None that I can tell you." He dropped his head and resumed sweeping.

Tarkio sighed. Nunkini was in one of his difficult moods.

"Is there news you can tell us someplace else, or news that someone else can tell us? Or is there news if we pay for it?"

"Or news that we have to beat out of you?" Waukomis smiled. "I like that kind the best, the kind we beat out of you."

"You wouldn't," Nunkini said, licking his lips, eyes darting back and forth, looking from Tarkio to Waukomis. A thin sheen of sweat appeared in the down on his upper lip.

"We wouldn't if we hear some news," Tarkio said. "What kind do you have for us?"

"The kind that gets told in the stables behind the Northern Inn. In half an hour. Go away before anyone sees me talking to you." Nunkini flapped his hand at them, turned his back and put his broom back in motion, stirring up the dust.

"Make sure you show up alone, Nunkini," Tarkio said.

"And don't forget your news. I don't mind waiting for it, but it better be good," Waukomis said.

They ambled away from Nunkini, looking at the town hall and inn with sidelong glances. No one seemed to be watching.

"He's nervous. More than usual," Waukomis said.

"Something's up." Tarkio rubbed his thumb along his fingernails. "Maybe I'm picking up something from Nunkini, but I'm feeling a little jumpy. Let's see what's going on at the stables, shall we?"

THEY WALKED to the end of the street and ducked into an alley. Following a twisting route, they made their way to the stables Nunkini mentioned. They watched for a few minutes, waiting to see if anyone went in or went out the wooden doors which were standing open. All appeared to be quiet. While Tarkio remained watching the front of the stables, Waukomis went around to the back, to listen for sounds other than horses snorting or eating or rustling the hay.

Tarkio used the time to think. What could have unsettled Nunkini? Why didn't he want to be seen with them? And what happened to Poales? Had he been taken? Were other traders in danger of being taken?

He was so lost in thought he barely noticed Waukomis return.

"That's not good, my friend," Waukomis said. "I could've slit your throat before you knew I was upon you."

Tarkio nodded, then pointed. Nunkini was walking toward the stables, carrying his broom. They watched him enter the building, then waited several minutes. No one followed, so they walked across the street and entered the stables, breathing in the smell of horse and hay and manure.

Nunkini was mucking out a stall, tossing the filthy hay in a pile, muttering to himself. Tarkio and Waukomis stood near the entrance to the stall, both with hands on the daggers in their belts.

"Nunkini. The news," Tarkio said.

Nunkini started and dropped the pitchfork.

Waukomis grabbed it and leaned on it as if he was preparing for a leisurely chat. "I'm ready," he said.

Nunkini closed his eyes, then opened them wide. "I shouldn't be talking to you. To any traders."

"Why not?"

"You're unsafe."

Tarkio frowned. "Since when?" When Nunkini didn't answer, he said, "You've known us for years. What changed?"

Nunkini kicked at the dirty straw, sending a shower of dust motes into the air. "You just threatened to beat me. I'd call that unsafe."

Tarkio felt a pang of guilt. He hated having to torment Nunkini, but he was desperate for news of Poales. "I'm sorry about that. If you please, put it down to concern about our friend." Tarkio tried and failed to catch Nunkini's eye. The boy was too busy staring at his shoes.

"Besides," Waukomis said, "you weren't too friendly before we even started talking. What's up?"

Nunkini closed his eyes. "I shouldn't tell you."

"If you please, Nunkini," Tarkio said. He held his breath, watching Nunkini's eyes dart back and forth, from the stable door to the straw at his feet, to Waukomis and the pitchfork.

"Poales came here yesterday. Last night the guardsmen took him from his room at the inn."

Tarkio stared at him, then at Waukomis. Why would anyone go after Poales? He turned back to Nunkini with raised eyebrows. "Why?"

"I don't know. All I've heard is they are suspicious of him for some reason. They've been talking a lot about unsafe traders, whatever that means."

"Is that all?" Waukomis asked.

"Yes, it's all. Will you go?" He flapped his hands at them. "I don't want to be seen with any traders, not 'til they figure out who is unsafe."

"We're going," Tarkio said. "We never spoke to you."

"Not unless you give us a reason to find you," Waukomis threatened, pointing the pitchfork at Nunkini. "No one need ever know you saw us."

"Fine. Just go."

Waukomis speared the floor with the pitchfork. Tarkio noticed a flicker in Nunkini's eyes. Fear, maybe. Or was it anger?

TARKIO AND WAUKOMIS walked away from the stables, aimlessly following first one alley, then another, ducking into doorways, skirting piles of refuse that all reeked in their own way, some smelling of burnt offal, others of manure.

When they were certain that no one had tried to follow them, they made their way back to the market. By this time, most vendors had packed up their wares. Only a few remained, chatting with the few shoppers who wandered the rows in search of bargains.

"Friends, this is your last chance!"

Tarkio and Waukomis ignored the seller's plea and ambled to a row of empty stalls. They sat down in front of the third one from the front entrance, settling themselves in the waning afternoon sun, sitting facing each other on tattered pieces of burlap, discarded by some vendor. They scooped out a circle of twelve little circular pits in the dirt, and moved pebbles from one pit to another, playing a game of strategy. Tarkio hoped they looked like people with nothing in particular to do.

After a few minutes, Waukomis asked, "Now what?"

"I'm not sure. I think Nunkini is telling the truth. I also don't think he's betrayed us, yet, anyway."

"If they question him, he'll crumble like a dry leaf, that's sure. Your move."

Tarkio thought for a minute, then moved two stones from one pit to another, skipping two pits in between. "Accepting that it's fact Poales was taken last night, do you think it's because he's been trying to organize a complaint about the guardsmen?"

"Hard to know. I sure hope not."

Tarkio forced himself to think slowly. "We've all been very careful, almost too careful. Maybe it was some other reason they took him." He moved three stones, dropping one each in a different pit. "In any case, we need to get him out fast, before they ask him too many questions."

"We could probably break him out."

"We could. But then they'll have a reason to be looking for him. He's our best contact in the south, and I don't want to lose him."

Waukomis laughed and scooped up all of Tarkio's stones. "Keep your mind on the game, will you?" He divided up the stones and handed half back to Tarkio. They arranged the stones in the pits and started another game. Tarkio picked up a stone and absently turned it over in his hand. “Hey, was that rumor true, that Poales started trading with the pirates?”

“It sure is.”

Tarkio dropped the stone in his hand. “How did that happen?”

“He went a little too far south, trading with some fishermen. A pirate ship sailed up and the pirates rounded up all the fishermen, and with them, Poales. They were about to kill them all when Poales offered a trade.”

Tarkio wrinkled his forehead. “What kind of trade?”

“It seems Poales had one of his inventions with him.”

“What would pirates want with children’s toys?”

“They’re not all toys. This was a tube with glass covering both ends.”

“What good is that?”

“Supposedly, you can see things far away through it.”

Tarkio stared. “No.”

“Yes. It took Poales a few minutes, but he was able to convince the pirate captain to not kill them, in exchange for his Farsight tube and the promise of more gadgets in the future. The captain agreed. They sealed the deal with some wine, and now Poales has some new trading partners.”

“That slippery fish. He gets out of the tightest spots.”

“Let’s hope the fish’s luck holds. Do you think they took him for that?”

“What, trading with pirates?” Tarkio bit his lip. “Let’s hope not.” He moved two stones from one pit to another.

A few traders walked by, stopped to watch them play for a few minutes, hurling abuse when either made a mistake. Two guardsmen stalked up to see what was drawing so much attention, puffs of dust rising from their tramping feet. “Just another pair of lazy traders, playing games.” They moved on, barely looking at Tarkio and Waukomis.

After the watchers left, Tarkio said, "I hope they all think we're that harmless."

"We really are."

"They don't think so. I'm sure if they knew what we're up to, we'd all lose our trading licenses."

Waukomis grimaced. "Then what? Can't imagine myself fixing roads the rest of my life."

"Or worse."

"If we were taken, that would be a short life." He moved two pebbles. "Your turn."

Tarkio sat motionless, staring at the pebbles in their pits. "I think we need to ask Juquila for help. We've never asked her for anything before."

"I'd hate to use her before we really need to."

"I know."

"Besides, it'd be more fun to break him out."

Tarkio laughed. Waukomis, true to form, was always out for entertainment. He turned his attention back to the game.

The afternoon shadows lengthened as they continued to play. A lone trader, hood pulled over his head, walked slowly up the row of stalls, carrying a large bundle. He set it down near Waukomis and sat on it. "Greetings," he said. "What's new under the sky?"

"Much that is new is not good," Tarkio said.

"We hope for good from the sky," the stranger said. He pushed the hood back from his face. "I'm Muzquiz, a trader of Trofmose."

Tarkio looked into the stranger's blue eyes that were so pale they were nearly white, eyes that didn't directly meet his gaze. "I'm Tarkio, also of Trofmose. That's Waukomis, from just about anywhere."

"Sorry it took me so long to find you. I heard there were some traders the guardsmen suspected, so I waited until I found out who they were."

"Did you?"

"I did. I think it was you two. That is, until they found you playing with rocks. When I heard them all laughing about it, I thought it was safe to approach you." He gave them a half-bow. "Clever means to arrange things so you could talk without being overheard, yet looking like you have nothing to hide." Tarkio thought he heard a trace of sarcasm in his voice.

Waukomis looked up at Muzquiz with raised eyebrows. "Why did you want to find us?"

"Galeano sent me to tell you about a trader called Poales."

Tarkio froze, waiting. "You know what happened?"

Muzquiz nodded. "I saw him yesterday. He did make contact with someone in the south, but whoever it was reported him to the guardsmen."

"Why didn't—?" Tarkio stopped himself.

"They take him in the south?" Muzquiz brushed his strawberry-blond hair out of his eyes and rubbed his nose. "They either wanted him to bring his goods here, or to find out who else is stirring up trouble."

"Where is he now?" Tarkio asked. He noticed Muzquiz wasn't looking him in the eyes as he spoke.

"As far as I can tell, he's still in the jail below the town hall. The ephor just returned from Anbodu this afternoon, so he'll probably question Poales tomorrow."

"Then we've only got tonight," Waukomis said.

"Don't tell me your plans," Muzquiz said, holding up his hands. "Poales and I only spoke for a few minutes, but they could suspect me. I'd rather not have much to tell them." He stood up and brushed the dust from his bundle, then hoisted it to his shoulder. "If you move two pebbles to that pit, you'll win," he said to Waukomis, pointing.

"Thanks a lot," Tarkio said. "I was hoping he wouldn't see that."

"I owe you one," Waukomis said.

Muzquiz shifted his bundle, held up a hand in farewell,

and continued to the main gate of the market. Tarkio and Waukomis returned to their game.

"What do you think?" Waukomis asked.

"I think I don't know. He knew the guild passwords. Galeano could have sent him."

"But they could have gotten them out of Poales by now."

"True. Unless they really are waiting for the ephor, then maybe not."

Waukomis rubbed his hand over his mouth, then selected a pebble and tossed it in a pit. "Are you thinking this may be a trap?"

"Yes. Muzquiz, if that really is his name, just about told us to break Poales out. He was sweating and wouldn't look me in the eye. Which makes me wonder why."

"Why he was sweating, or why does he want us to spring Poales?" Waukomis shrugged. "Let's try, it will be exciting."

Tarkio shook his head. "Maybe too exciting. Juquila may be a better hope."

Waukomis grinned. "Maybe. But from what you say, in some moods, she could be worse."

Nodding, Tarkio moved a few stones. "We'll have to hope she's in a good mood, then."

"Agreed. How much longer do we have to play this cursed game?"

"Just 'til I beat you one more time. Then we'll go see what games Juquila wants to play."

15

Sweat dripped down the back of Tarkio's neck, a warm trickle that traced a trail halfway down his spine. What they were about to do was risky, no doubt about it. He and Waukomis had spent the last few hours finding an inn and some supper, doing their best to act as though they had nothing on their minds other than the next day's trade. When the crowd in the inn's dining room thinned, they strolled out and made their way to the river.

From there they crept along the shore to the place where the walls of the ephor's house plunged into the river. Dabrey's full orb gave them enough light to see. Few people knew there was a narrow ledge that ran along the wall, as it was underwater even when the river was low. Tarkio poked a stick into the water, feeling for the ledge. He snorted in disgust and tossed the stick into the river. "At least three feet! It's going to be a wet walk."

"You had to pick early spring for this," said Waukomis.

They lowered themselves into the river, gasping as the cold water assaulted their legs and splashed their groins. They felt their way along the narrow ledge which barely provided a few inches of support for their feet. They clutched at projections in the rock, digging their fingers into the spaces between the stones, clinging tightly to keep the current from pulling them away from the wall.

As they inched along, they could hear the tramp of guards on the parapet that circled the top story of the ephor's house. Two stopped just above Tarkio and Waukomis.

"And so I—"

"What then?"

"—traders—"

Tarkio and Waukomis looked at each other, wide-eyed. From the few words they could hear, they didn't know if they had been spotted, or some other traders were the subject of conversation.

Waukomis mouthed to Tarkio "Stay or go?"

"Wait," he mouthed back.

They held their breath, fingers aching, legs cramping.

The guards laughed, and tramped on.

"Go," Tarkio mouthed.

Halfway along the wall they came to a door with no handle, its dim outline just visible about a foot above the water. Tarkio felt along the beam that formed the left side of the door, smiling when he found the hidden release that allowed him to push the door inward. He held his breath as he eased it inward, hoping the guards didn't hear the faint creaking. Halfway, the door stuck, just ajar enough for them to climb in, splashing water and grunting.

"Did you have to make so much noise?" Waukomis asked.

"Can't help it." Tarkio shut the door behind them, blocking the moonlight. The scent of mildew and stagnant water assaulted his nostrils and he sneezed. He lowered himself to the floor, then pulled his boots off.

"What are you doing?" Waukomis asked.

"Getting the water out of my boots. You should do the same." He dumped the water, hearing it splash against the stone floor. He set them against the wall and stood to wring some of the water from his trousers. From the grunts and splatters, he could tell Waukomis was doing the same.

"What's the point?" Waukomis asked. "We're not going to be dry any time soon."

"At least we won't be dripping all over Juquila's apartments."

"Where are we, anyway?"

"This is one of the emergency exits the first ephor put in. Just in case Trofmose was attacked, he could escape."

"Courageous fellow. I hope the present one isn't bolder. I'm not sure he'd like us visiting his wife this way. Are you sure this will work?"

"No, not really. Do you have another idea?" Tarkio pulled his boots back on and stood up. "Ready?" He put his left hand on the wall and began counting the stones as he walked. "One, two, three—" When he reached seventeen, he felt around. "Found it!" With one hand on the doorknob, he felt along the other three stones to the right for the hidden latch that would unlock it.

He pressed the lever. Nothing. He pressed it down again, straining to turn the handle on the door, which abruptly turned with a grating noise and he pushed the door open.

"Sure could use some oil on that one," Waukomis said.

"Hope no one heard that."

"Maybe they'll think it was the dying gasp of the chicken they're having for dinner."

Tarkio shook his head, stepped into the narrow passage, and placed a hand on the wall. He started counting again. At twenty-three he poked around with his foot. "Here, I found the steps." He led the way up and smiled when he heard Waukomis trip over the first step.

"Eighty-six, eighty-seven, eighty-eight. Now, on the right." Tarkio ran his fingers over the wall and felt another door. He eased it open, letting out the scent of spicy perfume. He paused, listening, then crept through.

"Where are we?" asked Waukomis.

"The inside of Juquila's wardrobe."

Tarkio crept to the front of the wardrobe, pushing aside the hanging silk gowns. A vertical line of light penetrated the gloom, light shining through the crack between the doors of the wardrobe. He blinked to adjust his eyes to it. He pressed his ear to the narrow opening and waited.

Hearing no sounds from the room, he pushed the wardrobe door open cautiously and peered out. The room was empty. He pulled the door shut. "Better get comfortable. I don't know how long we'll have to wait. If it's the ephor's first night back, he may be enjoying his wife for a while." There were some scuffling noises as the two of them settled on the floor of the wardrobe, leaning against its sides, silk gowns hanging in their faces.

"Have you been here before?" Waukomis asked. His voice sounded muffled in the darkness.

"No."

"Then how did you know exactly how many steps and where to find the doors?"

"Groa; she's Juquila's twin." *I wonder if Juquila's forgiven me,* he thought. She'd tried to stab him at his wedding, angry he'd chosen her less attractive sister. They both had auburn hair, coppery skin and dark eyes. But somehow a faint difference in shades and the shape of features made what was pretty on Groa seductive and exotic on Juquila. She'd never had to take second place to her sister before. Worse, she'd always had a temper and tended to hold grudges.

"Oh. That's the connection," Waukomis said. "But why wouldn't she lock her wardrobe? Is this a trap? Or is she expecting other visitors?"

"With Juquila, all you know is she always has a reason. Just be ready for anything."

The men sat in silence, the air in the wardrobe growing steadily staler, their senses dulling from the stuffy warmth.

Tarkio jerked his head up at the sound of the door to the room opening. He eased his dagger from his belt, ready to spring to his feet if the wardrobe door opened. *Fool*, he thought. *We should have waited on the stairs. We would have been able to hear well enough from there.*

"Go fetch me some wine," he heard Juquila say. He heard the door close. A soft rustling sound moved toward the wardrobe and the door opened. "You can come out now, Tarkio."

Blinking in the sudden light, Tarkio and Waukomis staggered to their feet and climbed out of the wardrobe.

"How did you know we were here?" Tarkio asked.

"The smell of the river and wet leather. There's been all kinds of talk about traders and conspiracies and clandestine gangs the last few days. A few traders even got taken. When I came into the room and smelled the damp, I knew it had to be you. I figured you'd show up one day. When you wanted something." She raised her eyebrows at Waukomis.

"Juquila, if you please, this is Waukomis." She didn't seem to remember having met him before, which was just as well. And typical of Juquila, to not pay attention to people of no use to her.

She nodded at him, then turned to Tarkio. "And who else could it be but you? The only person I told about this door was my sister. What do you want?"

Tarkio shook his head. "You always were quick, Juquila." He held out his hands, palms up, and shrugged. "Much smarter than I am."

"Is that what made you choose Groa over me? I always wondered." She put a finger under his chin and looked into his eyes.

Tarkio forced himself to meet her gaze, searching her obsidian eyes for signs of hatred or forgiveness. He wasn't sure what he saw.

She shrugged. "I'm far better off now, don't you think?" She waved a hand at the room.

Tarkio stepped back and looked around at the woven carpet on the wood floor, the tapestries on the walls, the polished furniture, the silk hangings on the bed, candelabras with burning candles placed around the room so generously the space was nearly as well-lit as if the sun were shining brightly.

He took in the vivid colors of Juquila's gown, made of some material he had never seen, a fabric that reflected the light in such a way that at times it looked black and at others appeared to be a dark pine-green. He sensed Waukomis was openly staring at the way the gown accentuated her lush figure.

"Yes, I'd have to say you are."

Juquila moved silently across the thick carpet, the only sound the rustle of her gown. She sat down at a low table and picked up an ivory-handled hairbrush. She pulled the brush through her long, thick auburn hair. "You were very bold, to come here not knowing if I was still keeping a dagger ready to stick in your ribs, Tarkio."

"I had a plan." Be careful, he told himself. Get this right, or it could turn out badly. Very badly. And not just for Poales. He felt the sweat form on the back of his neck.

"I see. Are you going to tell me this plan?"

"I might not need to now. Don't you want to know why we're here?"

"Tell me now, before my maid returns."

"A friend of mine, Poales, a trader from the south, has been taken. We think Valday will hear his case tomorrow. Can you get him freed?"

"Why would I do that?"

"Because he's a good man, and has done nothing to deserve getting taken."

Juquila set down her brush and looked down at her hands in her lap.

At least she hadn't refused immediately, he thought. "If you please, Juquila."

"Why should I?"

Tarkio's heart pounded. How to answer her? "I'll tell you the truth. There's nothing in it for you. I know you always felt people who got taken deserved it. But this is different. Poales has done nothing wrong."

"And why should I care?"

"You used to care about fairness." He held his breath, waiting for her response, not sure if it was a mistake to turn her thoughts to the days when she wanted him for her own.

She turned to look at him. "Fairness?" She smirked and shook her head. "A lot has changed in the last two years. I've seen a lot I wish I had never seen."

"Oh?"

"I was so zealous, so sure that the dream of a safe and prosperous society could be made real." She shook her head and sighed.

"Go on."

"Then I married Valday. Nothing changed, at first; he seemed as sincere as I was. It bothered me a little the way he angled for promotion, but I believed that was because he wanted to work hard for the good of all, to be in a position where he could do more."

Waukomis stepped forward. Tarkio shook his head and motioned for him to remain silent.

Juquila resumed brushing her hair. "Then a year ago, Valday became ephor and we moved into this house. In one day all my illusions shattered."

"How?"

"We no longer had a house the same size as everyone else. We even have servants. How is it fair that we have people waiting on us? Everyone knows the konameis all have housekeepers to help them. But we have kitchen maids and scullery maids, even maids to bathe and dress us. I asked Valday why. He said because we have more responsibility, everyone understands why we live a little better, why we need to have richer food, finer clothes."

"What responsibility do you have?" Tarkio asked.

"Exactly. I have none, other than to make Valday's life pleasant. I am not permitted to work. The maids live in terror, because I don't allow them to dress me. Valday rages when he catches me doing for myself."

She put down the brush and began braiding her hair in one thick plait that curved over her shoulder. "I'll tell you something else. These servants we have, most of them are never allowed to leave the house. Only the housekeeper and steward. No one can know the others exist. No one."

She stared at Tarkio and Waukomis as she spoke. She didn't continue speaking until they nodded their agreement.

"Do you want to know what annoys me the most? I no longer have to cut my hair short the way everyone else has to, with those choppy bangs. But I can't let my own family know. Whenever I visit them, I wear the gray turban that female konameis or konameis' wives wear. The turbans don't just mark our position. They hide the fact that we don't have to conform like everyone else." She wrapped a gold band around the end of her braid to hold it in place. "Valday says it's so they don't feel unequal. I think it's an absurd lie to cover up a sham."

Tarkio nodded. "I understand what you're saying." Do I? What is she really telling me?

"But that's not the worst," she went on. "That happened the first day I sat with Valday in court." She paused, then asked, "Do you know what happens to people when they are taken?" She looked from Tarkio to Waukomis. "Do you?"

Waukomis coughed, then said, "I try not to think about it."

Bad answer, Tarkio thought. "They just get killed, don't they? Or put to work somewhere?" He couldn't figure out where Juquila was going with this.

"The first court, the public court, decides the sentence of Taking," she said. "Then there is a second trial, a secret one. The lucky ones, they get put to death."

Tarkio's eyes widened. "The lucky ones?"

"The others, well, they do get put to work. Some go to work in the mines. Or in fields closer to the coast, where the pirates raid. They don't last long. But they aren't the most unfortunate."

She bowed her head, as if talking to the hairbrush lying on the table in front of her. "The truly unlucky become house servants for ephors and others in power. There's no way out for them. Their faces are branded with the word 'taken.' Their names are taken away. Like my maid. I don't know her name. I call her 'maid.' That's it."

Tarkio swallowed hard, trying to get rid of the sour taste in his mouth.

Juquila kept talking. "All I know of her is she's about fifteen and from Gishin."

He'd heard something about that, an underage girl from Gishin getting taken. He just couldn't place the memory. He listened in horror to Juquila's next words.

"She said something she shouldn't have, so they cut out her tongue. Which happens to most of the house servants."

Tarkio stared at her, feeling his stomach churn. A girl's tongue cut out?

Before he could say anything, Juquila continued. "Since she's pretty, big dark eyes, wavy auburn hair, they decided to not send her to hard labor but keep her for something else." She looked up at Tarkio. "Lucky for her, the day before she was taken, my former maid decided she couldn't take any more of this life and killed herself."

She paused to search Tarkio's face. "Imagine a life with no

name, unable to speak, never to leave the walls of this house, basically a possession. I couldn't blame her." She bit her lip. "And as for the girl who serves me now, she's better off here. They were probably going to send her to the capital."

"To do what?"

"Don't be such an innocent, Tarkio. The Prime Konamei keeps a few girls to amuse himself and others in favor."

Tarkio and Waukomis both gasped.

So much for safe and fair, Tarkio thought.

Juquila shrugged. "I've come to think that you were right all along."

"Right about what?"

"That passing more laws won't create a perfectly safe or fair society."

Tarkio tried not to let his surprise show. He never would have expected Juquila to sour on her new life, let alone so soon. If he could just say the right thing so she'd cooperate. "Will you help us?"

She tipped her head to the side and smiled. "Valday was very pleased with the welcome I gave him tonight, so I think he'll grant my request for mercy for a prisoner. He likes it when I sit with him in court. What grounds should I give?"

"Say that Poales has a clumsy tongue and speaks very poorly. He's not guilty, just unable to defend himself. Maybe you can convince Valday he's a bit slow, that his stammer is proof of that."

"That could work. I can say he seems too stupid to get involved in any kind of plot."

"Right."

"I'll do it. But you'll still owe me, Tarkio."

"What do I have that you could possibly want?"

"True. My servants live more richly than you do." She removed a strand of glittering emeralds from around her neck and tossed it on the table. "There is one thing." She stood up to face him. "Love my sister. She's unhappy and it's your fault. Make her happy, or I'll have to talk with Valday about you."

Tarkio sighed. How could he make a woman determined to be miserable be happy? "I'll do my best."

"Be sure you do." She smirked at Waukomis. "You and your silent friend can go."

"If you please," Waukomis said, with a grin.

Juquila laughed, then returned to her seat. She tipped her head and drew her brows together. "If you ever tell anyone what I have told you, you'll be the ones with branded faces."

"We understand. And thank you, Juquila. You won't regret it." Tarkio motioned for Waukomis to retreat through the wardrobe.

"Oh, Tarkio?" Juquila said. "I think from now on I'll keep that door locked."

"Fair enough." He stepped into the wardrobe. "Enjoy your wine." Without waiting for an answer, he pulled the door shut behind him.

16

"Then the Prime Konamei made a treaty with the Riskers. What were the terms of the treaty?"

Iskra opened her eyes and sat up to listen more attentively. It was two days after she'd been to the honey harvest, and she was back for another Oppidan lecture. She'd closed her eyes to avoid having to look at Tavda's empty place. The twice-weekly lectures, something she used to enjoy, were now a source of pain, and not just on Tavda's account. The room felt hot and stifling, like the very air was hemming her in.

Oyamel answered Edalia's question. "The Riskers were to keep separate from the villagers. They were to help fight the bandits. In exchange, they didn't have to follow all the Prime Konamei's rules."

"But—" The word was out before Iskra could stop it.

"But what?" Edalia asked.

Iskra frowned. "If the rules are meant to keep us safe, then why would the Riskers not want to follow them?" Surely, they don't think the Riskers *want* to be shot at or eaten by wild beasts, do they?

"Can anyone answer her?" Edalia looked around the room.

With a smirk, Oyamel responded. "Because the Riskers are barbarians who don't know any better." He folded his chubby arms across his chest and nodded. "They live like savages."

"Perfectly correct," Edalia said. "Because of that, we all understand contact with Riskers is dangerous."

"Then why do some traders deal with them?" Iskra could hardly believe she had the boldness to ask the question.

It seemed Edalia couldn't believe it, either. With wide eyes, she asked, "Why? Because of the treaty. The Riskers wouldn't be able to survive without our trade, our food, and other goods. We need them to help keep the bandits in check, until we have completed building a safe, fair, and prosperous country. Do you understand?"

"I understand why our first leaders wanted peace and fairness. And why they want the country to prosper. But why is everyone so worried about safety?" She knew she was asking the question badly but couldn't think of a better way to express her thought.

Edalia shook her head. "I'm disappointed in you. You used to be the most tractable student in this group. Now you have all kinds of silly questions. Does anyone have anything to say?"

Iskra wrapped her arms around herself, wincing under Edalia's sharp tone. She braced herself, knowing her classmates wouldn't be about to compliment her.

Oyamel stood, and said, "I agree. Iskra, you know that asking for explanations of matters the Prime Konamei has made clear is a waste of time. Why are you being so stupid?"

Maizie, a girl with black hair and olive skin chimed in. "Stupid or crazy. Which is it?"

Slumping in her seat, Iskra hung her head as the rest of the group added their abuse.

"People who ask questions don't fit in," Oyamel said.

"Do you hear that, Iskra?" Edalia asked. "You want to fit in, don't you?"

As Edalia's lecture drew to a close, Iskra began to relax. Maybe no one had reported her for skipping Volunteer Day. Maybe her fears were nothing. She lost herself in a daydream of walking with Xico in the sunshine.

The sound of her name brought her back to the present. "Iskra. Stand up," Edalia commanded.

Iskra drew a deep breath and rose to her feet, clenching her hands together tightly. All eyes were on her, staring, clear from their expressions they all knew what was about to happen.

"All of you know by now, Iskra chose not to participate in Volunteer Day. Will you be so kind as to explain to us why you failed to do your assigned duty?"

Iskra tried to answer but could not force words over her dry tongue.

"Speak up!" Edalia slapped her palm with her pointer, then waved it at Iskra. "Or do you want to hear from everyone else first?"

When Iskra didn't answer, Edalia pointed at Oyamel. "Name the first day of the week."

"Sanbe. Named for the joy of living in safety and fairness."

"Correct. Maizie. The second day."

"Yeksanbe. Named for the rhythm of our work to build a safe, fair, and prosperous land."

Edalia pointed at the girl sitting next to Maizie, who answered promptly. "The third day is Dosanbe."

The students continued answering in turns.

"The fourth day is Sesanbe."

"Charsanbe is the fifth day."

"The sixth day is Pansanbe, when we ramp up our efforts to meet our goals for the week."

"The seventh day is Sheshanbe, the day to achieve all we set out to at the week's start."

Edalia had now made her way around the room and had come back to Iskra. "Tell us, Iskra, if you can, the name of the eighth day."

"The eighth day," Iskra said, repeating a lesson she'd memorized years before, "is Hafsanbe, when we take the time to assess what we have accomplished toward the goal of creating a safe, fair, and prosperous society, and determine what we are to do in the coming week."

"And what else is Hafsanbe for?"

"The third, meaning the last Hafsanbe of the month, is Volunteer Day. Everyone performs some voluntary service to hasten the day when we will have built a safe, fair, and prosperous land."

"Then why did you not participate?"

Iskra tried again. "Edalia, if you please, I chose not to participate because I thought that if it is voluntary, that means I don't have to do it. Not unless I want to."

There was a sudden stillness in the room. A few students looked puzzled, like they thought what Iskra said made sense. Others frowned in disapproval.

Edalia's face turned red. "Why didn't you want to do it?"

Iskra remained silent.

"Answer me!"

"I just didn't." She fixed her eyes on motes of dust floating in a sunbeam. Don't get her mad, she told herself. "If you please."

The flush on Edalia's face turned purple. "You've been listening to malcontents. Does anyone have something to say to that?" Edalia asked.

Maizie stood up. "That doesn't seem fair to me. I had to do her work for her. No one helped me. What if I decided I didn't want to?"

Oyamel rose. "This is bad thinking. We all choose to help

because without everyone helping to build the safe society, we are all at risk. It's very selfish to not want to volunteer."

Another girl added, "Without everyone's cooperation, it will take longer to build a safe society, putting off prosperity for all. Maybe she wants that to happen?"

"And," Oyamel added, "people who are selfish don't belong. In fact, we don't want them."

Others added their insults and accusations, condemning Iskra. She forced herself to hold back tears. *I used to be like them,* she thought. *I was always the first one to rebuke someone else. I deserve all they give me, and more.* Finally, no one had any more to say.

Edalia asked, "What consequences should she bear for her selfish behavior and listening to troublemakers?" She reached up and tugged at her teacher's pink band on her shoulder, as if it gave her confidence in her authority.

"Make her sweep the entire square by herself on the next Hafsanbe," Maizie said.

Others nodded their agreement. "That will be fair. We'll have the day off, and she'll have to work."

Iskra tugged at the neck of her dress and swallowed hard. She felt as though the room were closing in on her, growing warmer and more airless.

"That will show you, Iskra, that you don't choose your days off," Edalia said. "We are given Hafsanbe, one day out of eight, when we don't work. Giving one Hafsanbe back each month in gratitude to our leaders is not a lot to ask. Do you all agree?"

The students nodded. "Do you?" she asked, turning to Iskra.

Iskra nodded.

"Good. I hope we never have this conversation again. You may all leave," Edalia said.

The group got up and left the room, no one speaking to Iskra. She waited until she was alone, then sank onto the bench. She blinked the tears from her eyes and willed herself to not cry. Time enough for that when she was alone. Better not to let them see how much they'd hurt her.

She took a few more deep breaths, then started to get to her feet. The door to the room opened, and Edalia returned, followed by Kaberco.

"This is the girl?" Kaberco asked. He stopped, mid-stride and shook his head. "Iskra?"

She hung her head, saddened by the disappointment she saw in his eyes.

He stepped toward her. "Sit back down."

Iskra sat on the bench, waiting while Edalia and Kaberco studied her. She felt like a cornered mouse, waiting for a pair of stalking cats to pounce. His hazel eyes had grown hard and cold, feeling to Iskra like they could read her every thought. Just asking a few questions was harder than sneaking off. At least then no one made fun of her.

Kaberco spoke first. "I'm really disappointed in you, Iskra. When Edalia told me someone had skipped Volunteer Day, you were the last person I would have guessed. What's gotten into you?" He looked soberly at her, almost kindly.

She hung her head, trying to think of something to say. She shook her head. Not a word came to her mind.

"You didn't think you had to help your village, your country, your leaders on Volunteer Day?" Kaberco's tone hardened. "Just because we don't force you to work, you think you can shirk your duty?"

"No."

"Tell me how you think it is fair to everyone else who works hard that you don't help out." He sat down on a bench opposite Iskra.

"I wasn't thinking about fairness," Iskra said.

"What were you thinking about?" Edalia asked.

"I don't know."

Kaberco sighed. "You can't expect me to believe that you have no idea what you were thinking when you chose not to help your village." He shook his head. "Don't be afraid to tell us. We're here to help you understand what you did wrong." The gold chain draped over his shoulders clinked softly as he leaned toward her.

He spoke those words in a gentler tone. Iskra raised her head. Maybe Kaberco would answer her. He'd always been kind to her before. "It's all so confusing," she said.

"What is?" Kaberco asked.

"Just that, if it's a Volunteer Day, we shouldn't have to do it."

Kaberco's eyes narrowed. "I've heard talk like that before. You want to know the last person who said something like that? Your father." He stood up, towering over Iskra. "I'll try to explain it to you. We ask for one day of the month in voluntary service to help build a safe and prosperous land. To be fair, everyone needs to do their part."

"I understand that. But—"

"But what? What don't you understand?"

"Like . . .." She searched her mind for a question that would make sense. "Like, why are we not allowed to do much cooking at home?"

Edalia gasped. "Why would you want to do something so dangerous?"

"Is it really?" Dangerous for some people, maybe. She looked up, chin quivering but not quite willing to give up.

Kaberco stared at her. "Perhaps you have forgotten. Edalia, can you review why such a law was made?"

"Certainly. Because early in our history, several people burned themselves. Severely, to the point they were unable to work, work to build our safe and prosperous country. A few even accidentally burned their houses down, which not only endangered themselves, but the whole village. In response, the Prime Konamei made a law that most cooking would be done by those specially trained. In this way, we will all be safer."

"Do you understand now?" Kaberco asked Iskra.

She flinched at his harsh tone. "Yes." *I understand they think we are all idiots who can't manage a fire. And no matter what they say, I'm not free to ask any questions I want to.* She hung her head, then looked up at Kaberco. She didn't know which was more threatening, his broad stature or steely gaze. He'd never looked at her that way before, never been anything but someone who was kind and made her feel safe. Now he was frightening her.

He turned to Edalia. "Watch her. Watch her closely. And you," he said to Iskra, "know that I'll be watching you."

17

Later that evening, Kaberco recounted Iskra's story to the other four members of the Gishin village council, known as the Gishin Konament. "She's only a scared little girl. I don't think we'll have any trouble from her."

As ephor, he was the highest-ranking member. He was also the newest—and youngest—member, youngest by over a decade. He still had to prove himself to the other four. Especially to Murash, the questor, second in rank, in charge of the courts, settling disputes, and punishing minor crimes in a public forum.

He also disposed of those who were taken. Kaberco's stomach twisted just thinking about Murash and the secret, unsavory part of his job.

The konament gathered in the ephor's house, not in the plainly furnished public rooms, but in the ephor's private quarters. Brightly colored woven carpets covered the floor of the council chamber, cushioned chairs offered soft comfort, and a large fire took away the chill of the spring evening. After two months as ephor, Kaberco still wasn't completely used to the luxury of his quarters.

As Kaberco poured red wine he noted that each of the

other four konameis always arranged themselves in order of precedence. All of them bore the general title of konamei, but each had a specific title which indicated an area of responsibity.

The ludi, Rotena, in charge of schools and community events like marriages, and the lowest ranking, sat the farthest from the fire, even though she was an old woman with a hacking cough.

The syndic, Zurvan, who oversaw trade, and the adile, Yasumin, who took care of village property and streets, as the third- and fourth-ranking konameis, waited to see where the questor Murash and Kaberco sat before choosing their seats.

No matter where they met, whether the meeting was formal or just a casual dinner, they all stuck to precedence. All of them were afraid of stepping out of line, of offending one of the others.

Would they have more trouble from Iskra? Kaberco hoped not. He had a bad feeling about her, but for the sake of their long friendship tried to make light of her offense. "Edalia made sure the group told her off well. She won't step out of line again."

Murash looked down his long nose. "She'd better not. We've had enough trouble from malcontents lately." He was sitting to one side of the fire, and it was hard for Kaberco to read Murash's weathered face under his graying hair, half in shadow, half lit by flickers of light.

The others all started talking at once, sharing stories of complaints they'd heard or criticisms of the Prime Konamei.

"Peace." Murash quelled them with one word spoken quietly but with a hint of impatience. "There have always been rebels and agitators. This I know from experience, something others may not be aware of."

Kaberco bit his lip to keep from responding. Murash never missed an opportunity to remind the others how new he was to the job.

Murash turned his cold gray eyes to Kaberco. "The key is to keep a firm hand, not a ruthless one." He leaned forward, the silver chain of his office clinking softly on his shoulders. "It was ill-advised for you to take that other underage girl. Have you forgotten the protocol? You took her without going through my courts."

Three heads jerked to stare at Kaberco. He felt his stomach lurch but kept his face impassive. He cursed inwardly. He'd been a fool to think Murash would let that go without trying to use it against him. He fixed his eyes on Murash, ignoring the appalled and fascinated faces of those who were watching this confrontation unfold.

Kaberco took his time to respond. "It's true. It is within my discretion, as I'm sure you know, for certain cases, to take subjects who are younger than sixteen." He gazed blandly at Murash. "I followed the protocol for taking underage offenders. I executed the proscribed punishment for those who speak of forbidden things." Clenching his jaw, he hoped Murash couldn't sense his nervousness.

"What would a fifteen-year old say that was forbidden? Did she challenge your authority?" Murash's quiet tone didn't match the challenge in his eyes.

"This girl asked all kinds of questions about Riskers. It sounded as though she'd been to a Risker camp, even though she denied it. She knew things she shouldn't have known."

Rotena, the ludi, spoke up. "You couldn't have had Edalia let the group rebuke and correct her?" From her eager tone, Kaberco could tell she'd been waiting a long time to ask that question.

"Taking an underage girl for asking about Riskers?" Murash sneered. "Bit of an overreaction, I'd say."

Kaberco clamped his jaw shut. He knew what Murash was implying, that only a young, inexperienced ephor would make such a blunder. Taking a slow breath, he said, "My first move was to interrogate the girl. I thought once I found out what she wanted to know, I could tell her enough to satisfy her. But when I asked her what prompted her interest in the Riskers, she started babbling about an old woman in the market who was talking about the Desired One. What else could I do?"

If he'd ever wanted to create a sensation in a konament meeting, he'd done it now.

Zurvan spit out a mouthful of wine, eyes wide, the bronze chain on his shoulders rattling with his sudden motion. The others reacted as Kaberco expected, frozen with horror at the words of the old prophecy, words they thought had been stamped out of living memory.

Murash carefully set his wine glass down and broke the silence. "I see your position." He let out a long breath. "But the Prime Konamei won't like it. Not at all."

Kaberco grit his teeth. He didn't need Murash to remind him that he served at the Prime Konamei's pleasure, until he decided whether or not to make Kaberco's appointment permanent. Murash, he was sure, was hoping the Prime Konamei's decision would go against Kaberco.

Murash looked around the room. "Have any of you heard others talking that way?"

The others shook their heads.

Kaberco let out the breath he'd been holding. "Then let's hope it was only one girl talking crazy. We don't want the Prime Konamei to think we can't keep our village safe."

Murash placed his hands on the table. "I assume you sent a report about that incident to the Prime Konamei. Valday in Trofmose deserves one as well, if you've overlooked him. After all, he'll be the one to advise the Prime Konamei on appointing a permanent ephor here."

Kaberco felt a surge of hot anger burn his face at Murash's taunt. "Valday is well aware of the incident. I have done all that my position requires. And I will ensure the village is safe. If you please."

Kaberco could hardly wait for the konament members to leave. After seeing them out, he returned to his high-backed armchair and stared at the dying embers of the fire, sipping a glass of wine. Murash was looking for any reason to complain to the Prime Konamei about him. Now was not a good time for trouble. Kaberco had taken over as ephor when his predecessor died defending a caravan from bandits. The Prime Konamei allowed twenty-four-year-old Kaberco, the ephor's apprentice, to take over, saying he'd make a decision within a year whether Kaberco could keep the job or not. Kaberco couldn't blame the Prime Konamei for not immediately making his appointment permanent. Most ephors were thirty or more before they were given the position.

Murash, for one, had resented such a young man being given the title. Kaberco knew Murash had waited for years for the previous questor to die. He was well into his forties by the time he took his place as chief of the courts. He couldn't stand to see Kaberco elevated at such a young age.

Kaberco took a deep breath. He'd worked hard to get Murash on his side, but the man seemed determined to hate him. Perhaps the rumor that Murash had been grooming his own candidate to take over as ephor was true.

No matter. Perhaps the konameis would support him with the Prime Konamei, though he knew Murash wouldn't.

Which wasn't fair. He'd done a good job, Kaberco mused. He ran his fingers along the carved arms of his chair, tracing the leaves and limbs of a birch tree. The village had been quiet for the past several months. He clenched his fist around the carved knob at the end of the chair's arm and squeezed as if trying to get wine from the wood. His work should speak for itself, without these nonsensical political games.

He relaxed his grip when his fingers began to ache. Murash wasn't about to let Tavda's taking go unexploited.

Hopefully she was the one old Cassie was ranting to about the Desired One. And asking her to produce him. He shuddered at the thought. He never did find out who that girl was, the witnesses didn't remember. Maybe it was Tavda, maybe that's how she'd heard the name. Just mentioning the old myth that had been outlawed long ago was enough for someone to be taken. He was glad Murash saw that, understood he had no choice but to take Tavda, young as she was.

But he understood Murash's message only too well. The Prime Konamei would probably overlook one underage girl getting taken. But not two. He'd have to find some way to keep Iskra in line.

He closed his eyes when he thought of Iskra. Sweet Iskra. What got into her? She'd always been so compliant. Luza did a good job raising that one, he thought. It would kill Luza if something happened to Iskra, after losing her husband. He shook himself. Luza had bee n a good friend to his sister. Iskra had been something like a niece who'd adored him. He pressed his lips together. Friendship only goes so far. If Iskra turned out to not be as docile as he thought she was, she'd need to be kept in line.

The question was how best to go about it. He reached for the bottle and poured himself another glass. Probably by playing on her desire to be safe and follow the rules. She'd always looked up to him. He could play this like the favorite uncle. Timid people liked approval. He'd give it to her.

He swirled the dark red wine around in his glass, mimicking the spinning of his thoughts. There was something in Iskra's eyes today, when she asked why people couldn't cook at home. Something not quite rebellion. Disturbing, was what it was.

Tapping his fingers on the arm of his chair he replayed the scene with Iskra and Edalia in his mind. At the end, Iskra seemed to submit. "Seemed" was the word.

Her feigned compliance could cause big trouble for him if

she ever decided to rebel. He'd just have to watch her closely. He could come down hard on her, make an example of her, if he needed to. For her own safety, and the safety of the village.

He took a gulp of his wine, draining the glass. He didn't like the idea of hurting Iskra. But if she didn't comply? Murash would take his complaints all the way to the Prime Konamei.

He wondered what would happen if Murash did succeed in replacing him. His face reddened, thinking of the shame of failure. Not to mention losing his house, his servants, the rich food, and the wine. He stared into the embers of the fire, watching it cool and die.

If he failed, then he'd be faced with the difficulty, no, the impossibility of finding another position. He'd have to face the humiliation of being deposed and having to go to another region with the hope of finding another aged ephor without an apprentice. Hardly. Most likely, he'd end up in the Prime Konamei's Guard, keeping traders safe. That is, if his replacement didn't take him first.

No, Iskra was just going to have to shape up. No other outcome would be acceptable.

Hours later, Iskra lay on her bag of straw, staring at the rafters, unable to sleep. Small animals in the thatched roof of the cottage made rustling noises. A bit of straw fell onto Iskra's face. She brushed it off, wishing she could dispose of the thoughts that troubled her so easily.

She had thought that once Kaberco left the classroom, she'd be left in peace. That was a mistake. Edalia insisted on escorting her home, and on giving her mother a full report. Then the two of them ganged up to scold her, making her feel like a small child caught in some vile behavior. Her mother thought asking questions was despicable. Iskra couldn't figure out why.

Her heart was still pounding. She rubbed the nape of her neck, then shifted, causing the straw to crackle. She warily raised her head, listening. Her mother lay a few feet away on her own straw, snoring lightly. The last thing Iskra wanted to do was wake her up and invite more abuse.

She bit her lip to keep from screaming. Guilt weighed on her like an anvil on her chest. She'd let Tavda down because she didn't want to be abused by the class, to attract any attention that made her feel small and unworthy. And now what happened? The thing she feared most. Just because she asked some questions.

The Riskers seem to know something, she thought, *so they are the only hope of finding out why we can't have anything to do with them. It can't be wrong to visit the Risker camp, it just can't. But how can everything I've learned my whole life, everything I've believed, be wrong? How can I be sure?* She let out a sigh, frustrated she'd gotten no answers.

Would she be brave enough to go back? Once she got the answers she wanted, she could settle back into life in the village, be the compliant and safe person everyone wanted her to be.

Her stomach churned. If Luza caught her sneaking off . . . Iskra didn't even want to think about it. A metallic taste filled her mouth, and she started breathing faster. She felt that she would jump out of her skin at any minute.

I'm so afraid, she thought. It almost seemed like Kaberco was threatening her. Maybe that was for Edalia's benefit, so she'd think he was being equally firm with everyone.

That thought gave her a moment's comfort, when she felt a little less panicked. *But maybe he meant it, that I had to get in line or else. What would he do to me?* Thoughts of getting taken filled her mind. She took a few deep breaths, trying to slow down her ragged breathing.

She sat up and rubbed her neck, then buried her face in her hands. Why are they all so angry?

She thought instead about the Riskers, their food, their music and laughter, and wondered why asking about them would be enough reason for Tavda to get taken.

She curled up tight in a ball and wrapped her arms around herself. *It's all my fault Tavda's gone.* She clenched her teeth to hold in sobs as the tears ran down her face. *I'll hate myself forever. Maybe I should just volunteer to be taken. Then maybe I can find Tavda and she won't hate me anymore.*

The tramping footsteps of a guardsman in the street made her open her eyes wide, and she lay, immobile, scarcely breathing until he had passed. *No,* she thought. *I can't ask to be taken. Who knows what they'd do to me? And there's no guarantee I'd find Tavda that way.*

Better try the Riskers again. What could be so wrong about knowing those warm-hearted people? They seemed to have such love for each other, a love Iskra knew she'd never receive from her mother; instead, all she could count on was shame.

She closed her eyes. That was the kind of family Iskra wanted. Maybe some things were worth taking a risk for. Her eyes flew open at that thought, the heresy. Nothing was worth taking a few risks for. That was what everyone said. How could she even think such a thing?

She rubbed her face, her arms, massaged her temples. *Next thing you know, I'll be believing in the sky-god.*

She smirked as she pulled the amulet out from under the straw, trying to keep the rustling from waking her mother. The amulet shone with a pale green light which Iskra took to be a reflection of the moonlight streaming in her window. She wondered how she could know which was the better way. Was it in the village, and staying safe, or with the Riskers, who seemed to be free to love life and each other?

The only way to know would be to go back. As soon as she

could. Maybe some time with Cillia would give her some answers. She turned the amulet over in her hands, trying to stifle the thought that Xico was the person she really wanted to see. He was the one who gave her the courage to defy the rules, and to find out if there was another, better way to live. Him, and those brilliant green eyes that lit up her soul.

The glinting of the dim light on the amulet's green stones drew her attention. Maybe there was some way to test the amulet, to see if it had some power, some way to help her.

"Sky-god," she mouthed the words, wanting to make no noise, *"if you're there, help me."* She held the dragonfly in her hand, waiting. No answers jumped into her head, no surge of courage sustained her. She fell back on her pillow, limp and disappointed.

Then she felt it. A warm sensation washed over her, like a wave of a gentle sea. Wave after wave poured over her, seeping deep into her soul. She had no answers, but she did not care. What was it she was feeling? Peace? That didn't seem right, it was more than peace. The only word she had for the sensation overwhelming her was love.

18

The month of Toplu drew to a close and Zarku began, heralding the height of summer. Green leaves covered the white branches of the birch trees. The pines were a richer green, deepening almost to black in the shadows of their limbs. The vegetable plots surrounding the Risker camp were a study in shades of green, from the pale cabbages to the darker green of herbs and the red-streaked leaves of the beets.

Tarkio and Xico sat in Osip's kitchen, fletching arrows. A large heap of goose feathers lay on the table. Tarkio chose a feather and cut off the thick part of the quill. Then he sliced the feather in half, longways along the quill.

The door flung open, bringing a sudden gust of warm air that sent the feathers flying. "Quick, shut the door," Tarkio said without looking up.

"Why do you have the door shut on such a gorgeous day?" Iskra asked, as she pushed the door closed.

Xico jumped up to grab her hand. "Iskra! I didn't think you'd come today."

"I got up early and did most of my volunteer work. When

we stopped for lunch, I left." She placed her basket on the table. "Hello, Tarkio. I haven't seen you for a long time."

"It's been a few months, that's for sure." His forehead creased over his narrowed brown eyes. "You've been coming here?" Please say you haven't.

She sat on the bench next to him, gave him a direct look. "Yes. Just about every week."

"I'm just surprised at you, breaking the rules like that. What was it you used to say? 'It's not safe.' What happened to that?"

"These days, I'm not so sure what safe means." She shrugged. "Besides, I'm careful. There're lots of ways to get out of town without being noticed."

"You mean without being seen."

"No. Without being noticed." She picked up a feather and ran it through her fingers. "You know how it is. When the caravan leaves Gishin, aren't there usually people walking out with it?"

"Yes." Tarkio frowned.

"They're going to pick flowers or berries or nuts, depending on the season. Or some just walk about in the fields. You've seen them when you leave with the caravan, but you really don't notice them."

"Is she right?" Xico asked.

Tarkio nodded. "There's always a group of people. Since they aren't part of the caravan, I don't pay any attention. Go on." He noted that the girl he had thought of as a timid rabbit had more to her than he realized.

"Well, the first time, I left with the caravan like I wanted to walk a little. You know, the way you showed me when we went to the wedding. I strolled down the road after the caravan. You know the end of the Guarded Path isn't too far away from the town gates, hidden by the trees. I took my time getting there, like I had no particular plans, just picking some flowers. When no one was looking, I got on the path and started climbing."

"But if you did that week after week someone would notice."

She snorted. "Of course! That's why I found a different way to come every time. Some weeks I went out with the caravan. Sometimes I went to the market first, made sure someone noticed me there. Then I'd wait for a group of people to go out of the gates and tag along after them. There're always people coming and going on Hafsanbe, people taking their children for a walk, picnickers, people gathering straw, that kind of thing."

"And going back?"

"I make sure I'm not gone long, or for the same amount of time. If I come here early, then I go to the market after." She looked down at the feather in her hand. "People see me coming and going, but no one really notices me. I'm good at not being noticed."

There was a moment of silence, then Tarkio said, "Well, I'm impressed. I wouldn't have guessed you have such a talent for deceit."

She flinched. "What's wrong with avoiding problems? Tell me you've never tried it."

"Help me pick up these feathers, will you?" Xico asked.

She got down on her knees and started collecting feathers from under the table. He leaned toward her and put a finger gently on her cheek. "I notice you," he said.

Tarkio, observing, bit his lip and suppressed a sigh. He'd seen this kind of thing before, and it led to trouble. This time, he was to blame for starting it. Now he had to figure out a way to stop it.

Iskra resumed her seat, blushing, and asked, "What are you doing with these?" She put a handful of feathers on the pile.

"Fletching arrows," Xico answered.

"Fletching arrows? You mean you are making weapons?"

"Of course."

"But that's against the rules."

"Rules for the villagers," Tarkio said.

She sighed. "Rules for the *villagers*."

Tarkio frowned. He dragged his knife longways along the quill of the feather in his hand. "In case you haven't noticed, things are different here." After a pause, he halved another feather. "Iskra, have you ever wondered why the Riskers are allowed to live separately, with their own rules, not like the villagers?"

"Lately, yes. Not before. I suppose I always thought the Prime Konamei was just being patient, waiting for them to want to join us. After all, the Riskers were savage barbarians before the civil war. They followed our ancestors over the mountains to gain what they could from us and to prevent us from building a safe society. They didn't know any better."

Xico burst out laughing. "That's quite a *jargaggle*."

"*Jargaggle*?"

"Mixed-up story."

"It's not a story. Everyone knows it. We learned it in school."

Tarkio noticed the defensiveness in her voice and smiled. "Do you think now that that's what the Riskers would tell you happened?"

"How else could it have happened?"

Tarkio twirled a quill in his fingers, then laid it on the table and sliced it in two. How much do I tell this girl? Will it cause trouble for her, or keep her from worse mischief?

"Well," he said, "it's like this: Three or so centuries ago, there was war in the land. Not just here in Tlefas, but over the mountains, as well. Most of the men from this side of the mountains went to fight in the war. Pirates sailed up the rivers, almost to the mountains, and killed or kidnapped almost everyone who was left. The few survivors were driven closer to the mountains, where most of them died of starvation or were eaten by warboars.

"The war dragged on for years, tens of years. Some of the men who'd gone to fight realized it was a war that would only end when everyone was dead. They didn't want to be part of that end. They mutinied, gathered up some women and children, and fled back over the mountains. Others followed. People from all the countries involved in the war came, seeking to escape the horror."

"I know all that," Iskra said. "That's what they told us."

"Soon after they settled here, new conflicts arose. While most of the people just wanted peace and safety, a few questioned how the leaders were going about achieving that. These people didn't agree that the cause of the civil war was the fact that some people were rich and others poor."

"If that wasn't the reason, what was?"

"It was that some of the rulers were richer and some were poorer," Xico said. He lined up three feathers together and trimmed the ends to make them the same size. "Some didn't like having less power and wealth than the others."

Tarkio nodded. "It was a little more complicated than that, but you're right. One of the kings, the most powerful one, wanted to control the entire land. The other three didn't want him to, especially the one who controlled this part, that we call Tlefas. The result was, they all went to war. By the end of twenty years, all four kings had lost their thrones and all the territory was controlled by warlords. They got into a stalemate that ground on for over fifty more years."

"How horrible. No wonder our ancestors fled."

"And it's no wonder, after decades of living in terror of raids and killing, that they prize safety. But some of the people who came with them weren't so sure everyone had to be the same. They also didn't think you could just write some rules and make everyone completely safe."

"That's true," put in Xico. "Warboars and thunderstorms don't pay attention to rules."

Tarkio flicked a feather at him and went on. "So, they started their own settlements."

"And became the Riskers?" asked Iskra.

"Yes. At first the villagers tried to force them to come back. But the leaders saw a use for the Riskers, and made a treaty. See, they'd already created the Prime Konamei's Guard, and forbade the villagers to have weapons."

"Well, of course," Iskra said. "Weapons are dangerous. People can get hurt. And that was how the war started so fast. When the kings started killing, a lot of people were armed already." She shook her head. "Which is another reason we don't have a king, but the Prime Konamei, who is just the first leader among many."

Tarkio nodded. "The problem here, Iskra, was that the forests were overrun with warboars. And other people were fleeing the conflict as well, people who really didn't want to build a new life."

"What did they want?" Iskra asked.

"You've met some of them, or at least their descendants," Xico said. He looked up from the arrow he was fletching. "You call them bandits."

Iskra looked at Tarkio. He nodded. "The ancestors of the bandits felt it was easier to let someone else work to grow food or to make something, and just steal it from them. The Riskers, who were armed, have served to keep the bandits, warboars, and other wild animals from attacking the villages, at least in the areas closest to the mountains. That's why the bandits mostly go after the caravans."

Xico finished his arrow and reached for more feathers. "There are other reasons we have the treaty."

"True," Tarkio said.

"Is it the honey trade?" Iskra asked.

Tarkio nodded. "That, and some of the other things the Riskers make."

"Then why aren't we allowed to associate with Riskers?"

"That's a good question, Iskra." He looked down at the pile of feathers he had already cut, pushing and poking them with his finger. He stirred them a bit, then chose two of them. "Do you see these feathers? Notice how there is a slight curve like a cup. This one curves one way, that one the other way. If you put them on the same arrow, it won't fly properly. They need to be the same to work together to create the right spin to keep the arrow in flight."

"Are you saying we *do* have to all be the same?"

"No, just that sometimes things don't mix. What the Riskers and the villagers believe don't mix too well. Their beliefs are so different they interfere with each other. What the Prime Konamei and his konament decided was that it was better to live separately. This way they could maintain peace and order."

He picked up his knife and went back to cutting feathers. She must understand by now that coming here will just cause trouble for everyone, upset the uneasy alliance the Prime Konamei maintains with the Riskers. "Why make enemies of those you need? From the Riskers' point of view, they get to live in freedom without having to continually fight for it, knowing they are vastly outnumbered. From the konameis' point of view, they have their allies, but by keeping the groups separate, they can maintain their control over the rest of the population."

Tarkio watched Xico tie three feathers to the shaft of an arrow with a strand of suet, and hold it up. Frowning, he nudged one of the feathers with his thumb, trying to align it to his satisfaction. Tarkio looked up to see Iskra gazing at Xico like she was staring into a fire. Tarkio didn't like her fascination with his friend.

"Does that make sense to you?" he asked.

Iskra started, then looked down at the table. She fidgeted with some of the wood shafts lying on the table. "What I don't understand," she said, "is why they tell us there is no sky-god."

"That's the other reason they think the civil war started. One kingdom believed in the sky-god, and used the amulets they said came from him for the good of the kingdom. Another made their own amulets, to have their own power. Another believed in a host of gods, some good and some evil. I'm not sure what the fourth believed."

"How could they believe different things? Only one can be right."

"Yes," Tarkio said. "The ancient faith in the sky-god."

"Then why do our leaders say he is a myth?"

Tarkio looked up at her, startled by the high-pitched whine in her voice. "Because they saw the religions and their differences as the root of evil. They reasoned if there is a true religion, everyone would believe it. Since they didn't, and instead had all kinds of conflicting beliefs, all of them must be false. To create a safe and peaceful society, all false belief had to be stamped out." He cut a few more feathers.

Iskra bent to pick up some feathers that had blown to the floor. "That doesn't make a lot of sense to me."

"To me, either," Tarkio said. "Just because one is wrong, doesn't mean they all are. But it made sense to them, and they fought a long and bloody war over it."

Iskra shivered. "And to think we are the only ones left."

"You mean, after the war?" Tarkio asked. "No one knows for sure."

She stared at him, wide-eyed, then opened her mouth.

Tarkio cut her off. "What I've told you is dangerous. For you, I mean. If people in the village found out you knew this—"

"But they'd want to know the truth!" She frowned. "You know all this. How?"

Tarkio met her gaze but didn't answer.

"You trade here, so you've talked with the Riskers. If you know this, don't others? More traders have to know!"

Reluctantly, Tarkio nodded. "Yes, others do know." She's

quick, I have to give that to her. Out of the corner of his eye, he saw Xico looking at Iskra with something like admiration on his face.

"Then why don't you do anything? Tell someone?"

Tarkio looked down at the knife in his hands, then back at Iskra. "Well, you see, there's this little matter of getting taken."

"But it's not a problem that people are living a lie?" Her lip curled as she stared at him.

Tarkio felt his face grow hot. This girl, scared of everything, was scorning him for not wanting to be taken? He tried to sort out his thoughts. What was the best thing to tell her?

"Well, someone needs to say something." Iskra sounded determined.

Tarkio's eyes widened in alarm. Now what would she do? He had to stop her. "Look, Iskra, people are—"

A clatter on the table made them both jump. Xico had dropped an arrow. "You're going to tell her?" he said.

"Tell me what?"

Letting out a sigh, Tarkio said, "I see I have no choice, now that Xico has spilled the hayseed." He looked steadily at Iskra. "But you cannot tell anyone, even breathe a hint of what I'm about to say."

"I won't. Ever."

Hoping she'd be true to her word, he began. "Many of the traders do want to change things in Tlefas, let people know the truth about the Riskers and to have more freedom. But we have to act carefully, to avoid getting taken. Do you understand?"

She nodded.

"As a first step, the trade guilds are banding together to ask for more protection for the caravans against the bandits."

"That's all?" She shook her head. "What good will that do?"

"It's a cause all can agree is just and has nothing to do

with changing anything major. If we succeed, then we've established that a group of people can ask for change without threatening the established order. This eases the control the Prime Konamei has over all of us, without creating chaos. Then we can tackle the bigger issues, slowly, so as not to cause a nervous ephor to start a wave of mass takings." He looked hard at Iskra. "That's happened, you know. No one wants to see those times again."

She sat staring at him, jumping when the door opened. Tuli stuck her head in. "Good, Iskra, you're here. Mam thought she saw you. We're going berrying, do you want to come?"

Tarkio noticed how Iskra looked longingly at Xico before she nodded. "Yes, I'd love to."

Tuli picked up three baskets from the corner and handed one to Iskra. "We'll be back soon. Pie for dinner tonight, little brother."

"Then I won't go anywhere." He smiled at Iskra. "And I'll see you later."

After the girls left, Tarkio stared at Xico with a frown. "That girl's in love with you, Xico."

"Really? Why do you say that?"

Tarkio was surprised to see the pleased smile on Xico's face. "She looks at you as if she thinks you can do anything." *Doesn't he see this could only lead to trouble?*

"That's what my parents tell me, that I think I can do anything."

"Sometimes I think you believe that."

Xico picked up one of the strange red arrows Tarkio had picked up after the bandit attack. "Look at these fletches, they're so short."

Tarkio stifled his irritation at Xico's change of subject. "I know. That's why they were able to shoot from so far away."

"That gives them distance, all right. But their arrows flew straight and true, without wobbling. How'd they do that?"

"I thought of that. And did you notice? They aren't painted red. The wood is red. What tree has red wood?"

Xico nodded. "None that I know."

"Me, either. Wish I'd picked up one of their bows. It must be something in the design." He pressed his lips together. What does he feel for Iskra? Is he unsure of his feelings, or not sure he wants to tell me?

Xico scrutinized the placement of the feathers on the red arrow. "How did they do this?" When he looked up Tarkio gave him another hard stare. Xico met his gaze and laughed. "You're still there, are you? Do I believe I can do anything?" He shook his head. "No, it's only when Iskra gazes into my eyes that I *know* I can."

Tarkio pressed his lips together. He didn't like the sound of that. He pushed the feathers he'd cut into a pile and threw his knife down on the table. "Here, Xico, that's the end of them. I'll go see if your mother has any more." He stood up and walked out of the cottage.

19

Iskra took a breath and held it. She pulled the bowstring taut and sighted the target Xico had set up behind his father's barn. She let the arrow fly. "Oh!" She couldn't help but let out a disappointed cry when her arrow bounced off the edge of the target.

"Don't worry, you'll get it," Xico said. "You need to pull back more on the string, so your shot flies faster. Then it will go in the target and not bounce." He handed her another arrow. "Try again."

She looked at the arrow, somewhat horrified that she was handling weapons. *This isn't safe, what I'm doing. Any of it. But here I am.* She frowned and shivered.

"What's wrong?"

"Does everyone learn to shoot?"

"Of course, all of us. Even the girls." When she shook her head, he asked, "Does that bother you?"

"Of course it does. Weapons are dangerous. And if bandits attacked us, could you fight them off alone?"

"I'll show you." He pulled three arrows from his quiver and shot them one right after another. All three hit the center of the target he'd aimed for, clustered together. "You see," he said, "I know what I'm doing." She watched as he strode to the target, retrieved his arrows, and shoved them back into his quiver.

When he rejoined her, he said, "Want to try some more?"

"I don't know, Xico. It's getting late. I've been here too long already." After going berrying with Tuli and Fialka, she'd stayed to watch them bake pies with the hopberries. Then Xico wanted to test some of his new arrows, which led to her archery lesson.

He opened his mouth to argue, then nodded. He ran to the target to pick up the scattered arrows and shoved them in the quiver at his hip. Then he rejoined Iskra and they ambled toward the Guarded Path.

Iskra walked as slowly as she could, not wanting to hurry off. Xico picked a few daises from the side of the path and handed them to her. She smiled her thanks and ambled on, enjoying the warm feeling his gift gave her, a feeling that gave her the courage to ask a question she'd been pondering. "Xico, I'm confused."

"About what?"

She wrinkled her forehead. "At first, it seemed to me that all the Riskers live better than we do in the village. Your family certainly does."

He shrugged. "We work hard." He tilted his head to look at her. "And?"

"Today, when I was with your sisters, we passed a run-down cottage. The windows were broken, the yard was full of weeds. The man sitting outside looked, well, like what I thought a Risker would look like." The last words came in a rush. She looked at Xico, almost apologetically.

Xico shook his head and laughed. "I think you saw Bronnit."

"How can he live like that?"

"Bronnit doesn't like to work. He fishes a little in the river, lives off that and some hunting. Trades a few pelts when he wants something else. The way he lives is good enough for him."

"It doesn't seem fair that he lives in a hut. It looks like it could fall down on him."

Shrugging, Xico said, "It might."

She frowned. "But it's not fair. You have a nice, solid, comfortable house. Why shouldn't he have one?"

"He could have one any time he wanted to. People would be happy to help him fix it up, if he ever got the notion to."

"Why don't you just fix it for him?" She pulled a few petals off one of the daisies.

"Because he never offers to help with the honey harvest or to build barns or fletch arrows or even stand guard duty. This is our way, Iskra. People who don't work, don't eat."

"But what if they're sick or old?"

"Oh, that's different. We all help out then. But for a young man like Bronnit, there's no excuse. We leave him alone. If that's how he wants to live, then so be it."

"I can't believe you'd let someone live like that."

"It's not my decision." He looked at her, frowning. "Don't you understand? He chooses to let his fields go fallow and his roof to fall on his head. The elder has spoken to him, and Bronnit understands."

"He might be hungry." She saw the irritation in Xico's eyes, but couldn't stop. How could he be so unfeeling, so unfair?

"Then he can work," Xico said. "It wouldn't be fair to someone else to work hard to feed someone who doesn't want to do anything for himself, when he's more than capable. There's a good living to be made here for anyone who wants it."

"But you have more than he does." She tore the petals off another daisy.

"So?"

"That's not fair."

Xico stopped to stare at her. "You mean, you think everyone has to have the same house and same horses and same everything, no matter how hard they work? What if one person worked all day and another one hour a day, then what? The worker ends up with the same as the *faineant*, the slacker? Should they both have the same reward?"

"Of course not. That's why people are limited in how much money they can make. If they make more, then they can donate the extra money to the ephor for the defense of the village." She folded her arms across her chest. "That makes it all fair." She could tell from the amusement in his eyes that he thought what she was saying was ridiculous. Her face reddened and she flung the ruined flowers to the ground. "I have to go home now," she said.

"Why now?"

"Because I do." She didn't understand why he didn't see how upset she was.

"Now you're in a hurry to go? Sure you can't stay longer?"

Iskra hesitated, then let out a deep breath. "No, Xico, I can't. I need to get back around the time Volunteer Day ends. I can finish my work, and get home when my mother is expecting me. It's easier this way."

"Why don't you just tell your mother the truth?"

Because she'll scream at me. She'll tell me I'm no good like my father and am an ungrateful daughter. Then she'll cry. "You wouldn't understand."

"No, I don't understand. Why do you follow all those silly rules? Chop your hair off. Only wear gray clothing. Do the work they tell you to do. Everybody be the same."

"Xico—" She wasn't sure if her frustration was more because he was pressing her, or because he was saying the same things she'd been thinking for months.

"Then they tell you a pack of lies for history, and tell you that the stories from the past that are truth are nothing but myths and children's tales." He slashed at a bush with his bow, startling a rabbit which darted across the trail into the brush on the other side. "I thought you were smarter than that."

Iskra sucked her cheeks in and lowered her chin, blushing. "Xico, smarter people than me believe what I do. We all learned it in school. The leaders who were smart enough to build Tlefas believe it."

"They were smart enough to convince you to believe it."

She put her hands on her hips. "How do you know what you believe is true?"

"Because I have seen the sky-god's power. You have, too. Admit it. Didn't my mother heal you the first time you came here?"

"Something did. How can I know that was the sky-god? Maybe it's some other spirit, or, I don't know, my imagination?"

"Imagination that you were healed?"

Iskra had no answer for that. She narrowed her eyes and pressed her lips together. How could Xico not understand how hard all this was for her? Tarkio was right, the villagers and Riskers just couldn't mix. They would never understand each other. She walked in silence until they reached the top of the path. "I need to go. You don't need to help me down. I'll be fine." She turned away and started the descent down the rocky path.

She ignored the sounds of Xico following her down the path.

With each twist in the path her anger grew. *Why do I come back here? Stupid people, they believe in myths and half convinced me to believe in them, too.*

She slipped on some loose stones and skidded a few feet down the trail. A strong hand gripped her elbow, steadying her.

"Are you all right?"

She shook off Xico's hand and didn't answer. She stalked down the trail, wanting to snarl at him.

"You need to choose how you want to live, Iskra," Xico said. "You're a slave and you don't know it."

"Leave me alone." *What do you know? All of you are stupid. You do dangerous things and laugh while you do them. Hanging off ladders just to get honey. Making weapons.* She shook her head. *There's plenty to be afraid of in life. Good thing we have leaders who believe in protecting us.*

Even as she scoffed, she could see Xico, dangling from the ladder, fearlessly competent. She knew no one like him. She hurled his image from her mind. *He's not anyone I should waste my time thinking about. He doesn't understand anything about sacrificing for other people, or not making trouble for others.*

As she neared the foot of the trail, she couldn't hear Xico following her. She didn't ask herself why a tear trickled down her face.

20

Kaberco leaned against an oak tree, screened by some tall bushes. He cautiously shifted his weight from one foot to the other, hoping he wouldn't have to wait much longer. How long can Iskra possibly spend with the Riskers?

Soon he heard faint scuffling noises. Someone was coming down the Guarded Path. *One person,* Kaberco thought. *Not a very large one. Must be Iskra. If it is, I'll have to reward the guardsman who saw her sneaking off. Clever of her to do most of her voluntary service first.*

He inched around the bushes, making sure whoever was coming down the path wouldn't be able to see him. He pulled down a branch of the pine tree he hid behind to give himself a better view.

He thought about how best to approach her. Gently, like an old family friend? He wrinkled his brow, considering. He had to get this right, to get the truth out of her and minimize the damage.

The noises slowed, then he saw her. Iskra peered out from around the rock walls, looked from side to side, then gingerly stepped out onto the trail that led to the road. She stood up a little straighter, then began walking briskly.

Kaberco waited until she was just passing him before he jumped out and accosted her. "Where have you been, Iskra?" he asked softly.

Iskra screamed and spun around, dropping her basket. Her eyes widened when she saw Kaberco and her mouth fell open. She covered her mouth with her hand and gulped.

Kaberco took a step back and waited, giving her time to recover from her surprise. "Will you tell me where you've been?"

"I-I was walking," she said.

"Who have you been walking with?"

She stooped to pick up her basket, hiding her face from his piercing stare. "Right now, with you."

"And before?"

"I'm alone other than you."

Kaberco pressed his lips together and clenched his jaw. "I think you and I need to take a walk of our own." Good; I've scared her. I'm going to have to take a tougher approach.

"My mother—"

"Can wait. Now walk." He motioned for her to move along the trail. When they reached the first bend, a guardsman was waiting for them. "Now you don't have to walk alone any more, Iskra."

He laughed as she looked from him to the other man with wide eyes and hung her head. "Just walk."

KABERCO STALKED DOWN THE TRAIL. He studied every move Iskra made, observing the droop of her head, the shuffling of her feet. *What's gotten into her? She was always so sweet, so docile. I hope her rebellion doesn't ruin her life.*

The guardsman halted at a fork in the trail and looked over his shoulder at Kaberco. "To the right," Kaberco said.

The right-hand path led straight into a doorway cut into the side of the rocky hillside. Iskra stopped in her tracks. "Keep going," Kaberco said. "Boreje, a torch." They waited while Boreje reached into the darkness, felt around, and pulled a torch down from a bracket. He struck a flint and lit the oil-soaked wood. He blew on it gently until the flame caught and black smoke streamed upward. Then he held it up and walked into the doorway.

Kaberco pushed Iskra forward. She stumbled into the cave. "Sit down."

When she made no move to comply, he grabbed her arm and shoved her down onto a rough seat formed from rock. She crouched over, rubbing her arm, clutching her basket, shivering in the damp chill.

Kaberco settled his bulky frame onto a similar seat facing her. "Now, are you going to tell me who you've been walking with, or not?"

She pressed her lips together and closed her eyes.

Kaberco sighed. "I wish you would trust me," he said softly.

Iskra opened her eyes and stared at him. "What do you mean?"

"I'm trying to help you." He sighed again, and resumed, using what he hoped was a fatherly tone. "I know you've been up to the Risker camp. That's the only place you could have gone, following that path you took. Am I right?"

Iskra bowed her head.

"So, I am. Who did you visit up there?"

"Just some people," Iskra said. "No one important."

Kaberco reached over and put a finger under her jaw and lifted her chin. "Look at me and say that, Iskra."

She raised her eyes to meet his. "No one important."

"Good. Are you planning to go back there again?"

Iskra hesitated. "No. No, I'm not going back."

"You had better be telling me the truth."

"But what's the harm in it?" Iskra blurted out the question before she realized she'd spoken.

Kaberco grabbed her jaw and pulled her face close to his. "It's forbidden, that's why. Against the rules. Dangerous. Is that clear?"

He released her and stood up. He paced around the cave. *That was stupid. Great way to get her to tell you what you want. Now I'm going to have to go mean.* He circled Iskra, now huddled on her rock. "What is it that draws you there, Iskra?" The flickering torchlight made it hard for him to read her face.

"I don't know, really." She put her face down on her knees.

Kaberco shook his head. "You're willing to risk everything for what? Something you don't know why you want to do? Does that sound very smart to you, Boreje?" He felt a sour taste in his mouth as he said the words, like his body was revolted at what his mind was forcing it to do.

Boreje snickered and rolled his small, mud-brown eyes. "Maybe she wants to live like pigs, or warboars. That's what those Riskers are like."

"I'm disappointed in you, Iskra. I thought we were friends." Kaberco watched her sit up and stare at him, mouth trembling.

"Can you promise me you won't go back there?" Kaberco kept his tone low and even.

Iskra nodded.

"Good." He pressed his lips together. Now to make sure she keeps her word. "Do you want my help?"

"To do what?" She drew her eyebrows together.

"Look, you skipped Volunteer Day once already. Today you left early, before all the work was done. What do you think Edalia will do to you?"

"She'll be angry, but—"

"You need to think hard about this. You're fifteen, right?"

"Yes."

"In a few weeks, Edalia will be making job assignments. Your job assignment, for the work you will do for the good of the village for the rest of your life. Do you think this is a good time to have her doubting you? To be on her bad side?"

Iskra's eyes widened and her mouth fell open. "She wouldn't—"

"Don't be so sure. If you want to spend the rest of your life mucking out stables, or feeding pigs, by all means, go back and visit the Riskers."

He let Iskra think about that for a moment. "Edalia is also the person who makes the marriage arrangements. You don't want her annoyed with you and give you a husband no one else wants, do you?"

Iskra dropped her head on her knees again and moaned softly.

"There are a few men, older men, men with grandchildren who would love a young bride to replace their wives who have died. Edalia might just think you would be a good choice for one of them."

He watched her shake her head and rock back and forth.

Boreje chuckled. "Yeah, my old grandad says he wants a new woman. I'll tell him you might do."

"No," Iskra said. "Please, no."

Her voice quavered, Kaberco noted. Good. "Some people never find a place to fit in. You know they don't end up among us for long."

A whimper from Iskra told him his threats were sinking in.

"Now, if you do what I tell you," Kaberco said, "I'll make sure Edalia doesn't let any of these little misdemeanors of yours affect her decisions."

"What do I have to do?" Iskra looked up at Kaberco, meeting his eyes for the first time.

Maybe she's about to cry. Don't mess this up now. "What

I'm asking you to do will help keep everyone safe. You'd like that, wouldn't you? To help me keep Gishin safe?"

She stared at him, wide-eyed, then nodded.

"I just need to know if you saw anyone up at the Risker camp who wasn't a Risker."

"Who else would be there?"

"Bandits. Traders. Or someone from the village."

Iskra looked at him for a moment, then at the stony floor. "I already told you. I saw no one important."

Kaberco bit his lip. He thought he saw something flicker in her eye, like she was lying. But he couldn't be sure. "That had better be the truth. If I find out differently, you'll be sorry. Very sorry."

He narrowed his eyes and looked at her hard. "Listen closely. You are not to go to the Risker camp again, until I tell you. Then I want you to go. When you return, you need to tell me who was there and why they were there. Do you understand?"

"I think so."

"Don't forget. Help me in this, and I'll fix it with Edalia. I want you to be happy, Iskra." He paused. "If you won't help me, and your life doesn't work out the way you want it to, you will have no one to blame but yourself." He studied her face a moment, then went on. "I suppose I don't have to explain to you that no one is to know of our conversation?" He waited for her to nod. "Boreje will see you back to the village." He motioned for her to follow Boreje from the cave. He followed behind them. Now if Boreje can play his part well.

Boreje didn't disappoint. He took Iskra by the arm and pulled her close to him. He towered over her, overpowering her with his bulk. "You know," he said to Iskra, "no one would care what happened to someone who snuck off to see Riskers. If someone found her wandering the hills, where she wasn't supposed to be, well, who could blame them if he decided to have a little fun with her?"

Kaberco nodded as Iskra gasped and pulled away from Boreje. If reason didn't work, maybe a little fear would. He ignored the heaving in his stomach and tried to put the image of Iskra's scared face from his mind.

As he walked behind Iskra, Kaberco ran his tongue around his teeth. *This was almost too easy,* he thought. *She's a frightened little chick, but a clever one. She didn't answer my questions directly. What is she hiding?*

21

The cave was dark and damp and smelled of smoke. Ragged shadows darted from crevice to crevice, hiding whatever lurked within. Iskra inched deeper into the cave, cringing with every sound. She ran her trembling hands over the wall, searching, seeking, what was she seeking? She had to find it, before—

She sat bolt upright on her straw, sweating and shaking. Another dream of being trapped in a cave. She bent her knees up and wrapped her arms around them. Of course, this time it was just a memory of being questioned by Kaberco.

Or was it? The cave in her dream was the same as the last dream, and it looked nothing like the cave Kaberco took her to. The dream cave was high on a mountain, with gusts of warm air blowing through it. The other cave was airless and still. There was also a sound in the dream cave, a high-pitched wailing whimper, like the cry of a baby.

She lay back down on her crackling straw, tossing and turning to find a comfortable position. What is Kaberco up to? Why does he want to know who's in the Risker camp?

He's playing me like a cat toys with a mouse. That wasn't like him, the kind friend who'd bought her sweets and offered wise advice. Now it's like he's watching me.

What is he using me for? He's using me just the way our leaders are using us, keeping us afraid of everything, trapped by their rules. Whatever Kaberco's plan is, I need to go along with him. I have to stay on his good side. Maybe if I do, he'll be kind to me again. No, he wouldn't ever hurt me. Perhaps he'll stick up for me against my mother or even Edalia. They'd listen to him.

Kaberco, so brave and confident. Like fearless Xico, but in a different way. Xico was so unlike anyone else she'd ever met. The boys her age, and even the young men of the village, all seemed so timid, so cowed when compared to Xico. Precious few of them would take honey from bees, let alone climb a ladder to do it. "It's not safe," they'd say. None of them laughed at the rules. None of them had ever fought a warboar. Or had vivid green eyes.

She pounded her fist deep in the straw. *No more green eyes.* She supressed the yearning to see the smile in those green eyes. *No. He just makes me unsettled and thinking dangerous thoughts. My only hope is doing what Kaberco wants. If he sends me back to the Riskers, I'll ask about the sky-god. That's all I'll go there for. Whoever is telling the truth about the sky-god is telling the truth about everything else.*

22

Three weeks later, Iskra watched as Cillia punched a lump of dough, then folded it over on itself and squeezed it. As always, Cillia's sunny kitchen smelled of baking bread, stewing meats, and flowery herbs. Sun streamed through the windows and a gentle breeze flowed through the open *ikkuna*.

"Cillia, can I ask you something?"

"Not sure I can answer, but I'll try."

"Can you tell me about the amulet you gave me?"

"What's there to know?" She looked at Iskra's disappointed face and smiled. "I'm sorry, I forgot you're not one of us." She sprinkled a little flour on her dough and worked it in. "Well, the first amulets were made centuries, maybe thousands of years ago by followers of the sky-god. These people lived in the early days, before a faction rebelled against the sky-god."

"What did they do?"

"No one knows. All the old writings were lost in the war, and it's hard to know what's legend and what is truth anymore. But I'm pretty sure about this part: The sky-god gave his followers amulets, so they could draw on his power. They couldn't manipulate events, but they did have more power to do what they needed to do. Like healing. Or hunting. Or making wise decisions."

"Doesn't seem like much magic to me."

"It wasn't meant to be. They were a way to keep a close connection, a bond, with the sky-god." She kept working the dough as she spoke, letting her words come out in the same rhythm her fingers used as they squeezed and pressed.

"Do many people have amulets?"

"Just about all of us have at least one. Mostly the small ones." She dusted off her hands and reached up to take her basket from the shelf. She pulled two amulets from the basket. "See this one? It has one bead, like the one I gave you. This is what most people have. Mostly the amulets enhance the abilities you have, but sometimes they help you in other ways. Like the healing ones, they give the power to heal when you cannot. Or they give knowledge you wouldn't have otherwise. Each one is a little different, depending on who uses it. And most amulets only amplify one or two abilities." She replaced the amulet and pulled out another. "See this larger one? It has two purple beads dangling from its tail. It gives its user more power. Its power is what enables me to heal wounds and sicknesses no one has any cure for." She replaced the amulets in the basket and turned back to her dough. "We all are given our first amulet around the age of ten at the Giving of the Amulet. Some earlier, some later. The parents and the Elders decide who is ready."

"What happens at the ceremony?"

"We hold them on a clear night. Anyone can come, but usually it's just the family. We sing to the sky-god and ask him to show the child how to use their amulet."

"That's it?"

Cillia smiled. "Sometimes a green light shines on the child, a mark of the sky-god's favor. In rare cases, a purple light shines, which means even greater favor. Meaning they will be able to use their amulets in many ways, not just one or two."

"Do you know anyone that happened to?"

Cillia paused in her work and looked out the window. "I've seen the green light a few times, the purple once."

Iskra got the sense Cillia wasn't going to tell her who that happened to. "Are the amulets with two beads the most powerful ones?" she asked.

"I've heard there are amulets with three beads, which are more powerful yet. This might just be a story, though. Supposedly there are three of them, and—"

The door opened and Xico, Tuli, and Fialka burst in. Iskra pressed her lips together. Just when she was getting somewhere with Cillia, they get interrupted.

Xico smiled broadly with wide eyes. "Iskra! I'm so glad you are here!"

She looked at the floor, not wanting to answer.

"We're about to go for a swim," Fialka said. "Care to join us?" Without waiting for an answer, she seized Iskra's hand and tugged her to the other room. "You can wear an old dress of Veressa's."

Iskra stood motionless. She couldn't help smiling at the thought that Xico seemed pleased to see her. At the same time, she was annoyed he seemed to have forgotten their quarrel. She hadn't forgotten, and wouldn't have bothered to come today, except Kaberco ordered her to. And now they want her to go swimming? That was forbidden. Like everything else in Gishin.

Before Iskra knew what had happened, Fialka had pulled her into the other room. She and Tuli helped Iskra take off her clothes and replace them with a garment that looked like the pants men wore, but of some softer material and cut to fit tightly to her legs, and an old yellow-green dress of Veressa's, one that fit her better than anything she'd ever worn. The dress nipped in, hugging her waist, and was cut off short, barely covering her knees.

"Well, look at you," Fialka said when she was dressed.

"The color of that dress makes your eyes look almost green. Very pretty."

"I agree," Tuli said.

"Really? But I'm not pretty, not like you two." She looked at the two girls, admiring their dark curling hair and large blue eyes.

Tuli smiled. "Thank you. Really, I think you would look better if you didn't cut your hair that way."

Iskra put a hand up to her hair. "This is how everyone does it."

"Hey, what's taking so long in there?" Xico called from the kitchen.

"We're coming already," Tuli said. "And what's the rush? The water isn't going anywhere."

Iskra followed her and Fialka from the room, laughing as Tuli seized Xico's head in a hug.

Cillia handed Xico a bundle to carry, saying, "Here's some food to *knabble* on. Enjoy yourselves, but don't stay too long. I'll need some help later."

XICO LED the way up the slope of the hill along a path that wound between graceful trees with slender white trunks. Iskra's heart was pounding, and not just from the exertion. She was going swimming? In water? Everyone knew that was dangerous. People could catch horrible diseases from the water. Or drown. She determined to stay as far from the water as possible, to stay safe. And yet, tugging at her resolve was an odd fascination for doing dangerous things, like learning to use a bow and arrow.

As they walked toward the lake, Iskra was grateful for Tuli and Fialka being with them. They kept up a stream of banter with Xico and did not mark her silence. He, however, kept glancing her way, like he was trying to catch her eye. She pretended she didn't notice. She did take stock of the motion of the muscles in his legs and arms, visible below his cutoff shirt sleeves and pant legs.

They reached the crest of the hill and looked down. A small lake lay in the valley below, cradled in rock walls that formed nearly sheer cliffs of over one hundred feet high.

"What is this place?" Iskra asked.

"They say that hundreds, maybe thousands of years ago, people mined this place for the rock. Built cities with it, they say. Not much sign of any cities anymore, and the water filled up the quarry," Xico said.

They continued along the path as it turned to the left and wound down the hill, curving back and forth, forcing them to walk single file. The cliff walls became lower as they walked along the shore, and soon they came to a level place just a few feet above the water, shaded by trees. Several other Risker families were already there, splashing in the shallow water.

Iskra watched with horrified eyes as Xico bounded into the water and swam out into the lake. He dove down, waving his feet as he disappeared.

"He's gone!" she said.

"No," Fialka said. "See, he's come up over there." Xico's head was just visible over the gentle swell of the water. "Are you ready to go in?"

"No, not yet. Fialka, I'm not sure I want to swim."

Fialka gave her a long look. "Have you ever been swimming before?"

"No, of course not. It's—"

"I know. It's not safe. But what would you do if you ever fell into the river? It's not safe to *not* be able to swim." She walked down to the water and motioned for Xico to swim in. Turning to face Iskra, she said, "He's the best swimmer in the family. He'll show you."

Iskra tried to think of the words that would convince

Fialka and Xico that she could not get in that cold, dark water.

"Oh, look, there goes Tuli," Fialka said.

Tuli was climbing up an outcropping of rock that jutted out into the lake, rising about fifteen feet above the surface. She stood on the top for a moment, a sudden breeze puffing her hair in all directions. Then she jumped.

Iskra screamed and clutched Fialka's arm. "She'll be killed!"

"Not Tuli. She's another one who swims like an eel." Tuli's head broke the surface of the water. A young man clambered up the rock, followed by a few others.

Xico swam to the shore and walked out of the water, shaking the water from his hair. Iskra couldn't help noticing the way his clothes clung to his body. "Did you see Tuli jump? She's fearless, my sister is," he said.

Iskra wanted him to say that about her, with the same admiration in his voice. Fearless. Not a word she could use to describe herself. Not a word anyone would use.

"Xico, Iskra wants you to teach her to swim," Fialka said.

"Really?" He turned to Iskra with a wide smile.

Her eyes widened and she opened her mouth to say no. Before she could speak, Xico took her hand and led her to the water.

23

An hour later, Iskra sat on the shore, wrapped in a thin blanket. She closed her eyes, tipped her face back, and let the sun warm her skin. Never would she be frightened of anything ever again, she told herself. The water that looked so cold and dark from above turned out to be warm once she was in it. Heated by hot springs, Xico told her.

After putting her face in the water, she could face anything. And the sensation of relaxing into the water and allowing it to support her, what a crazy thing to do. Once she swallowed her fear, swallowing a little water wasn't so bad. And the swimming itself was actually pleasant. As was the memory of the way Xico looked at her body with the borrowed dress clinging to every curve.

Her reverie ended when Xico flung himself down next to her, water dripping from his dark hair. He dug around in the basket and handed her a piece of bread and a slice of cheese. Tuli and Fialka joined them. Fialka handed around round orange fruits with thick peels that turned out to be white inside. The fruit itself was made of sections that split apart and contained tiny pockets of juice.

After they'd eaten, Tuli and Fialka drifted off, talking and swimming with some of their friends, leaving Iskra alone with Xico. For a while they sat in silence. Iskra wanted to break open the subject of their last conversation. Her heart pounded and she couldn't think of any words to say. To her relief, Xico saved her from having to think of any.

"I am really glad to see you," Xico said. "I thought you were angry the last time you left."

He was so bold just to say what was on his mind, she thought. "I was."

"And now?"

Iskra tossed a pebble into the water. "I guess not. I don't know. It's so confusing."

"Because we're not what you'd been told we are?"

"Yes, and so many other things."

Xico began building a tower with small stones. "I'm sorry. My da told me I shouldn't have pushed you. He says it's a lot harder to accept that all you know is a lie than to learn it in the first place."

Iskra nodded. "What makes it so upsetting is no one answers my questions. They just say Riskers are dangerous. Or to believe other than what they say is stupid."

"What do you think?"

She began her own pile of rocks. "I don't know. I wish there was some way to know the truth." She looked up at the sound of cheering and laughing. Tuli and Fialka were on top of the rock, holding hands. They swung their arms, then took three running steps and jumped, splashing down into the lake together.

Xico chuckled. "Fialka usually doesn't jump. She's not like Tuli, not fearless."

"You admire fearlessness."

"I do. What's the point of being afraid of things? Face them, and they're usually not as bad as you think."

"But, Xico, some things are dangerous."

He looked at her, then down at his tower of rocks. "The lake can be dangerous if you don't know how to swim. Warboars are dangerous, if you don't know how to fight them." He raised his chin to look her in the eyes. "Face your fears, learn to overcome them. Why be a slave to them? Why let them bind you like a bird in a snare?"

She felt like he was issuing some kind of challenge to her. To face fears? She'd never done that in her life. She'd been brought up to flee, to find protection, to hide. She thought of cowering in the cave when Kaberco was taunting her, and the joy she felt when she first went under the water of the lake and felt the water's warmth cradling her in its rocking waves. She bounced a pebble in her hand as she watched several people jump from the rock.

"Iskra, do you want to jump, too?" Xico asked.

She gasped and blurted, "Oh, no, I couldn't. It's just so high."

"I can see you want to." He took her hand. His touch sent a flicker of electricity down to her toes. "I'll jump with you. It will be fun, you'll see."

"No, Xico, please." She jerked her hand from his.

"Are you sure?" He looked at her, tilting his chin down and smiling.

"Yes. No." She watched as Tuli jumped again, arms outstretched, her hair flying around her head as she plunged into the water. "What makes her do it over and over?"

"I can't explain it. You'll just have to try it."

Iskra was seized with a sudden desire to jump, to do another something she knew was risky, even dangerous. This was different from breaking the rules about visiting Riskers, this was doing something that could hurt. This was different from climbing the Guarded Path, which scary as the steep trail was, her feet stayed on the ground and the rock walls offered some support. Throwing herself off a rock to hurtle to the surface of the water below, that was a real risk, a real danger.

She got to her feet. "I want to try. But you'll have to jump with me."

Any doubts she had were taken away by the approving smile Xico gave her. He leapt to his feet and took her hand. They walked over to the rock. Fialka was climbing up, so they waited for her to reach the top and jump. Iskra scrambled up the rocks, using the level spots as footholds until she gained the summit.

She stood back from the edge, waiting for Xico to join her. He tipped his head back, allowing the breeze to blow his dark hair back from his face.

Iskra looked around in panic. The rock didn't look that high from the ground, but now it seemed like a towering cliff. The water looked cold and forbidding, a dark green that likely hid jagged rocks waiting to break her bones or concealed unnamed monsters that craved human flesh. Her heart raced and she wanted to be anywhere but this high up on that rock.

Xico took her hand. "Ready?" He took a step toward the edge.

She edged back and held her breath.

He raised his eyebrows. "Look at you, look at those shaking knees." He touched her cheek gently with his finger. "Don't worry, you're with me. Nothing bad will happen to you, I promise."

She looked into his eyes and wanted to believe him. But she just couldn't seem to make her feet move. She felt as if her feet were glued onto the rock, and was powerless to take a single step.

He tugged her hand. "Put one foot in front of the other." She took one step, then another toward the edge and looked down. She could see the water splashing against the base of the rock, leaving a dark stain on the pale gray surface. She took a big step backward.

"Iskra. Just jump. Don't think? Ready?" He took a firm grasp of her hand. "Close your eyes and run. Now!"

Without thinking she did as he said. Blind, she took two quick steps, Xico pulling on her hand. One step, two steps on the rock, then the third into open air. The air whipped her hair and clothing up as she fell, then she splashed into the warm embrace of the water.

She kicked her way to the top, stroking with one hand, the other clinging to Xico. Her head broke the surface and she shook the water from her eyes. She felt as though she would drown in joy, the sense of triumph and victory.

"Let's do it again!" she said.

Her smile was matched by Xico's grin. "I'm not against it."

They swam to shore and climbed to the top of the rock. A few others were already there, laughing as they each took a turn leaping to the water below. Iskra looked around at the people sitting on the grass eating, children running in the shallow water, splashing each other and giggling. All relaxed and easy, unbound by fears or rules or edicts from on high.

"Xico, when I hesitated to jump, why didn't you just push me off?"

He jerked his head to face her. "Why would I do that?"

"You know, to make me jump."

"I couldn't do that to you." He took a step closer to her. "I wasn't sure you really wanted to."

"But I said I did."

"I know. But I'd been watching your face." He smiled. "When you were watching Tuli and the others jump. First you were afraid, then surprised, then longing. I didn't know which was the strongest." He touched her cheek with one finger. "And besides, I could help you, I could encourage you, but I couldn't face down the fear for you. You had to do that."

Iskra blinked at him, not sure if the water in her eyes was from the lake. He wanted her to choose? She couldn't remember anyone giving her a choice about anything before.

"Now what?" Xico said. "You want to brave it alone?" He pointed to the water. "Or to hold my hand again?"

"Not this time." She stepped toward the edge of the rock and turned to face him. She spread her arms wide and with a wild, shameless boldness that surprised herself, said, "I want you to hold all of me."

A smile spread across his face all the way to his eyes as he looked at her face, then the wet clothes clinging to her body. "If you please." He took two quick steps toward her, threw her over his shoulder and sprang off the rock.

Iskra grabbed his shoulder and pushed herself up, reveling in the strength of his arms around her as they flew to the water. A second later they plunged into its depths. He moved his hands to caress her waist and to pull her toward him as they sank.

When they surfaced, he moved his hand around her back and looked into her eyes. She saw the joy on his face, joy that she knew was reflected on her own. She couldn't speak, could barely breathe, lost in the warmth of Xico's eyes.

And choked when a wave hit her in the face.

Xico let go of her, laughing. She splashed him and grinned when he ducked and sputtered. He recovered and seized her in a hug. "Want to try again?"

"I'll race you."

Half an hour later, Iskra and Xico sat on the rocky shore, eating bread and cheese again. *This is joy,* Iskra thought. Such exhilaration, such a sense of being able to do anything. She shivered as she re-lived her first jump. The terror of looking down at the water. The sense of being in flight. The plunge into the warm water. The freedom of having faced down a fear. *Now I understand. Taking a risk stretches you, so you can find out what you can do, instead of being sure you cannot. What is it about him that makes me feel so light, so free? He helps me be better than myself.*

"Xico, why do *you* think it's forbidden for villagers to visit Riskers?" she asked.

"Good question. I never understood that. Maybe they just want you all to work hard and be content with what they give you."

"Or maybe they're just afraid of what they don't know."

"Could be." From his tone, Iskra could tell his mind was on some other topic. He pulled a small piece from his bread and flung it to a sparrow, laughing as it pounced, only to have it snatched away by a crow.

"Iskra, I'm eighteen now, and am starting to trade for myself."

"What do you mean?"

"Up to now, I've been helping Da or Tikul. Now I'm trading my arrows and furs. Tarkio and some of the other traders take them all over Tlefas for me. They take a cut of whatever they sell, and bring the rest to me."

"That's nice."

"It is. Most don't branch out quite so young. Da told me I can start building my own house now."

"Your da said that? Not the leaders?"

"You mean the elder? No. We own the land, we do with it what we want." He paused to throw another piece of bread to the waiting birds who gathered before him like an audience watching a performance. "Once I build a house, I'll want to share it with a wife."

Iskra felt her heart skip a beat. "Do you have anyone in mind?"

"I do."

The sun seemed to dim at his words, the joy of the day weakening at the thought of Xico settling down with a wife. She stared at the ground in front of her, unable to ask the obvious question.

"But I'm not sure she'll have me."

She swallowed hard and made the effort to speak. "Oh, I think she will." *Who wouldn't want you?* "Does she live in this camp, or another?"

"She doesn't live in any Risker camp," he said, taking her hand in his.

She gasped when she understood his meaning, then tried to catch her breath enough to reply. "Xico, I'm sure she'd like to take you, but if she's not a Risker, then it would be impossible. To marry a Risker, that's the worst crime I can imagine."

His fingers tensed in hers, but his voice was steady when he asked, "Why a crime?"

"That's what I don't know. I need to know why it's so horrible, before—" She looked at him sideways, out of the corners of her eyes. He seemed almost pleased with that answer. To her relief, he tossed the rest of his bread to the birds and stood up. "I don't want you to get in trouble again. Are you about ready to go?"

24

As Xico walked her back to the camp, Iskra walked in a daze of happiness mingled with shock. Did she hear right, that Xico was thinking about her for a wife? How could someone so confident, so bold, so wildly good-looking, be attracted to her, plain, timid Iskra?

She changed her clothes at his house and gave his mother a hug. Then they headed for the Guarded Path, taking their time strolling through the camp.

Xico carried his bow, his quiver slung at his side. Iskra couldn't stop thinking about the warm feeling she had when Xico looked at her, when he touched her, the feeling as he supported her body in the water, the desire for him to touch her more. She didn't want him to know what else she was thinking.

"Why did you bring your bow?" she asked.

"I always do. We never know when bandits or wild animals will come this way."

"Then why don't you build a wall around the camp? Like we have a wall around the village?"

"We could do that. But our fields and animals would be outside. We'd still have to patrol at night to protect them." He turned his head casually, scanning the line of trees that marked the edge of the forest. "If we had a wall, we'd have to spend a lot of time keeping it in good repair. We also wouldn't be able to see what was on the other side."

He smiled at her doubting expression. "We do build in some defenses. Most Risker camps, like this one, are built in valleys with only a few ways in. Take the Guarded Path. It's so narrow only one, maybe two people can come up at a time. The path is just as narrow to the lake." He pointed with his bow. "We've dug deep pits and placed spikes in the bottom along the trees. That traps the wild animals. If bandits tried to get over, our guards would know in plenty of time."

"Have the bandits ever tried?"

"Not for a long time. Sometimes, like when there's famine or a really hard winter. I've heard of them trying to steal a girl. That happened down south. But you never know. We always have guards on patrol, too. But not enough to fight off a large group of them. Everyone has to be ready all the time."

Iskra wasn't sure she wanted to live that way. Always on guard? Always ready to fight off an attack? At least in the village, she could walk around not looking over her shoulder or listening for danger in every crack of a twig.

They rounded a corner. Over by the blacksmith's forge, Iskra caught a glimpse of a tall, dark-skinned man showing samples of leather goods to Osip and some of the other men. From his brown clothes and short boots she knew he was a trader. She'd never seen him before, she was sure of it.

"I'll see you next week." Xico wasn't asking.

"I don't know."

"Why?"

She wondered if she should tell him, if she could trust him with her secret. She took a deep breath, gathering her courage. Opening up to someone was like jumping off a rock into the lake. *I trusted him then, maybe I can trust him now.* "I need to tell you something." She walked a few more steps with her head hanging. "Last time when I left, the ephor was waiting for me at the bottom of the Guarded Path."

"What did he want?"

"He asked me why I skipped volunteer day, where I'd been, said he knew I'd been up here." She shivered at the memory and her steps faltered.

Xico put his hand on her arm. "He didn't hurt you, did he?"

She smiled, hearing the protectiveness in his voice. "No, but he made threats. Lots of them."

"Like what?"

"That soon they'll be assigning jobs. If I get on the wrong side of the wrong people, I could end up in a job I don't like."

"Anything else?"

"Or they could assign me to marry an old grandfather."

Xico stopped and stared at her. "They wouldn't."

"They've done it before. I always wondered why the blacksmith was married to someone forty years younger than he is. Now I think I know." She grimaced. "It's horrible."

Xico turned his head, staring intently into the trees, holding up a hand for her to be quiet. A minute passed, then he shrugged. "Just an animal." He turned back to her. "When do they make marriage assignments?"

"Oh, I have a year, maybe more. Usually by the time someone is seventeen they have it settled."

"Do they let you choose?"

"No, but they do ask who you like. Most people end up with someone they're happy with."

"And if they don't?"

"What choice do they have? Make the best of it, or cause a fuss and get taken."

"You mean you're stuck for life?"

She shrugged. "Or until you produce at least three children. Then you're allowed to live apart. You're still married, but don't have to live together." She noticed his wrinkled nose.

"This is how they keep everyone safe. Marriages are to last as long as both people live. If they aren't happy, they can at least do their duty to help increase the population, so we have more workers. Then they can separate. It's the best way to be fair to everyone."

Xico scuffed at the ground with his shoe. "You believe that, do you?"

She walked in silence for a few minutes. *He doesn't want me to.* "I'm not sure anymore." Which, she told herself, was the truth.

He held a tree branch that extended over the path so she could walk past without stooping. "What about you? Is there some village boy you want to marry?"

She looked down at the path, hesitating, afraid she had misunderstood what he told her at the lake. "No, Xico, there isn't."

"What will you tell them, when they ask you who you like?"

She stared at him sadly. "I'm not sure." They stared into each other's eyes, Iskra feeling like she could lose herself in the green depths of his eyes forever. Then she shook herself. "I didn't finish telling you about the ephor. He made a deal with me. If I help him, he'll fix it so I don't get an awful job."

"What do you have to do?"

"To not come up here, unless he tells me to."

Xico frowned. "Is that why you came today?"

"Well, yes. I couldn't have come otherwise. But there's a catch. I have to tell him who I saw up here, other than Riskers."

"That doesn't make sense. The only people who would be here would be traders, and that's allowed."

"I know. Still, I didn't tell him that I saw Tarkio here before. I'm glad he wasn't here today. Something seemed funny about it, why Kaberco wanted to know who was here."

"Sounds odd to me, too. Da might understand it. I'll ask him."

"Good idea." They walked in silence, considering Kaberco's request.

Xico reached for her hand. "Iskra, when will you come back?"

"I don't know. I can't come back unless Kaberco tells me to, and they are watching the Guarded Path." She inclined her head toward him. *Oh, I want to. But do I dare?*

Xico pursed his lips. "There is another way. Look." He squatted and drew in the dust with his finger. "Here is the Guarded Path, the trail to the road, and the village." He drew a few more lines. "Over here is the village dairy, right? If you go behind it and follow the stream, you'll come to a waterfall up the hill. On the right of the waterfall, as you are facing it as you come up the hill, understand, the water comes out from the rock just a tiny bit. Go behind it, and you'll find a cave. We can meet there."

She stooped to look closely at what he'd drawn. "I can't go there alone." Her hands began to tremble as her eyes locked on the rough map, staring but not seeing.

"Sure you can. It's close enough to the dairy that you won't run into any warboars. And no one knows that cave. Just me and my da."

She dropped her voice to a whisper. "How do you know about it?"

"Da and I used to walk down that way about once a week, when he started taking me on patrol with him. We found that place one hot summer day when we stopped there for a drink, only because I started exploring and was small enough to get behind the waterfall without getting wet."

Heart pounding, sweat beading on her neck, she hesitated. "I'll be there," she finally said. "In the afternoon." She slowly looked up at him, and relaxed when she saw his relieved smile.

He helped her up and gently touched her hair. "I'll be

waiting." He stroked her cheek, then under her jaw. She stared up into his eyes as if she was staring into a flame, unable to move, almost unable to breathe.

He cupped her face with his hand and gently kissed her mouth.

Her knees felt weak and she felt the sting of a tear in her eye. *He loves me,* she thought. *I love him back.*

25

I*'ll wait as long as it takes,* Kaberco thought. He and Boreje were settled comfortably at the foot of the Guarded Path. At least, Boreje was. He dozed in the summer heat, lulled to sleep by the drone of insects.

Kaberco rubbed his hands over his trousers and bit his lips. This just had to work. He didn't want to think about having to take her.

He was so deep in his musings he didn't hear Iskra's approach. He sprang to his feet when she appeared, startled by the noise she made when she nearly tripped over Boreje's legs stretched across the opening in the rocks.

"You're back," Kaberco said. "See anyone important?" He pulled his eyebrows together and watched her face carefully as she replied.

"I don't know about important," she said. "But there was one trader there."

Kaberco frowned. Her tone was as playful as if she had brought him a surprise from the market and wanted him to guess what it was. "Who?"

She shrugged. "I don't know. I've never seen him before."

"You didn't ask his name?"

"I only caught a glimpse of him as I was leaving."

He raised an eyebrow at her, then sighed deeply. Using her as a tool wasn't as simple as he thought it would be. "What did he look like?"

"He's tall, dark-skinned. I think he was selling things made of leather."

"That's all? Did you notice anything else about him?"

She wrinkled her forehead and pushed her lower teeth out in front of her uppers as she thought. "No. He was dressed just like any other trader, leather boots, brown pants, and shirt."

"He was the only one?"

"Yes."

Kaberco studied her face, wondering if she was telling him the entire truth, or only part of it.

"Kaberco?" Iskra asked. "If you please, may I leave?"

"Yes. I'll let you know if I need you to go back again."

She nodded and strode away.

Kaberco noted how she was trying not to run, but walked faster the farther she got down the trail. Good. She's nervous. But not intimidated. She's not hunched over, her head's up like she owns the world. What's changed? He waited until she'd turned onto the road, then looked at Boreje. "I think I know who she saw: Poales."

"Who's that?"

"He's the one they took in Trofmose a few months ago. They suspected he was involved in some kind of plot to undermine the Prime Konamei. That fool of an ephor let his wife convince him Poales is a halfwit and they set him free. Halfwit or not, now I'm sure he's up to something."

"Why?"

"Since when does Poales come to a backwater like this? All those southern traders stick to the bigger towns, and let the local traders go to villages and Risker camps around here." He clenched his fist. "Mark my words, Boreje. Something is up. We need to find out what it is."

"And the girl?"

"She doesn't know anything, I'll wager. But she's served her purpose. Now it's time to teach her a lesson."

Iskra hurried along the road, shaking her head to empty it of the stabbing fear that filled it during her encounter with Kaberco, and wrapped her thoughts around happier memories. Jumping from the rock, leaning into Xico's kiss. The hard look in Xico's green eyes when he thought of her married to an old man. His broad smile when she agreed to meet him again. And now that she'd told Kaberco what he wanted, he'd fix everything with Edalia.

She stopped by the market and flitted through the stalls, searching for her mother's favorite foods. She needed to find something to explain how long she'd been gone, Kaberco's idea or not, and to get her mother in a good mood.

She bought some dried apricots and pears from one old woman, and two pasties from another, then headed home. Humming, she flung open the door and stopped with one foot in mid-air, stunned at the sight of her mother and Edalia seated at the kitchen table, deep in conversation, the battered teapot in front of them. She made a move as if to turn and flee.

"Finally. You're home. Where've you been?" Luza asked. "Get in here and shut the door." She set her mug down on the table with a thump.

Iskra did as she was told. It seemed everyone was very interested in where she went these days. "I was at the market." She walked to the table and set her basket down.

"All day you were buying dried fruit?" her mother asked with drawn brows.

Edalia stood up. "I don't have much time. I've waited for you long enough, Iskra." She paused, then said, "I've come to tell you what your job will be. Your mother agrees that it is a good one for you."

Iskra sucked in a breath. What her mother thought was good for her and what she thought were two different things. "What is it?" she asked.

"You'll be working for Mazat on the chicken farm. He needs someone to feed the hens, gather eggs, and pluck chickens. You'll also fetch lunch for him and the other workers, and clean his cottage."

Iskra stared at Edalia, her good spirits draining into her feet. The air felt close and musty, making it hard for her to breathe. Her knees went weak and she thought she might fall. She put a hand on the table to steady herself. She focused her eyes on the pink band around Edalia's shoulder, the pink that showed her as a nurturer of the young. This didn't feel like nurture to Iskra.

It was more like a punishment. Working for Mazat, a foul, toothless old man. And on the chicken farm. She had wanted to work with the tailor, or even the baker. The vegetable farms would have been better than this. "I don't want to work there."

"You don't have a choice," Edalia said. "I talked to all the people you've apprenticed with, and Mazat was the only one who would take someone who's skipped Volunteer Day."

Iskra let out a slow breath. *I'm sure you talked with them all,* she thought. *What did you say? That I was lazy? Careless? Even the ones who liked me weren't going to contradict you. They'd be too afraid to defend someone who is out of favor.*

"Don't be stupid, Iskra," Luza said. "What if no one had wanted to take you? That would have been so shameful for me." She picked up the teapot and refilled her mug, spilling a little on the table.

"Listen to your mother. The decision has been made. Go there tomorrow morning."

"This is it? If you please, is there no chance I could change jobs?"

"No, not for you. Kaberco told me specifically that you got yourself involved in things that were not your place to meddle with. 'She needs a lesson,' he told me. Show yourself to be a good worker, and maybe in a year or so, if you make the right marriage and your husband does something you could help him with, you might be able to change and work with him, if he's agreeable. But for now, this is it."

She looked directly at Luza. "Don't you agree?"

"Of course. I've not been able to make you obey me, so Kaberco and Edalia have offered to help. You'll do a good job for Mazat, or you'll be sorry."

Luza didn't look at Iskra as she spoke, and Iskra heard the quiver in her mother's voice.

Iskra forced herself to keep her face still, to show none of the fear and anger surging within her. "And if I don't?"

"Oh, we have jobs you'll like even less," Edalia said.

"And I might not have room for you here anymore," added Luza.

Edalia nodded. "Thank you, Luza. Safety and fairness to you." She walked out of the cottage and shut the door behind her.

"Well, what's wrong with you? Are you going to stand there all day? Do something with your fruit." Luza paced back and forth. "I don't know why you took it in your head to buy pasties. We're better off eating at the inn."

At the sound of her mother's voice, Iskra mechanically took the fruit and pasties and placed them on a shelf.

Luza shoved her chair back. "Make yourself useful and sweep the floor." Iskra fetched the broom and silently went to work. Her mother was muttering in the background, but Iskra paid her no attention. She'd learned over the years to let her mother talk until she'd worn herself out. Until then, Luza wouldn't expect much of a response from Iskra.

Which gave her time to think. Something was going on here, something more than just her breaking some rules. She tried to imagine what Kaberco was up to, but gave up after a few minutes. Whatever it was, she was best staying out of his way.

"You're not doing it right," her mother snapped. "Sweep away from your feet." She grabbed the broom from Iskra's hands. "Look, this is how you do it. How many times do I have to tell you? Or do you think you know everything and don't have to listen to me?"

With a sigh, Iskra took the broom back and continued to sweep, returning to her own thoughts. Xico was right. I am a slave. Slaves have no choice over what jobs they do. They get stuck for life in a hopeless place. She rubbed her forehead with the back of her hand.

He also told me to choose the life I want. Which do I choose? The life I know, the one that is safe? Or the one with risks that could be dangerous? Safe slavery, or chancy freedom? Which is better?

She considered her mother, her friends, the stability of the village. No one in Gishin incited her to do things that frightened her, like jumping off rocks.

Instead they forced her into fearful situations. She was terrified of working for Mazat. The last two girls who'd worked on the chicken farm became beaten down shells of themselves, cowed and flinching at every sharp word. They did manage to escape, one by marrying a trader, the other the dairy farmer's son, both men much older than themselves. *It must be bad with Mazat, if that's their idea of a change for the better,* Iskra thought grimly to herself.

Then there is Xico. Her heart beat a little faster, thinking of jumping off the rock with him. Frightening at first, but the joy of facing down a fear made the terror worth it. Then the heart-stopping moment just before he kissed her, when fear melted into joy. Isn't that what Xico had been trying to tell her all these months? That you can't remove all fear and danger from your life. But if you fight it, and face it, you are stronger and don't need to fear so much.

She wondered if she really could leave the village to live with the Riskers. No more silly rules, no more Edalia and Kaberco watching, waiting for one wrong move. No more threats of being taken.

It took her a while to face that snippet of the truth, the bit she'd avoided. That her friend Kaberco, the one she relied on for protection, was the one who had betrayed her. It seemed there was a limit to what he would allow. He would only keep her safe if she let him box her into the confines of the rules. No questions allowed.

The village is where I belong, isn't it?

She considered that. The village was really the only life she knew. But more and more, she didn't feel like she belonged. She had too many questions, had seen too much of another way of life to accept all she'd been told her whole life. *And it's not like I have a family that loves me, like Xico does.*

Then she had to ask herself, was Xico seriously talking about marriage to her? Maybe he was just caught up in the moment. Maybe he was just daydreaming, or saying things he thought she wanted to hear. Or worse, perhaps she had completely misunderstood him. Her face burned at the thought of him suspecting she had feelings for him when he had none for her.

Iskra stared at the wood floor before her, barely conscious of her mother still talking. *Maybe his parents will take me in if he doesn't want me.*

I don't think I can live like this much longer.

26

By the middle of the next morning, Iskra was ready to face bandits and warboars and even Kaberco's wrath if she could only run away. Mazat had dogged her every step, leering as she bent to pick up baskets of corn. She felt her skin crawl every time her gray eyes met his tawny brown ones. He watched as she tossed grain to the hens and searched for eggs, snickering as she timidly put her hands under the setting hens, laughing when she gasped with pain when they pecked her hands.

Then he sent her to the village inn for a bucket of stew for their noon meal. She thought she'd be free from him for a while, but he insisted on accompanying her, to make sure she knew the way, he said. As if she couldn't walk the half mile from the farm to the village on her own. If he only knew how far she'd gone on her own.

On their return, he led her into his filthy hut to prepare the noon meal. He sat on a bench and watched her warm the stew and set out bread.

"Mazat, if you please, I can call you when this is ready. Do you not have something else you need to do?"

"I've got to keep my eye on you. That's what Edalia said to

do. You skipped out on volunteer day. Shirkin' your duty. Lazy. I'll make 'er work, that's what I told Edalia." He had repeated this to Iskra three or four times in the course of the morning. Snickering, he pulled off a boot, placed his large bare foot on the table, and began scraping his corns with a dull knife. "I been wanting help for a while, but no one stays long. Sly girls, all of 'em. They find a way to slink away." He blew on his knife. "Edalia promised me you're here forever."

She shuddered and turned back to the stew. That couldn't be true, that she'd be trapped on this farm until either she or Mazat died. The way things were going, the way people seemed to lie about everything, she wasn't so sure. She gave the stew a stir, gritting her teeth in an effort to hide her disgust with the squalor in the hut.

Chickens walked in and out of the door, pecking at insects and crumbs on the floor, leaving oily brown droppings behind. Grease clung to the table, the plates, the pots, the knife, the walls. Chicken feathers were everywhere, some bloody. She ignored the heaving of her stomach and fixed her thoughts on the idea that this torture would not last forever, that maybe someday she would be free of Mazat and his chickens. Maybe a better job. Or maybe life with Xico. She felt a surge of hope at that thought.

After lunch was more of the same. Mazat chose a few hens who had stopped laying and showed Iskra how to wring their necks. Then he set her to plucking them.

She hated the messy work, the sharp quills that poked her fingers, the blood that stained her apron. She searched her mind for some way to ease her misery. *Some day I'll be as good at this as he is. Then I'll get the job done faster. But I don't think I'll ever be able to kill a chicken without wincing.*

Late in the day, Mazat dragged a cart to the barn. Shortly he returned with it loaded with corn. Iskra couldn't help staring as he approached. The cart was missing one of its front wheels. Mazat walked hunched over, supporting the corner with the missing wheel against his shoulder, balancing it so he could drag it along. She had to marvel that such a tall man could bend so low and still drag the cart. He must be very strong.

"I s'pose you wanna know why I don't fix it," he asked her.

"Well, yes." *Of course you should fix it, stupid old man.*

"But first, you haf ta go to the wheelwright's guild an' ask fer a wheelwright. Then you haf to bring 'em your cart or whatever you want fixed. It'd take me half the day to drag that thing all the way into town." He spat, aiming for Iskra's feet but not quite making it. "Then, you wait weeks or months or however long it takes 'em to get around to fixing the wheel."

"But then it's fixed."

"No, not quite. Then you haf to haf the wheelwright and the wagonmaker agree to come out to watch you use the cart, to make sure you are using it safely."

"You seem like you know what you're doing. They would just come and pass you and that would be the end of it." To her surprise, Iskra was telling the truth. As foul as Mazat was, he wasn't incompetent. With his high cheekbones and sun-bleached hair, he might have been handsome when he was young. Maybe that's how he managed to convince three different women to marry him.

"That's what you think." He snorted. "If they see somethin' they think might not be safe, they'll bring all kinds of other people pokin' around, askin' questions, tellin' you what to do." He looked around, as if making sure no one else could hear him. "Better to avoid that trouble in the first place."

Iskra nodded. There was a lot about Mazat's house and yard that could be considered unsafe. She looked at the green band on his shoulder, green for agriculture. That meant he was under the supervision of Zurvan, the syndic, who would send his inspectors with their orange bands and account books. They'd find plenty to ask about, and make life miserable for Mazat.

For a moment, she thought of a way to get back at Mazat: she could report him to the syndic as being unsafe. Then maybe they'd let her have a different job as a reward for trying to maintain safety.

She shook her head. In spite of herself, she had an odd sympathy for Mazat, feeble and fleeting as it was. No, she wouldn't tell anyone. *Besides, they probably already know,* she thought. *They just use Mazat and his chicken farm as a way to punish people. My only hope is to work hard so he has no complaints. Maybe later I'll be able to find something else.*

Finally, she heard the faint sound of the horn they blew in the village, announcing the end of the work day.

Mazat told her she could leave. "I went easy on you today. Tomorrow you'll really work."

ISKRA STUMBLED TOWARD THE VILLAGE, her hands throbbing from the wounds made by the hens' sharp beaks. *His hens are as mean as he is.* She wondered how long she'd have to endure the drudgery of the chicken farm. *A few months, maybe a year, and they'll let me have a different job. In the meantime, I can see Xico at the cave and have a few hours of happiness.*

Her way home took her through the market. A few traders were still there, winding up the day's business or getting a jump on tomorrow's. She stopped to look at an old woman's pears, wondering if Luza would be pleased or not if she bought some. Buying pears could either be a peace offering or cause for another war. If they were old and wrinkled, Luza would berate her for being a fool to buy garbage. If they were fresh, her mother would moan over the extravagance. If she came home empty-handed, her mother would accuse her of wanting to starve her to death.

The pears looked smooth, but felt overripe when she held one. Sighing, she put it down.

"You won't find any others," the old woman said. "Usila was taken last night." Iskra stepped back. Usila was taken? She was such a sweet lady, always a kind word for everyone.

A rough hand grabbed her shoulder and jerked her around. "You! You should be ashamed to show your face here!"

Iskra pulled away from Tavda's mother. "What have I done now?"

"It wasn't enough you got my daughter in trouble. I've heard about you, still asking questions. Think you're above the rules?"

Her face reddening, Iskra tried to think of some way to calm the woman. A few people stopped to listen.

Another woman chimed in. "My son says she asks the most outrageous questions in the Oppidan lectures. She's trouble, all right. It's good they've sent her to work for Mazat. He'll get her into line."

Others joined in hurling abuse at Iskra. "What's wrong with you?" "Do you like danger?" "Do you like unfairness?" "You must want our country to stay poor and weak. Not the kind of person we want living here."

Iskra backed away and hurried to put as much distance between the women and herself. She turned a corner and bumped into Tarkio.

"Well, hello, Iskra," he said.

She stared at him, then hung her head.

"What's wrong?"

She sagged limply against the side of a market stall.

"Was that you they were yelling at?"

Nodding, she let out a deep breath.

"I'm sorry. What happened?"

She held a shaking hand to her mouth as if to stifle a sob. "I need to tell you something."

She paused as two fat women carrying baskets of thick woolen socks passed by. In a few words, she explained about her encounters with Kaberco and the deal she made with him, the deal he did not keep.

"What did you tell him?"

"The first time, I told him I didn't see anyone important at the Risker camp. I'm not sure why, but I didn't want him to know I saw you there."

"Thank you for that. The less he knows of where I am, the better."

"Yesterday, I did tell him something. There was a trader I didn't know at the camp, so I didn't think it would matter if I told Kaberco about him."

Tarkio's eyes widened. "What did this trader look like?"

"Tall, dark-skinned, selling leather."

Tarkio drew in a quick breath. "You say you told Kaberco this yesterday?"

She nodded. She could tell he was disturbed by the way he broke eye contact and rubbed his hand over his mouth. *That's another person I've hurt.*

A moment later he spoke. "Maybe it's not too late," Tarkio said. "Listen, don't tell anyone about this. You haven't seen me, and never see that trader again. Agreed?"

"Yes, but I don't understand."

"It's better this way, believe me. And it's probably better if you stay away from the Riskers. Don't go back there." He turned and hurried away.

She felt a sinking sensation as she watched him. If she did as he said, she'd lose the only joy she had in life.

TARKIO STROLLED THROUGH THE MARKET, trying to look unhurried. He turned down one street, then an alley, and eventually made his way through the gate to the dairy farm. He gave the buildings wide berths, making sure he didn't disturb the dogs, and sought cover under the trees at the edge of the forest.

Once under the trees, he walked a little straighter. He found the stream and began to follow it up the hill, skirting the waterfall. Higher up, the stream cut deep into the side of the hill, forcing Tarkio to jump from stone to stone and even to use his hands to climb up the sheer face of the hill. It was a good thing it was a clear night and Dabrey was still full; without the moonlight, he'd have a hard time seeing in the darkness.

What a fool he had been to tease Iskra into going back to the Risker camp. Just to see if just for once he could get a woman to do something she didn't want to do.

Now innocent little Iskra will pay the price because I married on impulse, out of loneliness. I married a woman who was unsure of herself, who has no business being a trader's wife. Groa would be far happier married to a man who was home every night. Nothing I do is good enough for her, all because she wonders what I'm doing when I'm traveling. He rubbed his thumb over his fingernails, full of pity for his wife. *She deserves better than me. I've failed her.*

Now he'd proven himself to be twice a failure. A meddling, bumbling fool who couldn't keep his wife happy and may have ruined another girl's life. And Xico's, too. Tarkio groaned. Xico, the best friend he'd ever had. Cillia filled his mother's place, Xico and his siblings the brothers and sisters he'd never had. His stomach lurched and knotted. *And this is how I repay them. I'm such an idiot.*

Now Poales could be in trouble. His license to trade with the Riskers didn't include the northern camps. Why Poales was risking his license, and why Kaberco was spying on the Riskers were questions he didn't have answers for.

What he did know was that this could all come crashing back on him. If Iskra decides to come clean to Kaberco and tell him everything, well, that would be the end. Tarkio knew it would be hours, not days before he was taken.

Half an hour later, Tarkio was sitting in Cillia's kitchen, listening to Xico tell him about a warboar hunt. It seemed the Prime Konamei wanted a set of warboar tusks from a northern warboar, which were bigger and thicker than the southern ones. Xico and Poales had been tracking a warboar, when another warboar attacked it. The hunters waited until the warboars had locked tusks and had wounded each other, then they let their arrows fly. Poales had taken the tusks, Xico the skins and the legs.

"What are you going to do with them?" Tarkio asked.

"I'm not going to eat them, that's for sure," Xico replied. "Dying of rotgut isn't how I want to go. But the skin does make good leather, rough, but useable." He rubbed his hands together. "And I thought the sinew might be useful, maybe be stronger than the cow's." He pulled the candle closer. "See how it's thicker? Worth a try to find out, don't you think?"

"Clever, aren't you?" Tarkio smirked. "Only you would think of something like that. Where is Poales now?"

"He went back to Shinroo."

Tarkio smiled slowly. "That's good. I'm not sure if Kaberco is looking for him, but better if the two of them don't meet. At least if he's questioned, he's got a reason for being this far out of his usual route."

"If Kaberco is trailing him, he'll find that Poales, that slippery fish, as you call him, has escaped the net once again." Osip laughed. "He's pretty clever, for a supposed halfwit."

"Which is why he needs to stay out of sight for a while. I don't think anyone suspects him down south."

Osip nodded. "If I see him, I'll let him know."

"And I'll go to Shinroo tomorrow." Tarkio rubbed his chin and tugged on his lower lip. "Xico, you need to know something. I saw Iskra in the market today."

"How is she? Did she tell you about her job?"

Tarkio crossed his arms when Xico's face lit up at the mention of Iskra. "No. She had something else to say." He told them Iskra's story, watching his listeners' reaction. Cillia, at least, clearly saw the danger. Her hands were pressed to her mouth, eyes opened wide. Osip's lips were pressed firmly together. Xico was frowning, but there was no sign of surprise on his face.

"Did you know this?" Tarkio asked him.

"Not about Poales."

"But you don't seem too surprised that Iskra's having trouble in the village."

"She told me some of it." A muscle twitched along his jaw. "I need to stop them from bothering her."

"Xico, you can't and you know it," Cillia said. "We have an uneasy truce with the villagers. They don't get involved with us, nor we with them."

"I know. But this isn't right."

"That's not for us to decide. She belongs to the village and needs to live under their rules."

Tarkio leaned forward. "Since Kaberco is watching the Guarded Path, then she won't be able to come here anymore. Is that right?"

Xico studied his long fingers as he flexed and stretched his hands. "That's right," he said. "She won't be coming up the Guarded Path again." He picked up the pieces of warboar and walked out of the cottage.

Tarkio and Cillia looked at each other for a long moment after Xico left. She shook her head. "I wish I could say I'm relieved, but—"

"But what?" he asked.

"I love that girl. She's been such a help to me, so eager to learn, so quick with her questions. I hate to think of her trapped like a little bird in a cage, hemmed in by all those rules and all the fears she's been taught. And I see how happy Xico is around her. He's acting more like a man because of her."

Tarkio started to speak, then stopped when she held up

her hand. "I know, Tarkio. I know it's forbidden. But I can't explain more clearly to Xico. You know him. He wouldn't let a little thing like a prophecy foretelling the end of the realm stand in the way of something he really wants." She rubbed her face. "I just don't see a good end to this."

Osip nodded. "The problem is, Xico thinks he can do anything. What's impossible for others is just a challenge for him." He rubbed his hand over his eyebrows. "He's been cursed with too many talents. They'll get him into trouble some day."

Tarkio felt a cold sensation in the pit of his stomach. "If Kaberco keeps Iskra from coming back, then maybe Xico will forget about her."

"That would be mercy from the sky-god, if that happens. I just can't imagine Xico giving up that easily."

Cillia was right. Xico wasn't going to give up Iskra. Tarkio knew for everyone's sake he was going to have to.

27

Iskra gripped the handle of her basket as she strode up the steps to Kaberco's house. She tried not to think too hard about what she was doing. Otherwise her nerve might dissolve like a sandy riverbank in a thunderstorm. In the week she'd been working for Mazat, she'd had plenty of time to think about the mystery she'd been swept up in. First Cassie and the dezeerudun. Then Tavda. Then Edalia, who didn't answer questions. Even her mother. Everyone seemed to be afraid of something. What good was safety if you're always afraid?

Guilt made her wince as she thought about Tavda. Where did the taken go? It didn't seem like they ended up with the Riskers. Cillia seemed to have secrets, but Iskra had the feeling these were about something else, not people who got taken.

Which left Kaberco. He used her, betrayed her, and was punishing her now. There was no point asking him any questions. That would just get her in worse trouble. But how could she find out what she so desperately needed to know?

It was the clucking of the chickens that gave Iskra the answer. One afternoon she was cleaning Mazat's hut, fighting a headache. She could hear him, talking to his chickens, making fun of the syndic and his fussy rules. When Mazat spoke, the chickens clucked in response.

"Yes, Zurvan would make a good chicken, my friends. He pecks, he clucks, he pecks again. All to get more food for himself."

Mazat would be horrified to know I'd overheard him, she thought. *And I'm appalled to realize I agree with him.*

Thinking of the syndic led her to think of Kaberco. He was certainly not like a chicken. More like a bear. The idea struck her like a rock falling from the roof of a cave, letting in a glimpse of light from above. If anyone knows what happens to people who get taken, it would be Kaberco.

Her plan exploded in her mind. All she'd need to do was go to Kaberco's house late afternoon on a Charsnabe, just as the clerks would be leaving. The village konament met a few times a week, usually in the morning. But on Charsanbe, the fifth day of the week, they met in the afternoon, just after the clerks went home.

Then it would get scary. She'd been in and out of the ephor's house for years because of her long friendship with Kaberco. Many of the clerks would recognize her and not think anything of her being there. The trick would be getting to the konament chamber without being seen and finding a place to hide where she wouldn't be discovered.

The other problem had been getting Mazat to let her leave early. In the end, it hadn't been too hard. He'd come in from the barns, complaining that the latch on his chicken coop had rusted through.

"Now I have to get it repaired. Such a waste of time. I don't have time to wait all day while they make me a new one."

"If you please, I have a suggestion," Iskra said.

"You?"

She ignored his sarcasm. "If I took the broken latch to the market, I could leave it with the blacksmith. He could probably have it ready by morning, and I could bring the new one back then."

Mazat drew his bushy gray eyebrows together. "What if it's not ready by then?"

Iskra bit her lip. "Well," she said, "I'll find out when it will be done. And go back for it when it is." She hoped Mazat wouldn't decide to do the errand himself. "I'm sure you'll agree, that way you don't have to be bothered."

"Hm. I'll think on it."

Which is why a few hours later Iskra was walking up the steps to Kaberco's house, having left the rusted latch with the blacksmith. She tried to stride with a firm tread, as if she knew where she was going and had every right to be there.

A few people hurried past her on the way out. Many had business with the ephor's clerks, reporting the neighbors who broke the safety rules. Or else they came to defend themselves against the accusations. Minor complaints that weren't resolved were sent over to the questor's courts, for a trial and usually some kind of punishment. Major complaints, well, those people got taken.

She stopped near the corridor that led to the back stairs to the second floor, the ephor's private rooms. She'd never been up there, but a much younger Kaberco had shown her the way. A clerk she recognized as one of Kaberco's by the black band on his shoulder pushed past her, eager to leave after his work day was over.

She took a deep breath, hoping he was the last to depart. She walked down the corridor, stopping at the sixth doorway. Trying to ignore her shaking hand, she pressed the latch and pushed the door open. She jumped up onto the first stair and pulled the door shut behind her.

Now she was committed. Before, she could have come up with some story of looking for a friend. Now if she was caught, there wasn't much she could say. She crept up the stairs, listening for the sound of anyone approaching.

She hesitated at the top, mouth hanging open. Gone were the rough stone and plain wood of the lower floors. The walls of the corridor were smooth and white, with bright-colored tapestries hanging at intervals. Elaborate iron sconces held massive candles, waiting to be lit when the sun set. The floor was polished wood, with a carpet running down the center.

She stared at the luxury, feeling an even greater sense of betrayal. How could Kaberco talk about fairness, when the rest of the village lived in such poverty, and he had such comforts? She lost her fear in her anger, and started to explore.

She opened the first door, and saw a cozy sitting room, with cushioned chairs all in vivid shades of green and yellow, bright accents against the dark wood floor. Another room held a massive bed, heaped high with pillows, covered in a thick, dark-blue spread Iskra couldn't call a blanket. It was thicker than any blanket she'd ever seen, and soft to the touch.

The fading light made her realize she needed to hide herself quickly. She opened a few more doors, then found what had to be the konameis' chamber. Five cushioned chairs arranged in a rough semi-circle stood on a brightly colored carpet near the massive fireplace. A round wooden table surrounded by more chairs filled the middle of the room. Hearing voices in the distance, she darted inside. Two high and deep cabinets stood on either side of the fireplace. She opened the door to one. It was crammed full of shelves. No place to hide.

A man in the corridor laughed and called something. They were coming. She ran to the other cabinet, her hands trembling to open the door. This one had fewer shelves, all near the top. The bottom held rolls of paper, standing up like a forest of white tubes. She jumped in the cabinet and pulled the door shut behind her.

She sank to the floor, pulling her knees up to meet her chin. The door to the corridor opened and she heard people enter the room. She clamped her teeth hard to prevent herself from making a sound. *Good thing it's a hot night and they won't light a fire. It could get warm in here.* Already the stuffy, airless closet was making her sweat.

Heavy footsteps accompanied by the creak of leather and clink of chainlinks moved from the door toward the chairs. Kaberco. Others joined him. There were a few minutes of the rustling of clothing and the scrape of chairs along the floor.

"Pelma, pour the wine."

That was Kaberco, Iskra thought. But who was Pelma? She listened intently, noting each clink of the glassware.

After five glasses had been poured, Kaberco spoke again. "Leave us, Pelma."

Pelma must be some kind of servant. But how can that be? We're all supposed to be equal. Iskra tried to make sense of what she'd heard.

A raised voice jerked her attention back to the meeting. "The traders are angry, and I can't blame them." That scratchy voice had to be Zurvan the syndic, overseer of trade and guilds.

"Angry at the bandit attacks? I would be angry as well." The smooth and oily voice with little emotion, that was Murash, the questor, Iskra was sure of it.

"I am angry as well," Kaberco said. "Believe me, I have impressed upon the guardsmen the need to preserve the safety of all the traders. Even the ones who complain the loudest."

Murash spoke again. "Do you need help reining in the complainers?"

"What do you mean?" Zurvan asked. "The guild is within its rights to request that its members be kept safe."

"Our friend, Kaberco, could take one or two of the worst troublemakers." Murash laughed. "That should get the rest in line."

Iskra's eyes widened. The man in charge of justice and fairness suggested that they take people for asking to be safe?

"There will be no need of that," Kaberco said, his deep voice exuding calm. "My guardsmen have this under control."

"Then perhaps we revoke some trading licenses?" Murash said. "We can't allow traders to think they have more power than anyone else."

There was a pause, then Zurvan said, "My traders know their place in working for fairness and prosperity. I will manage them. Not you."

"See that you do," Murash answered. "Otherwise, I'll have to step in."

By this time Iskra's hands were shaking and she thought she would jump out of her skin. She could barely believe what she was hearing. To distract herself, she untied the ribbon on her basket and retied it, feeling her way in the dark. The repetition of the mindless task helped her calm down enough to listen.

"But would that be fair?" This was a high, thin woman's voice. Probably, Iskra thought, the ludi, the old woman who'd been in charge of schools and the healers for over twenty years.

"Whatever keeps the village safe is fair," Murash said, his tone harsh. "Now, what about the potter? He's been complaining that with every bandit attack, he loses half of what he sent to Shinroo. Can't you keep him in line?"

"What would you have me do? He's an old man and speaks his mind," Zurvan answered.

"We could make an example of him," Murash said. "Like we do with most troublemakers."

Iskra bit hard on the sides of her mouth to stifle a gasp. Is that what her mother was so scared of, that they'd make an example of her? She untied the bow she'd just finished and started over, swallowing hard.

"Like that little girl a few months ago?" This was a younger woman's voice, Yasumin the adile, Iskra figured, who took care of the village property and roads.

Tavda, Iskra thought. She's talking about Tavda.

"She quoted the myth, the prophecy that had to be suppressed." Kaberco's voice had an edge to it, like he was suppressing irritation. Iskra could imagine the lines in his forehead deepening, his eyes narrowing. "You know that in order to preserve safety we have to keep people from rallying around myths or anyone who sets himself up in opposition to the Prime Konamei."

Iskra couldn't help thinking that if they put a little more energy into actually helping people instead of preaching safety, they wouldn't have to worry about people seeking other leaders.

"But that girl was only fifteen," Yasuvin said.

"We've discussed this. What she spoke of was forbidden, against the law." Murash spoke with finality.

Iskra pressed her hands to her mouth and held her breath. Her eyes widened and she sank against the back of the cupboard, weakness spreading through her body.

"But we won't do that, at least not now," Kaberco said. "We can't take any more underage people, not so soon."

Iskra let out the breath she was holding, slowly so as to make no sound. He wasn't planning on taking her.

"They're too young to be of any use, in any case. Don't you agree?" Kaberco asked.

Iskra frowned, wondering what they would use taken people for.

"So, what will you do?" Murash's tone sounded like a challenge. "If others start talking about the prophecy?"

"We will make an example of them in other ways." Kaberco sounded grim and determined.

"How?" Murash asked.

"Do you really need me to tell you?" Iskra could tell Kaberco was annoyed now by the way he spat out his words. "Like the tailor. We put him in your jail for a few days. Now, shall we get to the real business of this meeting?"

They must have agreed, because Zurvan started talking about pottery production and goods made from metal. "Trofmose has extra metal candlesticks. Shall we allow them to be brought here?"

"The villagers don't need them," Murash said.

"Agreed," Yasumin answered. "The pottery ones are safer, anyway."

Iskra could barely believe what she was hearing. All her life she'd been told that what they had in the village was all there was. The bigger towns might have more things more often, but still the same things. Then she'd seen how the Riskers live. That she put down to people just not knowing. But this! The people were deliberately being kept poor.

By now her limbs were cramping and she shifted her foot. She pushed it out, and brushed against one of the paper rolls, making it crackle. She froze, holding her breath.

The konameis began debating trade routes and what goods came from which town, and which goods should be traded out. None of this was interesting to Iskra. Her breath came faster and she felt dampness on the back of her neck. She wished they'd hurry up and finish their meeting so she could escape. To keep her nerves steady she tied and retied the bow on her basket.

"Should we look at a map?" Kaberco asked.

A chair scraped against the floor and heavy footsteps approached her hiding place. With a jolt she realized the rolls of paper were maps. She clapped her hands over her mouth to keep from screaming. Jail or taken, which would it be?

"No, I'd like to consult with my counterpart in Trofmose before we go further with this," Zurvan said.

Kaberco's footsteps paused, then retreated. "Then we have nothing more to discuss. I'll see you all out."

Iskra let out a cautious breath as she heard the chairs scrape along the floor, and the konament members taking their leave, the door closing behind them. The room grew silent. She waited, then pushed the cabinet door open. To her relief, the room really was empty. She seized her basket, then scurried for the door. This was the terrifying part. If she could just get out of the room, then no one would know what she'd overheard.

She eased the door open and peeked out. The corridor was empty, dimly lit by the candles in the sconces hanging on the walls. She ran for the stairs she'd come up and started down. Then she heard a sound that caused her pulse to race, pounding the beats in her ears.

"Pelma!" It was Kaberco, who'd somehow returned up the front stairs. Iskra swallowed hard and scampered down the stairs, hoping to get around the bend before Kaberco took it into his head to look down.

Then what she was most dreading happened.

She ran right into a girl a few years older than she, dressed in soft gray with no band on her shoulder, holding a basin of water. Iskra felt a warm splash that soaked the front of her dress. She and the girl stared at each other.

"I'm sorry, if you please," Iskra stammered, edging herself around the girl.

"Pelma!" Kaberco was calling from the top of the stairs.

The girl's eyes widened and she scurried up the stairs.

Iskra didn't hesitate. She raced the rest of the way down to the main floor. If only Kaberco hadn't locked the main door. She ran down the corridor, her footsteps echoing in the empty halls. One look at the main door dashed her hopes. The heavy bolt was in place, a thick beam that ran the whole width of the door. Heavy footsteps on the main stairs told her Kaberco was approaching.

She ran back the way she'd come and plunged down the back staircase. Two steps down was a side corridor. She ran down it, following a vague memory of Kaberco showing her a side way out that led to the ephor's stables. Her memory held true and she found the door that led her outside.

She breathed in the scent of horse and hay, and marveled at the darkening sky. She'd only been inside for a few hours, while it felt like weeks. She sagged against the wall, the rough wood scratching her cheek, reminding her she had to summon what strength she had left and get herself home.

Thankfully, her mother wasn't at home. The village konameis weren't the only ones to meet on Charsanbe. The market vendors met every other Charsanbe to discuss prices and profits, new items and which traders had the best products. Iskra had always liked these quiet evenings at home alone.

She pulled a pastie and apple out of her basket, congratulating herself on remembering to get herself something to eat for her supper before venturing into Kaberco's house. She sat and ate, mind reeling at what she'd learned. First, she thought of how Kaberco lived, with such luxury. And even, it seemed, a servant. That must be what Edalia meant when she said leaders deserve to have a little more than the rest, since they carried more of the burden of building a safe and fair society. But why not just tell people? Why pretend everyone was the same, when the differences were so great?

In all fairness, she thought, Kaberco of course wouldn't cook or clean for himself. She'd heard of him having a housekeeper, but this girl seemed like someone who waited on him. And there was something strange about Pelma, how she didn't speak. Even when Kaberco called to her, she didn't respond.

She pondered that until she could no longer put off thinking about the worst bit she'd learned. People get taken as examples, to keep others in line. That is not fair or just. *Tavda said something dangerous, something about a prophecy. I wonder if she said it to me.*

She thought back to the konament meeting, and took comfort in the idea that they wouldn't take another underage girl. *Which means I'm safe, at least for the next few months. That gives me time.*

Time to find out what Tavda said and what happened to her. Time to persuade Edalia I'm a safe and productive citizen who deserves a better job. And maybe enough time to figure out just what that stirring pleasant feeling Xico stirred up in her was all about.

28

Iskra looked up at the waterfall, enjoying the cool spray that misted on her face. Three days had passed since she'd ventured into Kaberco's house. Now she sat with Xico, huddled next to him for warmth in the chilly cave. They faced the waterfall, watching the sunlight play with the streams of water as they fell. Xico stroked her cheek. "Then what happened?"

"Mazat hurled chicken droppings at me. He screamed that's all I'm worth, chicken dung. All because I broke an egg putting it in the basket."

"Maybe it was cracked already."

"No, it wasn't. I dropped it when Udbash snuck up behind me."

"Who's Udbash?"

"Mazat's son." She shivered. "I don't want to think about him." She clenched her eyes shut, as if to blot out the memory.

Xico put his arm around her, pulling her close to his side. She leaned her head against his shoulder for a moment, then opened her eyes and looked at him. "If working for Mazat isn't bad enough, this week we all have to help with the early harvest. Four hours a day. Most bosses don't expect people to work a whole day during harvest, but not Mazat. I'm up early to gather eggs and get them ready for market and feed the hens. Then off to the fields. Then back to Mazat, bringing his lunch. Then back to the fields. Then back to feed the chickens again. I'm worn out going back and forth so much."

"I'll take you away from this, I promise."

"How?"

"I have most of my cottage built, Iskra. The walls are up, and the roof will be done by winter. I'll work on furniture over the winter. I'll make it *couthy* for you."

"Couthy?"

"You'd probably say cozy." He smiled and brushed her hair back from her face. "Then we can be married in the spring."

When she didn't respond, he put a hand under her chin and tipped her face so he could look into her eyes. "I'm asking you to marry me, Iskra."

She gasped, overwhelmed by the intense look in Xico's green eyes. She blinked. Her heart started to race. "Marry you?"

"I know, you never thought you'd marry a barbaric Risker. You'd stay in the village your whole life."

"You're not barbaric."

He put his hand behind her neck and kissed her. "Are you sure about that?"

She smiled and pulled back. "Usually." She tapped her finger on his lips. "But you're right about one thing. I never thought of any life but in the village."

"Do you love me?"

She dropped her eyes. Trembling at the thought of revealing herself to him, she found she couldn't say a word.

He stroked her cheek with one finger. "I love you, Iskra. Do you love me?"

Did she love him? He scared her at times, with his boundless confidence and lack of concern for safety. She couldn't possibly approve of the way he lived his life. But then, he didn't approve of hers, not entirely. Yet he said he loved her. Was it possible to love someone you didn't completely approve of?

Xico put his finger under her chin. "Do you love me, sweet girl?"

Did she? The longer he looked into her eyes, the more she knew she wanted to be with him. Was that feeling love? She took a deep breath, her heart pounding harder than when she was about to jump from the rock. He put one hand on the side of her face and stroked her hair with the other. His touch gave her the courage to speak.

"I do, Xico. I do love you."

He leaned over and gently pressed his lips to hers. "Then will you marry me?"

She drew her breath in, but before she could answer, he kissed her again. "You don't have to answer today. Think about it. We could have a good life together. It's a life you can choose."

She rested her head on his shoulder and they sat in silence. *I would have to choose,* she thought. She mused on this thought, watching the sunlight dance on the waterfall. *Once I decide, there's no going back. If I refuse Xico, he won't give me another chance. He'll find someone else. Plenty of Risker girls would take him in a heartbeat. I would if I were one of them.*

Could I live as a Risker? Always on guard, watching for bandits and warboars. She shuddered, thinking about having to learn to shoot well. *Would I ever really fit in, belong?* She shivered and Xico's arm tightened around her. *With him, I don't think I'd be so frightened. We'd laugh a lot, enjoy life. Not like in the village. A happier life, but less certain, less safe.*

Idly she noticed the light coming through the waterfall was dimmer. She pulled away from Xico and jumped to her feet. "I've got to go," she said. "I've been here too long already."

He followed her to the waterfall, then pushed ahead of her and slithered out from behind the water onto the rocks beside it. He motioned for her to come as well.

Usually he watched her walk down the trail to the dairy farm, creeping through the forest, making sure she made it to the farm below unmolested. Today she clung to his hand as they walked.

Just before they reached the fields, they stopped for a long embrace.

"Next week?" he asked.

"I'll be here." She let her fingers linger on his cheek, adjusted her basket on her arm, and turned to walk along the edge of the field.

She hadn't gotten very far when Mazat came around the side of the barn. He spotted Iskra and walked toward her. "What're you doing here?"

Iskra gulped and tried to think up a story. Mazat gripped her arm. "Answer me!"

She cried out and struggled to free herself.

Xico burst from the shelter of the trees and ran toward them. "What are you doing to her?"

"And what business is it of yours?" Mazat said. "You're just a Risker." He sneered. "And a law-breaking one, at that." He pulled out a small horn and blew it. Two guardsmen with drawn swords rushed from behind the barn.

"Let him go," Iskra said. "He didn't do anything."

Mazat gave her a piercing look and curled his lip. "Seems to me you're very interested in someone who didn't do anything." He motioned to the guardsmen.

One seized Xico's arms and marched him toward the village. The other followed with Iskra, gripping her arm so his fingers were nearly touching the bone.

29

Kaberco peered through the tiny window of the door to the cell. Iskra sat slumped on the stone floor, head on her knees. Her shoulders were shaking, whether from cold, fear, or silent sobs, he could not tell. But no matter. Any or all would serve his purpose. He narrowed his eyes and hardened his resolve. Liking or not, she was causing trouble. Sending her to work at the chicken farm hadn't been enough. He had to be harsh, to teach her a lesson. He resisted the urge to shout or pound the door. *Patience. Another hour alone will be enough to make her talk,* he thought. *Time for me to have a drink.*

He climbed the stairs to the main floor and opened the door to the room he used to meet with people. He unlocked a small cabinet and pulled out a bottle of Porrimian whiskey. He took a large mouthful and belched.

Now about Iskra, he thought. The boy was no problem. He'd questioned him, threatened him a little, had him escorted to the foot of the Guarded Path. It didn't seem like he knew Iskra at all. Just a Risker wandering the forest, got too close to the village, and stuck his nose into something he shouldn't have. But odd, if Iskra has made several trips to visit the Riskers, that this boy would have no knowledge of her at all.

Something had changed with her. Something had turned her from the timid, docile girl he knew into this young woman who walked with her head high and a smile on her face like she treasured a joyful secret. It had to be the Riskers. She's going to have to be kept away from them at all costs.

He didn't want whatever happened to infect the rest of the village.

The people were jittery, there was a restless undercurrent in the village. Like dry tinder in late summer, all it would take would be one spark to set the whole place ablaze.

Fortunately, most villagers were sheep who did what they were told. They understood the need to preserve safety at all costs. Or they were afraid of the consequences. Either way, they didn't break the rules.

He took another swallow from the bottle, enjoying the burning sensation as it flowed to his stomach and warmed him from the inside. Traders, now, traders are different. They weren't quite so concerned about safety. Maybe because they had to take chances every time they went on the road. Worst of all were the ones with licenses to trade with the Riskers.

He pulled a glass from the cabinet and filled it, then sat at the table, sipping the lavender liquid. He thought of the traders in the area who dealt with the Riskers. There were just three, two old men from Shinroo and that other one from Trofmose. Tarkio. The one who brought Iskra home after the caravan was attacked. *Maybe he knows something. I'll have to ask him.* He swirled the glass, watching the motion of the whiskey. *Kaberco, my boy,* he said to himself, *this has to stop. That old fool in Trofmose is getting soft, probably worn out by that young wife of his. The ephor in Shinroo has no desire to leave there. The others to the south follow like geese wherever they're driven. There's no one in my way if the Prime Konamei decides Trofmose needs a new ephor, one who knows how to keep the peace and the people under control.*

His eyes blazed as he thought of himself, ephor of Trofmose, living in that big house on the river, ruling a large town rather than a backwater village, enjoying the wealth that went with the post. Then he'd really be in a position to keep not just a village, but the whole region safe. No rebellious whippersnapper would get in his way. He sipped his whiskey, content to wait. Iskra could wait.

When an hour had passed, he returned to the basement jail, creeping along the dimly-lit corridors so Iskra wouldn't hear him, one hand on the chain around his shoulders to keep it from jingling. He was counting on scaring her into a confession. When he reached the cell door he peered in the window. It didn't seem as if she'd moved, but her trembling was a little less.

He put the key in the door and flung the door open. Iskra, sitting on the stone floor, jerked her head up so abruptly she banged it on the stone wall behind her. She gasped with pain and put her hand to her head.

"You'll have to be more careful, won't you?" Kaberco said. "Careful about so many things." He closed the door and leaned against it. "What were you doing with that Risker in the woods?"

"Nothing."

"Nothing?" His eyes met hers, searching for any signs of a lie.

"The wild flowers are so pretty now, they've gotten so full. I was walking past the farm and saw some beautiful blooms, with such vivid red petals, and thought I'd gather some. He—the boy, saw me, and we talked for a minute."

He studied her face. *Her lips aren't quivering like they used to when I questioned her. She seems stronger. Not a good sign.* "You talked for a minute?"

"Yes."

Kaberco laughed. "The two of you should agree on your stories before you tell them." He paused to let her think about that. "Don't try to come up with a new tale to tell. I'll tell you what the boy said. He said he'd never seen you before and had never spoken with you. He came to your aid when he thought you were being attacked. Now he's sorry he did, since he thought you are ugly and stupid. A scared rabbit, that's what he said." He watched in satisfaction as her lower lip trembled and her face reddened. "Well?" he said.

She wrapped her arms tightly around herself.

"What puzzles me," Kaberco said, "is how you met the Riskers in the first place."

She looked up, frowning. "I told you. We—"

"No, you didn't." He tried for a gentle tone. "I'm disappointed. You used to tell me things, to trust me. Now you're keeping a secret from me." He shook his head slowly. It wasn't hard for him to infuse a sad tone into his voice.

"Kaberco, if you please, I wanted to tell you."

"Why didn't you?"

"I was afraid."

He took a step closer to her. "Let's start at the beginning. When was your first visit to the Riskers?"

She folded her hands together in front of her and squeezed them together. "The day the caravan was attacked and I had to run up the mountain."

"I see. From what I recall of that story, a trader helped you and brought you home."

"He did."

"But first he took you to the Riskers? Why?"

She pushed her lower teeth out and clamped them in front of the others, pressing her lips firmly shut. At first Kaberco thought she wasn't going to answer.

Finally, she spoke. "I was scared and shook up, and my arm was bleeding. He thought I needed to eat something before walking home. He got the wife of one of his trading partners to feed me and bandage my arm, then brought me back."

"Didn't he know he was breaking all kinds of laws?" Kaberco tried to keep the anger from his voice.

She tugged the hair on the back of her head. "Probably. But he thought I needed help. I'm sure you'll agree he was thinking of my safety." She nodded her head as if to emphasize her point. "He was afraid other bandits were around."

"He decided to violate some of our strictest laws because you had some insignificant wounds and you were scared?" He clenched his fist. "Even if you were dying, he should have known better."

She jerked her chin up. "You're saying it's better to bleed to death or allow bandits to capture me than let a Risker help? Fine way to promote a safe society!" She glared at him. "If that's your idea of what's right, maybe it's better to die than to break the rules!"

Kaberco stared into her blazing eyes, shocked by her outburst. He'd never heard even a sharp word from Iskra before. What had gotten into her?

He put his hand in his pocket and withdrew it slowly, his fist clenched. She watched with wide eyes as he opened his hand to reveal a yellow-green ribbon. "Does this look familiar?"

"It's a ribbon."

"Whose ribbon?"

She shook her head. "How would I know?"

Kaberco ran the ribbon through his fingers. "It's just the right length to tie around a basket handle. And isn't this the color you use?" When she didn't answer, he pointed to the floor beside Iskra. "Is that your basket there? Where's your ribbon?"

He watched her carefully, noting her face grow pale when she saw no ribbon tied around the handle.

"I must have lost it somewhere."

"Don't you want to know where I found this one?"

Iskra opened her mouth but made no sound.

"It was in the closet where I keep my maps. Now how could it have come there? And what do you want with maps?"

He couldn't be sure, but she seemed to relax a little. "I don't care about maps." She sat a little straighter. "Lots of people use that color. Mine's probably on the path to the chicken farm."

"Yes. Maybe. Somehow, though, I doubt it." He studied her face, searching for any sign of defiance or deception. "You know that trespassing into the ephor's house and stealing documents is a taking offense." He paused for a moment. "As is talking about anything you saw there."

"Where do people go when they get taken?"

The suddenness of her question shocked him, and from the way her hand flew to her mouth, it startled her as well.

"What?"

"My friend Tavda was taken. What happened to her?"

He let out an irritated huff. She was bringing that up again? "If you know what's good for you, you'll stop trying to find out." He frowned. "Is that why you've been going to the Riskers? Well, you should have just asked me. The Riskers wouldn't take in our criminals. The Treaty won't allow it." He raised his voice slightly. "Don't you see? We have to do what it takes to build our safe and fair society."

"Safe and fair for whom?"

His eyes widened and he paused to consider what next to say.

A knock on the door broke into his deliberations.

Kaberco opened the door and put his head out, then stood back to admit Luza.

"Kaberco, I had no idea," she said, wringing her hands.

"You don't know all of it," he answered. "There's something funny going on. Your daughter says she wanted to collect some wild flowers, and met a Risker by chance. He says they never spoke."

"Flowers? Since when has she been interested in flowers?"

Luza shook her head. "She's been like this lately, secretive, strange, you know." She scowled at Iskra. "Look at you, a prisoner in a jail cell. You think of no one but yourself. You don't care what shame you bring on me."

Kaberco watched Iskra flinch at her mother's words and lay her head on her knees. She's weakening, he thought.

"You are her mother," he said to Luza. "She shouldn't have secrets from you."

"I try to talk to her, to correct her, to keep her safe, but she still runs off. She never considers me."

"And meets Risker boys in the forest." His tone became hard and accusing.

"Shameful," Luza said, shaking her head. "Shocking."

"Do you not understand that is forbidden?" he asked Iskra. "Do you understand why?"

She nodded.

"I don't think you do. Edalia has told you only part of the story. Yes, they live differently, and are barbarians. But do you know what happens when a Risker mates with one of us?"

Iskra turned her face toward him and he knew he had her full attention. "The child, if it lives, is a monster. Sometimes born with no head. Or no arms. Or extra arms. The mother usually dies in childbirth. What do you think of that?"

Iskra closed her eyes and mouthed the word "No."

Kaberco watched her closely, then turned to Luza. "What do you think we should do with her?"

"I don't know. I can't control her," Luza said.

He shook his head and spread a scowl across his face. "What's going on, Luza? First your husband, now her." He gestured at Iskra.

Luza shank back. "Kaberco, you know I've been loyal to the Prime Konamei and our country my whole life. I've tried to be safe, keep my family safe, work hard. You know that."

"Things aren't always as they appear." He pulled his dagger from his belt, held it up to the light, then replaced it.

"You need to work with me. Keeping your daughter in line is your responsibility. If you keep order in your own household, you help me keep order, so the village stays safe."

Luza thought for a moment. "Maybe an early marriage would settle her down?"

Kaberco put his hand over his mouth and rubbed the lower half of his face, concealing his smile. This was too easy. He nodded slowly, as if considering Luza's question. "You know, that's a good idea. Early marriage. I'll talk to Edalia. If you give your consent, we can get this arranged before the year is out."

He yanked Iskra to her feet. "Go home with your mother. You'll do as you're told, get married, have some children, and stop running off. Do you hear? Because the next time, there will be no coming back. You will be taken."

30

Iskra rose before dawn five days later. She hadn't slept much for almost a week. She'd tossed and turned each night, burning with shame, replaying the humiliating scene with Kaberco. Did Xico really say she was ugly and stupid? Her heart raced, her mouth went dry. She knew if she didn't act now, she'd doom herself to a lifetime of misery, of never knowing the truth.

She dressed silently, in agony the whole time that her mother would awaken and catch her. Was her mother stirring? Iskra held her breath, then let it out slowly when she heard her mother's even breathing. She crept out of the cottage into the street. Her one thought was to get to Xico, to find out what he really told Kaberco. She had to know. He lied about not knowing her. *Was the other part, that he thinks I am ugly and stupid, a lie as well?* Just thinking of Xico saying those words about her lit a burning sensation in her stomach. *Probably when Kaberco questioned him, he realized I wasn't worth all the trouble marrying a villager would cause, that we'd have a monster child. He realized I'm not good enough for him.*

Mist swirled between the cottages, obscuring everything more than a few feet away. *Good,* she thought. *I just might be able to do this. I can get up to the camp, talk to Xico. If he doesn't love me, then I'll know. I can maybe get to Mazat's before it's too late and do what I need to do to make peace with the village. But if Kaberco lied, then I need to think hard about becoming a Risker. There won't be anything for me here.*

She flitted cautiously from cottage to cottage, making her way to the edge of the village, to the back gate. Presently she saw the guardsmen open the gate and go out to patrol the outside.

Clenching her teeth, she walked to the gate and slipped through. She sought cover under the trees of the forest and headed for the dairy farm. The chilly breeze made a hissing sound in the leaves, like thousands of snakes readying to attack.

Xico had told her there were other ways to the Risker camp, but she only knew one. The Guarded Path was watched, and not just by the Riskers. She'd have to take a chance on going by the waterfall, even though she didn't really know the way. She assumed the stream would lead to the top of the hill, and from there she could find the camp.

As she approached the dairy, she moved cautiously, not even wanting to breathe. The mist parted and she saw a guardsman leaning against the wall of the barn. She inched her way toward the stream. She crept deeper into the woods, and only got onto the trail when she was well out of sight of the forest's edge.

She took a deep breath and began the climb. Then she heard the sound that set her pulse to racing: footsteps on the path behind her. She began to run.

"She's moving," she heard a deep voice say.

"She won't get away," answered a raspy one.

I'm such an idiot, she thought. *Of course Kaberco would have his men following me.* As she raced up the slope, she wondered. *Should I hide under the waterfall? But what if they see me go in? Then I'll be trapped.* The wind picked up, making a dull roaring noise that intensified like the bellow of a wild animal, then ebbed to a softer moan. Her heart pounded as she clambered up the hill. She came to the waterfall and began scaling the rocks. She had nearly reached the top when her pursuers reached the foot of the waterfall and climbed after her.

"She's a goat, this one," the deep voice said.

She slipped when her foot dislodged a loose stone. A cry of pain from below told her it had struck one of the men behind her.

"You'll pay for that," he shouted.

Gasping for breath, Iskra reached the top and looked around. Now where? She saw a trail and sprinted up it. A stitch in her side made every breath a stabbing pain. The trees were silhouettes in the mist. She put her head down and ran.

Glancing over her shoulder, she saw that the men chasing her had reached the top of the waterfall. Their footsteps grew louder. They were gaining on her, about to catch up with her.

Something farther up the hill was crashing through the underbrush. Xico, come to her rescue? She veered toward the noise, then jumped back when she heard the roar. That wasn't the wind, she realized. A moan escaped her lips. A giant warboar with three-foot tusks rushed at her, its tiny eyes blazing red in its massive head. Iskra froze in place, afraid to flee, knowing she couldn't outrun the charging beast. It leapt over a downed tree, its hoofs cracking fallen branches under its weight. She lunged to hide behind a tree but was too late. One of its enormous pointed tusks grazed her thigh, sliced through her clothing and slashed deep into the flesh. She fell, shrieking, clutching her leg.

The warboar paused. It turned and pawed the ground. Iskra stifled a scream. The two guardsmen approached, shouting at her. The warboar roared and charged the guardsmen. They turned and fled down the trail, the warboar in pursuit.

Iskra pulled herself to her feet and limped up the trail.

Blood ran down her leg and the ground lurched under her feet. She clutched a tree for support. The last thing she remembered was seeing a figure appear out of the mist on the trail above her.

ISKRA HEARD murmuring voices somewhere nearby. Afraid to open her eyes, she lay still, listening. What is this place? There was a familiar odor, a pleasant one that gave her a sense of well-being, fresh bread and drying herbs. She was lying on some kind of bed. Not made of crackling straw like she was used to, but something softer that cradled and warmed her. She felt herself drifting back to sleep but willed herself to stay awake. The warboar had cut her leg. Why didn't she feel any pain? She was about to move her hand to her thigh but stopped when she heard the door open.

Light footsteps came into the room. A cool hand rested on her forehead. "No fever."

Iskra opened one eye to look at the speaker. "Cillia?"

"Yes, it's me. You've had quite a morning. Let me see your leg." She pushed the blanket over to the side. Iskra blushed as she realized she was wearing only the top of her shift. The rest had been cut off and she had no clothing on underneath.

"I'm sorry, all of your clothes were soaked with blood. We had to take them off you." Cillia began to gently peel a bandage that went from Iskra's knee all the way to her groin. "Can you spread your legs a little so I can reach to the inside of your thigh? This may hurt a bit."

Iskra clutched a handful of blankets and grit her teeth. "A bit" was putting it mildly. She was grateful for the pain so she didn't have to wonder who the other part of the "we" was who took her clothes off. The bandage pulled at the drying blood, bringing to life the nerves that had been mercifully silent up to now.

"Good, the bleeding has almost stopped." Cillia tossed the bandage into a bucket. She wiped the blood from Iskra's leg with a damp cloth. Then she pulled her amulet from her pocket and passed it over the length of Iskra's wound, chanting softly. When she finished, she dabbed some herbs mixed with oil on the wound, dabbing gently to make sure the mixture adhered to Iskra's skin. "If you don't mind, it would be best to let that wound be open to the air, just so it can dry a little." She adjusted the sheet to cover Iskra as much as possible, but Iskra still felt very exposed. "I'll get you something to drink."

"Cillia, how did I get here?" Iskra asked.

"We'll talk later," Cillia said. "You need to rest. Try to go back to sleep." She left the room and closed the door behind her.

Iskra stared blankly at the door. She heard Cillia say, "She's awake now." She was answered by deeper voices, men's voices.

Her eyes widened at the thought of anyone else coming into the room, seeing her exposed. Xico. What if he came in? Funny how that thought didn't cause the same embarrassment she felt when Cillia was working on her wound. The thought of Xico was a tingling one, an enticing one. Then the memory of what Kaberco told her came back. The sting of the wound on her leg was nothing to the stab in her soul at the idea Xico had changed his mind. Or never loved her in the first place. She closed her eyes tightly. She couldn't bear to think of Xico any more.

THE WARMTH in the room woke her. Another hot summer day, she thought. Then she noticed she was buried under a heavy blanket. Someone's been in here while I've been sleeping, she thought, alarmed. She shifted, and realized she felt no pain in her leg. She threw the blanket back and gasped at the sight of her leg. No gaping wound, no throbbing flesh. Just a thin red scar that ran from knee to groin, thin as if it had been cut with a fine knife rather than gouged by a warboar's tusk.

She covered herself hastily with the blanket at the sound of the door opening, holding it tight under her chin. Cillia entered the room, carrying a pale blue dress over her arm. "Are you feeling better? Your wound has healed nicely."

"Yes, thank you, Cillia. I can hardly believe it."

"Don't thank me, thank the sky-god. He's the source of the power." She set the dress down on the bed. "I'm afraid your things are ruined. Here's an old dress of Fialka's you can have, and an underskirt." She paused, frowning. "The dress is old and faded and might pass for gray in the twilight. As soon as you get home, you'll have to hide it." When Iskra nodded, she continued, "Why don't you get dressed and come have something to eat?"

Iskra was suddenly hungry. She sat up, letting the blanket fall to her lap. "Right away, I'll be there."

Five minutes later she walked into the kitchen, feeling a little lightheaded and weak. Xico jumped up and seized Iskra in his arms and held her as if he would never let her go. She clung to him with a sob.

"All right, Xico, let the girl sit down. Seems to me she'd like some food," Osip said.

Xico released Iskra and helped her to a seat at the table. *Maybe he doesn't hate me,* she thought. He sat next to her, not letting go of her hand.

"I'm so grateful for your help," she said, looking at Cillia. "How did I get here?"

"Tikul was guarding that approach to the camp," Osip said. "He heard a warboar and went to see if he could kill it. They usually aren't this low in the mountains, not in Rozhal. Next month, maybe. But not now." He smiled at Cillia as she set a bowl of stew in from of him and picked up his spoon.

"Tikul heard the roaring, then the sound of a charging warboar. He knew it was after someone. Then he found you, clinging to a tree, barely conscious, blood pouring from your leg. He bound your leg as best he could, then brought you here."

"Just in time," Cillia said. "You were as white as the petals of a daisy. I had a time, getting the bleeding to stop. But you're mended now, as much as you will be."

Osip leaned forward. "What we want to know is why you came here at all. Xico told us what happened last week."

"He doesn't know all of it. They've decided to arrange a marriage for me."

All three of her listeners gasped. "They can't do that, you're only fifteen," Cillia said.

"They can if my mother agrees. And she does. She says an early marriage will settle me down." She stifled a sob and stared at her yet-untasted stew. "How could she do this to me?"

"Have they said who they want you to marry?" Cillia asked.

Iskra closed her eyes. "Not yet. But when they do, I won't have any choice." She pushed her bowl away from her and put her head in her hands.

"No!" Xico dropped his spoon into his bowl. "You can't."

Osip narrowed his eyes. "What I don't understand is why they are going to such lengths? That seems a little extreme, don't you think, to arrange a marriage for a fifteen-year-old?"

"Kaberco knows Xico lied when he said he didn't know me," she answered, not raising her head. "Not knowing what Xico had said, I told Kaberco that we met by accident in the forest and talked for a few minutes. He laughed at me, said we needed to agree on our stories."

"I'm so sorry, Iskra," Xico said. He put his hand on her shoulder. "I thought it was better just to deny everything, rather than just part of it. Then I wouldn't have to remember any story I made up."

But did you have to tell Kaberco you think I'm ugly and stupid? If you didn't love me, you should have told me. She longed to be alone with Xico, to question him, but dreaded his answers. She sat up straight, picked up her mug, and drank. *I have to know.*

As soon as Cillia finished her stew, Osip said, "I need your help with one of the cows. She's acting funny, won't stand up."

Cillia nodded and stood up. "Xico, you sit with Iskra while she eats. Don't go anywhere; wait for us to come back." She picked up the basket with her herbs and amulets and followed Osip out of the door.

31

Cillia followed Osip to the stalls where the cows sheltered. It was no surprise to her to see a perfectly healthy cow, standing placidly, chewing her cud. She raised an eyebrow at Osip.

"It was the best excuse I could come up with," he said. "I didn't want the boy coming along to help. We need to talk."

"I know. Before this happened, I was ready to do whatever I could to send her away." Cillia stroked the cow's face. "I still think it would be best."

"For Xico, that's for sure. But an arranged marriage at fifteen? I've heard they sometimes marry young girls in the village to older men. Not a fate I'd want for little Iskra."

Cillia shuddered. "Nor I." She sat down heavily on a bale of hay. "But she and Xico have got to stay away from each other. Did you see how he hugged her?"

"That wasn't the first time, I'll wager. She clung to him like she was coming home."

"It will break his heart." Her throat ached, hurting for her youngest son.

"He won't be the first young man to have a broken heart. He'll get over it."

Cillia shook her head. "You don't sound like you believe that."

"Woman, why is it you can see right through me? You're right, this will cut deep."

Cillia thought of how to dredge up the will to tell her son to give up a girl he clearly treasured. She looked at Osip, seeing her own torment echoed in his blue eyes. Cillia noticed the silver threads in Osip's dark hair, the smile lines around his eyes. *Xico is much like him,* she thought. *Xico will never reach his age.*

She jumped at the thought and shivered. Where did that come from?

Osip looked at her. "What's wrong?"

"Nothing." She twisted her hands together. "Osip, is it really impossible for them to be together?"

"Cillia, there's no way. The village will never allow it. They don't want to allow for any chance of the prophecy coming true." He held out his hands, palms up. "Do you think our elder would allow it, either? Not likely." He shook his head. "And our Xico, what kind of life would he have? He'd have to take little Iskra and make their own camp somewhere high in the mountains. That's a hard life, and a lonely one. Not what I want for either of them."

She let out a long sigh. "Well, we'd better go tell them to end it now. Better sooner than later."

MEANWHILE, Iskra told Xico about her time in the cell, how Kaberco questioned her, and the decision to marry her off. She couldn't summon the nerve to mention the things Kaberco claimed that Xico had said.

"Is that all?" Xico asked.

"That's what happened."

"Are you sure about that?"

She looked down at her hands, hands she held clenched in her lap, trying to keep her fingers from twitching. "Why?"

"Because you seem so upset. Were you really that frightened when he questioned you?"

"I was. He could have had me taken, you know." She shivered at the thought.

Xico pulled her to him and pressed his forehead against the top of her head. "That's a horrible thought."

She heard the anger and fear in his voice and pulled away from him, wrinkling her forehead. "Really?" She wished she could believe him. "Would you really be sad?"

"Yes, really." He answered her sharply and frowned. When she made no response, he said, "I don't know how I'd go on without you."

"Then why—?" She stopped, biting her lip, too afraid of the answer to ask the question.

"Why what?" He put his hand under her chin and raised her face so he could look into her eyes. "Please tell me."

She gulped and opened her mouth to answer. No words came. Her fear that he would laugh, that he would admit to all Kaberco had said kept her silent.

"What did he do to you?" Xico's voice hardened. "Did he hurt you?"

"No, he didn't."

"Then what? You can tell me." He leaned in and kissed her forehead. "Just one word at a time, just say it."

"Did you have to tell him that you think me ugly and stupid?" Her voice trembled a little as she repeated Kaberco's words. Once she started, the words tumbled out like water racing over a waterfall. "And nothing more than a scared rabbit, worthy of scorn?"

"Iskra!" Xico grabbed her hands in his. "I didn't say that. None of that. What I did say, as sarcastically as I could, was that I was surprised he would think I would waste my time on a village girl, and one as young as you, to boot." He looked deep into her eyes. "Believe me. I love you. I was trying to protect you. I never thought he would twist what I said and spin it into a tale I never told." He cupped her cheek in his hand. "I want you in my life however long it is. Once my parents agree, there's nothing to stand in our way. Nothing." He tipped his forehead to gently touch hers.

His nearness was affecting her breathing, making it come in shorter, quicker breaths, almost as if she were running for her life. She wanted so much to believe him. She'd become braver, less afraid, since she'd met Xico. Being with him made her feel more alive; sharing her thoughts with him made her feel more complete. And touching him made her feel an intense desire she never believed possible. She'd never be able to love anyone else.

They sat in silence, arms around each other until Cillia and Osip returned. Then Xico rose and carried the dirty dishes to a shelf along the wall.

"Sit down, Xico," Osip said. "We need to talk with you both."

Xico resumed his place on the bench next to Iskra, and his parents sat across from them.

"I'll get straight to the point." Osip looked at Iskra, then Xico. "You know villagers and Riskers are forbidden to mingle, and you both know why."

"Yes," Xico said. "It's against the rules."

"It's worse than that," Iskra said. "Any babies they have will either die or be monsters with no heads or extra arms."

Cillia and Osip looked at each other, shaking their heads. "Where did you hear that?" Cillia asked.

"Kaberco and my mother."

Cillia sighed. "As much as I hate to say your mother told you something that's not true, I have to. Way back, when the land was being resettled and Tlefas was being formed, there were many mixed marriages. The children were perfectly fine." She raised her hands in the air and dropped them with a shake of her head. "Think about it. We all came from the same country, hundreds of years ago."

"But why did they tell me that?" Iskra looked from Osip to Cillia, puzzled and confused. She felt the weight of the lies she'd been told like a rock on her soul.

"They are trying, in any way they can, to get you to follow the rules."

"But why do we have to follow these rules anyway?" Xico said.

"Son, we do. This is bigger than you, or Iskra, or Kaberco, or our camp, or the whole village of Gishin."

"I don't see how."

"I'm not sure I fully understand, myself," Osip said. "But think about it this way: If it wasn't terribly important to keep you two apart, would they be going to all this trouble? There must be some horrible consequences that you can't see. They just want to save you from them."

Iskra thought of Kaberco's mocking laughter and found it hard to believe he was interested in helping her.

Next to her, Xico stirred. "I don't think so. I think all they want is for the villagers to have no idea that life can be any different for them. Then the people in power, like Kaberco, can keep it."

"He's right," Iskra said. "They aren't trying to save us from anything. Except from them, what they'll do to us."

"It's not just what they do, but what you do, Iskra," put in Cillia. "It's not their fault you had your leg gouged by a warboar. You chose to come here." Iskra blushed and looked at the floor. Cillia had a point. Just leaving the village was dangerous. Had she followed the rules, she wouldn't have been hurt.

Osip studied his calloused hands and the dirt under his fingernails. "Xico, we worked hard to build what we have. If you keep on this way, then what? Will the Prime Konamei decide to go back on his agreement with us, with all the

Riskers? Or will he just decide to make an example out of our camp? We can't fight off his entire army." He took a deep breath. "Are you really willing to violate the Treaty and put all of us in jeopardy?"

Xico clenched his fists. "But this is just not right."

"I'm not saying it is. I'm just telling the two of you that it would be better for you, for everyone, if you don't see each other again." He stood up from the table. "We'll leave you alone to say goodbye. I'll step over to your brother's house. Tarkio's there, and he can see that Iskra gets back safely."

Cillia stood and walked around the table. She laid a hand on Iskra's shoulder and kissed the top of her head. "I'm so sorry."

She and Osip walked out the door.

Iskra stared at Xico for a long moment after they left. "Now what?"

"We say goodbye."

She felt the strength fall from her, not gradually like the leaves drop from a tree in the fall, but suddenly, like a boulder falling from the face of a cliff. She sagged forward and clenched her eyes shut, her breath coming in shallow gasps. She felt as though she were drowning, that all the life was draining out of her.

Xico put his hand on her shoulder, massaging it gently. "Not forever. But I have to do as my da says. I'll just have to convince him to change his mind. When he does, you can move here."

"I'd have to leave the village? You couldn't move there?"

He stroked her cheek, his green eyes regretful. "No."

That he didn't bother to explain told her what she asked was impossible. But so was her leaving the village. The Riskers wouldn't take her in. No one would break the treaty.

Her head drooped as a feeling of desolation seeped through her as she realized she had to return to the village, to smooth things over with her mother and Kaberco. But then what? The best she could hope for was a delay in whatever marriage they were arranging for her. She shuddered as she tried to imagine being married to anyone but Xico. They'll probably give me some weasel like Oyamel. Not someone I could love. Or even respect. Her stomach twisted and cramped at the thought.

The door opened to admit Osip and Tarkio.

Iskra stood up. "Goodbye, Xico," she muttered. She stroked his face gently, feeling as though she were ripping her soul in two as she turned away.

With a deep breath, she staggered to the door. She turned for one look and saw the promise in his eyes, a promise meant to reassure her. She turned away, unable to stop from feeling it was an empty promise, never to be fulfilled.

32

He's angry with me, Iskra thought. *He won't even look at me.* The rustling leaves overhead sounded like the voices of accusers, spitting vile abuse on her head. *I've lost Xico. Now Tarkio hates me.* She looked at the back of Tarkio's head as he strode along the trail, putting his feet down hard on the ground. He was walking so quickly she could barely keep up.

"If you please, Tarkio."

He stopped and looked over his shoulder at her with a hard expression on his face.

"Tarkio." She paused, fumbling for words. "I'm so sorry I got you into this."

"You?" His jaw dropped. "You got me into this?"

"Well, yes. You shouldn't have to keep escorting me back and forth. I'm sure you have other things to do."

Tarkio let out a harsh laugh and turned to keep walking.

"Wait," she said. "I want to know something."

He paused, and without turning, asked, "What?"

She tried to look into his face but the afternoon sun was in her eyes. "I know you said you have a license to trade with the Riskers. 'Just business' is what you called it. But your relationship with Xico and his family seems like more than that."

Tarkio sighed, then turned to face her. "When I was young, my mam got sick. Very sick. She could barely get out of bed. My da did all he could to care for her. He didn't trade as much so he could be home more." He looked past Iskra in the direction of the Risker camp. "He had a license to trade with the Riskers and had been dealing with Osip for years. When he and Cillia heard about my mam, they offered to help."

He reached up and pulled a leaf off a low-hanging branch. "You can imagine how my da felt. He knew Cillia could possibly heal my mam, but if anyone ever heard of it, they could both be taken. In the end, my parents decided to let Cillia help in another way."

"Which was?"

"By that time, I was twelve, and old enough to be my da's apprentice. He took me with him, trading. Instead of taking me on all his trading runs, he brought me here, to Osip and Cillia. They let me stay with them and taught me all about honey and archery and living in the wild. Cillia, well, she wasn't exactly my mother, but she did for me what my mother would have, had she been able."

He took a deep breath. "Meanwhile, da started spending more time with mam. He came and got me one day, so I could say goodbye." He let out a long sigh. "Cillia gave my mam her last wish, that I wouldn't have to watch her waste away before my eyes. Xico and his sisters and brothers took the place of the ones I never had; in a way, they are my family."

"I see."

His face darkened. "No, you don't see. I don't want them hurt. It's one thing for me to come here, I'm not breaking any rules. But you?" He snorted. "I'm the fool who brought you here in the first place, which makes this my fault. But now you need to stop. Think about the danger you are putting all of them in." His eyes were cold and hard as he stared at her. "Think about someone else other than yourself. Grow up and do your duty."

He crumbled the leaf in his hand and flung it to the ground. Then he strode down the trail.

She realized that if he wasn't furious with her before, now he was. What could she say or do to make things right? She brushed angrily at her bangs, not sure if her anger was more at Tarkio, Xico, or herself. She certainly deserved it, falling for a Risker, getting everyone in the village all riled up. *Now I've lost Xico.* Her lip curled as a sour heat churned in her belly. *I'm such a failure. I deserve whoever they make me marry.*

When they got within sight of the edge of the forest, he stopped. "Now listen," he said. "I need you to do what I tell you. Go straight home, don't try to hide yourself. When they ask you, tell them you got up early because you couldn't sleep. You went for a walk. Then someone started chasing you and you were frightened, so you ran. Then the warboar chased them away. You got lost and have spent the rest of the time trying to find your way back. You didn't see anyone or talk to anyone. Is that clear?"

"Yes. That's what I'll say."

"Iskra." His tone softened. "Please. You have to stay away from Xico, from the Riskers. For everyone's sake." He pointed toward the village. "Now go. I'll wait here until you get to the lane."

She gulped, then tried to nerve herself up to leave the shelter of the woods. She watched the back of the dairy farm. Put one foot in front of the other, she told herself. Seeing no one gave her enough courage to take the first tentative step. No shouts, no barking dogs. She took one step, then another. Still nothing. She concentrated on one step after another until she passed the farm and reached the lane that led into the village.

With a sigh of relief, Iskra approached the door to the cottage. *At least this time I'll get home without causing a scandal.* She opened the front door. She had one foot inside when she froze, her muscles tensing, her stomach clenching. Sitting on stools around the table were Luza, Edalia and Kaberco.

"Come in," Luza said. "And sit down. We've been waiting for you."

Kaberco stood up and walked toward her. "Yes, we have." He pulled the still motionless Iskra into the room and shut the door behind her. He pushed her toward the table.

She wrapped her arms around herself and walked to the table, hunched over. She sank onto a stool and closed her eyes. The air was warm and stuffy, increasing her sense of being trapped.

Luza began. "Where were you, Iskra? I was so worried when I woke up and you were gone."

Iskra didn't open her eyes. "I couldn't sleep, and I got up to take a walk."

"That's a long walk you took. It's nearly sundown." Luza pointed her finger at Iskra. "Mazat needed your work today, and you didn't show up. How could you do that?"

"I was walking. I heard shouting and was frightened. I ran into the forest. Someone was chasing me. I ran, I don't know where I ran. Then a warboar charged whoever was after me, and they ran off." She opened her eyes wide and looked at her mother. "Maybe they were bandits."

"Bandits?" Kaberco said. "I don't think so." He took a step closer to her. "Then what?"

"Then I was lost. I wandered around, got tired. Sat down under a tree and must have fallen asleep. After I woke up, I didn't know which way to go. It took a long time to find my way back."

"You're sure of that? That's what happened?" Kaberco

spoke softly, which made Iskra more nervous than if he'd shouted.

"Yes." She dug her fingers into her arms and huddled on the narrow stool. Why were they all staring at her?

"This is hard for me to understand," Kaberco said. "You say you got lost. All you had to do was walk downhill, and you'd end up in the village. Didn't that occur to you?"

"Yes, but if you please, when you get high enough up, there are valleys. I must have gotten confused about how I got there."

Kaberco raised his eyebrows. Iskra held her breath. What did I say wrong?

"And you say you saw no one? You spoke to no one?"

She sighed. "That's right."

Kaberco turned and spoke to Edalia and Luza. "I think we have a problem here. Do you see what it is?" Without waiting for an answer, he continued. "She says she was frightened but ran the opposite direction of where she'd find help. She says she got lost in a valley. But you have to hike half an hour or more to find the valleys. What do you know of the valleys up in the mountains?" He stared at her for a moment, then continued. "Just to let you know, you weren't chased by bandits. They were my men, guarding the dairy farm. There have been reports of people by the stream that comes down the hill. One that looked like a girl."

She willed herself to not respond, to not let her eyes flicker or her mouth quiver.

"When they saw a girl sneaking through the woods, they chased after her. They got a good enough look at her to know it was you."

"I told you I was there and was chased. I didn't know they were your men."

"But here's the problem. They say the warboar charged twice. The first time at you."

"Oh?" She forced herself to look at Kaberco with wide, innocent eyes.

"What's more, they saw it gouge your leg. And they saw all the blood."

She shrugged. "They must be mistaken. It all happened so fast."

"Really?"

His smirk made her heart pound faster and her hands sweat.

What does he know?

"My men returned later, with five others. They thought they would try to find you and bring you back, if the warboar hadn't eaten you first. Imagine their surprise when they found a trail of blood that led a few steps along the path, then a pool of blood under a tree, and marks as if someone had collapsed there. But no body. Just some muddled footsteps. A mystery, don't you think?"

Iskra clenched her hands together, trying to keep them from shaking. "That would be mysterious, if they were telling the truth. But if I was gouged by a warboar and lost so much blood, then why am I able to walk? Why am I not in pain?"

Kaberco walked around the table and put a hand on Luza's shoulder. "She asks some good questions, don't you think? Maybe we need to investigate this further."

Luza nodded and crossed her arms. "Yes, we need to know the truth. I'm not so sure she's telling it."

Iskra stiffened and looked at her mother with wide eyes. "Mam, don't you believe me?"

"Why should I believe you? You sneak off in the early morning and are gone for hours. Then you come back here with some story of getting chased by a warboar and being lost in the woods."

"But that's what happened."

"You also say you saw no one, spoke to no one. That's clearly a lie."

She flinched at the harshness in Kaberco's voice and gripped her hands tightly together under the table. "What do I need to do so you'll believe me?"

Edalia spoke for the first time. "Stand up."

Iskra complied.

"Pull your skirt up." Edalia pointed at Iskra's dress.

"What?"

"Pull your skirt up. We want to see your leg, where the warboar cut you."

"But it didn't."

"Then prove it." When she hesitated, Edalia repeated her command, more sharply. "Prove it."

With shaking hands, Iskra pulled her skirt up over her knees. "Higher," Edalia said. Iskra inched the skirt higher, closing her eyes when she heard her mother gasp.

"She's never had that scar before," Luza said.

Kaberco grabbed her leg. "Look at this scar. Where did you get this?"

Iskra started to sputter but could get no words out.

"How high does it go?" Luza jerked Iskra's skirt up, exposing Iskra's nakedness and the scar that ran nearly up to her groin. She twisted a handful of the material in her hand and jerked Iskra toward herself, putting her face up against hers. "Where did you get this?"

"I—"

"You saw no one, huh?" Kaberco pulled Iskra from her mother and gave her a shake. "Luza, is this one of Iskra's dresses?"

He let go of her so suddenly she fell back against the table. Iskra felt the room spinning around her and she thought she might fall. She looked at her mother, begging her silently for help.

"No, it is not. Sure, the color is about right. But it's not the gray we wear. That's a faded blue. Look at the cut, the way it nips in at the waist. That wasn't sewn by any village tailor." Luza took a step closer and pulled at the skirt. "See this underskirt? White, not gray." She pushed Iskra against the table. "Risker clothes, and no shift. What am I to think?"

Iskra pulled her chin up and stared straight ahead. So now they know, or at least they guessed.

Kaberco jerked her again. "The warboar gored you. Then what?"

Iskra remained silent.

"You may as well tell us. It's obvious you went to the Riskers."

Her heart hammering, Iskra considered. They knew where she'd been. Would the truth help, or hurt? "I did," Iskra admitted.

"You see?" Kaberco turned to Luza and Edalia. "You didn't want to believe me." He looked at Iskra. "Why did you go there?"

"Well," Iskra said, "it's like this. After the warboar charged your men, I passed out. The next thing I knew I was in the Risker camp. One of the women used herbs to heal my leg. My clothes were torn and covered in blood, so they gave me this dress to wear." She held out a foot. "You can still see the traces of blood on my boot."

Kaberco sneered. "You expect us to believe that? You've had plenty of time to concoct a fairy tale for us. I see it all now. You went to the Riskers, and they used their evil spells to heal you."

"I'm sure you'll agree the spells were hardly evil if they healed me." She shook her head. "Far better than any supposed healer here."

Luza shrieked. "How can you speak to our ephor like that?"

"How should I speak to someone who threatens me and twists my words?" She noticed a flicker in Kaberco's eyes, like a fleeting sensation of fear or doubt. Then it was gone.

Kaberco stepped toward her. "If that's the whole truth, then why didn't you just tell us?"

"I-I was frightened." That, at least, was the truth. Iskra raised her face to look Kaberco in the face. "I know it's forbidden to go to the Riskers, and I knew you'd be angry if you found out where I was."

"It's a little late for you to expect us to believe you."

Iskra stared at Kaberco, mouth hanging open. What had happened to Kaberco, who had been such a kind friend her whole life? How could he speak to her with such a harsh tone, glare at her with such accusing eyes?

Kaberco laughed, the mocking sound cutting through Iskra like a spear. "The time for us to listen to your lies is over. We don't know what you've been doing, but it's going to stop. If you were sixteen, we would have taken you. Since you are underage, and your mother can't control you, we'll deal with this another way."

Iskra swallowed hard and sat up a little straighter. "What do I need to do?" *I'll have to go along with whatever it is,* she thought, *just to get them to calm down and give me some time.*

Edalia answered. "We've arranged a marriage for you. Your mother has given consent, and you'll be married on the next village wedding day."

"But that's next month," Iskra said.

"In just over two weeks. You'll be too busy to be sneaking off to do who-knows-what," Edalia said.

Kaberco leered at her. "It's a good thing your new husband won't be bothered when he hears you came back from the Risker camp half-dressed. He's just happy to be getting a young bride."

Iskra felt the walls of the room closing in on her. "Who am I marrying?"

"You'd like to know, wouldn't you?" Kaberco paused. "Should we tell her, or let it be a surprise?"

Edalia answered. "You'll be marrying Udbash."

Bits of straw poked Iskra as she lay on her bed, each provoking a memory from the day. Her flight up the hill. The warboar attack. Cillia's healing touch. Xico's sad eyes as he said goodbye. Tarkio's anger. The humiliating scene with Kaberco. The horror of her looming marriage to Udbash. She writhed at the thought, wishing she could sink into her straw and never emerge.

They don't see, Iskra thought. *All they've done is convince me they are wrong. If the Riskers have evil magic, then magic is real.* She got up from her straw and looked at her mother snoring gently, sound asleep. Iskra turned to peek out the window. Dabrey was high in the sky, a perfect half moon on its way to becoming full. Zlu was just rising, a half moon starting to wane. Together they gave enough light for Iskra to see the shadow of a man standing near the house across the alley, watching her house.

Yes, Kaberco's making sure I don't go anywhere.

She looked again at the night sky, at Dabrey's shining half.

Half. That's what I am without Xico. She choked back a sob. *Now that his parents won't let me see him, now I know how much I love him.* She felt numb and empty, desolation replacing the joy she'd felt only hours ago.

Udbash. They want me to marry that filthy man with yellow teeth. A man who delights in making chickens die a slow and painful death. How long before that's what I want for myself? She swallowed hard to get the taste of bile out of her mouth.

Xico's parents will take me in. They have to. She shook her head. *They won't. They can't. Maybe Tarkio will help me get away, maybe all the way to Anbodu. If only I could get there, I could lose myself in the capital. Maybe there's someone who could make me fake papers. But how do I leave? They'll be watching me now.*

She returned to her straw and lay down. *The problem is how to escape. If I try and they catch me, they'll take me for sure. If I get away, I could run into another warboar. Or a bandit.*

Her thoughts ran around her head, chasing in circles like a whirlwind, dizzying her with false hopes and possible disasters.

Even if I make it to the camp, Cillia and Osip might turn me away. I wouldn't blame them. They only want what's best for their son. She stifled a sob as she realized that's not something she could say about her mother and herself.

She forced her thoughts back the to Riskers. *The elder wouldn't let me stay. Xico at least has a family, people who love and support him. How wonderful life would be, to live surrounded by people who really care for you. He'd get over me soon enough.* She buried her face in her straw and screamed, hoping her mother wouldn't hear. She clenched her teeth tightly to keep from sobbing.

When she was calmer, she realized she had only one other hope. She reached under her bag of straw and pulled out her amulet. It glowed softly green in the moonlight.

"Oh, sky-god, please help me." She felt as though a tiny drop of peace dripped into her troubled mind. She wiped away a tear and clutched the amulet in her fist, staring at the faint moonlight on the floor until she fell asleep.

33

A few hours earlier, Tarkio stroked the rough wood of the bench he sat on, wondering about those who'd sat there before him, waiting for Kaberco. He didn't like the whole situation with Iskra and Xico. He pounded the heel of his hand against his forehead. Stupid, stupid Tarkio, for getting all this started. There must be something he could do to help Iskra. Kaberco was fair, that much was sure. But Tarkio was after mercy, not justice, and he wasn't sure he could expect that from Kaberco. He hoped the ephor's absence had nothing to do with her.

He didn't have much of a plan to help Iskra. But maybe, if Kaberco was interested in the news Tarkio had for him, it might give him an opening to speak on Iskra's behalf. It wasn't long before he heard the door open and saw Kaberco stride in, chain jingling, a scowl on his rugged face.

This doesn't bode well, Tarkio thought.

When Kaberco saw Tarkio, his scowl deepened. "It's late, trader, and I'm tired."

"If you please, I have news you'll want to hear," Tarkio said. "News that shouldn't wait any longer." He had a sense of unease. Kaberco usually wasn't that curt with people.

With a resigned shrug, Kaberco pointed to the room he usually received visitors in. It was starkly furnished with rough wooden furniture, simple matting on the stone floor, and bare uneven plastered walls. "Will this take long?"

"I don't think so, if you please." Tarkio waited for Kaberco to bring a torch from the corridor to light the candles on the table and to settle into his ephor's wooden armchair. Then Tarkio sat on a nearby bench. He leaned forward. "Some weeks ago, as I was on my way to Trofmose, the caravan was attacked."

Kaberco said, "You need to tell me about that now?" He spit the words out like he was hurling stones in Tarkio's face.

"If you please." He studied Kaberco's face, sensing Kaberco was disturbed about something. "The guardsmen valiantly fought off the bandits, and only a few traders died. But there was something odd."

"Odd?" Kaberco looked at Tarkio with raised eyebrows.

"Odd. As usual, after the bandits had been defeated we gathered up all the arrows that were usable. There were some that had obviously not been shot by the bandits."

"How do you know?"

Tarkio pulled an arrow from his bundle. "You can see for yourself. It's red."

Kaberco reached for the arrow. He seemed to be trying hard not to show any shock, but Tarkio hadn't missed the widening of his eyes and how Kaberco held his breath for just a second.

After a pause, Kaberco asked, "Who have you told of this?"

"No one. I didn't think anything of it at first, but later realized that no one uses red arrows, not guardsmen, not traders, not bandits, not even Riskers."

"Right. Why come to me? Why not Valday?"

Tarkio shrugged and looked into Kaberco's eyes. "I

wanted to bring it to someone who would take action. Valday does a good job maintaining safety and fairness, but—"

He had the sense that Kaberco was watching him closely, observing every move.

Kaberco held up a hand. "Valday is a careful and precise leader, a good subject of the Prime Konamei."

Good, Tarkio thought. *We understand each other, but neither of us said anything incriminating.* "I thought of you, since you put such energy into your office." He looked at Kaberco. "It's quite remarkable, really, to have an ephor who works as hard as you."

Kaberco pulled his eyebrows together, and looked into Tarkio's face, searching. "Do you know why? I had an older sister. She raised me after our parents died."

"What happened to her?"

"About six years ago, she was on a caravan from Gishin to Shinroo when it was attacked. The bandits kidnapped her and took her to their camp, deep in the woods." He shuddered, then made a fist. "I tracked them for days, and finally came upon her body, tied to a tree. She hadn't been dead long, more's the pity. The bandits used her abominably." His face darkened. "I swore then I'd do all I could to hunt down the bandits and keep everyone safe. No matter what. No more girls kidnapped; no more caravans attacked." He leaned forward. "I'd been apprenticed to the ephor for a few years by then, so I set myself to learn all I could." He gestured to the surrounding room. "And here I am today."

"I had no idea." *No wonder he takes any threat personally. Which means there's no chance he'll let up on Iskra.*

Kaberco looked sternly at Tarkio. "I am serious about keeping Gishin safe. That means protecting the caravans that come in and out, and keeping the peace, so that all are safe and are treated fairly. And I will go to whatever means necessary to do so." He nodded and settled back into his chair.

Tarkio nodded. *All very well, if you make sure your men do their part.* "If you please, I think you've done quite well."

Leaning forward, Kaberco studied Tarkio's face, his hazel eyes dark and cold in the dim light, giving Tarkio the feeling he was being stared at by a panther about to pounce. He clearly didn't take Tarkio's words as a compliment.

"Keeping everyone safe also means enforcing the rules. All the rules. And punishing those who break them, or even just bend them."

Tarkio fixed a bland expression on his face, ignoring his pounding heart. "As you should. I've always known you to be fair and just, ready to show clemency to those who are sincere in their willingness to change their ways."

Kaberco's lip curled. "I hope that means you won't be taking any more girls to the Risker camp. In distress or otherwise."

Tarkio felt the sweat bead on his forehead. How much does he know? "At the time, if you please, I was concerned for the girl. She was badly shaken and bleeding. I wasn't sure that other bandits might be pursuing her. If there was more than one, I doubted I could fight them off; the Risker camp seemed like the safest place at the time." He looked at Kaberco's narrowed eyes and met his hard stare. "Later events have led me to consider that may have been a lapse of judgement." When Kaberco didn't answer, he swallowed hard and went on. "I crave your patience, if you please."

Kaberco's face hardened. "There is a limit to my patience, something that should not be forgotten."

"I won't test it."

"Make sure you don't." Kaberco compressed his lips. "Is there anything else you have to say?"

Tarkio stood up. "I don't want to take up any more of your time. If I can help you in any way, please send word to me."

"Just let me know if you come across any more red

arrows," Kaberco said. He waved at the door, a clear command for Tarkio to leave.

Tarkio strode out of the room, restraining himself from hurrying. He felt a cold sweat on his neck and clenched his jaw. With every step he expected a guardsman to stop him, to seize him, and drag him off to wherever the taken ended up.

After Tarkio was back on the street, he took a deep breath and looked up at the half moon. He believed Kaberco, that he was out for vengeance against the bandits, that he truly wanted to make people safe. What bothered him was the fact that Kaberco was willing to go to great lengths to do it.

He let out a long breath. *Have I just made things worse?* At the very least, it was clear Kaberco had just given Tarkio a warning.

THE NEXT MORNING, Kaberco met with the village konament. This time they ignored the cushioned seats by the fire and sat on wooden ones around the table, Kaberco at one end, Murash at the other.

After they'd discussed the business of the week, Kaberco announced, "I have something of import to share with you all."

"Not the need to take another underage girl," Murash said.

Kaberco looked at him blandly. "No, I think this is a more troubling matter." He threw the red arrow onto the polished table, sending it skidding toward Murash.

The questor stared at the weapon. "Where," he asked, "did you get that?"

So, he sees, Kaberco thought. The others, all wearing puzzled frowns, didn't.

Kaberco said, "That's not important. What concerns me more is we've never seen a weapon like this before. The Prime

Konamei sends arrows to all his guardsmen, and to all the ephors. None of them are red." He looked around the room. "To answer your question, a bandit fired it. My question is, where did the bandits get it?"

"Could they not have made it themselves?" asked the ludi. She was a timid woman who rarely spoke up at meetings.

Murash turned to her, smirking. "Yes, in the schools they opened last month for their children." He let out a harsh laugh as the ludi reddened and dropped her gaze. "I've never heard of the bandits making anything they couldn't steal."

"Pirates?" Zurvan asked. "Maybe the bandits started to trade with them." He drummed his fingers on the table.

"Would you trade with the pirates?" Kaberco asked. "I wouldn't."

"Our good ephor declines to trade with the pirates, as he should," Murash said. "But who knows the minds of bandits and pirates?"

Kaberco allowed them to debate the point. *Let them think I'm listening to what they have to say,* he thought. The only one who matters is Murash. He waited patiently until Murash finally said, "There's still another possibility."

"The Riskers?" Zurvan asked, his eyes wide.

Murash laughed. "Oh, come on. You don't think it's them?"

Kaberco nodded. "That's right. Not the Riskers. It must be someone from over the mountains." He looked around at his listeners, gratified by their horrified expressions.

Then they all began shouting at once. "That's impossible!"

"Everyone over the mountains is dead!"

"Do you think they'll attack us?"

"You speak treason!" came from Murash.

Kaberco pounded on the table, making his shoulder chain jingle. "Konameis! If you please." When he had their attention, he pointed at the arrow. "Look at it closely. The wood isn't painted red, it is red. Tell me what tree it came from."

They sat in stunned silence, some with wide eyes, others with hanging jaws, until Murash asked, "Just out of curiosity, where did you get this red arrow?" His eyes narrowed as he stared at Kaberco.

"People in this town look to me as someone to trust. A trader, Tarkio Sabidur from Trofmose, sought me out. He'd picked it up after bandits attacked the caravan he was with."

The syndic nodded. "Good man, that Tarkio. He can be counted on to do the right thing."

Maybe, Kaberco thought. Aloud, he said, "Friends, we need to report this to the Prime Konamei. Then we need to take precautions, be alert for any disturbances."

"Absolutely not," Murash said. "We shouldn't disturb the Prime Konamei for this. What do we have? Mere idle speculation about one arrow." He curled his lip. "Fools, that's what he would think of us."

"That's a good point, Murash," Zurvan said. "We should wait until we are more certain of our information."

Kaberco let his eyelids droop to hide his growing anger. *Wait for what? Until an invading army is at our door?* He laid his hands flat on the table before him. "Konameis, we are agreed that the red arrow means we have an unknown enemy among us, are we not?"

He looked around the table at the other four, waiting for their nods. "While speculating about what is over the mountains can be treasonous"—he paused and looked straight at Murash—"facing the facts in front of us is not. Nor is it less risky than not acting on the truth."

"Agreed," Murash said, his tone as smooth as Kaberco's had been. "We need to discover who this enemy is. Then we can make our report to the Prime Konamei."

Kaberco noted the vein in Murash's neck was throbbing. It always did that when he was up to something. "And just how do you propose we find out?"

Murash rubbed his nose, covered with the red lines of tiny blood vessels.

His fingers are swollen, Kaberco thought. Maybe a sign his health is declining? Can't count on it. He waited as Murash looked around the room as if to ensure he had everyone's attention.

"I'm sure our ephor knows best," Murash said. "But if it were my decision, I would first ask the Riskers. They are our first line of defense to the east. If any enemies have come from over the mountains, wouldn't they know?"

Kaberco nodded and forced a small smile. For once that snake had a good idea. "Of course. That was going to be my next move. I'm so glad you agree." He looked around the room. "One way or the other, by the end of the week, I will report to the Prime Konamei. It is our duty to keep him informed of anything that could endanger peace and safety. The Prime Konamei's peace must be kept at all costs."

THE MEETING ENDED SOON AFTER, and three of the konament members left quickly. Not Murash. He shuffled his papers, as if searching for a certain document. Kaberco pretended to be absorbed in his own documents, watching Murash out of the corner of his eye, trying to ignore the heat rising up his neck as he waited.

At last, Murash pushed back his chair. "I see what you are doing, Kaberco."

Kaberco looked up, eyebrows raised. "What do you mean?"

"You know the Prime Konamei will decide very soon if you'll keep your position or not, so you concoct a crisis with your red arrow, to justify any irregularities, like taking underage girls." He smiled. "Very astute of you, to come up with something that will overshadow any other concern in the Prime Konamei's mind. I'm impressed." He shook his head. "But isn't causing panic in the village too high a price for achieving your ambition?"

Kaberco allowed himself to scowl. He spoke evenly and low as he responded. "This crisis is not concocted. Unless you believe the traders have discovered a new kind of tree." He jutted out his jaw. "After the trader left, I questioned a few of the guards, and they told me they've found red arrows, as well." Seeing Murash's frown, he went on quickly. "I convinced them the Prime Konamei was testing a new kind of arrow, and the bandits must have stolen some. I don't think the village is about to dissolve into hysteria." He tried to breathe calmly to keep his face from growing red. Murash would love to depose him. All he needed was an excuse to complain to the Prime Konamei.

"I see." Murash stood up. "Well, keep things under control. Safe and fair, and the Prime Konamei won't need to know of all the disturbances around here. Wasn't a girl caught visiting the Riskers?"

Kaberco's brain exploded with every foul word he could think of while he kept his face rigid. How did Murash hear of that? He'd tried so hard to keep it quiet, for Iskra's sake as much as his own. "I have the situation well in hand. We won't have any more trouble from that girl again."

Murash nodded, then walked to the iron-trimmed door. As he went out, he said over his shoulder, "That's good. I would hate to have to disturb the Prime Konamei." He banged the door shut behind him.

Kaberco let loose the curses he'd suppressed in front of Murash. He was so close to achieving his goal of being appointed permanent ephor, and one stubborn girl threatened his hopes. He paced around the room, forcing himself to think, to plan.

It was clear Murash hadn't complained to the Prime Konamei—yet. But he was looking for a reason to. If Iskra made one more visit to the Riskers, or asked a few more dangerous questions, Murash could claim Kaberco was unable to control the village. Add to that another taking and a little murmuring, then Murash would send a messenger to the Prime Konamei. Two, most likely. Just to make sure one of them got through.

Kaberco sucked his cheeks in between his teeth and considered. Luza. He knew she could be counted on. Luza had even turned in her own husband when she thought he was a threat to peace and safety.

Those were dark days for Luza. The questor had questioned her mercilessly, certain she shared her husband's discontents. It was only Kaberco's intervention that saved her. Since then, her loyalty was more to Kaberco than anyone else.

He shook his head. Loyal as Luza was, she could not control her daughter. He couldn't allow Murash any tool, most of all a disobedient girl, to use against him. He thought back to Tarkio and his platitudes about mercy. Could he have anything to do with Iskra's rebellious ways?

He considered Tarkio, his reputation for wisdom and caution. *No, Tarkio wouldn't do anything to jeopardize his trading license. Probably. I'll have to watch him. Odd that he showed up with the red arrow right when Iskra was in deep trouble, though.*

And Iskra? Murash may want to use her against me, but it's he who will go down. Controlling Iskra may just be the way to prove myself to the rest of the konament, at least. An image of Luza's face flashed through his mind. He shook his head. *I have no choice. Personal concerns are not as important as safety.* As much as he didn't like it, he was going to have to clamp down on Iskra. Hard.

34

Iskra wiped the stinging sweat from her forehead. The rain wasn't helping. It made the summer day feel even more stifling, the steam in the kitchen denser, the odors smell fouler. She hung a pot of soup over the fire, then took a slice of bread and spread butter on it. Thankfully, a trader had come by and he and Mazat were quibbling over the price of eggs. *A few minutes of peace, that's all I want. Working with him is worse than being chased by a warboar.*

Kaberco had obviously spoken with Udbash. All morning Udbash had tailed her, asking her if she'd lost her shift somewhere. He spoke in great detail of his longing to see her without it, and just what he planned to do when he'd taken it from her. She cringed every time she thought of him looking at her, touching her.

"Two weeks," he said. "Two weeks 'til we're married. But mebbe we won't wait that long. You know you want it, if you gave yourself to Riskers."

"I didn't," she'd insisted.

His response was a mocking laugh. "That's right, stick to your story if ya want to. But in two weeks, you're mine."

She stifled an impulse to vomit, swallowing hard to keep

the acid in her throat from forcing its way out of her mouth. Udbash loved to see fear. She wasn't about to show it to him. *Just go along, don't cause trouble,* she reminded herself. *You've still got a little time to find a way out of this.*

The door creaked open. She whirled around, expecting Udbash. To her surprise, Mazat entered the hut. Rain sluiced from his hair and down his dirty face. Mazat eased his skinny frame onto a bench and stretched his legs out in front of him. Mud from his boots dripped onto the floor. "I hear you and my son're gettin' married."

"That's what they tell me."

There was a long pause, so long that Iskra looked up from her work at Mazat. He was gazing at her with something almost like pity.

"My son, my boy, he's not quite right. Got dropped on his head when he was little."

"That's horrible! What did the healers do?"

"They tried to get me to let them take 'im. 'Just overnight,' they said. Nothin' doing."

"Whyever not?"

"That's what they said when his ma took ill. Just overnight. I never saw her again. Wasn't about to let that happen to Udbash." He shook his head and stood up. "Don't really see him as the marrying kind, though."

Iskra felt a surge of hope. "Can you stop him?"

Mazat looked at her, the corners of his mouth drooping. "I can't stop them." He stood up, shaking his head. "They say everyone has to do their duty and produce three children to work for the safety and fairness of the land. Udbash has to do his duty. And so do you." He stalked out, muttering.

Iskra leaned on the table with both hands, staring unseeing at the scarred and stained wood. *Them?* She took a few jagged breaths. That must mean Kaberco, Edalia, the konament, everyone. She knew what Mazat meant about children. Since he'd only produced one child, his son was expected to make up the difference. To have five children. She moaned at the thought of bearing not one, but five of Udbash's children. Her knees went weak and she sagged against the table.

The boiling soup reclaimed her attention. She gave it a stir. Udbash really isn't right in the head, that was sure. *If I can't get out of this wedding, would I be able to control him?* She ran her hand through the hair on the back of her head and gave it a tug. *Maybe I can.*

Half an hour later, Udbash stomped in, his bulk crowding her in the tiny room, his loud voice demanding "something hot."

"Here's soup, if you please." Iskra ladled soup into a bowl and set it on the table.

He ran his eyes over her, lingering on a spot just below her waist. "Lucky girl you are, don't ya think."

Iskra couldn't even think of a response. She put her head down and reached for a slice of bread.

"You're not so keen on marryin' me? Would be worse if it was my old da."

Iskra looked up in surprise. If anything, middle-aged Udbash with his blotchy skin and rolls of fat under his neck was more repulsive than scrawny Mazat. At least Mazat had a sliver of kindness.

"I know, not too many people would want you, after you've been pleasuring the Riskers."

"That's not true!" She spat the words at him.

Udbash winked. "Sure, that's what ya say. But I still want ya. Someone like you will do anything I want. Anything."

She blinked, unsure of his meaning.

He must have seen the puzzled look on her face. "I don't mean cookin' and cleanin', either. You'll do all that for me and more. You'll work for me all day, and then all night."

She pulled her arms around herself, trying to stop from shaking.

He studied her for a minute. "Doncha like the idea?" He

chuckled and rubbed his hands together. "I don't care. You'll be mine, an' if I'm not pleased, you'll pay. You'll wish that warboar had killed you. And no one will notice. It'll save 'em the trouble of taking you." He looked up at the sound of Mazat stomping his feet on the doorstep. "And don't tell my da any of this. I'll say you lied, like you do. He'll believe me, not you." He bent his head and shoveled some stew into his mouth, leaving Iskra staring at the bread in her hands, a piece of bread she'd crumbled into bits without knowing what she was doing.

Head hanging, Iskra closed the door to Mazat's hut behind her. The late summer sun was still high in the sky, beating remorselessly on her head. Weary from the day's work, worn down by ceaseless leers and threats, she was grateful for the few minutes of solitude she would have as she trudged home. She'd use them to try to think of some way to escape marriage to Udbash.

She was not to get them. Her mother was waiting with a frown and crossed arms at the entrance to the chicken farm. "It's about time," she said. "What took you so long?"

"Mam, there's a lot of work to do." She plodded along the dirt road next to Luza. "Why are you here? I know the way home."

"Kaberco asked me to escort you to and from work. And to keep an eye on you when you are home."

Iskra frowned. Now her mother was going to be her jailer?

"I hope you aren't tired," Luza continued. "We have some sewing to do."

"Sewing?"

"You need a wedding dress. You don't think I'll let you get married in something old. That would be shameful."

"Don't you think it's shameful marrying your daughter to a man old enough to be her father?"

Luza looked around, then pulled Iskra into an alley. "Kaberco was right. You are out of control. You haven't learned anything and are as rebellious as ever." She curled her lip, glaring at Iskra. "That means you leave me no choice."

Iskra didn't like the sound of that. She felt beads of sweat form on her forehead and took a step back, feeling the rough wood of the side of a building press into her back. "No choice? Choice about what?"

"Kaberco and I have been talking. We're going to move your wedding up, to the next Hafsanbe. The first day of Oznobal."

"That's in four days!" Iskra wailed. "No!" The nausea that had plagued her all day twisted her stomach. She heaved and felt sourness fill her mouth. Marry that foul man in four days? And sleep with him? She forced herself to swallow the bitter mess that was forcing its way to her teeth. Her eyes flitted up and down the alley, looking for a place to escape, somewhere to hide. Why had she ever asked even one question?

"You listen to me." Her mother poked a finger into Iskra's chest. "I'm trying to keep you safe. If you don't marry Udbash, underage or not, you'll be taken." Her face crumpled. "I'm trying to keep us both safe."

Iskra pushed her mother's hand away. "That's the real truth, isn't it? You're willing to sacrifice me, just so you can be safe." She felt a sudden release at those words. While it hurt to think her mother would be so selfish, it was a relief to finally quit stifling the truth.

"All you think about is you. If you'd had any thought of me, you'd never have gone to the Risker camp in the first place."

Iskra blinked, then stared at Luza. "You're right, Mam. Next time bandits are chasing me through the forest, I'll be sure to think of you, rather than how to get away from them."

Luza stared at her, her icy scowl more unsettling than Udbash's leers. "You're not my daughter. You're all your father, him all over again. There's nothing of me in you. So be it. No more talk." She pushed Iskra back onto the street. "Walk."

Iskra felt like she was venturing into a dark cave, a cave whose walls narrowed and confined her in darkness and despair.

HOURS LATER, she was blissfully free from her mother's barbs. She sat on her straw, arms wrapped around her legs, leaning her face against her knees. She thought of Edalia and her mother. Of Osip, Cillia, and Tarkio. Everyone seemed to be willing to sacrifice her just so there would be no trouble anywhere.

Falling back on her straw, she let the tears flow, gritting her teeth to keep from sobbing and waking her mother. Her sense of being abandoned by everyone and her terrors of marrying Udbash kept her from sleep. She compared Udbash, fat and hulking, mean and foul, with healthy, vibrant Xico, who made her feel confident and joyous instead of weak and worthless.

Xico is the one I want.

She thought back to the first time she saw him, bravely killing the bandit chasing her. Of his confidence. The way he never made fun of her fears, but helped her through them. Of the way he looked at her, the way he hugged her and she wanted him to never let her go. Of the way he touched her that set her skin on fire so she longed for him to touch her everywhere, or she'd die.

But she could never have Xico. She felt numb throughout her body, everywhere except the ache in her heart.

She rolled over on her straw. Even Oyamel, prig that he was, would have been better than Udbash. She grabbed her head with her hands to keep from screaming. She was terrified of marrying Udbash. Even leaving the village for good was less horrifying. She stifled a sob.

She lay on the straw, dozing. Then she saw the green light, and grabbed for it. She was startled when it vanished. She unclenched her fist and rubbed her hand over her eyes. Another dream, the same as before. In a cave, holding a baby, frightened for some reason, searching for something. She was running her fingers over the walls of the cave, looking for . . . what?

The dream had been so real, she was surprised she felt no pain where she'd scraped her fingers on the rocky walls of the cave. This time it was different. The green light had been guiding her, showing her the way to go.

"Sky-god, help me."

She didn't know any other way to pray, if that was what she was doing. She reached under the straw and found her amulet. The moonlight reflected off the green and purple stones, making little points of light that danced on her blanket. She shivered, remembering the terror she felt in her dream. *The Riskers said dreams have meaning, that the sky-god used them to speak to us.* She smiled wryly. *This was easy to figure out. I'm trapped in a dark cave. My mother is my jailer, Udbash my punishment. There's no way out.*

But what about the green light? She held the amulet up to the moonlight. The soft green glow was oddly comforting. "What do I do, sky-god?"

She felt it, like someone had slipped a word into her mind. One word: *Wait.*

35

T*wo days,* Iskra thought. *Two days left to the wedding. Two days before my punishment begins, a sentence that will last the rest of my life.*

She was sitting at the table in her cottage, squinting to see by candlelight. *Just a few more stitches on this hem to go, and my wedding dress will be done.*

The past two days she'd thought of all kinds of crazy schemes to escape. Beg Edalia for forgiveness, offer to take on the worst job, or marry anyone, anyone except Udbash. Hide in a trader's wagon and let him whisk her far away. Climb the village walls at night. Steal a guardsman's horse and ride out. Each one was less likely to succeed than the last.

She thought back to Veressa's wedding. No pearly-gray dress for Veressa. She got married in vivid green. Cillia said that was for fertility. Risker girls chose their own colors for marriage. Some picked yellow, for prosperity, others chose blue for serenity. Then there was pink, for love. Iskra snorted in disgust. I wonder if there's a color for those who want an early death. My only hope, being married to Udbash.

Luza came over and scrutinized her work, nodding her

approval. "I'm glad you've accepted the situation. We were all so worried."

"What choice do I have?"

"Kaberco's very happy that you have come around. He—"

"Kaberco?" broke in Iskra. "You've been talking to Kaberco?"

Luza flushed and shuffled her feet. She coughed, then cleared her throat. "Well, yes. He's been asking about you. He was concerned."

Concerned about keeping himself safe. "Was he?"

"Oh, yes. He asked if you were sleeping and eating."

"Did you tell him?"

"Of course. He said you look a little peaked, dark circles under your eyes."

"That's kind of him to notice." Iskra didn't try to keep the bitterness from her tone.

"It was kind, even if you don't think so. He also said that if maybe you are too sickly to get married, perhaps you need some time in the house of healing. I told him I didn't think so. You're just a little nervous. Once the wedding is over, you'll be fine. That's what I told him."

Iskra stared down at her sewing so her mother couldn't see her face. *Is she that stupid? Does she not know what Kaberco is saying? That I could just be taken? I don't believe all this concern for my health. Or is he feeling guilty over sentencing me to life with Udbash and thinks taking is a better end for me?*

The cottage suddenly felt oppressively hot and the walls seemed to be closing in. She pressed her hands down into her lap to keep them from shaking. "Mam, if you please, it's getting dark. I can't see anymore. May I stop? I can finish tomorrow."

"Why, yes, of course."

Iskra rose and carefully folded the wedding dress and placed it on a shelf. "I think I'll just go to bed."

Luza nodded. "Sleep well."

Once in the bedroom, Iskra sank to her straw, hugging her knees, sitting motionless in the dark. *Will they come for me tonight? Or do I have one more day?* Being taken was beginning to seem better than marriage to Udbash. *Maybe then I'll find Tavda.*

Or will they give me two days, and then let me live to be Udbash's slave? She stayed motionless as she listened to her mother come into the room and lie down on her own rustling straw. Soon Iskra heard her gentle snore.

How can she sleep? Doesn't she care what's about to happen to me? No. She wrinkled her face. *Maybe she hadn't cared what happened to Da, either.*

My father. He'd never have let this happen. Da, what happened to you? Did Mam betray you, too?

Footsteps crossed the yard behind the cottage. She froze, waiting for a knock at the door. The footsteps continued on. Silly. It's too early for them to come to take someone away. They always wait 'til after midnight.

I need help. Every night asking the sky-god; every night getting the same answer: *Wait.* And every night, the dream of the cave and the baby, searching for something, feeling the fear.

She reached under her straw for the amulet. The green glow was stronger. She held it to her heart. "Sky-god, I need help. Won't you help me?"

Go.

Did I imagine that, or was that the answer? She waited. Another word came into her mind.

Now.

Her heart pounded and she felt the sweat on her palms. *Dare I?*

Leaving would be dangerous.

Staying would be worse.

She eased herself off the straw. Her mother didn't stir. Hands shaking, she picked up her cloak and boots and crept to the door to the other room. She looked back at her mother. No movement.

Ignoring the fluttering in her stomach, she slipped to the door that led outside. She put on her boots and put a trembling hand on the doorknob. Her fingers refused to turn it. She thought of Udbash and shuddered. Taking a deep breath, Iskra opened the door and walked into the night.

Once outside, Iskra looked around the sleeping village. Now where do I go? She spotted a small green light down the street. She walked toward it, noticing that the light from Dabrey, now full and high in the sky, was bright enough to see by. If anyone is looking, they might see me. A thought that did nothing to help her fight the weakness in her legs and to keep walking.

Her breathing was loud and rasping in the silence. She struggled to breathe slower, more quietly. Better. She moved along the street, eyes fixed on the green light. As she drew closer, it moved toward the back gate of the village, which oddly was wide open. She followed the light through the gate, into the woods, and through the underbrush, jumping at every breath of wind and twitch of a leaf. An alloe rat scuttled away from her. She stood still, waiting for a cry, a shout. Nothing. She went on.

The green light led her to a narrow trail, barely wide enough for her to place her feet. She had to set one foot down directly in front of the other, as if she were walking on a narrow board.

The trail zigzagged up the hill, skirting boulders and clumps of pine. Always the green light shone in front of her. It led her for almost an hour. Iskra was beginning to feel she'd really get away from the village.

Then the light suddenly vanished.

Iskra stifled a scream, and waited, holding her breath. She

could hear the sounds of two men coming down the trail. She stepped behind a tree and pulled her cloak around her, ducking her head. The men were coming closer.

I shouldn't have come. When they leave, I'll go home. She squeezed her eyes shut, willing the men to keep moving.

To her surprise, they did. She didn't dare look to see who they were. Traders, Riskers, bandits, guardsmen, she had no idea. She let out a slow breath and waited until the noise of their descent had died off. Her heart was pounding in her chest and she suppressed a whimper. She stayed crouched behind the tree, unable to move.

A rustling in the leaves behind her made her jump. A small animal darted across the path, scurrying too quickly for Iskra to see what it was. She shook herself. *I've got to go on. There's no going back for me.* She looked at the path. Fears of bandits and guardsmen and warboars paralyzed her.

She leaned her head against the tree, placing a shaking hand against its rough bark. Minutes passed as she tried to decide what to do. Another rustle in the leaves made her bite her lip. *I can't stay here forever. Put one foot in front of the other. That's all I can do. One in front of the other.* She stepped back onto the path, glancing first down the hill, then up. She gasped with relief to see the green light patiently shining ahead.

Swallowing hard, she gulped back her fear and the sourness in her throat. She followed the green light, barely able to see the trail in the scant moonlight that penetrated the trees. She reached the summit of the hill at last, and as she did the light dimmed, then went out.

A man stepped out of the shadows, his bow ready with an arrow on the string. "Who approaches?" he asked.

"Please, my name is Iskra. I want to find Osip and Cillia's house."

The man came closer. "You. I know you," he said. "The last time I saw you, a warboar had come a bit too close to you."

"Tikul, is that you?" When he nodded, she held out her hand. "Thank you, I can't thank you enough for helping me that day."

He took her hand briefly, then dropped it, frowning. "The last I heard from my da, they told you to stay away."

"They did. But I'm in terrible trouble. I was afraid—" She stopped, unable to say the words.

"Speak your fear. It won't seem so evil."

His gentle tone bolstered her courage. "I thought they might come for me tonight, to take me."

"I've heard that happens, down in the villages." He drew his eyebrows together. "But not with one so young."

She hesitated, not wanting to go into the whole story. "It seems I am a special case. Will you help me once again?"

Tikul shrugged. "You really don't need my help. The camp is that way. Through that gorge ahead. There were two bandits prowling around, but they turned back when I sent a few arrows their way. You'll be safe enough, I reckon. Now go."

She thanked him and set off in the direction of the camp, running in the moonlight.

36

Half an hour later, Iskra sat in Cillia's kitchen, sipping tea. Some herb that calms the nerves, Cillia had said. It smelled wistfully sweet. If she drinks this, it must work. She's remarkably calm for being rousted out of bed in the middle of the night.

After Iskra had finished telling her story, Osip said, "Xico, go fetch Tarkio. He's staying at your brother's house." Xico started to say something, but Osip interrupted him. "Just go, and hurry. We don't have much time."

Xico gave Iskra a long look, then left the cottage.

Osip turned to Iskra. "The way I see it, you've got about four or five hours before your mother notices you are gone. She'll look for you, then go to Kaberco. He'll send a man up the Guarded Path. We can stall them a little, but before then, you need to be long gone."

"Where will I go?"

"We'll have to think on that."

Cillia sat next to Iskra. "We know how Xico feels about you. He's told us over and over and has heard all of our objections." She rubbed Iskra's cold hand between her warm ones and looked into her eyes. "We need to know, do you feel the same? He's ready to risk everything to marry you, even though it is forbidden."

"I do." She could barely get the words out of her dry mouth.

"Are you sure it's Xico you want, and not just an answer to your troubles?"

Iskra stared at her, pleading with her eyes. She worked her mouth, trying to moisten it enough so she could talk. "I know you won't believe me, but I don't think that after knowing Xico, I could love any of the boys in the village. Not anymore."

"Even though Xico is forbidden to you?"

"If I can't have him, I don't want anyone."

Cillia and Osip exchanged a look. "We'll wait for Xico and Tarkio, then," Osip said.

Iskra sensed they weren't going to answer any questions, so she took another sip of tea. Cillia was right. She was feeling calmer, the sensation of being trapped and hunted receding as the warmth of the tea spread through her body.

The door opened to admit Xico and Tarkio. Iskra shrank from Tarkio's angry scowl.

"What's all this?" he asked. "Xico's told me quite a tale."

"Yes," Osip said. "What are we going to do? She can't go back."

"She can't stay here," Tarkio said.

"She and Xico want to marry," Cillia said.

"Have you told them why they can't? Told them everything?"

"No. We thought you'd be the best one to do that," Cillia said. When he frowned at her, she went on. "You understand both worlds, Riskers and villagers."

Tarkio sighed, then nodded. "You're right." He paused a moment as if collecting his thoughts. "Iskra, Xico, have you ever heard of the prophecy of the Desired One?"

"The what?" Xico said.

Iskra frowned. "No. I've heard nothing of that."

"Back when the war was raging and the first settlers came to Tlefas, led by the man who became the first Prime Konamei, there was some mixing between the different groups, the ones who later divided into Riskers and villagers."

"Did some of them marry?" Iskra asked.

"Yes, back then it was allowed," Tarkio said. "But the Prime Konamei and his advisors were concerned that the Riskers and their insistence on freedom would make it impossible to create the ordered society they dreamed about. They forbade any mixing between the two groups. They allowed only the traders to go back and forth, using them as a means of communication, as well as trade."

"That seems very wrong," Iskra said.

"You need to understand. The people who came here had just endured a bloody and brutal war, a war that lasted over a hundred years. Four generations had grown up knowing nothing but bloodshed and destruction. Their dream was to find a remote place they could settle and have peace. They didn't want to ever again go through the slaughter and grief they'd left behind." He sighed. "Their motives were noble, no doubt. I'm not sure it worked out the way they planned."

"And the prophecy?" asked Xico.

"Soon after the treaty was established, several Risker women who possessed some of the more powerful amulets began having dreams and visions. The vision was always the same: One day a Risker and a villager would wed and have a child, the Desired One. The child would bring a new order to the land and free it from its chains."

Iskra looked at Tarkio, wrinkling her brow. "So?"

"So the Prime Konamei made it a terrible crime for a Risker to marry a villager. And they began teaching the village children that Riskers were savages, there was no sky-god, no magic, the amulets were fairytales—well, you've heard it all, I'm sure."

"But they never told us about this Desired One."

"Of course not. They were afraid people who were unhappy with the Prime Konamei or their leaders for any reason would make a mixed marriage just to try to produce the Desired One. The Prime Konamei's goal was to stamp out all memory of the prophecy and to make sure if anyone did bring it up, the rest would laugh it off as a myth."

"The problem for them is that you can't kill an idea," Osip said. "Too many people knew about the prophecy and told their children. As time went on, more people liked the thought of a new order and freedom. The prophecy got mixed with stories of the Desired One. It's impossible to know what's truth and what's myth. But the tales were passed down from generation to generation."

Tarkio looked from Xico to Iskra. "Because of that, laws were passed that decreed stiff penalties for anyone who broke the ban on mixing with Riskers. Or for even mentioning what they called the myth of the Desired One. This isn't about just you two. All of us could be in danger, even this entire camp."

Xico turned to his parents. "Why didn't I know about the Desired One? I understand why Iskra wouldn't, but why didn't you tell me?"

"Because of other parts of the prophecy. One is that the father of the Desired One will not live long enough to see his child's first steps, and that the mother will not hear her child's first words." Osip paused and rubbed his hand over his face. "The Riskers keep the prophecy secret until a couple decides to wed. If they have chosen to marry another Risker, well and good. In the rare instances it is a mixed marriage, they then need to decide if they will take a chance that they could produce the Desired One. No one has ever dared."

"But why keep it a secret?" Xico asked.

"To keep idiots from being tempted by forbidden love," Tarkio said.

Xico glared at him and opened his mouth to respond.

Before he could, Cillia reached over and took his hand. "Do you see why we tried to separate you and Iskra? If we'd told you the real reason, would you have listened?" She waited for Xico to shake his head. "We feared for your lives."

Xico frowned. "But the prophecy doesn't have to mean us, does it?"

"No," Cillia answered. "But there are three other pieces. One is that the Desired One will be fathered by a green-eyed man."

Iskra gasped. Xico shrugged. "Well, what of it? I'm not the only one with green eyes."

"A green-eyed man who is a skilled archer," Osip said, "who will pass his gift on to his child."

Xico drew his brows together. "And the other part?" he asked.

"That the three amulets of power will find the Desired One. The first early in life, the others at times when they are needed most."

"How can an amulet find a person?" Iskra asked.

"No one knows," Cillia answered. "And no one knows if the prophecy is really from the sky-god, or if all the pieces are true. It's been three hundred years since Tlefas was resettled. There's been plenty of time for the story to be exaggerated. It could all be nonsense, a baseless myth, like they say it is."

"But the Prime Konamei takes it seriously," Tarkio said. "Just mentioning the Desired One is enough to take someone."

"And then . . .." Cillia let her words trail off.

Iskra noticed the tears in Cillia's eyes, the sadness of her drooping mouth.

"There's one more piece of the prophecy." Cillia sighed and hung her head, then looked resolutely at Xico. "The Desired One will be conceived in the month of Rozhal, just before the fields ripen for the harvest."

"That's this month," Osip said. The room grew silent.

Iskra sucked in her breath and wrinkled her forehead. She rubbed her hand in her hair, trying to remember. Something seemed familiar about this, something she needed to remember. She clenched her jaw and pulled her brows together until her eyes were nearly shut. "The Desired One," she whispered. "Dezeerudun! That's it!"

"What is?" Tarkio asked.

"Do you remember the day you and Xico rescued me from the bandits?" When he nodded, she continued. "The night before, Old Cassie was taken. The day before that, Cassie grabbed me and asked when I was going to give her the dezeerudun. I had no idea what she meant." She looked around the room.

Tarkio scowled, Cillia closed her eyes, Osip rubbed his hand over his forehead. Only Xico met her gaze.

"That must be why Cassie was taken." She looked at Tarkio. "And Tavda."

"Tavda?" Tarkio asked.

"Yes. My friend. I told her and the trader we were riding with, about Cassie. The trader got very angry and told me never to talk about the dezeerudun. Kaberco said something about Tavda talking about a prophecy. This must be what he meant." She put her face in her hands, feeling the shame of how she'd let Tavda down weigh on her like a heavy cloak. "This is all my fault. Tavda would still be here if it wasn't for me."

Tarkio's eyes opened wide and he blinked at her a few times, as if he'd received some kind of shock. "The fifteen-year-old who was taken was your friend?"

"Yes." She wondered why he seemed so disturbed by that news. "It's all my fault."

"Your fault?" Tarkio asked. "Why do you say that?"

"Because she asked questions about Riskers in the Oppidan lecture. I was supposed to back her up. When they started making fun of her, I didn't speak up. That made her angry, and she kept pressing for answers. She never would have done that if I hadn't let her down."

"And you thought coming to the Riskers would help?" Tarkio curled his lip.

"I had to know what she said that was so bad. At the time, I thought it was her questions about Riskers. When I saw you that day, and you invited me to the wedding, I thought that was my chance. I'm not sure I would have found the courage to come here on my own."

Tarkio stared blankly at her. After a long pause, he said, "No, Iskra, it's my fault. I brought you here and encouraged you to come back." He stood up abruptly. "None of that matters now." He looked at Osip and Cillia. "Now what? She can't marry Xico."

"What?" Iskra stared at him, unable to believe what he'd said.

Tarkio took a few steps back, glaring at her, looking around at Xico and his parents, then fixing his eyes back on her. "Your friend is gone. Gishin was unsettled for weeks after she was taken. Do you think Kaberco will just let you go? You and Xico will be fugitives, always on the run. I'm begging you, don't do this."

"But I have nowhere else to go." Her voice trembled and she felt the sting of tears in her eyes. "And I can't marry Udbash. I can't. This is my only way out."

Tarkio narrowed his eyes. "That's all Xico is to you, a way out?" He spit out a vile curse. "You want him to leave his home, his family, his friends, just so you can have a way out? Pathetic, that's what you are." He spun to face Xico. "And that's what you want to marry? A selfish coward?" He pointed at Iskra. "At least if she was pretty, I could understand. Maybe."

"That's enough!" Xico jumped to his feet and pulled his arm back as if to strike Tarkio. He let out a gasp, then dropped his fist to his side. "I love her, and she loves me."

"You deserve better than marriage to a child who just sees you as an escape."

"That's not what's happening here," Xico said.

"Don't be a fool! Can't you see she's using you?"

Xico crossed his arms across his chest. "You need to leave. You've insulted us both."

"Tarkio, please," Iskra said. "I really do love Xico." She faltered, blushing. "I loved him from almost the first time I saw him."

Tarkio shook his head. "One thing about you is you're clever enough to say the right thing."

She rose to her feet and faced him. "Then hear this. I'm not going back to Gishin. If Xico won't have me, I'll have to find some other life."

"But of course I'll have you!" Xico put his arm around her.

"Are you sure?" She looked up into his face. "It's only going to mean big trouble for you."

"What's a little trouble? It won't be that bad. I can handle whatever happens, as long as you are with me."

Tarkio moved to the door, shaking his head. "Well, Xico, if you don't want my advice, then I'll be leaving." He opened the door, then turned to look directly at Xico. "Peace and safety to you," he said sarcastically, banging the door behind him.

Iskra rubbed her hand over her mouth, stifling a sob. Drawing a deep breath, she said, "Xico, I'm so sorry." A tear formed in the corner of her eyes when she saw the pain on his face. "He's right. I can't do this to you. Maybe I should just go away on my own and leave you out of it."

"Is that what you want?"

"I want what's best for you. I can't ruin your life just to save mine because I was stupid."

For answer Xico wrapped his arms around her. "If you're stupid, so am I."

Osip held up a hand. "We could go on all night, sharing blame. There's enough to go around. We all made choices, and now have to live with the aftermath." He looked from Xico to Iskra. "Now you know. And you need to make a decision. Do you still want to marry each other?"

Xico tightened his arms around Iskra. "I do," he said. "We don't have any idea that this prophecy means us. You say the part about green eyes might not even be true."

"And Cassie really could have been crazy," Iskra put in.

"Even if the myth is about us, I don't care. I love Iskra."

Osip turned to Iskra. "Do you feel the same? You are very young to get married."

"I am, but I was going to be married in two days anyway. Better to wed someone I love."

With a sigh, Osip turned to his wife, who nodded. "If the prophecy does mean them—" he began.

"Who are we to get in the way?" Cillia finished. She turned to Xico and Iskra. "I'll not lie, we're not happy about this. But it seems we have no choice."

"Cillia. . .." Iskra held out a hand to the older woman, wishing she could say something so that Cillia wouldn't resent her. The next thing she knew, Cillia had gathered her into a strong embrace.

"I love you and my son, and always will."

Iskra's knees went weak. She was taking this woman's son, putting him into danger, and all Cillia could say was that she loved her? Osip's arms went around the two of them. "And I love you," he said. "I can see what my son sees, that you'll be a good wife for him. I only wish you'll have many years to make him happy."

"That's what I want," Iskra said. "All I want."

Osip nodded. "If that's so, then we have to get moving. Get them ready, Cillia, while I draw a map."

"A map?" asked Iskra.

"So you know the best way to go through the mountains."

Iskra's lip trembled. "We'll be leaving?" They wouldn't get to stay, protected and supported by Xico's family? Deep down, she knew her dream of settling into life in a loving family wasn't going to happen. She still felt Osip's next words like an unexpected blow.

"You can't stay here," Osip said. "They'll come after you. Once they know you're married to Xico, treaty or no treaty, they'll make sure you never have a child."

Osip stood up. "I'll get Tikul and his wife, and inform the elder. Xico, get yourself ready."

Cillia took Iskra by the hand. "I'll heat some water so you can wash. Then we'll have to see about a dress for you."

37

Iskra stood in a daze as Fialka and Tuli wove pink and yellow flowers into her hair, forming a crown. "It's a good thing Da let me plant them so close to the house. It'd be hard to find anything blooming in the middle of the night," Tuli said.

The door opened and Cillia poked her head in. "Is she ready?"

"Yes, come and see."

Iskra stood up and turned to face Cillia. She was wearing Tuli's best dress, a yellow-green color, the color of fields just before they ripen for the harvest. She traced a finger along the embroidered trim that ran down the sleeves. Never had she dreamed she'd ever wear anything this ornate. She caught a glimpse of herself in the mirror. Her cheeks were flushed, giving her a healthy glow. Her gray eyes had taken on a green tinge, and their expression was an odd combination of joy and fear.

"You look lovely," Cillia said. "The girls did a good job, trimming your hair. It doesn't look so choppy. Now, hurry. Tikul's already started on Xico." She took Iskra's hand and pulled her into the kitchen.

Xico was sitting at the table, his right arm outstretched with the inside of his wrist exposed. Seven burning candles stood nearby, giving light to Tikul, who was poking Xico's wrist with a needle. With every stab, a muscle twitched in Xico's jaw.

"What is he doing?" Iskra asked. Whatever it was, it looked painful.

"Sit down," Cillia said. "This is Zamora, Tikul's wife. She'll do your tattoo."

"What tattoo?"

Cillia pushed her down onto the bench. "I'm sorry, I forgot you don't know our customs. When Riskers marry, they tattoo the name of their *selladria*, their beloved, on the inside of their wrists. The tattoo is forever, and so is the marriage bond." She pulled up her sleeve and showed Iskra the word "Osip" on her wrist. "I'm glad you both have short names. It won't take long."

Zamora took Iskra's arm and stretched it out. "Are you ready? This can be a bit painful." With that, she made the first stab of the needle.

Iskra gasped and tears came to her eyes. One rolled silently down her face, but she kept her arm still.

"Good girl," Zamora said. "I'll be quick, we only have four letters." She bent over her work, spelling out Xico's name, her brown hands moving confidently. "We usually do this a week or so after the wedding, so no one's in pain for the wedding night. You'll just have to put up with it."

Too stunned to respond, Iskra sat, flinching with every jab of the needle. No one had said anything about a tattoo.

She wondered what other rituals she was in for. And what risks. Here she was marrying a man she really didn't know that well, and a Risker, at that. One she was going to have to flee with. Her eyes widened as she realized that prospect seemed like a lesser risk, a less terrifying future than marriage to Udbash and staying in the village.

Xico leaned over. "We have to do this, so the other camps will know we really got married. We wouldn't want them thinking we're just some rebellious lovers who ran away from home in the middle of the night, would we?" He winked at her, then yelped when Tikul jabbed him roughly with the needle.

"Sit still, will you?" he said. "Don't want to hurt my crazy baby brother."

Iskra didn't know what to think of that. Was Tikul angry with Xico, or just teasing? Or was that anger directed at her? From the way he frowned at her she was sure he thought she was the demented one.

To punish herself, she focused on the stabbing sensation of the needle Zamora used to create the tattoo. *She's surprisingly gentle for a girl with such big hands,* Iskra thought. By the time Zamora had finished, Iskra's wrist felt like it was burning.

Zamora gestured to Cillia to look at Iskra's wrist. "The letters are a lot thinner than I usually do, but we don't have time for more," Zamora told her.

"It's fine. Osip, we are ready." Cillia led the way out of the cottage.

Xico stood up from the bench and held out his hand to Iskra. She put a trembling hand in his and got to her feet and followed him outside to where the elder stood waiting. He was a little shorter than Osip, his left arm in a sling. Osip and Cillia stood next to him, facing Xico and Iskra. Fialka, Tuli, Tikul, and Zamora stood to the side.

The elder took a step forward and leaned on his walking stick. He began to chant. "Sky-god, we seek your blessing. Sky-god, bind Xico and Iskra, bless them."

Osip and Cillia joined him. "Sky-god, we seek you. Guide them and protect them. Make them fruitful. Make them loving. Make them yours." The others joined the chant.

"Xico," the elder said. "Do you pledge yourself to Iskra, to love none other, to protect her and provide for her, all the days of your life?"

"I so pledge," Xico answered.

"Iskra." The elder turned to her. "Do you pledge yourself to Xico, to love none other, to honor him and care for him, all the days of your life?"

Uncertain of the proper response, she hesitated. Xico looked at her with a raised eyebrow and a smile.

"I so pledge," she said.

Cillia smiled. "What does the color of your dress signify?"

This time she knew the response. Fialka had taught her well. "I wear yellow-green for peaceful harvests and fruitful marriage."

"Do we acknowledge them as wed?" Osip asked.

"We so swear it," said the others. A lavender light shot down from the sky, illuminating Xico and Iskra for a moment, then faded.

Osip said to Xico, "Take your bride."

Before Iskra could wonder what that meant, Xico pulled her into his arms and kissed her. "My *selladria*," he said.

Cillia gave Iskra a hug. "I'm glad to welcome you into the family, but sorry we have to send you right off. Go get changed. You'll need to leave as soon as you are ready."

ISKRA WENT into the bedroom with Fialka and Tuli feeling like she was walking in a fog. She barely noticed when Fialka began pulling the flowers from her hair.

Tuli removed a blue dress from a shelf and dug around for a shift and underskirt. "Here, these will do," she said.

"I don't need to take the shift," Iskra said.

"You do. Don't you get it? If you go out as a villager, married to Xico, it will be too easy for you to be tracked. You have to pose as a Risker. Down to your skin. Just in case they catch you. And I'll find you some swimming things."

"What?"

"Just the leggings. If you're going to be crossing the mountains in winter, you'll want something warm on under your skirt." She rooted around to the back of the shelf. "Here, these can go in your pack for now." She looked at Iskra, who was planted in one spot, staring at her. Tuli flapped her hands in the air like she was herding geese. "Hurry. Mam wants to put something on your arm before you put the dress on."

Iskra quickly shed her clothes and pulled on the shift.

Fialka collected Iskra's village garments. "I'll pack the green dress for you, so you have a spare." She added the dress to the pile of clothes in her arms and left the room.

Before Iskra had a moment to herself, Cillia bustled into the room, carrying a small basket.

"Let me see your wrist," she said. She smeared a brown paste on Iskra's flaming skin. Then she passed her amulet over it, chanting softly. Taking a clean strip of cloth, she loosely wrapped Iskra's wrist. "It's usually better to leave it exposed to the air, but since you'll be in the woods, you'll have to cover it. If you can, take the bandage off at night and put more of this paste on. You'll be fine in a day or so." She smiled at Iskra. "Do Fialka's shoes fit you? Good. Finish dressing and come out."

She paused on her way out of the room. "You do know what is expected of you, as a wife?"

For a second Iskra didn't know what she meant. When she realized Cillia's meaning, she blushed and said, "Oh, yes. Mam told me."

Cillia smiled kindly. "There's no need to blush, and no need to be nervous. Osip made sure his boys know how to be gentle."

Iskra watched her leave the room. She hadn't thought much about the physical part of being married in all the talk of escaping. She wondered what Xico was intending to do about it. She pushed the thought away to finish dressing. Nothing was happening the way she'd thought her wedding would go. Even the fact that she married someone who made her feel things she'd never felt before was unexpected.

A few minutes later, Iskra went into the kitchen. Osip and Xico were bent over a roughly-sketched map. "If you go around the lake to the north and go straight into the mountains, you'll see a pass. On the south side is a dry cave. Remember? We found it that time we got caught in a hailstorm." He tapped the paper. "But this is the most direct route."

Iskra caught the smiles between Xico and Osip over that shared memory.

Osip went on. "You can spend the day there, get some rest. Head south tomorrow."

"Then where will we go?" Iskra asked.

"There are Risker camps all along the mountains, about two days' walk apart, sometimes three. It might take you longer, since you'll have to stay off the lower trails." Osip said.

Iskra's chin dropped. She hadn't really thought beyond fleeing the village and marrying Xico. Traveling through the mountains, living in caves? For a frenzied moment she thought regretfully of her sheltered life in the village. Then she thought of Udbash. *Don't be such a mushroom. You won't be alone.*

Osip traced a line on the map with his finger. "Here, nearer the capital, the mountain range is at its thickest. There is a Risker camp, Altiad, over the first line of mountains, farther east. If you make it there before the winter, you'll be safe at least until spring. The trails are impassable once the snows start."

"When will that be?" Iskra asked.

"Most years, around the first of Urartu. That means you have about six weeks. You'll have to move fast, in case you're followed. And pray the snows come early, so whoever's after you can't follow you to Altiad." Osip paused. "I've never been there, but I've heard. It's a rough life, Altiad. Even though it's farther south, they're a lot higher in the mountains. Winter is brutal there." He looked sadly at Iskra. "But it's your one chance of surviving 'til spring."

"Then we'll have to make sure we get through," Xico said.

Iskra studied Xico. He didn't seem worried. Maybe she shouldn't be, either, she thought.

"Come spring, the beginning of Etla, make your way south through the mountains to Xabiad, the Risker camp south of Litavye. It's the farthest one, the one between the sources of the two branches of the river Oxa."

"Why there?" Xico asked.

Osip moved his finger along the river. "Because if Kaberco trails you that far, you'll have two possible ways to get away."

Iskra's heart sank. Did Osip really think Kaberco would go after her, all the way to Litavye?

Osip traced the river to the sea. "The first goes down the river to the coast."

"That's where the pirates live," Iskra said, knotting her forehead.

"True. But there are traders who know them. Poales, for one. And the pirates might be interested in a skilled trapper and arrow-maker."

"What's the other way?" Xico asked.

"Through the mountains to the east." Osip grimaced. "That would be going into the unknown. There's been no news of anyone from the other side of the mountains for three hundred years. No one knows if anyone is alive. There are stories of monsters and savages, but I think those are just tales to keep people from exploring."

"Probably so," Xico said. "If anyone survived the war, they most likely didn't want to attempt crossing the desert, let alone climb the mountains. We'll just have to find a way to live off the land."

"Will we ever be able to come back?" Iskra asked.

"When we're sure they've given up looking for you, we'll come after you. Leave word in Xabiad which way you go. It'll be easier for us to find you if you take your chances with the pirates, but you'll have to decide that if the time comes." He looked at Iskra's trembling lips and smiled. "Cheer up, that's only if they keep tracking you. Once you leave here, we'll set up some false trails. If they believe you're dead, they'll give up. You won't be able to come back here for years, but maybe you can settle in another Risker camp."

Xico grasped Osip's arm. "Thank you, Da. This gives us a good chance."

Osip clasped Xico's arms and stood looking into his eyes. "My son, you've been gifted in many ways. But don't make the mistake of trusting in your own abilities. Look to the sky-god; he will show you the way." He pulled Xico into a firm hug. "Now thank me by getting yourselves away."

Cillia brought a long scarf to Iskra and wrapped it around her head. "Make sure no one sees your hair until those bangs grow out." She helped Iskra into a cloak and strapped a large bundle onto her back. "I'm so sorry there's no time for a wedding feast. But I gave you the best I could come up with."

Xico had a similar bundle, in addition to his bow and arrows.

Xico's siblings hugged her, then gathered around Xico. Tikul held his younger brother for a long moment. He released Xico, and said, "If you didn't want to help with the honey harvest, you could have just said." He cuffed Xico on the back of the head, his smile faltering as he spoke.

"Maybe next year," Xico said. "I'll still harvest more than you."

"Next year, I'll race you across the lake," Tuli said. She flung her arms around him, then pinched his cheek. "Who would have thought baby brother would get married before me?"

Iskra couldn't help noticing the muscle twitching in Tikul's jaw and the shine in Tuli's eyes. Her own eyes filled and she looked away, not wanting to see the sadness she was the cause of.

Fialka laid her head on Xico's shoulder and wordlessly gripped his arms as he embraced her. She took a step back, a single tear trailing down her face.

Cillia clung to Xico for a long moment, then released him. She looked long at his face, into his green eyes that mirrored her own, as if memorizing his features. She cupped his face in her hand. "My last born. May the sky-god protect you." She bowed her head as Osip put an arm around her shoulders. Iskra felt a pang, thinking of what she was taking Xico away from. Never had the cottage seemed more like a haven of peace.

"Go now," Osip said, and swallowed hard.

Xico nodded and embraced him, then took Iskra's hand and led her out into the misty dawn.

Tarkio sat limply in a stuffy pub in Shinroo later that evening. He'd trudged all day through the forest in the foothills of the mountains, not wanting to be seen anywhere near Gishin. An untouched mug of beer warmed slowly as he stared unseeing at the fire. He dimly heard the scrape of someone pushing a bench back, the shouts of someone calling for beer, the carefree laughter of men who hadn't betrayed all they'd loved best.

What have I done? My best friend is fleeing for his life. Xico should have married some Risker girl, settled down in the camp to a life of harvesting honey and fletching arrows. Now he's married to a villager, one I brought into his life, and he and Iskra have little chance to survive the next few weeks, let alone the winter. Or longer. He winced as he considered that the day might come when Iskra wished she'd stayed and married Udbash. He closed his eyes and shuddered.

A hand on his shoulder caused his eyes to fly open. He relaxed when he saw the innkeeper's chubby daughter. "You don't seem too interested in your beer," she said. "Or anything else for that matter."

Tarkio shrugged.

The girl looked at him for a moment, then turned on her heel and walked away. *Yes, leave me alone.* He folded his arms across his stomach, digging his fingernails into his arms, his thoughts filled with self-loathing and blame.

A few minutes later the girl returned with two tankards of beer. "You look like you could use a friend," she said. Her black eyes were soft, her expression sweet.

"You don't want to be my friend."

"Why not? You're not here often, but you've always seemed like a kind sort." She slid onto the bench next to him.

Tarkio looked down at the beer and shook his head. "A fool. An arrogant idiot. Always thinking I know best."

The girl sighed. "We've all been that at one time or another."

"But it doesn't always mean disaster for others."

"Tell me of this disaster."

Tarkio took a deep breath. It would be relief to talk, but talk had proven to be dangerous. He considered what he could say, without putting himself or the girl in danger. "Where do I start?"

"Wherever you like." She waved a hand at the room. "We're not busy, and most have gone home." She leaned forward slightly. "So. Your disaster."

"I convinced a girl to do something she didn't want to do."

The girl leaned back with raised eyebrows. "You don't seem like the type to do that."

"No, it wasn't like that. I-I convinced her to take a little trip. Manipulated her a little, so she'd agree."

"And?"

"She met my best friend." Tarkio felt a stab in his stomach at the thought of Xico. He picked up a tankard and drained it. "I didn't mean for anything to come of it. But they fell in love."

"Your friend should be grateful."

"Except she'd already been promised in marriage to another."

"Oh." The girl leaned forward, propping her elbows on the table, resting her chin in her hands. "Then what?"

"You can imagine." He paused as a burst of laughter erupted on the other side of the room. He waited as a few traders left, making their noisy farewells with the innkeeper. "They fought to be together. Now they are in trouble. Big trouble."

"You mean—?" The girl looked at Tarkio with huge eyes. She dropped her voice to a whisper. "Taken?"

"That's what I think." Tarkio hung his head. Close enough.

The girl took his hand in hers. "I'm so sorry. But how could you have known?"

"I should have known better. I'm such a fool. Always have been." He sighed. "I'm so sure I'm right. Then I bring such pain to everyone around me, like a farmer brings his harvest."

"What do you mean?"

"Like my wife." The girl dropped his hand and moved back slightly. "We married the year my father died. I was all alone. She was so lively and fun, she brought warmth to me like hot bread on a cold morning." He sighed. "I didn't realize she saw me as a way out, a way to escape living with her old drunk uncle. I wonder if she ever loved me."

He picked up a second tankard, took a long drink of beer and set it down with a thump. "But she has no business being married to a trader. She's jealous of everyone I meet, and it makes her angry. Had she married the baker, who she could keep under her eye all the time, she'd be happier." He hung his head. "She wasn't like this before, always finding fault. But now, it seems, I can do nothing right in her eyes." He rubbed his mouth and chin. "Maybe she's right."

"Is she really that miserable? And you?"

"We both are. But she's not to blame. I am. My da taught me to keep my word. I promised to marry her, to care for her always. That's how my da was with my mother, even after she got sick and couldn't get out of bed. He nursed her himself, all the way to the end. That's how I want to be. But I can't. A failure. And a fool." He put his face down on the table.

The girl patted his shoulder. "Here," she said. "Drink." She raised Tarkio's head and pushed his beer toward him. He drank it down in one gulp. "I don't think you're so bad."

"You don't?"

"I think you make mistakes like the rest of us." She pushed her untouched beer toward Tarkio. "Drink."

He picked up the mug, and drank deeply, looking deep into the girl's face. She had flawless brown skin and a warm, sympathetic smile.

When he finished the beer, she asked him, "Where are you staying tonight?"

"I don't know," he said. He stood, and wavered. Three mugs of beer on an empty stomach and drunk very fast made him a little unsteady on his feet.

"Come with me," she said. "We have an empty room." She took him by the hand, supporting him with a soft arm. She led him up the stairs and down the bare corridor, dimly lit by a flickering candle. She opened a door and guided Tarkio to the straw mattress.

He sat down and tried to pull off his boots, his hands sliding off the worn leather. The girl laughed and helped him, then began pulling off his clothing. He tried to stop her, dimly thinking there was a reason he shouldn't let her, but was having trouble remembering, or caring. He stopped trying when she sat on his lap, facing him with her legs spread so her knees were on either side of his thighs. She took his face in her hands and kissed him gently. "I can make your pain go away," were the last words he remembered her saying.

38

Kaberco's rage and frustration boiled within him, fueling his racing heart and burning his face. He stared at Iskra's pile of straw, a low spot in the center where she slept, where she should be lying.

Luza cowered before him, hanging her head.

"How could you be so stupid?" Kaberco shouted. "You know how crafty that girl is. You just went to sleep? You didn't keep watch all night? For what did I get you excused from work this week? To let you sleep all day, and all night, too? Have you no sense?"

Luza shook her head and rocked from side to side. "But these last few days, she's been so docile." She walked into the other room and took Iskra's wedding dress from the shelf. "See? She's been working hard on this and is almost finished. I thought she'd accepted the situation."

Kaberco raised a hand as if to strike her. "Fool! Of *course* she'd want you to think that. What else would she do if she was planning an escape? Tell you her plan?" He slammed his fist into his palm. "The question is, who helped her? Was it you?" He moved a step closer to Luza. "Was it?"

She cringed, then held her hands out to Kaberco. "Please believe me. I had no idea what she was planning."

Kaberco studied her through narrowed eyes. No, she probably didn't, he thought. Luza, for all her good qualities, was not the sharpest arrow in the quiver.

The door crashed open, banging against the wall. Udbash rushed in. "Where is the girl?" he yelled. "Where is she?"

"Udbash," Kaberco said, "it seems her mother has allowed her to escape."

Udbash clenched and unclenched his fists. Spittle formed in the corners of his mouth. He ran to Luza and seized her around the throat. "You did what?"

Kaberco grabbed Udbash's hands and forced him to release Luza. She fell to her knees, gasping for breath. Red marks appeared on her neck. "Udbash, don't be an idiot. She's the only one who can tell us anything about where the girl has gone."

Udbash kicked Luza. "Speak."

When she didn't reply instantly, he kicked again. Luza tried to talk, but choked on her words. Udbash went to kick her again.

Kaberco grabbed him by the throat and pulled him away. "If you hadn't tried to strangle her, she'd be able to." He pushed Udbash against the wall and motioned for him to stay there. He helped Luza to her feet, then poured some water into a tin cup and gave it to her.

She sipped the water, gripping the cup with shaking hands. "I already told you. I know nothing. As soon as I realized she was gone, I came for you, Kaberco. You know that." She took another sip of water and set the cup on the table.

Udbash's face turned a dark shade of purple. "Yer lyin'."

Kaberco looked at Luza, then at Udbash. "I don't think so. She wouldn't lie to me. The girl tricked her into thinking she was set to marry you and plotted her escape. Clever of her." He clenched his jaw. "Very clever. As far as I can tell, she took nothing of her own with her. If for some reason she'd been stopped, she could have come up with some story of taking a walk or going to work early." He folded his arms. "No, I think she planned this all on her own."

Udbash stalked around the room, kicking the bench and the stove. "How kin you be so sure?"

"Well," Kaberco said, "if Luza was trying to help the girl, she would have slept in and waited until later to report her absence. As it is, she rousted me out of bed long before my time."

"That girl won't get away with it," Udbash threatened. "I won't be made a fool of. I'll track her from one end of Tlefas to the other 'til I find 'er."

"I'll help you," Kaberco said. "And if we don't find her, well, then, I think Luza will just have to be taken."

KABERCO PACED BACK and forth at the foot of the Guarded Path. He and Udbash had climbed up to the Risker camp in the early morning. The guards, all armed with bows, had turned them back, saying they would bring their case to the elder.

"Wait at the bottom of the trail," the guards told them.

Udbash, the fool, had tried to argue. Two Riskers carrying large clubs appeared out of the trees and stood on either side of the guards. Kaberco pulled Udbash back down the trail.

One hour, two passed. The shadows on the road grew shorter. Kaberco used the time to think through the events of the past few weeks. The one puzzling thing was why Iskra went back to the Riskers after her first meeting. What made that timid girl go back on her own? She must have had help, and her helper had to be a trader. The one most on the scene was Tarkio. Kaberco sent one of his guards into town to find and detain him. Just issuing the order eased some of the nervous energy pounding through his veins.

His first problem was to find Iskra quickly. If that didn't happen, he'd have to come up with some way to hush this up, and to keep Murash from finding out. Or at least to keep him from sending messages to the Prime Konamei. His nostrils flared; he was angry enough to smash the side of the mountain.

He looked at Udbash slumped against the face of the cliff like a lump of mud that had slid from the side of the hill. *Somehow, I have to keep him quiet.* The sun filtering through the leaves cast much shorter shadows than when they'd started.

"Either they're digging that girl's grave or giving her a lot of time to get away," Kaberco said.

"You may ascend," a voice said.

Both Kaberco and Udbash jumped. Neither had heard the Risker approach. They moved to the foot of the trail.

"You may ascend," the Risker said to Kaberco. "You may not," he said to Udbash.

"You kin think that, but I'm going up. This is my bride, and I'm gonna find 'er."

An arrow flew past Udbash's cheek, just grazing the skin.

"He will not miss next time," the Risker said. He motioned to Kaberco to begin climbing.

Kaberco shrugged and said to Udbash, "You should go home. This could take a while. If she's there, I'll find her." Actually, this would be better without that oaf blundering around.

Udbash narrowed his eyes and glared at Kaberco. "Make sure ya do." He turned and stalked along the path back to the road.

Two hours later, Kaberco stood before the elder, holding his hands behind his back, fists clenched so tightly his nails dug into his palms. He had the sensation that he was the one on trial, the one who'd done wrong. The man was half a foot shorter than Kaberco, twenty or more years older, and had one arm in a sling. A walking stick lay on the floor next to him. But somehow this old man with piercing blue eyes who sat so easily in his carved wooden chair wielded a serene authority Kaberco knew he'd never have.

He bent his head to answer the elder's question politely. "No, I found no trace of the girl."

"You're satisfied? We're not hiding the one you seek?"

"She's not here now." He looked around the room. Strange, he thought. The polished wood of the table gleamed as softly as his own table did. The mats on the floor were thicker, the patterns more intricate, the colors more vibrant than any he'd ever seen. *These barbarians have a few comforts. I never would have imagined.* He turned to face the elder. "What I don't know is if she ever was."

"Believe what you will, just leave us," said the elder. "You know the law, that villagers are not to come into our camps unbidden." He looked up as Tikul entered the room. "What is it?"

"I was out hunting and found this." He held up a torn and bloody gray cloak. "It's not one of ours."

Kaberco grabbed the cloak. "This is a villager's cloak, all right. Where did you find it?"

"I'll show you," Tikul said.

Tikul led the way through the camp to the Guarded Path. They descended to the foot of the mountain, then followed the path to the road. Tikul led Kaberco along the road for a mile, then up the hill into the forest, doubling back in the direction they had come.

"Wasn't there a shorter way?" Kaberco asked through clenched teeth.

"There is. But our laws dictate that outsiders use only the Guarded Path, not any of our secret ways."

Kaberco thought about that. *Convenient rules they have, these Riskers. Maybe they've always existed, maybe they are an excuse to keep me busy.* He shook his head and chose to remain silent. He followed Tikul through the forest, feeling the sweat grow on his back as the sun grew hotter.

"Here is the place," Tikul said. Kaberco saw the trampling of the underbrush, the blood on the ground, some lighter footsteps surrounded by heavier ones. The footsteps led off toward the north.

"It looks like someone was taken captive," Kaberco said.

"It does," agreed Tikul.

"The owner of the cloak, most likely."

"That's what I would think."

"Who do you suppose took her? Bandits?" His tone grew sharp.

"Many bandits roam these mountains."

Kaberco studied his face, searching for signs of deception. He wasn't sure what he read in Tikul's face, other than weariness. His eyes drooped as if he'd been up all night. Which is what he'd have done if he'd been helping Iskra. "I'll take the cloak, and see if it belongs to the girl we are looking for. Thank you for your help."

AN HOUR LATER, Kaberco sat in Mazat's hut, filling him and Udbash in on the day's events. "I took the cloak to Luza. She says it belongs to Iskra."

"Kin we go after these bandits?" Udbash asked.

Kaberco snorted. "There are no bandits." *What a fool this fellow is,* he thought.

Mazat was staring at Udbash with a look of mingled pity

and scorn. "They want you to think bandits stole your bride," Mazat said.

"I agree," Kaberco said. "The man who took me to the place they supposedly found the cloak, Tikul, never gave me a straight answer."

Udbash stared at him, face reddening. "Then we go back and make 'em tell us where she is."

Kaberco sighed. Udbash was as stupid as he was filthy. Kaberco watched a chicken fly up to sit on the sideboard and peck around at the food left on the dirty plates. Sneering, he shook his head at Udbash. "We can't. I've told you before. That would violate the Prime Konamei's treaty with the Riskers."

"Are ya sure she isn't in the camp?" Udbash asked.

"Yes. Tikul told me so, although I don't think he realizes it."

"How'd he do that?"

Kaberco smirked. "He thought he was being so clever, leading me down the Guarded Path, then back up the mountain, taking up time. When I asked if there was a shorter way, he said it was forbidden to show outsiders their secret ways in."

Udbash frowned. "That makes sense. I'd do the same."

Kaberco slammed his hand on the table. "Idiot! Don't you see? If they have secret ways in, then they have secret ways out. Who knows where she is by now?"

"You're not gonna go after her?"

Kaberco let out a harsh laugh. "Of course I am. I'm leaving in the morning. Do you want to come with me?"

Udbash rubbed his hands together. "Gladly. As long as it takes. My da can take care of the chickens by hisself while I'm gone." He turned to Mazat. "Right?"

Mazat nodded. "I can. It's Iskra's help I'll miss." He looked at Udbash and shrugged. "Why don't you just let 'er go? There's plenty of other girls in the village, girls who'd be easier to manage."

"I want that-un. No girl runs out on me." He turned to Kaberco. "You sure we can find her?"

"Where will she go?" Kaberco asked. "She can't go to another village, no ephor will let a girl stay without documents from her old village. She'll have to go to the Riskers. We'll head north to make sure she didn't go to Calpiad. If we don't find her there, all we'll need to do is travel south, going from one camp to the next. We'll find her. Even if she keeps moving, she'll eventually run out of places to hide. The only way to fix this is to catch and take her. If she goes free—" He stifled a curse, thinking what would happen to him if he failed.

Udbash smiled and rubbed his hands. "Then I'll trap 'er, and never let 'er go."

39

Hand-in-hand, Xico and Iskra walked through the mist, the mist Xico called "a little *bryme*," and headed for the lake. Steam rose from the surface of the water, glowing in the light from the sliver of Zlu that had risen a few hours earlier. The leaves of the trees shone wetly in the moonlight. Iskra felt as if she were sleepwalking and would wake up at any time. She was married to Xico. She was on the run from Kaberco. She'd ripped Xico from his family. Her emotions—joy, fear, and guilt— mashed together like events in a nightmare, one sliding chaotically into the next.

Xico hummed as they skirted the lake. He seemed to be enjoying the adventure as if it were just an early morning stroll.

They turned to the north when they came to the river that fed the lake. "Walk on the rocks, Iskra."

"Why?"

"If they follow us this far, I don't want them to see our tracks along the trail. No point in making it easy for them. Once we cross the ford, there'll be more places for us to hide."

"How deep is the ford?"

"This time of year, only a foot or two. We've had a dry

summer, so the river's low. Some springs, it's too deep to cross."

When they arrived at the ford, Xico stopped to pull his boots and socks off.

"Won't the rocks hurt your feet?"

"They might. It's either that, or be wet and cold the rest of the way. It's up to you."

She stopped mid-stride, her eyes wide. This had to be one of the only times in her life someone let her make a choice between safety and something else—and didn't assume safety was the right answer. This new life was going to take some getting used to, she thought. *And I think I like it.*

Xico didn't seem to notice her hesitation. When he stepped into the water, she had to raise her eyebrows. His "foot or two" looked more like three to her, judging by how high on his legs the water splashed. Taking a deep breath, she stepped into the water and gasped at the cold. Holding her skirt high, she struggled to stay upright, sliding on the slippery stones. Her shoes filled with water and she fought to raise her feet enough to stagger across the ford.

Xico waited near the other shore. He put a hand under her elbow and helped her climb the bank, then jumped up beside her. She stared at the water oozing out of her shoes while he replaced his dry socks and boots.

He looked at her soaked shoes, opened his mouth, then closed it. He stood up and put his hand on her cheek. "Ready to move on?" he asked.

She nodded.

He leaned down and kissed her. "It's a glorious night, don't you think?" He turned to walk north, careful to walk on the rocky part of the river bank.

Three hours later, they were climbing a goat trail up the side of a mountain. Iskra's steps came slower and slower as she trudged along the twisting path. She couldn't even see Xico anymore. *What was I thinking to want to flee into the moun-*

tains? How long will we be fugitives? She wondered how long her strength would hold out.

Sweat dampened her back and under her arms. Her shoes were still drenched, squishing water with every step. *I should have listened to him and taken them off. Serves me right for being afraid of a few bruises or a stubbed toe.*

She glanced over her shoulder and felt her head spin at the sight of the valley far below, barely visible in the early dawn light. Just keep moving, she told herself. Don't look down. She had a wild thought of throwing herself off the path down the mountain. Then the worst would have happened, and she would have no reason to fear.

She shook herself, took a deep breath and pressed on. One foot in front of another. One more step closer. Push a branch out of the way. Crazy trees growing out of the side of the mountain. Roots grasping the rocks like claws. Her thoughts came in gasps, like her breath.

She rounded a bend and bumped into Xico.

"I found the cave," he said. "Give me your pack." He slid the straps holding the bundle off her shoulders. "It's just a little farther, so take your time." He touched her cheek lightly and strode up the path.

He doesn't even seem tired. "Come on, Iskra," she said aloud. "Put one foot in front of the other." She plodded on, ever upward.

A few more twists of the trail, and an opening in the mountain wall appeared. She peered in. "Xico?"

"In here." He had already spread their blankets on the floor near the back of the cave. "Take your shoes and stockings off, *selladria*. I'm going to get some wood."

Iskra pulled off her shoes and persuaded her soaked stockings to leave her feet. They clung like woolen leeches to her damp flesh, her feet white and shriveled. She huddled on the blanket and shivered. She wrapped her arms around her legs, head resting on her knees, too tired from the sleepless night and long hike to think about much of anything.

A crash woke her up and she jerked her head up. Xico had returned, and dropped an armful of brush and branches on the floor. He smiled at her. "I'm sorry, were you asleep? You must be worn out."

"No more than you," she said.

"Me? Nah." He grinned. "Why don't you look and see what food my mother sent? I'll get a fire going."

He moved to a spot in the middle of the cave and started breaking up the branches and laying a fire.

"Um, Xico? Won't the smoke—"

He held up a hand. "Can you feel the air? It's flowing up right here. There must be some kind of natural vent. And look at the floor." He pointed to a black circle of ashes. "Someone else lit a fire here." He soon had a small fire going and placed her wet shoes nearby.

Meanwhile, Iskra dug through the bundles and found two meat pasties, bread, cheese, and apples. There was also a small basket, carefully wrapped in cloth. She undid the cloth and gasped. A small cake lay inside. Tears tickled Iskra's eyes. Such kindness on Cillia's part. She thought of everything. She took the food and sat on the blankets.

Xico pulled a flask of water from his belt. "Welcome home, *selladria*, at least for today." Smiling, he offered the water to her.

After they ate, they lay back on the blankets, huddling together for warmth. Within a few minutes, she was asleep.

Four hours later, Iskra woke up. The fire had gone out and there was a chill in the cave. She could tell from the shadows that the sun had risen and was moving overhead. She lay listening to Xico's steady breathing.

It could have been Udbash, she thought with a shiver, *lying next to me.* Marriage to Udbash would have been intolerable. The worst would have been what happened at night. She closed her eyes. *But it didn't happen. I'm married to Xico.* Fear flickered in her mind, then she repressed it. Cillia said he'd be gentle. No need to be nervous. She held up her wrist with the tattoo and gently touched it. Whatever Cillia had used had worked well. Instead of stinging pain there was only a faint tenderness.

A burst of wind roared through the branches of the trees outside the cave.

Xico stirred beside her. He raised himself up on an elbow and shook his tousled hair from his eyes. He leaned forward to look into her face. Iskra nervously smiled at him. He smiled back, and gently put one hand on her face and stroked it.

"My wife. I can hardly believe it." Then he traced a finger along her chin. "Such *baquit.*" He touched her lips before she could ask the question. "Happiness." He moved his finger down her neck, along her collarbone. "Why are you so beautiful?" He leaned over to put his mouth on hers.

What had she been expecting? Whatever she'd imagined, it wasn't this, this tingling that coursed down to her toes. His fingers continued to explore her body. Her breath came faster. When he pulled back to take off his shirt she gasped, feeling it was an eternity before his mouth was on hers again. She couldn't get her body close enough to him, longing to press her skin against his. She'd die if he stopped touching her.

Some time later, Iskra idly traced her fingers along the muscles of Xico's back. He was lying on top of her, sound asleep. She drifted in and out of sleep, feeling as though the entire world had vanished other than the two of them in the cave, a cave that no longer felt cold.

She listened to the gentle hiss of the wind in the trees and tried to figure out what it was she was feeling. Happiness? She didn't think so. What she was feeling was beyond that most fleeting of emotions, the feeling that was tossed by circumstance like a ship in a stormy sea.

Pleasure, she thought with a smile. Yes, that, and fulfillment as well. But there's something more, something I've never felt before.

Her eyes widened with a sudden thought. *It's not what I'm feeling, it's what I don't feel. I'm no longer afraid. I faced my fears, and they fled.*

She put her arms around her slumbering husband and let herself slide into sleep.

40

Three weeks later, Kaberco took a gulp from the tankard of beer as soon as the servant set it before him. He wiped his mouth on his sleeve and drank again. He looked around Valday's dining hall, enjoying the rich tapestries on the walls, the long wooden table, the silver candlesticks, the rich food spread before them.

One day, this could be mine.

"I've waited a long time to taste your beer again," he said.

Valday smiled. "It's been a long time since you came to see me. Trofmose is not that long of a journey from Gishin."

"My duties have kept me close to home these days."

The light from the candles gleamed on Valday's bald head as he nodded. "I heard about the fire."

I'm sure you have. A fire that nearly destroyed the village would be gossip that would spread as if it had wings. "It could have been worse. Everyone worked together, and did what was expected."

"You included."

"I had to set an example for the village." Kaberco took a bite of chicken.

"I also heard that, over my objections, you use one volunteer day a year to hold fire drills."

Kaberco swallowed the partly chewed meat. "I meant no disrespect—" He spoke louder than he intended.

Valday held up a slightly trembling hand. He's aged, Kaberco thought.

"None taken," Valday said.

"People expect leadership," Kaberco said in a quieter tone. "Without a strong hand, they are like sheep. Aimless. Helpless." He bent over his plate to cut his chicken, trying to hide the thought that invaded his mind. *Only traders or eccentrics like Mazat can think on their own. No one else dares to. Is this what we've produced? A garden of stunted plants, only producing half of what they are capable of? He swallowed that thought with another gulp of beer. We need those rules, to keep people safe and ensure fairness. There's no other way.*

"And because of your disrespect, as you call it," Valday said with a smile, "there was less damage than otherwise. You did what had to be done to keep the village safe." He gestured with his fork. "In fact, some say you were the hero of the night."

"Did they?" *I wonder who,* Kaberco thought. Certainly not Murash. In any case, he was relieved Valday wasn't holding a grudge about the drills. "Well, that's good news, for once."

"Oh?" As always, Valday was as quick to pick up on the smallest hints of trouble as any gossip in the market.

Too quick for my liking, thought Kaberco. *Being the hero of the fire probably won't make up for my Iskra problem. I need to get him on my side, to be willing to help if the Prime Konamei asks too many questions.* "As it turns out, there has been a problem."

"Hence the visit. Somehow I knew it wasn't just for my beer."

Kaberco gave him a fleeting smile, then told Valday about Iskra and her family, her defiance, and her flight.

"Why did you let this go on so long?" Valday asked.

"At first, I thought it was just her age, or some rebelliousness toward her mother. The girl was always so timid, so compliant, it was hard to believe that she wouldn't come around. But something changed."

Valday picked up a roasted chicken leg and took a bite, raising his eyebrows at Kaberco.

"It's hard to say exactly what. She grew bolder. When we questioned her, she became more evasive."

"You say her father was like her."

"Yes, always asking questions."

"You should have just taken her."

"I see that now. I wanted to. But we'd had to take another fifteen-year old earlier in the year. We didn't think the village would stand for another underage taking." He ran his finger around the rim of his tankard. "Besides, it was hard to believe that someone who had always been so easy to bend would suddenly become so resolute. Neither the Oppidan teacher nor I, nor her mother, wanted to believe the girl wanted to destroy our way of life, all we've worked to build." *Not to mention, I considered her a friend, of sorts. I didn't want to take her.*

"Now what?"

"We gave her several chances, and she refused them." He cut a piece of potato into pieces. "We thought an early marriage with a man who would control her was the best solution. He'd get her in line, and it would be an example to anyone else." He laid down his knife. "Now we have no choice. When we find her, she's taken." He stabbed a piece of potato with his fork. "We have to do what is best for the village, to keep everyone safe."

"Yes, you do." Valday stroked the side of his tankard. "How did she meet the Riskers in the first place?"

Kaberco nodded. "That's a good question. We've been investigating, also trying to figure out how she got out of the village without being caught."

"Any ideas?"

"We suspect a trader helped her. But he wasn't anywhere to be found around the time she escaped, and couldn't have been involved some of the other times. I'm not certain. I'm watching the man, though."

"Hmm. Where is she now?"

"We don't know." Kaberco reached for the bread and tore a hunk off the loaf. "We think she's run off with a Risker."

"Do you have proof of that?"

"After we couldn't find her, I went back to the camp and asked to speak with the Risker boy we'd caught her with once. They couldn't produce him."

"Oh?"

"They said he'd gone trapping in the mountains and would be back in a few days. That was the first story. I've gone back many times. The story changes. He's at another camp, visiting his sister. Or I just missed him, he's checking his traps." He tore a small piece off the bread in his hands.

"Could that be true?"

"It could be. Except I never see any of his family, even though I've asked. I only talk with the guards and once the elder. That tells me they don't want the family giving him away."

"Why didn't you go after them?"

"If you please, that very next night was when the market and inn burned. We've been working the past three weeks to rebuild. We've made good progress and I think we'll finish in another week." He shrugged. "I couldn't leave right after a disaster like that."

Valday thoughtfully pulled some grapes off the stem and popped one in his mouth. He chewed and spat out the seed in Kaberco's direction. "What do you intend to do now?"

Kaberco didn't like the coldness in Valday's tone. He had to make sure Valday didn't see this as a failure of his leadership, the way Murash did. "The first thing, obviously, was to put out the story she was taken. Her mother's cooperating."

He shuddered. "It wouldn't do to let people know what really happened."

"No, it wouldn't." Valday spit a seed onto the floor. "You're not going to let her go, are you?"

"Of course not. But it's already the last week of Oznobal. The snows could start any day. I don't see any point trying to track them through the mountains in winter."

"How do you know that's where they are?"

"We've been watching the roads and rivers closely. It's pretty easy to tell Risker women from ours. They all have long hair."

"If you wait until spring, her hair will have grown out."

"Yes, but by then she'll be sixteen; no problem taking her then. And they might think they've shaken us off. They'll either stop moving, or go farther south. Either way, we'll catch them. The mountains end in the south, and there will be no more Risker camps to hide in."

"There is a flaw in your plan," Valday said. "Don't you see it?"

"Even if they try to double back and head north again, we'll still have them. The Riskers won't hide a mixed couple. Once we visit a camp and make an official complaint, it will be barred to them."

Valday nodded. "Make sure they understand the Prime Konamei would consider that a violation of the treaty."

"Yes, of course." He drank from his beer, then set the tankard down carefully. "Just in case you're wondering, I did consider sending someone to the other Riskers camps, the southern ones, to make the complaints now."

"Why didn't you?" Valday's eyelids drooped, making it hard for Kaberco to read his expression.

"Because come spring, when they move south, they'll know to hide in the mountains. I'd rather them think we've given up so they get careless. And it will be a lot easier to track them from camp to camp." He studied Valday's face, looking for any sign of approval. When he didn't see any, he continued. "By letting them move all the way to the camp near Litavye, it will be easier to catch them. If we miss them there, they'll have to keep moving. Between warboars and bandits, they won't be able to survive long in the wild. Not just the two of them."

"You hope it's just the two of them."

Kaberco clenched his jaw. "If it's not, I'll take the proper steps."

Valday put his hands together, matching fingertip to fingertip, forming a peaked roof. "The Prime Konamei would be most displeased if this marriage proves to be fruitful." He looked at Kaberco, and nodded. "I'm glad you understand that. The Risker and the girl, when you find them?"

"The Risker will have lost his life, defending her, of course. Then I'll let her intended have a few days with her, as a reward for his silence. Then she'll be taken."

"Very well." Valday studied the wine in his glass, then looked up at Kaberco. "Once she's taken, come back and see me. We'll have things to discuss." He looked at Kaberco's plate. "Have you eaten enough? Or are you ready for the sweet?"

Kaberco felt the tension in his stomach ease. Valday wasn't going to be a problem. "I'd love some, if you please."

Valday rang a bell on the table and leaned forward. "As long as the Prime Konamei accepts your handling of events, I'll be satisfied."

The knots in Kaberco's stomach returned as wrenching cramps. *That snake. He's with me, as long as the Prime Konamei doesn't have any issues. What a fool I was to think he'd back me up.*

41

Iskra slipped on the wet path and fell on her hands and knees. The heavy pack shrugged forward onto her neck, pushing her face down. She struggled to her feet, trying to ignore the bloody scrape on the palm of her left hand.

She stood, one hand against a tree, holding the wounded one up to the cold rain, letting the raindrops wash some of the dirt away. When she'd caught her breath, she shifted the pack and started to walk. One foot in front of the other.

Xico was waiting for her around a bend in the trail. "I think we're almost there. We're nearly to the end of the trees," he said, pointing up the mountain. "Da said the pass was just beyond that."

When she didn't answer, he put a hand on her shoulder and looked into her face. "What's wrong?"

"Xico, I don't know if I can walk any more today." *Forty-seven days we've been on the move. Six weeks. I'm so tired. Tired of running from warboars and sleeping under piled-up tree branches. Tired of eating alloe rats and black nuts.* She dropped her head and slumped her shoulders.

He pulled her close to him. "Sweet girl, we have to. I'm

sorry. It's already the last day of Camalu. If it gets any colder, this rain will be ice. Then we'll never get through."

She leaned her head against him. "Xico—"

"Please, can you try? We'll stop for a rest at the edge of the trees, then make one last push. There's not much daylight left, but I know we can make it."

She sniffed and wiped her face on her sleeve. "Lead on, oh taskmaster."

Xico bit his lip. "I'll take that as a joke."

She didn't bother to reply. She pushed past him and plodded up the trail.

By the time they reached the tree line, the rain had slowed. Xico settled Iskra in a dry spot under a pine tree, where the rocky ground was covered with years of fallen pine needles. He pulled some bread and cheese from his pack and offered them to her.

"I'm not hungry, just thirsty," she said.

Frowning, he handed her a flask. "You need to eat, that's why you feel you can't go on."

She took a sip of water. "Do we have any fruit?"

He rooted through the pack and came up with a bruised apple. "Do you want this?"

"Yes, please." She took the fruit from him and bit into it.

They chewed silently for a few minutes. "It's so nice here," she said. She thought longingly of the last camp they stayed in, just two days earlier. Everyone said they'd make it to Altiad in two days. It was taking them more like three. *Two days the way Riskers walk,* she thought. *Three for someone like me.* She felt a stab of guilt at holding Xico back, then stifled it. She was doing the best she could. And he needed to see that.

"If we sit longer, we'll be stiff. And it sure isn't getting any warmer."

She shook her head wearily, then took his hand and allowed him to hoist her up. She didn't try to help him. *He doesn't understand. I just can't go on. I'm not as strong as he is.*

Bending low under the pine branches, they stepped out from under the protection of the trees. The rain had stopped, and the sun, low in the sky, was just visible over the top of a mountain.

"That's the best sight I've seen all day," Xico said. "If the sky keeps clearing, we'll have some light to see by. Zlu will be full tonight." He gave her a smile, then started to walk up along the path. She followed behind, forcing her unwilling feet to keep moving.

An hour's walking brought them near the pass, but it also brought a return of the clouds and wind. The rain began again, this time mixed with ice. Xico made Iskra walk in front, so that if she slipped, he could catch her.

The wind threatened to shove her off the path. Her cloak, already wet, took on a sheen from the ice that clung to it. Her steps were slowing, her breathing labored. *We'll never make it.*

She looked over her shoulder at Xico. He was a few steps behind her, head down. Even his steps were slower, she noticed. He slipped and went down on one knee. He gasped, then pulled himself upright.

He looked up and saw Iskra, and hastily smoothed out the furrows in his brow and smiled. "We'll make it, sweet girl, you'll see."

He's worried, Iskra thought. *He's not so sure.* A small knot formed in her stomach. *More than that, he's afraid. He doesn't think we're going to make it.*

She gave him a tight smile and turned back to the climb. *I've never seen him fearful before. If he's scared, then what hope do we have?* She felt a heaviness that had nothing to do with her fatigue. Xico might not be able to protect her from every danger.

She plodded on for a few minutes, letting hopelessness wash over her. She looked up when there was a sudden break in the wind.

"Feels good, doesn't it?" Xico asked. He could have been

talking about a sip of hot tea on a cold morning. "Let's see how far we can get before the wind picks up."

In spite of herself, she felt a little more optimistic. He seemed to have shaken off his stumble with no trouble. She shook her head. *He's not super-human, Iskra. What did you expect? That he could calm storms and vault over mountains?* She smiled and took another step up the trail.

The path narrowed to nothing more than a track for goats, twisting its way between two cliffs. Ice built up on the path. If it were not for the rocks jutting through the packed soil, they would have had nothing to keep their feet from sliding. Iskra climbed bent nearly double, her face stinging from the icy rain that came in sheets, flung by gusts of wind.

One big gust knocked Iskra backward, and she stumbled into Xico. They fell and slid down the mountain, crashing into a boulder in a bend in the trail. She lay half on top of Xico, gasping, stunned by the fall. Her first thought was of the pain that shot through her body. Her second was relief that they hadn't slid all the way to the bottom.

"Iskra," Xico said. "Iskra. Can you move?"

She took a few more breaths. "Yes." She rolled to her knees, then staggered upright.

He lay on the ground, slowly straightening his legs.

"Xico, what have I done?"

He held up a hand. "I'm all right. Just give me a moment." He put a hand in his pocket, then pulled it out, clutching something in his fist. Iskra saw a glint of purple and green. Xico muttered for a few minutes, then touched the amulet to his neck and shoulder. He shoved it back in his pocket. With a groan, he rolled over and got on his hands and knees, then slowly got to his feet. He put a hand up and rubbed the back of his neck, wincing.

"Xico, are you hurt?"

"When I fell over, I landed on the pack. My head flew back and I felt something pop in my neck." He looked down at where he fell. "Good thing for the pack. Otherwise, my head would have landed on that rock." He pulled her into his arms. "Are you hurt?"

"No, I landed on you. Better than a rock." She smiled up at him.

He took a deep breath. "Then we'd better have another go at it. I'll lead this time." He led the way back up the path. Iskra noticed he was walking a bit slower and favoring his left leg.

Half an hour later, they heard the wind, howling and moaning, the pitch rising to a shriek.

"Good," Xico said. "That means we've found the pass."

They rounded a bend and the full force of the wind struck them, piercing their clothes like a frozen dagger. Iskra clung to Xico, and they staggered forward, barely able to make any progress against the wind.

Iskra lost feeling in her toes, her nose, her forehead. Her scarf, wound tightly around her face, grew wet where her breath melted the frost that formed around her mouth. The wetness froze, the icy spot slowly growing larger. She squinted her eyes against the wind and ice. One foot in front of the other. One more step

At last the path started to descend. "Keep going!" Xico shouted over the wind. "We'll make it."

The daylight was nearly gone and they had trouble seeing the path. They slipped and skidded on loose stones and icy patches. They finally reached the tree line and scurried under the shelter of the pine trees. The relief of being out of the wind lasted only a few minutes. Then Iskra noticed how badly her frozen face hurt and how cold she was. She put her head on Xico's shoulder.

"I know," he said. "But we did it. Let's keep moving, shall we? We'll get there sooner that way."

Too tired to plead for just another moment's rest, she

followed him down the trail. A few minutes later, they saw a flickering light in the distance. Altiad, the Risker camp.

Xico put his hand under Iskra's chin. "Remember, they might be a little primitive."

"But they'll have fire. And we'll be there in just a few minutes."

Xico stroked her cheek but didn't respond. He turned and began the descent to the valley below.

Iskra soon found out why he didn't answer her. Distances were deceiving in the mountains. The light seemed so close, but they never seemed to get any nearer. They followed the trail back and forth across the side of the mountain, the light sometimes to their right, then to their left, then directly below. But never closer.

The daylight was gone by the time they reached the floor of the valley. Iskra could just make out the outlines of cottages in the moonlight. They staggered to the nearest one and knocked on the door.

Iskra thought she had found paradise. At least, it would have been paradise had her thawing fingers not stung and burned so much. She wasn't quite sure how it happened, but she was sitting wrapped in a warm blanket, feet in a bucket of warm water in front of a fire. She sipped the tea the woman had given her. Xico had gone somewhere with the man of the house. At least, that's what she thought he'd told her. It was all a little fuzzy in her mind.

As she thawed out, she tried to make sense of her surroundings. The house had an earthy smell, as if it was underground. There was only one window near the door, covered with heavy wooden shutters. Two candles stood on the wood table. The center of the room was filled with a large, square oven with thick mats and blankets on top of it. The walls were rough stone, the floor more stone with worn woven mats covering it. She bit the inside of her cheek. Osip had said they'd be primitive up in Altiad.

She jumped when the door opened and a blast of icy air swept into the room, blowing in Xico and two men wearing fur hats and sheepskin coats. Iskra recognized the one as the woman's husband.

Xico walked to her. "Are you feeling better?"

"A little." She managed to give him what she hoped was a reassuring smile.

Xico turned to the men. "This is my wife, Iskra."

The men shrugged off their coats and shook the snow from their hats before answering. The sight of their clothing reassured Iskra. These Riskers were no less civilized than any others she'd met.

"I'm Kargat, the elder." He was tall, with straight, dark hair and dark almond eyes, skin the color of nuts.

"And I'm Baymak. Welcome to my home." Baymak could have been Kargat's twin, except his vest was red-and-black plaid, while Kargat's had silver buttons.

"Thank you." Iskra nodded timidly at them both.

Kargat looked at Iskra. "Your husband asks for shelter. It appears strange to me that two such young people would come here so late in the year, braving the ice and wind of the pass. There must be some good reason."

She blinked, trying to collect her thoughts.

Xico stepped forward. "I am from the far north, from Zafrad near Gishin. We were married two months ago. We had to flee immediately."

Kargat looked from Xico to Iskra. "And you, daughter? What camp are you from?"

She took a deep breath, looked him straight in the face, and said, "I am not from any camp. I am from Gishin."

"I knew there was something wrong," the woman said. "She wouldn't let me take her scarf off, wet as it is. She's got the short hair of a villager, mark my words." She shook her head, flinging the tail of the wool scarf she wore on her head over her shoulder.

"Peace, Maitla," Kargat said. He looked at Iskra. "Is she right?"

For an answer, she removed the scarf from her head, revealing her cropped hair and the bangs that now reached below her cheekbones. *If they won't take us both, maybe they'll let Xico stay. I can't let him suffer any more for me.*

"Did you receive help from other camps, or have they all turned you away?"

Xico looked straight at Kargat as he answered. "Every camp we came to gave us at least one night's shelter. One kept us over a week, when the rains came. We were grateful for what they gave us. They all said they could not keep us long, for it would violate the treaty."

"Neither can we. If the Prime Konamei sends his agents after you, we cannot harbor you," Kargat said.

"We understand," Xico said. "All we ask is shelter for the winter. No one will be able to follow us over the pass now. When the thaws come, we'll leave."

"You couldn't leave now, even if you wanted to. And I wouldn't send you to certain death. But we haven't saved up stores of food for unexpected guests. What will you give us, so that we can share what little we have with you?" He gestured around the room, at the strings of onions and dried apple slices hanging from the walls, the shelves that held sacks of flour and clay jars.

Xico said, "We have a few things to offer." He walked over to his pack and opened it. "Along the way here, I have been hunting. When we stopped for more than a day or so somewhere, I set traps." He pulled out a bundle of furs and handed it to Kargat. "These are good pelts that can help keep someone warm. I can trap for more, if need be."

Kargat stroked the soft gray fur and nodded. He handed the bundle to Baymak. "Do you have anything else?"

Xico reached into the pack again and pulled out a small packet. "A cup of peppercorns."

His listeners gasped. "Those're gold up here in the mountains. Few traders think to bring them this far," Baymak said.

Iskra noticed that Xico was avoiding her glance, forcing his expression to remain solemn. She tried to keep her face bland, to not show her surprise that a little packet of peppercorns would be worth so much.

"Will it be enough," Xico asked, "to buy house room for the winter?"

Baymak and Maitla exchanged glances and nodded. "It is enough for us," Baymak said. "You may stay here, and welcome."

"Good," Kargat said. "Everyone helps in winter, to keep the paths between cottages and the well clear. All the men help gather firewood. We go every morning in groups, some to chop the wood, some watching for wolves. They get hungry when the snow flies." He looked at Iskra. "You will help Maitla, yes?"

"Yes, with pleasure," Iskra said.

She suppressed a shiver. She'd fled Mazat's service. Now it seemed she'd found a new taskmaster. This grim-faced woman didn't seem like an improvement.

She felt a sinking feeling. It was the same in every camp they'd come to: Xico was welcomed, she as his wife was tolerated, and they were only accepted for a short time. Maybe they'd change their minds during the winter, if they showed how useful they were.

When Kargat spoke, Iskra realized she'd been lost in a fantasy. "Remember," he said. "When the thaws come, you will have to leave."

42

"The Spring Thaw Feast? What's that?" Iskra asked, looking up from the sock she was knitting.

"It's when we celebrate the first sight of grass under the melting snow." Maitla smiled. "Should be soon, one week, maybe two. It's the day we most look forward to all year."

"After this winter, I can see why."

"It's not just the cold and the dark we're glad to see go. By now we're all sick to death of dried fruit and pelchi."

Iskra nodded. She'd had her fill of pelchi herself, the little round dumplings stuffed with meat the women of Altiad made by the thousands in the fall. The pelchi were stored in lean-tos outside the house, where the freezing temperatures turned them rock-solid within hours. Every day, someone would go out to chop some pelchi off with an axe, however much was needed for the family that day.

"What will we have at the feast?"

"Rabbit and fish and jam and dried fruit. And of course bread and whatever else people can bake from what they have left." She shrugged. "It's a modest feast, but a joyful one."

She and Iskra were deep in a discussion of what they

would make for the feast when Xico burst into the cottage, followed by Baymak.

"Iskra, we have to leave. Today."

She stared at him and frowned. "Now? Are you sure we should leave now?"

"Yes." Xico put his hand on her shoulder. "I've just got word the pass is clear, a week earlier than expected. No one will be coming after us quite so soon. By leaving now, we'll be far enough from here they won't know we've left. Hopefully, they'll waste a lot of time searching for signs we died in the wilderness." He took her hand. "Besides, it won't get any easier if we wait." He peered into her face. "We'll just have to take our chances."

She bit her lip. Xico was right. She was already five months pregnant. Hiking through the mountains would be difficult enough now. Waiting would only make it worse. "Are you sure it won't snow again?"

"No one can be sure," Baymak put in. "But Xico's right. You can't afford to wait."

With a sigh, Iskra looked around the tiny cottage, grateful for the hospitality Baymak and Maitla had extended to them. Like most of the houses in Altiad, the oven was built large enough for two or more people to sleep on. Once Maitla learned Iskra was pregnant, she'd insisted she join them on top of the oven during the worst of the winter months. *Such good people,* Iskra thought, *to take us in for the winter, to share their food with us. How clever of Cillia to give us a few packs of peppercorns. How did she know spices would open doors for us?*

At first, Maitla had been cold, suspicious of the village girl living in her house. Over time, she became more accepting. Iskra's hard work was part of it. Some had to do with Xico's trapping abilities. He and Baymak had tramped far together through the mountains surrounding the valley, and never came back empty-handed.

Most of all, though, it was the peppercorns that had paved

the way. Baymak traded them to the others in the camp, earning far more than he spent in feeding Xico and Iskra. The sudden acquisition of wealth calmed Maitla's fears more than anything Iskra could ever do or say.

Over time, Maitla had warmed up to her, become almost friendly. Now they'd have to leave. Iskra suppressed a whimper. *Be strong, Iskra,* she told herself. *You chose this. Don't make it harder for Xico by complaining.*

By mid-morning they were packed and ready to leave. "Before you go," Maitla said, "let me trim your hair."

Iskra felt a sting of tears in her eyes at Maitla's thoughtfulness. A few months earlier, Maitla barely spoke to her. Now, she's looking out for her. She sat still as Maitla carefully tapered Iskra's hair, shaping it around her face so it didn't have the choppy look of grown-out bangs.

Baymak, Iskra knew, was truly sorry to see them go. Maitla, on the other hand, was smiling as she said her goodbyes, but her voice cracked in the middle of them. She wasn't as happy to see them go as she thought she'd be.

Iskra embraced them both warmly, then turned to follow Xico out of the village.

THE PATH they followed was still covered with packed snow, making walking easy. Iskra turned her face up, letting the warm sun caress it. She couldn't help comparing their leisurely stroll out of Altiad to the desperate stumbling rush to find it.

They came to the pass in the middle of the second day. Iskra was almost amused by the care Xico showed her. He shouldered both packs, and took them up the slope a bit, allowing Iskra to rest. Then he'd leave the packs and return to help Iskra up the slope, making sure she had no chance to fall. *It's almost like he thinks I've turned into pottery,* she thought.

They crested the pass late in the afternoon, splashing through puddles of melted snow.

"You see, Iskra," Xico said, "we were right to try."

By evening, she began to wonder. They'd made it down to below the tree line, Xico again carrying both packs and supporting her the entire way, trying to lessen her fatigue as much as he could. The relief they felt at reaching a lower elevation was short-lived. The wind shifted to come from the north. It picked up speed, rocking the branches of the trees, rubbing them against each other, making creaking groans like the sounds of a dying bird. The air felt distinctly colder and the sky clouded over.

Iskra looked at Xico, who nodded. "Yeah, it feels like a storm." He led the way into the pine trees. "I don't dare go in too far," he told her. "I can't see the sky in here, the trees are too close. We could easily lose our way and never find the trail again." He pointed to a large pine. "Let's camp under that one."

Wearily, Iskra set her pack down and sat on the pine needles next to it. The branches overhead were so thick no snow had filtered through, leaving the ground fairly dry. She bit her cheek. Fatigue overwhelmed her like a heavy fog, making it hard for her to even look at anything. Xico unrolled a blanket and wrapped it around her shoulders, then built a fire. He took a pot and collected some snow from a snowdrift still piled high off the trail. While the water was heating, he took his knife and began peeling bark from the pines.

"What are you doing?" she asked.

"Getting dinner."

"We have bread."

"We do. But we should try to make it last, don't you think?"

Iskra frowned. What did he mean by that?

She soon found out. By the time they'd finished eating the pine bark and drunk the tea Xico made with some of it, the wind was howling through the trees. Xico walked back to the trail, and came back, his head and back covered with snow.

"It's really coming down." He took off his coat to shake the snow off. "At least with all this snow, there's no *gallinippers* about." He grinned at her puzzled expression. "Mosquitoes." He put his coat back on and stretched himself on the ground next to her and put his arms around her. "Don't worry, we'll be fine. I'll make sure of that."

They ended up camping there for days. Xico scraped bark from trees, collected sap, and trapped a few animals. Melted snow provided water. The biggest danger was from cold, and they spent much time wrapped in blankets, huddled together. Xico heaped up pine needles so they could burrow among them, giving them even more protection from the bitter cold.

On the third day, Iskra watched in wonder and then amusement as Xico pulled out his shaving things. Funny the things you learn about a person after you marry them. Every second or third day, Xico found a way to shave. Usually that was how long it took to get from one Risker camp to the next. Once he'd arranged for a place for them to stay, his next stop was nearly always the camp's bath house. Who would have guessed that "the barbarian savage" Riskers would be so concerned with cleanliness?

And here they were, snowed in, camped under a pine tree and he was still intent on getting clean. He set a pot of water over the fire. While he waited for that to heat, he tested the blade on his razor, a metal edge set into one side of a bronze triangle that had three holes in it for his fingers to grasp. When his water was ready, he poured it into a small leather bag he apparently kept just for this purpose. She watched him, smiling as he carefully shaved his handsome face, using the fingers of his left hand to feel for spots he'd missed.

When he finished, he looked up and saw Iskra staring at him. "What?"

"I can't believe you're going to all that trouble."

"What else do we have to do? We've got food for another day or two. The snow's still falling, so we can't leave." He looked her full in the face, green eyes wide and serious. "And besides, it's safer this way. Never want to be unsafe."

She frowned, then shook her head as he burst into laughter. She stared at him, then laughed, a little surprised at herself. A few months ago, she'd have been mortally offended by a joke about safety. Now, she could revel in poking fun at what she used to take so seriously.

Xico wrapped up his razor and put it in his pack. Standing up, he blew on his cold fingers.

"Chilly work, shaving." He sat on the ground next to her and rubbed her face with his. "I know you like it smooth." He stroked her cheek, then pulled her down onto the pine needles. "Time to warm things up, don't you think?"

Iskra smiled. Even here, trapped by a blizzard.

He kissed her gently, and smoothed her hair back from her face. Then he frowned, and moved his hand to her swelling belly. "Unless, you don't want to. . .?"

For answer, she kissed him hard on the mouth. "As you say, what else do we have to do?"

43

Two days later, Iskra's mood had shifted with the wind. Sitting huddled by the fire, staring into the flames, she despaired that they would ever leave this forest. She was tired of cold feet and always feeling like she could eat more. She was sick of pine bark and pine tea, and stew they made from the food they carried, hard chunks made from fat and dried meat.

She was wearied by the constant searches for dry wood and pine needles for the fire. Bored with waiting for the snow to stop and the sun to come out. Fatigued by anxiety that a warboar would find them, worrying even though Xico said all the warboars moved down to the lower slopes for the winter. Her arm was sore from all the knife-throwing practice Xico made her do. "Just in case we meet some people we'd rather not get too close to," he said. She was tired of hearing the approach of a bandit in every snap of a twig. Annoyed with herself for not having the sense to know that no bandit would be roaming around in a blizzard.

She felt toyed with and frustrated by the snow that stopped just long enough to make her think they could get on the move again. Irritated that every time the snow slowed, Xico would look at the sky and say, "There's more on the way." Exasperated by the fact that every time he said that, more snow fell. Did he always have to be right?

Worst of all was having to push her way through the pines to the hole Xico had dug that served as a privy and the way it felt like the wind blew up into her every time she used it. She tried to hide her mood from Xico, but her irritation was growing like an inflamed tooth, a pain that throbbed and never left her.

Fueling her foul mood were her misgivings about Xico. He wasn't talking as much as usual, his usual buoyant mood subdued. Maybe he was regretting marrying her, having to leave his family for her. Did he feel like he was trapped into marrying her? *A little too late to ask that, Iskra.* She chewed on her lip until she tasted blood. If she knew he still loved her, it would be bearable. She didn't think she'd have the nerve to ask him the question.

He returned from hunting that afternoon, grinning as if he'd found a treasure. "Look, rabbits!" He held up the two small animals. "We'll have fresh stew tonight."

She made no answer.

He didn't seem to notice. "I think we should pack up and move on."

She jerked her head up to look at him. "Why now?"

"The wind has shifted; it's now from the south. We need to get past all this snow before it melts. Make it harder for someone to track us. And I don't know about you, but I'd like to dry my feet out."

He worked as he was speaking, packing up their possessions into one large bundle. He pulled her to her feet and gave her a hug. "I'll be glad to get on the move again. Sitting here was making me a little nervous."

Iskra made an effort to reply. "Me, too."

"We do need to be careful. If someone has come up from the south to look for us, all they'll have to do is wait for us just south of where this blizzard hit."

Iskra felt a twist of fear in her stomach. "If that happens, what do we do?"

"We try to convince them we're a pair of Riskers off to visit relatives. If we do end up in a fight, throw your knives and anything else you can grab at whoever is on your left. I'll take whoever's on the right."

She frowned. "How many people will they send after us?"

"I don't think more than five or six." He shrugged. "We can't worry about that now. I'm hoping they've given up finding us. If they haven't, we'll deal with that when it happens." He smiled. "We've made it this far, right?"

She nodded and followed him through the woods. Now that they were on the move again, their camp under the pine trees was looking a lot more appealing. After half an hour she was already tired and just wanted to lie down.

She began to lose all sense of what her body was doing. She repeated "just one foot in front of the other" to herself over and over, barely feeling the breeze on her face or the sweat on her brow.

Xico seemed to be heading due south and a little down the slope of the mountain. *At least we don't have to go up. I don't think I could manage that.*

She bumped into Xico. "What—"

He put his hand over her mouth and whispered directly into her ear. "Listen."

Voices. Shouting voices and the clang of steel. She began to shake and let out a whimper.

"We need to see who it is," Xico said. "Slowly, now."

Iskra crept after him, afraid to breathe. They came to a large outcropping of rock and peered over it. Four guardsmen were fighting five bandits. Three other bandits lay on the ground, dead, along with two guardsmen. Iskra gasped.

Xico frowned. "They're fighting right in front of the entrance to the trail to the next camp. We'll have to wait and see who wins." He put his arm around her. "We'll be fine."

A guardsman ran one of the bandits through with his sword. A bandit stabbed him in the throat. A second guardsman beheaded him. He happened to look up right into Iskra's eyes. "Hey, who're you?" he yelled.

The other guardsmen and the bandits all looked up. "They must be the ones we're after," one of the other guards said. He stepped back from the bandit he'd been fighting. "You know there's a reward for them. We'll split it with you."

Xico nudged Iskra with his elbow. "Get ready. I don't think they'll make any deals with us." He already had his bow strung and and three arrows in his hand.

She pulled her throwing knives from the pouch she carried them in. "Xico, I can't."

"You can. Just go for that bandit on the left. Ready?"

She was shaking so badly she was sure she wouldn't be able to hit the side of the mountain, let alone a person. And she had no illusions that she'd be able to hit a man any place that would really hurt him. Then he'd have her knife and just hurl it back at her.

"Don't make us come get you," the big guardsman said.

"He's lying about the reward, you know," Xico said. "Why should you trust them?"

The bandits looked from Xico to the guardsmen.

"As I see it, there are three of them, and three of you. I'll help whoever promises to let us go." Xico spoke confidently.

Iskra couldn't imagine why he'd say that. How would they be able to trust the bandits? She knew the guardsmen would turn them in.

The bandits seemed to think the way she did. Two started to laugh. "Kill them for us, go ahead," the third said. "Then we'll see what else you can do for us."

A second later she knew.

"Left!" Xico said. He shot once, twice, three times. Two of his shots lodged in the eyes of the guardsmen, the other went cleanly through the throat of the third. "Left!"

Iskra gripped her knife and grit her teeth. *I can do this. I can't fail him.* The bandits were moving toward the base of the rock. She raised her arm and flung the knife as hard as she could.

To her shock, it hit a bandit in the face, but only enough to make a scratch. Not the one on the left she was aiming for, but the big one, in the middle. He roared out a curse. She threw her second knife and hit him again. Then she heard the twang of Xico's bowstring, another quick three shots. All three bandits fell to the ground. Xico seized his knife from his belt and vaulted down from the rock. He ran to each fallen man on the ground, bandit and guardsman alike, and slit all their throats. Then he wiped the blade on one of the bandits' sleeve.

Iskra let out a sigh and slithered down to the ground. Sobs forced their way from her mouth.

"Iskra?" Xico somehow appeared in front of her. He dropped to his knees in front of her and put his arms around her. "We're fine. You were marvelous."

"I didn't do anything."

"You did plenty. You distracted them enough that I could get more arrows. That was all I needed, just a few moments."

She bowed her head and continued to shake.

He stroked her hair. "We really need to get out of here, before anyone else shows up."

She continued to look down and shook her head.

He took her hands in one of his. "What's wrong?" He stroked her face and put his head under her chin and tried to raise it.

She shook her head, not wanting to meet his gaze.

Xico rocked back on his heels. "Oh, Iskra, I'm sorry. I

know this was frightening for you. It's not the life you wanted to have. Are you sorry you're with me?"

"No." *But are you sorry you're with me?* She shook her head back and forth. "Xico, do you think we'll ever be able to live in peace?" She just couldn't bring herself to ask him what was really on her mind. To speak about it would be like jumping off a rock into the lake, something that might be good but could also end horribly.

"Somewhere, somehow, we'll find a way. It won't be easy, but we'll figure it out."

"Are you sure? It's just—" She felt like screaming, throwing things, doing something, anything so she wouldn't explode. All her frustration at being stuck in the forest and her fears that Xico resented her mingled with her fear of attack along the road and threatened to burst from her in an anguished scream.

"Just what?

She held her hands up helplessly. "I-I want . . . I don't know what I want."

"Are you afraid?"

She pulled her head up to look at him. "Only that you'll change your mind about me."

He looked straight in her eyes. "That's never going to happen." He drew his brows together and shook his head. "Do you really doubt me? Or think that a little difficulty would change how I feel about you?"

She felt relief as if he'd lanced a boil in her soul. All the things that had been bothering her seemed like petty complaints, fading away in the reassurance that he still loved her. "No, Xico." Taking a deep breath, she went on. "Or maybe Tarkio was right, I'm ruining your life." She'd never had the courage to bring up Tarkio before.

"My life would be ruined without you." A muscle twitched in Xico's jaw. "And I don't want to think about Tarkio." There was a hard note in his voice she'd never heard before.

She reached out and took his hand. "I think he just wanted to protect you."

"Funny way to protect me. I loved him as a brother, and he insulted you."

"Sometimes, when people try too hard to protect, they end up hurting."

"What do you mean?"

"Like in the village. We spent so much time trying to remove any possible danger from our lives. Think about it. We weren't allowed to do much cooking at home, just a little soup or tea, because we might get burned. Or cut ourselves."

Xico snorted. "What about the bakers or the cooks?"

"They are professionals, specially trained." She leaned back against the pine tree. "If they weren't telling us to be safe, they were warning us to avoid danger." She crushed the pine needles in her hand as she made a fist. "The thing is, we spent all our time imagining things to be afraid of. But they never taught us how to overcome the danger, how to face it when we actually ran into a real threat. What if the village was attacked? No one except the guardsmen would have the first idea how to fight back. All their teaching did was trap us, bind us by the fear. I know I didn't want to do anything, say anything, or even think anything because I was afraid of the consequences."

"Are you afraid now?"

"No. Not now." She sighed. "Sometimes I am, a little." She picked up a handful of pine needles and let them fall through her fingers. "I left most of my fear behind in the village." *The only thing I'm afraid of is life without you.*

"What do you mean?"

"All my life, I was taught to fear the world and everything in it. To expect danger at every turn. They said that was the way to be safe." She scooped up another handful of pine needles and smiled at Xico. "Fear is a snare. The only way out of it is to face it, to conquer it. That's what I learned from you." She flung the needles away and leaned over to kiss him. "And if for no other reason, I am infinitely glad to be here with you." She stroked his face, staring into his beautiful green eyes. "But there are a thousand other reasons, Xico. At least."

44

Five weeks after Iskra and Xico were trapped by the snowstorm, Kaberco wearily rode through the streets of Trofmose. His plans for tracking down Iskra had been interrupted by orders from Valday to lead a raid on the bandit camps. Now, after nearly a month of mustering troops, tracking bandits and orchestrating the battle, he was leading what remained of his patrol back to Trofmose.

Good, he thought. *We made it just before sunset.* He looked up at the clouds gathering in the sky. *And before the rain starts.* He shook his head. Half his men dead, most of the rest barely able to sit in the saddle.

He led the way to the stables behind the guardsmen's post and arranged with the officer in charge to house and feed his men and their horses. Then he plodded to Valday's house, arranging his thoughts, planning how to tell Valday what happened.

A clerk ushered him to wait in one of the public rooms. At least it had a fire, Kaberco thought. Even though summer was near, the nights were cold. He lowered himself to the wood bench, wincing from soreness. Leaning back against the wall, he closed his eyes to wait.

He was tired, weary to the bone. And not just from the hardships of battling bandits. *We have enemies all around us. Bandits without. Many within. Corrupt guardsmen like the ones who tried to kill me during the battle. Suspect like Tarkio: rule-benders. And rebellious like Iskra. Why so many? Why don't they see the wisdom of working together, for safety and fairness for all?*

He sat upright when he heard the servant return.

"If you please," he said, "you are to come upstairs."

Kaberco grunted in response. Upstairs. To the private rooms. That's better.

Valday was waiting in a room with large fireplaces, huge candelabras, and padded armchairs. "Come in, come in." He pointed to one of the chairs for Kaberco to sit. "Tell me everything."

"Did my messengers not get through?"

"Both of them did. But I want to hear from you."

Kaberco looked pointedly at the glass in Valday's hand, a glass half full of a pale yellow wine.

"Oh, you are thirsty. Hungry, as well?" Without waiting for an answer, Valday motioned to the servant. "Fetch more wine, and food for my guest." When the man left, Valday looked at Kaberco. "Well?"

"Well. We tracked them for over a week before we had any idea where their main camp was. It was difficult work, as we had no sign of them at all."

"How did you find them?"

Kaberco took a deep breath. "At his request, I sent your man Chadan and a few others ahead as scouts. They found the bandit's trail leading into the forest."

Valday nodded. "Chadan's a good tracker."

"Hmm. I assigned him to lead the attack."

"Good."

"But I also divided the force into three. Chadan led the first straight into the woods. The second I sent farther up the road, with instructions to enter the forest later and to cut over to meet us. The third, I led myself."

Valday set down his glass with a thump. "That was a terrible risk you took. What if bandits had fallen on any one of those groups in force? They could have wiped you all out."

"I thought of that. But we'd never come against them in large numbers before, so I hoped they would think the force under Chadan's command was all we'd sent after them."

"Go on."

"The main group took the brunt of the attack. The bandits approached on both sides of the trail, and had an easy time killing most of the men. My group came up on one side of the trail, and were able to kill quite a few before they regrouped and had us outnumbered."

"Then what?"

"The detachment from Shinroo caught up with us just in time. They'd heard the noise of the battle, but you know how it is in the forest. It's hard to tell where sounds are coming from, or how far away they are."

Valday drank deeply from his wine. "Are any bandits left?"

"Not from that group. But there are others. Many others. All this means is we'll have a little peace until others move in to fill the void. They won't be so bold in their attacks, at least for a while." He frowned, then leaned forward to look into Valday's face. "Chadan was killed."

Valday sagged in his seat. "He was a good man."

Had you fooled, didn't he? Kaberco thought. He tried to keep the anger out of his tone. "How long had he worked for you?"

"Not long. Why?"

"It's hard to lose someone you trust."

Valday's eyes narrowed. "You didn't trust him?"

Kaberco gratefully looked up when the door opened and three servants returned, bearing two blue bottles of Litavian wine, a tray heaped with bread, fruit, and cheese, and a tureen of steaming stew.

He let the men serve him, then held up his glass to Valday. "I thank you," he said.

Valday waved a dismissive hand. "It's a simple meal, but fitting for a soldier."

Kaberco frowned, attempting to make sense of Valday's meaning. He tore off a chunk of bread and dipped it in his stew.

That old spider, Kaberco thought, *watching me eat. What's in his mind?* He chewed steadily, trying not to cram as much food in his mouth as he could. This was the first good food he'd had in over a month.

He didn't have to wait long. Valday leaned forward. "When your first messenger came, I sent a bird to the Prime Konamei." Kaberco nodded. The Prime Konamei gave all the ephors trained birds that could bear messages to and from the capital. "I received word back today."

Kaberco tried not to show his interest, or his fear. "Oh?"

Valday smiled. "It seems the Prime Konamei has mixed feelings about you. He's thrilled you wiped out that gang of bandits. Clever of you to not be satisfied with wiping out the first band. Staying in the mountains for another week to ambush other bands who tried to raid the first bands' camp was brilliant strategy. The Prime Konamei was impressed. Called you a hero of the realm, how about that? But he's still not happy over the unfinished business from last fall."

"You mean the girl. I was about to go after her when you summoned me to go after the bandits."

Nodding, Valday continued. "The girl. Precisely. Well, the Prime Konamei said that if you can track down the girl and either capture her or bring proof of her death, then he will appoint you to your position permanently. But if you can't, well, he just can't have an ephor who lets people jeopardize the safety of the land without any consequences." He stared evenly at Kaberco. "You have some work to do." Valday stood up, using his hands to push himself up out of his chair. "I'm going to leave you; my konament awaits me. The maid will show you to a room when you're ready to clean yourself up." He ran his eyes over Kaberco's battle-stained clothing, then left the room.

Kaberco let out a long breath. He felt like events were rushing him along, giving him no time to think. He tore off a piece of bread, the soft, white bread only a powerful ephor like Valday would have on his table, and took a bite. *Think, Kaberco,* he told himself. *How did all this happen?*

It started with a bandit attack. When the guardsmen failed to prevent bandits from looting a caravan. Some were good soldiers, loyal and brave. Too many weren't. They followed orders out of fear, fear that they'd be shamed or disappear. Or else they'd become like Chadan, seeking power so they didn't have to fear and to instill fear in others. *Is this the harvest we're reaping, one that was sown in dread, watered by warnings? Have we tried to sow safety and prudence, and instead are raising fear? The people have become weak and timid, afraid of any danger. Too afraid to fight back or break any rules.*

Everyone is terrified, he thought. *Villagers, guardsmen, traders. He reached for his wine and took a gulp. Not everyone. Not all the traders, like that Tarkio fellow. Maybe because they have to face some danger, they aren't so afraid of it. Or maybe it's something else.*

He shoved that thought aside. What was clear was that he had enemies who were moving against him. Murash for one, possibly in cahoots with Valday. Or Valday might have his own game going on.

The only way out, he thought, *was to keep everyone safe. That's what the Prime Konamei wants more than anything.* He took another gulp of wine. *And the Prime Konamei thinks Iskra is a danger to the country. He would, if he really believes the prophecy. Which we all know is ridiculous. But because we're afraid someone might take it seriously, we have to hunt down a confused little girl who asked too many questions.*

Everyone is so afraid, they're no longer reasonable.

If we had less fear, we might have been brave enough to tell her the truth.

He looked at the bread in his hand. He could imagine Iskra's reaction if she saw this bread. A series of questions that would come as fast as hailstones on a roof. "Why does Valday have white bread? Why doesn't the baker make it for the village? Why can't we make our own bread?" With every question, she'd multiplied his doubts until they swirled through his mind like autumn leaves in a gale.

Iskra, with all her questions, was like a spark flying with the wind, a spark that could easily set the whole forest on fire. And he was running out of chances to stop her.

Would it really destroy the country if she was never found, never came back? He toyed with the idea of staging her death in the mountains, saying she froze to death. His last gift to the little girl he used to amuse by letting her run through the corridors of the ephor's house, exploring the twisting staircases and public rooms. He shuddered for a moment. *She's seen the private rooms, I'm sure of it. If she ever said anything about what she saw*— He didn't even want to imagine that.

He ladled some stew into a bowl and began eating, thinking about letting Iskra go free. It would be a major violation of the rules. The rules to make life safe and fair. Her angry face came to mind, the day she asked him, "Safe and fair for whom?" She was right, the rules didn't always make people safer and they weren't always fair.

He reviewed the events of the past months, trying to decide. Then he remembered the one event that made it all impossible. The time he caught her with the Risker.

He wasn't convinced that she and the boy didn't know each other. If Iskra was captivated by one of the Riskers, that would explain a lot. And would make it imperative that she was caught, before she had a child. Giving birth to a mixed child would really be the spark that set the realm ablaze with unrest and rebellion. If that ever happened, Kaberco knew his life would most likely be over.

No, he thought, *I have to find her. I have to keep everyone safe. Especially me.*

45

Iskra snuggled closer to Xico, enjoying the warmth of his body. Her back ached and she felt she was about to burst. The final month of a pregnancy was hard enough without the constant tramping through the mountains.

The night before, he'd said they had about an hour's walk to the next camp. With a sigh, she sat up.

Xico immediately woke. "What's wrong?"

"Nothing. Just thinking about moving on."

"Chilly, are you, *selladria*?"

"No, just stiff."

He rolled to his feet and helped her up. She staggered over to the side of the clearing where she could relieve herself.

When she returned, Xico was rummaging in his pack and found some dried fruit and cheese. He held it out to her. When she hesitated, he said, "It's not much, I know. Hot food tonight, Iskra."

They ate and packed up and started on their way. Xico, as always, had his bow ready with three arrows in his hand. Iskra walked behind him, noting the clouds gathering to her right and the chill in the air.

Xico stopped and held out his hand. She stopped and

waited. A sudden cramp pierced her abdomen and she bit the inside of her cheek to keep from making any noise. Men's voices, roughly laughing. Xico pointed up the hill toward the sound, then continued along the path. With the leaves fallen from the trees, they couldn't count on much cover.

Iskra followed, swallowing hard. They hadn't run into any more bandits up to this point. She couldn't tell how many men there were, only that it was more than two or three. That Xico was moving so cautiously told her he didn't think they were Riskers or traders.

They eased their way along the trail, the voices growing a little fainter. She leaned against a tree. Xico was by her side in an instant. She took a deep breath and straightened.

"Can you go on?" he asked.

She nodded.

He looked up the hill, toward where they'd heard the voices. There was silence around them, just the rustling of fallen leaves. He frowned, then leaned over and kissed her forehead. "We're almost there, *selladria*."

He moved down the trail, glancing from side to side.

Iskra followed, hoping the cramping wouldn't return, and to swallow down the fear. *I haven't felt this way in a long time. Not since they threatened me with Udbash.* She shivered at the memory.

A few minutes later they came to a ravine faced by two high cliffs. The only way across was a narrow bridge made of ropes and wooden slats. A few feet above the slats were other ropes that Iskra took to be flimsy handrails.

No, she thought. *I can't.* She closed her eyes.

She felt Xico's arms around her. "Are you feeling sick again? You're so pale."

"No. Yes."

"You can do this, *selladria*. Put one foot in front of the other, right?" He stepped onto the bridge and held out his hand.

Iskra felt rooted to the ground. But she knew there was no

choice. Go back, and risk the bandits. Go forward, and risk a fall. Better the fall, she thought. She put her hand in Xico's and stepped onto the bridge.

"I think you should go first," he said. He eased around her. "Go ahead, and don't stop."

For a crazy moment she had an image of him letting her get to the middle while he waited in safely, allowing her to fall. One glance at him made her realize that wasn't true. He was standing facing the way they had come, watching for anyone approaching. Protecting her. The least she could do was move.

She moved her right foot forward. Then the left. The bridge shuddered and shifted with each step. She clutched the side rope and forced herself to breathe.

"That's it, Iskra, you're doing great. Just don't look down."

"Now you tell me." She had already peered over the side, prompting a wave of dizziness. Was the drop one hundred feet, or just fifty? Either way, she wouldn't survive a fall. She took a deep breath. "One foot in front of the other." She concentrated on the next slat, then the next.

After what seemed an eternity but was really only a few minutes, she'd made it to the middle. Xico was a few steps behind her.

"This is good," he said. "Just keep doing what you're doing."

She swallowed and looked at the opposite side of the ravine. Maybe fifty more feet? She took a few more steps, feeling that she was getting better at balancing with the sway of the bridge.

A shout from behind made her heart lurch and she looked over her shoulder. Four scruffy stout men stood at the end of the bridge, all armed with bows.

"Come back, girly," one called.

"Iskra." Xico's voice was calm. "Just keep going. Don't stop. Get to the other side as quickly as you can."

"What about you?"

"Please. Just go. I'll be fine."

She knew he didn't want to worry about her while he fought the bandits. But what could he do against four? She took a few more steps, moving a little faster. She didn't want to jostle the bridge so much that Xico would fall. Forty feet to go.

She heard the twang of a bowstring, then an angry yell. She looked over her shoulder to see one of the bandits with an arrow through his eye.

"I have more arrows," Xico called to them.

The only answer was a few curses. Two of the bandits shot at him, both hitting the bridge.

Iskra took a few more quick steps. Maybe twenty-five feet to go. Keep moving, don't look down.

The bridge started shaking. She glanced back and saw one of the bandits sawing at one of the ropes, while another one was pulling on the handrail rope on the other side. Xico had twisted his arm around that rope and was kneeling on the bridge.

She turned and moved as quickly as she could. Twenty feet, now fifteen. The rocking motion was getting worse. Another scream from behind her. Xico must have shot another one. More curses filled the air. For a moment, the bridge seemed to be moving less. She used the chance to scurry to the end. She staggered onto the ravine's edge, gasping for breath.

"Xico," she called. "I'm over."

He was still kneeling on the bridge. Now both the bandits were sawing on the ropes. Xico shot one, then the other. One fell onto the bridge, his weight breaking the rope where he'd been cutting it.

The jolt sent Xico lurching forward. His arm wrapped in the rope saved him from flying over the edge. Iskra watched in horror as he teetered on the edge, then pulled back. He put his bow over his shoulder, untangled himself from the rope and began to pick his way along the bridge, staying low, always one arm twisted around the side rope.

Ten feet from the edge, the other rope gave out. The bridge dropped into the ravine. Iskra screamed, her heart falling to her feet. She crept to the side of the ravine and peered over. There was Xico, clinging to the bridge, climbing up the slats. She pressed a hand to her mouth, barely able to breathe as he inched his way slat by slat toward the ravine's edge. He clambered over the side and knelt on the ground, panting.

After a minute he stood up and stepped toward her. She flung her arms around him with a sob. He put his arms around her and stroked her hair. "See, it's not so bad when bandits shoot you. They usually miss, remember?" His arms tightened around her. "I think we could use a break, don't you?"

He led the way down the trail until they were out of sight of the bridge. Then they sat and pulled out their water skins.

She grit her teeth through another wrenching cramp.

Xico laid his hand on her swollen belly. "It's coming, isn't it?"

She nodded.

He pulled out his amulet and put it in her hand. Clasping her hand in his, he murmured a few words to the sky-god until the cramping eased.

"How far are we?" she asked.

"About half an hour. There's another rope bridge first, but that one's guarded. They'll help us from there."

She didn't think she could take another step. All she wanted to do was lie back and hope the pain didn't come back. She closed her eyes.

"We need to go now. Can you?" He helped her to her feet and put his arms around her.

She was relieved he was so calm. She didn't think she could keep from sobbing if he hadn't been.

He released her, slung both packs on his back, and pulled her right arm through his left. “Ready? One foot in front of the other. Look how far that’s taken you.”

She laughed. “Had I known then where I’d be now, I never would have left my house again.” She leaned her head against his shoulder. “How far I’ve come. And so very glad of it.”

The path led upward, but was wide enough for Xico to walk next to her, holding her steady and supporting her weight. It seemed to Iskra they were walking on a path that would never end. An hour passed and they hadn’t come to the second bridge.

Xico steered Iskra to a rock jutting out from the side of the mountain. “Here, sit a minute and catch your breath.”

She sank down, glad for a respite from the walking. Xico dropped the packs on the path and sat beside her. She smelled the salty tang of his sweat and heard his heavy breathing. Sensing his fatigue, her confidence in them making it to Xabiad ebbed. Were they following the wrong path? “Xico, do you know where we are?”

Xico picked up her hand and held it loosely. “We should be almost there. You’ll see.” He squeezed her fingers, then stood up. “Let’s get moving, before we stiffen up.”

She groaned as he helped her up.

“You’re not cramping again, are you?”

“No, that seems to have stopped. I’m just tired.” Weary to the bone was more like it. But there’s no hope for it. Got to keep moving.

She held her face up to a cool breeze, feeling refreshed.

Xico frowned. She looked up the mountain to follow his gaze. Black clouds were gathering. He looked down at her. “We might get a little wet, *selladria*.” He picked up the packs and took her arm. “Time to go.”

She continued plodding along the path. One foot in front of the other. The wind picked up. The sweat dried on Iskra’s face, then she felt chilled. She stifled a sob. If this kept up, they'd be spending the night on the mountain. And most likely, she'd be giving birth in a downpour.

Xico led her around a twist in the path, then stopped. "Look." Directly ahead of them was another rope bridge, swaying in the gathering wind.

She pulled back as he stepped toward the bridge. "I can't."

"You can. Please, Iskra. We do this now or we'll be stuck here all night."

She swallowed. Nodded.

He took a firmer grasp on her arm and they walked to the bridge. "Just hold onto me, right?"

She leaned on Xico, tottering, allowing him to pull her along through her daze of exhaustion. The bridge swayed and bounced under their feet. Xico kept saying, "One step at a time. One foot in front of the other."

At last they reached the far end. They took a few steps on solid ground. Xico stopped and put his arms around Iskra. She sagged into him, clutching his clothes to keep from sliding to the ground.

"Who are you and why are you here?" a deep voice asked from behind her.

Darkness came over her and she sank to the ground.

46

A crack of thunder woke Iskra. She was lying on a soft bed in a warm, dimly lit room. Rain pelted the windows. Xico slumped in a chair nearby, his chin on his chest.

A woman with a wrinkled face put her hand on Iskra's face. "You've had a time. How are you feeling?"

"Fine, I think. Where am I?"

"You're in Xabiad, in my house. I'm Doluru. Your husband brought you here an hour ago." She brushed Iskra's hair back from her face. "If I'm not mistaken, your time is about on you."

Iskra opened her mouth to answer, then gasped as another long cramp gripped her.

"I thought so." Doluru moved to the foot of the bed and pushed the blankets up. "I need to take a look at what's going on."

Iskra blinked, embarrassed to have this woman look at her in such an intimate place. But what choice did she have? She let Doluru position her feet so her knees were pointing to the ceiling. She stared at the ceiling, trying to pretend she didn't notice Doluru's fingers on her body.

Doluru straightened. "Things are moving along nicely. You'll be a mother by morning. Young man."

Xico stirred, then sat up. "Yes, what can I do?"

"Go to the kitchen and get the fire going. Put some water on to boil. Then go out back and get some more wood." When Xico hesitated, she flapped her hands at him. "She'll not go anywhere while you're gone. And while you're at it, help yourself to something to eat. You're going to need it."

He stood up and approached the bed. "Iskra—?"

"Will be fine. Now go."

Iskra had to smile at Xico's wide eyes and dazed stare. He gave her a weak smile, then left the room.

"Now, let's get you more comfortable." Doluru placed two large pillows behind Iskra's back and helped her sit up. "Are you thirsty?"

"Yes."

"I'll fetch you some tea."

After Doluru left the room, Iskra felt an overwhelming sense of being alone, lost, and adrift. She was helpless to stop what was about to happen and terrified of the pain. Another peal of thunder broke the sky.

Hours later she wished for the earlier pain to return. As the contractions came quicker, they also got harder. Xico held her hand throughout, letting her squeeze to the point of nearly breaking his bones.

She gave a sigh of relief as the contraction eased and slumped back on the pillows. Her eyelids drooped and she wished for sleep. Maybe she could just pass out and wake up when it was over.

She was barely conscious of Xico and Doluru talking. "Going to be rough," she heard Doluru say. "You'll need to distract her, talk about anything. This one's not going to come fast."

If she wasn't so tired Doluru's words would have frightened her. She shifted listlessly on the bed, trying to relieve the pressure on her back. She felt the bed sag. A hand touched her face. Xico's.

"What do you want to name the baby?" he asked.

She opened one eye. "I don't know. What were you thinking?"

"If it's a boy, I was thinking of Osip, after my da. Or would you rather name him after yours?"

"Osip is a good name."

"Da would be pleased to have a grandson named after him. Did I tell you the elder says we can stay here for a year? As long as no one comes after us, he'll let us stay. Then I'm thinking we can head north again, send word to see if we can go home."

"Do you think we could?"

"Sure, after a year they'll be sure to think we're dead. We go back, maybe not to Zafrad, but one of the other camps, take on new names, build a life."

She clenched his hand and moaned. This time the contraction was longer and left her sweating and gasping for breath.

Xico gently wiped her face. "And once we're settled, I'll start trapping again. And making arrows. I'll build us a house, better than the one in Zafrad. My parents will come see us. You'd like that, wouldn't you?"

She nodded, her eyes fixed on his face, feeling as if she would collapse if she couldn't look into the intense green of his eyes.

"Our little boy will learn to shoot as soon as he can walk. His Aunt Tuli will come and teach him to swim. What would you like to do?"

Besides love you? "I don't know. I really can't do anything. Except care for chickens. I can do that."

"Well, we'll have lots of chickens, if it pleases you."

Her breath was coming in ragged gasps. "Oh, it hurts. It does."

Xico sat behind her, wrapping his arms around her, letting her dig her fingernails into his arms.

Doluru stepped to the foot of the bed. "Let me just take a quick look." She pushed the blankets back and looked between Iskra's legs. "We're getting there. Time for you to get to work." She blew out the candle in her hand.

To Iskra's surprise the room didn't fall into darkness. She looked at the window to see faint sunshine.

"Yes, you've been at it all night. Just a little longer."

"I don't know if I can."

"Anyone who walked here from Zafrad can do this."

Doluru stared at Xico and raised her eyebrows.

"Oh, right," he said. "I was saying you could have chickens. Or would you rather pigs?"

"I don't know, I just want the pain to stop." She groaned and clutched his arm.

He slid off the bed onto his knees next to her. "It will, soon enough. But in the meantime, tell me what you want in a house. Sixteen rooms, or seventeen?"

"Don't be ridiculous."

"If you don't want to talk about the house, let me tell you how we'll live. Every day we'll get up, loving each other more. I'll go off trapping or hunting. You'll be home with our five children, each one prettier than the last." He stopped when another contraction came, gripping her hands as she screamed.

Doluru stood on the other side of the bed. "That's right, pull on his hands. Push, push, it's time."

"But it hurts!" Iskra wailed the words.

"I know, I know. But it will pass. Take a rest now, wait for the next one. Then push."

More time passed. Iskra could tell the sun was high in the sky. Every so often, Xico would spoon water into her mouth or dab the sweat from her face. The contractions were coming fast and hard but the baby hadn't moved. She began to sob.

"I'm dying, just tell me. I'm going to die and the baby, too. I can't push anymore."

"No one is dying here. You just need to stay calm and push when I tell you." Doluru's spoke firmly as if she expected Iskra to obey. "And you. Keep talking."

"Iskra, look at me." Xico put a finger under her chin to turn her face toward his. "You're not going to die. Doluru's a great healer. She's got her amulets out; I've given her ours. The sky-god has brought us this far, it will all be fine."

She gulped down a sob.

"Besides, who else will I go swimming with? You promised to jump from that rock again."

"Did I?"

"Yes. And we'll plant flowers all around our house, and keep the chickens from eating them. And our son will chase the chickens around to see if he could catch them. And he'll bring you berries and nuts and flowers every day."

She convulsed with another contraction. She barely heard Doluru speaking. "Push, push, there we are."

With her last strength Iskra pushed one more time. She felt sudden relief as if an enormous burden had been lifted. There was silence in the room. Iskra reached her arms out for the baby.

"Doluru?"

More silence. Iskra's mouth went dry. "Doluru? My baby?"

Xico stood up and walked over to Doluru. Iskra saw her shake her head. Xico's head dropped and he stumbled back to Iskra's side. He fell to his knees and dropped his face down on the bed.

"Doluru? Doluru!" Iskra shouted, trying to untangle her legs from the blankets. Xico was holding her down, trying to contain her as she thrashed. "What's wrong with my baby?" She saw Doluru with her fingers in the baby's mouth. "She's killing him!"

A loud cry pierced the room. Iskra fell back on the bed and moaned.

Doluru walked over, holding a squalling red baby. "Did you mean to say I was killing her?"

Iskra's eyes widened. *Her. A girl. We have a girl.*

"Give me a minute, let me clean her up, then you can hold her."

Xico pulled himself up on the bed and pressed his mouth to hers. "You gave me a girl. Thank you." He looked into her eyes and a tear ran down his face. He leaned down and pressed his forehead to Iskra's.

She wrapped her arms around his neck. A girl. Maybe there was nothing to this Desired One business, after all. Maybe they really could hide themselves someplace and be left alone.

Xico sat up when Doluru approached, carrying the baby all wrapped up in white cloth. He helped Iskra sit up higher and she took the baby in her arms. "She's so red," she said.

Doluru laughed. "That she is, like a ripe hopberry. Give her a little time, all that red will fade. Now, why don't you hand her to your husband while I finish with you. We've got a little more pushing to do and we'll be done."

Iskra regretfully handed the baby to Xico.

He took her in his arms, grinning. "I'll take our little hopberry for a walk."

47

Two months later, Iskra looked down at the baby in her arms. *Good,* she thought, *finally asleep.* She pulled her child away from her breast and cradled her against her shoulder, looking out the large windows of the cottage to the blazing sunshine. What a miracle, her daughter with blue eyes conceived in late summer, just as the fields started to ripen for the harvest during those first few days of her marriage. *A miracle that we are even here.*

She thought back to the events of the past year. Their wedding night in a cave. The trek over the mountains in a downpour that threatened to turn into ice and sleet. Refuge in Altiad. The week they spent camped in the pine forest, riding out a storm. Fighting off bandits by the rope bridge. Tears filled her eyes as she thought of Xico's patience with her. He never complained at her slow pace, that she couldn't carry her pack, that she was too exhausted each night to help set up camp. His good spirits never died, at least that he let her see. He just wanted to love her and care for her.

What a joy they'd found a woman as motherly and wise as Cillia to live with. Her home even smelled like Cillia's, full of fresh bread and herbs. *Finally, somewhere I feel at home, somewhere I belong.* Smiling, Iskra leaned over and kissed the baby.

She looked up at the sound of the door opening. Xico walked in, followed by Poales. She smiled and started to greet them, but Xico cut her off.

"We need to leave."

"What?" Her mouth flew open. "What do you mean?"

"I saw T-tarkio in Litavye a few days ago," Poales said. "He told me that Kaberco and Udbash were searching for you around here. It seems they never believed any of the false trails Osip left to confuse them."

"What's Tarkio doing here?" Xico asked.

"He w-wants to help you," Poales said. "He's willing to go with you, until you've gotten away."

"No." A muscle twitched in Xico's jaw.

"Xico, w-we don't know how many men Kaberco has. You need someone with you. If not Tarkio, then let me come."

Xico held up a hand. "I don't want to hear any more about him." He took a step toward Poales. "Make sure he understands we don't need his help." His face softened. "And Poales, thank you. But you had your own troubles up north. You don't need to get mixed up in this. We'll be fine on our own."

Iskra wasn't so sure about that, but the look on Xico's face told her it was better not to say so. She looked from Xico to Poales. "Do we have to leave now?"

"T-tarkio said they have probably made it to Guariad by now, just east of here. You're maybe a day ahead of them, if that."

"How did they find us so fast?" She turned to Xico as she spoke.

He shook his head. "They've had all winter to look for us. *Dixit* travels faster than any man." He looked at Poales, who was frowning. "Rumors."

Poales nodded. "I'd heard some myself in town. Mixed couple with a b-baby."

"Xico, where will we go?"

He looked up from the bundle he was packing. "Poales told me about a cave high in the mountains. We can hide there for a few days. It has a good view of the valley all the way to the river. If it looks like we can go downriver, I think the pirates are our best chance. After Kaberco and Udbash move on, Poales will find us and go with us."

"I've done some trading with the pirates. We just might be able to come to t-terms," Poales said.

Iskra laid the baby down and began gathering some clothes into a bundle. "I'm not sure I'm ready for this," she said. Her hands shook as she worked and she fought back the tears. Feeling a weakness in her knees, she sat down heavily on the floor and let her head hang forward.

Xico sat beside her and put his arms around her. "I know. I'm not ready, either. But we have no choice." He held her close for a moment, his face in her hair, then helped her to her feet. He turned to Poales. "Can you pack up the rest of our things? It would be good to have more to offer the pirates."

"Will do." He paused a moment, looking down at the floor. "Xico, I wish you'd let T-tarkio go with you. I've a bad feeling about this."

"We have packing to do," Xico answered.

Poales sighed. "Then I'll tell the elder you're going. P-peace and safety to you." He nodded to Iskra, and left the cottage.

Iskra looked up into Xico's eyes, then hugged him tightly. "I'm so sorry. This is all my fault. You should have married a Risker girl, settled down in that beautiful house you were building."

"No," he said. "I'm right where I need to be. With you." He kissed her hair. "We'll be fine. The sky-god has helped us get this far, right?"

She nodded, burying her face in his shoulder. They clung to each other for a few moments, then pulled apart and got back to packing.

When Poales returned, Doluru was with him. "What's this I hear about you leaving?" she asked.

"It's true," Xico answered. "We knew someday this would happen."

Doluru sank into a chair. "I did. But I didn't think so soon, not after the baby coming."

"You saved her life," Iskra said. "If you hadn't been here, known what to do—"

Doluru waved a hand, brushing away her words. "I did what any midwife would have done." She folded her arms across her chest. "Make sure you raise her well."

Iskra's chin trembled. "I promise." She knelt by the old woman and wrapped her arms around her. "I will miss you. You were more of a mother to me than my own mother ever was." After a long moment, she wrenched herself away from Doluru. Taking a long piece of cloth, she wound it around the baby, then around her back, forming a sling to hold the infant close to her chest.

Xico picked up a large pack and his bow and arrows. "Thank you, Doluru, thank you for everything." He leaned over and kissed her cheek.

"You've given me just as much, young man, if not more. I owe you."

He smiled and put a hand on her shoulder. "You owe us nothing." He looked at Iskra. "Are you ready, sweet girl?"

She nodded and followed him from the cottage.

48

They tramped silently through the forest, following the trail Poales had pointed out to them. *At least,* Iskra thought, *this far south the summer lasts longer. Up north we'd only have a few weeks before the leaves started turning colors under chilly rains.* She looked down at her sleeping child. *Please don't wake up. Please don't cry.*

Xico led them up the mountain, not bothering to stick to any trail. He followed one track for a while, then veered off, always seeking rocky ground where they wouldn't leave any traces. Then he'd switch to follow another trail. After an hour's walk, he turned south to travel across the face of the mountain.

They continued south another few hours, stopping at midday for a rest, seeking shelter from the sun under some trees. Iskra leaned against a pine tree and nursed the baby, dozing on and off. When she woke, Xico was pacing back and forth, muttering to himself.

She sat upright with a jolt, disturbing the baby. At the sound of the whimper, Xico spun around.

Iskra calmed the child, then looked up at Xico. "What's wrong?"

He grimaced. "Something feels wrong to me. I wasn't expecting them to find us so quickly. Either they are moving a lot faster than I thought they would, or someone has betrayed us."

"How could that happen?"

"People get careless. Or are overheard." He shook his head. "I don't know how they know. News like that would travel fast. Kaberco probably didn't spend the winter watching the snow fall, either. He probably sent word around to the other ephors to be watching for us."

She drew her eyebrows together. "Will they find us?"

"No, not if we get moving." He leaned down and took the baby from her, and helped her to her feet.

Not long afterward, they found the cave Poales had told them about. It was high up on the face of the mountain, the slit-like entrance invisible from above and below, screened by an outcropping of rock.

Xico sat down and rested his head against the wall of the cave. "This feels good, doesn't it?"

"Such a relief, to be out of the sun." She jiggled the baby on her lap, then rocked her to sleep. Xico watched her, rubbing his hands on his legs. Then he scratched his face and rubbed his neck. He pursed his lips, then bit them.

"Iskra, I'm going to go look for a spring." He leaned over and kissed her. "Don't worry, I won't go far." He stood up and walked out of the cave.

The baby let out a whine. "Don't be afraid, little hopberry." Xico's apprehension made her uneasy and unable to sit still, as much as she wanted the rest. She stood up and began walking back and forth in the cave, bouncing the baby on her hip.

An odd sensation crept over her, as if she had done this before. *But I've never been here in my life,* she thought. She turned around, looking at the cave walls.

My dreams. The walls of the cave were the same walls, the

sense of being in a cave up high, the baby in her arms, the sense of impending danger, all parts of her dreams. *What was I looking for?* She walked deeper into the cave, running one hand along the walls.

Then she saw a faint green light. She walked toward it, holding her breath. The light was coming from a small niche. She peered into the niche and saw the source of the light: a dragonfly amulet. She picked it up and gasped. It was larger than any amulet she'd seen before, and it had three purple stones dangling from its body to form the dragonfly's tail. She clenched it in her fist to keep from dropping it. Her knees felt weak and she thought she would fall. Her heart pounded and she forced herself to breathe calmly.

She heard footsteps in the front of the cave. "Iskra?" Xico called.

"I'm here." She went to the front of the cave to meet him.

"I need to tell you something," they both said in unison.

"Me first," Iskra said. She held up the amulet.

He held out a hand to touch it with one finger. "Where did you find this?"

"Do you remember the dreams I had last year? I haven't had them again, not since we were married. But this is the place, the same cave. I walked to the back, and saw the green light. Do you realize what this means?"

Xico fingered the amulet. "An amulet of power, that will find the Desired One when he needs it."

She shook her head. "But we have a girl. She can't be the Desired One."

He sighed. "That's what we thought." He rubbed his chin. "The prophecies never said the Desired One was male. We just assumed."

Iskra took a step back. "No. She can't be the Desired One." A lump formed in the back of her throat and her mouth went dry.

"But the amulet found her, just when she needs it most."

Iskra widened her eyes. "Do you really think so? That the prophecy does mean us, and that our daughter is the Desired One?"

"I don't want her to be. I just wanted to be left alone, to live in peace." Xico sighed and let his shoulders slump. "But it seems we don't have a choice."

She wrinkled her forehead. "What did you mean, she needs the amulet now?"

"People are coming, four or five of them. I could see them, off to the north just entering the valley. I'm going to head up that way and head them off."

"But Kaberco and Udbash are only two."

"They may have brought friends."

She grabbed his arm. "Xico, you can't. You can't leave me." She couldn't survive alone. Xico was the one who found the trails, the water, the food. He always knew what to do and had the boldness to see it through.

"I have to. If they are just a pack of bandits, I'll let them pass without them seeing me. We'll hope they aren't headed here. If they are, I have enough arrows to fight them off." He paused. "If it is Kaberco, then we need to make sure they don't come too close. If the baby cries, they'll find us. I'll lead them off, then I'll double back. Once they get to the river, they'll look downstream a bit. We'll use that as our chance to go over the mountains."

He took an arrow and laid it in the center of the cave, pointing south. "That's the sign Poales and I agreed on, in case we had to leave before he could get here. North for pirates, south for wilderness."

"Are you sure they won't catch you?" Her breath came in gasps and her heart was thudding in her chest.

"No one ever has, except you." He held her close, rubbing his face in her hair. "Be brave. We'll get through this, I promise." He ran a finger down her face. "I will always love you. And I'll prove it to you, every day, for the rest of our lives." He kissed her gently.

She looked deep into his green eyes, eyes that usually brimmed with confidence, eyes that now flickered with doubt.

He reached into his pocket and pulled out his amulet. He fingered it a moment. "Hang on to this for me, will you?" He pressed it into her hand, kissed her. "I'll want it back, you know." He smiled, then picked up his bow and arrows and slipped from the cave.

Iskra sank down to the floor of the cave. *Who do you think you are fooling, Xico? You know the prophecy.* She repeated the words to herself: "The father won't live to see his child's first steps. The mother won't hear her child's first words."

She swaddled the baby in her shawl and laid her on the floor of the cave. Then she went to the entrance.

By standing on a large rock, she could see the length of the valley. Xico was right, four men were making their way along the valley floor. She heard a whimper from the cave and jumped down.

She picked up the baby and started to nurse, walking up and down, singing under her breath. *Eat, my sweet, eat. Then sleep.* She tried to stay calm so her mood wouldn't distress the baby, but it was like trying to still the surface of a pond during a hailstorm.

When the baby fell asleep, she laid her on the floor again. Returning to the lookout point, she could see the men were approaching. One of them was pointing up, signaling to another to climb up the mountain toward the cave. Then they all started, and looked south along the face of the mountain. They ran toward whatever had startled them. An arrow hit one in the chest and he fell to the ground. The others paused, then took cover behind trees.

Iskra held her breath, watching with eyes so wide they

nearly bugged from her head. She couldn't see much of what was happening. There were a few shouts, some cries, then the largest one returned to the trail. Kaberco, she thought, no one else was that big.

Another staggered out of the trees, supporting a second, who was limping. Big and bulky, that had to be Udbash. Iskra wasn't sorry he had been injured. They were followed by four men, two holding the third tightly. The third was fighting to free himself. Blood ran down his face from a gash on his scalp.

Xico. Iskra pressed her fist to her mouth and bit hard. Anything to keep from screaming. She clung to the rock with her other hand, digging into it with her fingernails so hard she thought she might tear them off. She could hear shouts, but too faintly to make out any words.

Kaberco was asking questions, that much was clear. Xico wasn't answering. They hit him in the face, the stomach, the groin. With each blow, Iskra shuddered. Kaberco kept shouting questions. Xico fell to the ground. Finally, Kaberco stopped. He motioned to one of the men who had captured Xico. The man drew a sword and ran Xico through.

Iskra let herself slide down from the rock until she was sitting on the rocky ground. She felt her muscles weaken, like her strength was ebbing out of her body as Xico's life left his. She struggled to breathe, to fight the sensation that her world was ending. She let her head sag forward while the tears ran down her face. Even the light seemed different, all the colors muted, as if even the sun was mourning with her. *Oh, Xico. How can I live without you?*

She pressed her fists into her eyes. She thought of Xico, his easy confidence and buoyant spirit. And his dazzling green eyes, the eyes that captivated her from the start. She felt the pain rip through her as she realized she'd never see those eyes again. *What do I do now? What would he want me to do?*

She swallowed her sobs, pulled herself up, and returned to

the cave. She picked up the baby, cradled her, kissed her face. She pulled the three amulets from her pocket, Xico's, her own, and the big one, and tucked them into the shawl she'd wrapped around her child. Then she laid her back down, her fingers lingering to stroke the petal-softness of her face. Then she turned and silently moved to the entrance of the cave.

49

Iskra peeked cautiously over the top of the lookout point. Kaberco and his men were arguing.

They know I'm around here somewhere.

She gripped her trembling hands together. *I'm so afraid. But I can't let them find the baby.* She took one step away from the entrance of the cave.

It's time for me to choose. What do I do?

She looked down the hill at the shouting men. *I can't. They'll hurt me. I'm sixteen now. They'll have no problem taking me.* She shuddered, feeling a knot form in her stomach. *Udbash is down there. I can't let him see me.* She rubbed her hands over her arms and rocked back and forth. *Maybe if we're very quiet, they'll just go away.* She stood motionless, agonizing over what she had to do, unable to force herself to start. She bent her head forward and tugged at the hair on the back of her head.

Fearlessness, Iskra, she told herself. *That was a quality Xico loved. Can you be fearless for him? For the baby?* She thought of how Xico loved her enough to die for her. Now she had to do the same for her daughter.

But she couldn't. Heart pounding, she sagged against the

rocky cliff. She'd felt this same way in the Oppidan lecture, when Edalia was mocking Tavda. Pounding heart, wobbly knees. A low moan escaped her throat. What a coward she'd been, and let Tavda down. That ended in disaster. *Tavda was right, I'd do anything to save my own skin. I am a mushroom, like she said.*

But no longer. Xico's counting on me now. Taking a deep breath, she thought back to the day she jumped from the rock. Terrifying for a moment, difficult to take that step off the rock, and to commit to the flying leap. Then feeling the surge of radiant joy afterward.

There will be no joy this time, leaving the safety of this rock. She brushed her hand over its rough surface, then leaned her face against it as if to pull some strength from it. Sky God, protect my baby.

Put one foot in front of the other. Do it for Tavda. One foot in front of the other. For Xico. Tentatively, she stretched her foot out and leaned forward. One step. For our child. Then another.

Stealthily, she walked along the face of the mountain, flitting from tree to tree like a small animal seeking cover, striving to avoid being seen as long as possible. Every rustle of the leaves, every crackle in the undergrowth made her jump, expecting to be seized by one of her pursuers.

She made it to the place Xico had been captured, and swallowed hard, thinking of him dying to protect her. She kept walking, her teeth clenched. As she passed through a grove of oak trees, some crows rose up, cawing. She strode on, angling down the hill toward the path.

It did not take long for one of Kaberco's men to find her. He leapt from behind a tree, arrow on the string. "You can stop there, girl," he said.

Iskra sighed and bowed her head.

"Walk down the hill," the man said. He motioned with his

bow for her to go before him. As she started moving, the man let out a shrieking whistle.

Soon enough they joined Kaberco, Udbash, and the others.

"It's been a long time," Kaberco said.

"Not long enough," Iskra answered.

Udbash smirked. "Still the ornery one, aren't you? Well, we've got somethin' to show you." He grabbed her by the arm and pulled her north along the trail.

They led her to Xico's body, lying broken and bloody on the valley floor, a raven already plucking at one green eye. The raven paused, watching as they approached, then resumed pecking. She closed her eyes to shut out the sight, clamping her teeth together, willing herself to make no sound.

"Now, unless you'd like to join him, you need to tell me a few things," Kaberco said.

She was motionless, eyes shut, listening to the sound of the wind in the trees, the sound of all the joy in her life rushing away.

"Where's the child?" he asked.

She did not answer. She felt without Xico, she had no strength to even breathe. If not for the baby, she'd just lie down and never get up.

"Oh, we know there's a baby," Udbash said.

Iskra winced at the sound of his harsh voice.

"We heard all 'bout it in Litavye. A mixed couple from the north living at one of the camps nearby. They had a baby who just about died. You may as well start talking."

"Shut up, you fool!" Kaberco said. "Answer the question, Iskra."

She understood Kaberco's wrath. Udbash had saved her from trying to lie and say there was no baby. "Well," she began, then stopped.

Kaberco shook her by the arm. "Talk. Now."

"You heard right, I was with child. And I did have a baby,

who nearly died at birth." She did not have to fake the tears that came at the thought of losing the baby.

"Where is it?"

"It was sickly. It lived while we were still with the Riskers, but didn't survive once we left." She forced herself to look at Xico's corpse so the tears would keep flowing. She sobbed a few times, burying her face in her hands.

"I don't believe you," Kaberco said. He grabbed her chin and pulled her face to his. He stared into her eyes. "Show me the body."

She jerked back, freeing herself from his grip. "What do you think, that we carried a dead child around with us? My husband buried her high on the mountain."

He shoved her from him. She fell to the ground. "Show us the place."

"I can't. I was mad with grief and didn't want to give up the child. He took its body and buried it somewhere, I don't know where. He was gone for hours." A sense of numbness crept through Iskra's body. *Xico's dead.* She still couldn't believe it.

Kaberco bent and seized her hair, jerking her to her feet. He slapped her across the face. "That had better be the truth."

She let her misery burst from her in sobbing breaths. "It is." *Please believe me.*

Udbash shook a finger in Kaberco's face. "You need to beat the truth out of her. And search these mountains for her brat."

Kaberco's face turned red and he shoved Udbash's hand away. "You. You don't tell me what to do." He pulled Iskra a step away from Udbash. "If you hadn't been so quick to want to kill the Risker, we could have made him dig up the corpse." He studied Iskra's face with narrowed eyes. "I've got a few more questions for you," he said. He turned to Udbash. "She's your promised bride. When I'm done with her, you can do with her what you will."

Iskra squeezed her eyes shut and began to shake. *Xico's dead, and I'll be Udbash's toy.* Her knees went weak. The last thing she heard was the squawk of a raven.

50

Tarkio crept through the underbrush. He spotted four men walking along the valley floor. They must be with Kaberco and Udbash, he thought. Were there any others?

He froze when he heard shouts. Then two of the men ran into the woods, and returned with two others, and a captive. Xico. Tarkio smiled grimly to see that one of them had been injured. His smile faded when he saw another two men join them from farther up the trail. Eight altogether. Xico probably only saw the four. That's why he thought he could fight them off.

I'm such an idiot. I should have let Poales come. But I just had to be the one to rescue Xico and Iskra. I started this, I needed to fix it. And I was so sure I'd get here first, and that Xico and I could take on Kaberco and his men. He clenched his teeth. Now how to rescue Xico? He inched forward, trying to get a better view. He stifled a shout when he saw the sword pierce Xico's chest.

He clamped a hand over his mouth and closed his eyes. *Xico is dead. Because of me. He's dead because I made a stupid joke, just had to tease Iskra into going back to the Riskers.* He sank to his knees, feeling as weak as a mushroom under a hot sun. He bent over and let his head rest on the ground, welcoming the stabbing pain of a sharp rock pressing into his forehead as if it were a punishment. *My friend is gone.*

A sudden thought made him straighten. *Iskra. Think, Tarkio. Where is Iskra? I have to save her. And the baby. Just where is that blasted cave Poales was talking about?*

He soon got the answer to his first question. A little down the slope off to the south he saw Iskra appear, steadily walking through the woods. She headed west, angling toward the valley. Her progress was easy to mark even when she walked under the trees. Dark crows, startled, rose up with harsh caws.

He wasn't the only one to notice. Soon enough, Kaberco caught her. Tarkio looked around for the best place to stand to start shooting. If he could kill Kaberco and Udbash, and maybe one other, would the rest run? *Do I try to save her, or just the baby?*

He saw Kaberco knock Iskra to the ground as if he was felling a tree, then pull her up by her hair. His stomach wrenched, watching them torment her. Then she fell to the ground lifeless. Udbash kicked her in the head. She lay motionless on the rocky ground.

Tarkio gripped his bow. Why did I wait? Could I have saved her? He watched helplessly as the two of the men grabbed Iskra's ankles and dragged her along the trail, heading back north. They left Xico's body where it lay, leaving the ravens to their feast.

Tarkio remained crouched for a long time, eyes closed, rubbing his fingernails. *My best friend is dead. I should have come sooner to help him. Little Iskra is dead, or as good as. Because of me. So many people hurt by me. Xico and Iskra. Osip and Cillia lost a son, their children lost their brother. All because I'm an idiot.*

He chewed his lip as he thought about what would happen to Iskra. *Will she tell them all she knows? Have I doomed myself, and my brother traders by telling her our secret?*

He swallowed hard, as if he could swallow the guilt he felt.

Then I made it worse. To forget my shame, I was unfaithful to Groa. How ironic I finally did what she accused me of doing so many times. But there's no excuse. Never.

He stayed hidden in the bushes, torturing himself, heaping shame on himself, waiting.

He watched the sun on the leaves of the trees, the shadows dancing as the wind moved the branches, making a soothing whisper.

It was my mistake that started this, but I'm not to blame for the decisions Xico and Iskra made. I made my own choices, and have suffered for them.

The weight in his stomach lessened only a little at that thought. *That's true, but I still feel so guilty, so responsible. I was wrong to tease her, to bring her back to the Riskers. All I can do is the best I can to make amends.*

After an hour, he stood cautiously, listening. He heard nothing other than the gentle rustle of the leaves on the trees and the caws of the ravens. Iskra's pursuers must have gone by now, he thought. He headed for the place he first saw her. Backtracking up the slope, he searched for the entrance to the cave.

His first attempts were fruitless. The few paths up the slope skirted trees and wound around areas of sheer cliffs. He returned to the grove of oak trees where he first saw Iskra and tried again. He looked up at the cliffs, searching for anything that might be an opening. Going to have to search everywhere. He climbed to another area and made his way along the rock, following anything that could remotely be considered a trail.

An hour, two passed. His mouth had gone dry and he felt a tightness in his chest. Where was that cave? He bit hard on his lower lip.

Finally, he found the slit hidden by the stone that jutted out. He staggered in, blinking in the dimness, almost afraid he was too late.

There by the wall, he saw the small bundle. The baby still slept. Tarkio picked it up and touched its cheek, cradling it in his arms. He felt something hard under the shawl wrapped around the child. Loosening the shawl, he probed underneath with a finger. He pulled out first one amulet, then a second, then the third. His eyes widened when he saw the amulet of power.

"Oh, no, it can't be." He shook his head. "No."

He sat down on the floor of the cave, clutching the baby, his body trembling.

"So, little one, you just may be the Desired One after all."

I hope you enjoyed reading **Flight of the Spark** as much as I enjoyed writing it!

If you liked this book, please send me a tweet @evelyn_puerto

Book reviews mean a huge amount to a self-published author like myself and helps other readers to discover my stories. If you enjoyed this book, please take a minute to leave a short review on Amazon, Goodreads or other sites.

Follow this link to
The Flight of the Spark's page on Amazon:

https://www.evelynpuerto.com/reviews

Even one sentence will help a lot. Thank you!

ACKNOWLEDGMENTS

First, a big thank you to you, my readers. Thank you spending time in the world I created for you.

Flight of the Spark was a long time coming, and many people helped me along the way.

I wrote the first draft in about sixty days. Then I spent the next six years revising, editing, and generally learning all I could about the craft of writing.

Five or six beta readers read an early version and pointed out places the story could be better. You know who you are, and I thank you for slogging through that early draft. Countless others critiqued the first several chapters.

Members of the Fox Valley Writers Club patiently listened to me read chapters, and freely gave their opinions. Then there were some sharp-eyed critiquers at Inked Voices, and the gang over at Write Practice who gave feedback and ideas. Alice Sudlow gave me priceless editorial advice and pointed me to the Story Grid, one of the best editing tools out there. My developmental editor Theodora Bryant helped me solve story problems and other issues I didn't even know were there, making the story much stronger than was before. Sherry Chamblee did the final proofread and found a bunch of stubborn typos that refused to go away.

I'm also grateful to Giancarlo and Emily. When I shared my story idea with them way back when, they both said it sounded like something they'd want to read. That gave me the encouragement I needed to actually sit down and write the story.

Most of all I'm grateful to my husband Tony, whose support, encouragement and love keep me going when I can't find the words.

And lastly, thanks be to God, who gave me what ability I have to string words together into a story.

ABOUT THE AUTHOR

Evelyn Puerto entered the world around the time of the unveiling of the microchip, the introduction of Japanese cars to the US, and postage stamps that cost four cents.

Her Saturday morning friends were Mighty Mouse, Dudley Do-Right and the Jetsons.

Growing up, school was merely an interruption of her exploration of the worlds of Grimm's Fairy Tales, Louisa May Alcott and, later, JRR Tolkien.

When she married late in life, inherited three stepdaughters, a pair of step-grandsons, and a psychotic cat. Currently she writes from northeastern Wisconsin, but soon will be heading south for shorter winters.

She's the author of the award-winning **Beyond the Rapids.** To read more of her short fiction or to subscribe to her blog, visit www.evelynpuerto.com.

facebook.com/Author.Evelyn.Puerto

twitter.com/evelyn_puerto

instagram.com/theevelynpuerto

CPSIA information can be obtained
at www.ICGtesting.com
Printed in the USA
BVHW081911071219
565888BV00004B/17/P